JUST ONE BITE

S. L. COKELEY

Just One Bite

Copyright © 2025 S.L.Cokeley

All rights reserved.

No part of this publication may be reproduced, distributed, or transmitted in any form or by any means, including photocopying, recording, or other electronic or mechanical methods, without the prior written permission of the publisher, except in the case of brief quotations embodied in critical reviews and certain other non-commercial uses permitted by copyright law.

To request permissions contact the publisher at contactslcokeleybooks@yahoo.com

This is a work of fiction. Names, characters, businesses, places, events, and incidents are either the products of the author's imagination or used in a fictitious manner. Any resemblance to actual persons, living or dead, or actual events is purely coincidental.

Title page illustrations by Tinailustra

Cover illustrator by Adduani

Typography by Designs by Charlyy

Map illustrations by Holly Dunn

Chapter Headers by Charlotte Slegers

Line and Copy Editing/Proofreading by Dee Houpt, Dee's Notes:Editing Services

ISBN 979-8-9906188-7-9(Paperback)

Second paperback edition April 2026.

Slcokeleybooks.com

Big Bear City

For my grandma, who keeps asking me to write a children's book. This isn't it. This is just another vampire romance, but at least I added werewolves this time.

Trigger warnings can be found on my website
where I have a live updated list.
slcokeleybooks.com

Playlist

Calling After Me by Wallows

I Was Made For Lovin' You by YUNGBLUD

Endgame by Taylor Swift

New Perspective by Panic! At The Disco

Call It What You Want by Taylor Swift

Mystical Magical by Benson Boon

Delicate by Taylor Swift

I Love You, I'm Sorry by Gracie Abrams

back to friends by sombr

All song recommendations are solely for inspiring readers' imaginations when reading and sharing the love of music.

Doxlothia University

PROLOGUE

Olivia

There has to be an explanation.

Why else would I let some masked stranger touch me? The mask would probably be scary if the memory of him playfully waving at me in the hallway wasn't replaying in my mind. The night sky is blanketed by hundreds of stars, and I am backed against a tree with nowhere to go.

I've been touched by a man before, but it never felt like this. His eyes are hidden beneath the sinister mask, but his touch is tender.

His lips graze my ear, and he draws in a long, heavy breath, while my chest heaves in response. The slow caress of his fingers slides under my sweater and below my navel.

What is this visceral urge keeping me fastened here, pressed up against him like the stars might come crashing down if I leave?

He isn't human, that much I can tell. Humans don't look at other humans that way, with ferocity and necessity—like he is seconds away from sinking his canines into my flesh.

Desire lingers in my sigh and expands between us, and when my eyes threaten to flutter shut, I land on the description of the feeling.

Home. His touch reminds me of what I'd abandoned the hope of long ago. Safety. Wholeness. Comfort. That must be why I want to wrap my arms around him and bury my face into his chest.

The fear of that realization hits me as my sister's scream rings through the air, and I snap from my daze, press two hands to his chest, and push.

I run away, dodging the trees, not bothering to turn around to see if he follows.

With each step, I force him from my brain. All while hoping I never have to see him again.

CHAPTER ONE

OLIVIA

A few hours earlier

"Hurry and find our names," I shout over the crowd.

My little sister dives for the bulletin board within the bustling crowd of other students. I try to keep track of the pastel-pink ends of her blonde hair, but she's out of sight in seconds.

The entire system is inefficient. An almost four-hundred-year-old school hasn't found a better way to announce dorm assignments than a piece of paper on a board in the courtyard. Second by second, the crowd shoves me back as I examine the castle in the distance. It's the tallest building I've ever seen, so it's hard not to stare at the turrets stretching into the sky to figure out the symbol on the end of each spire. It's a star, I think. Then someone else pushes me, so I grab onto my other sister for support.

Evangeline—the only thing I've ever called her is Eva—is sickly pale and biting her cheek. I wrap my arm around hers, and she smiles sheepishly. She may be the oldest, but taking charge was never her thing. She prefers for my younger sister and me to take the lead. Unless it involves any type of athletics, then she'd rather not be involved at all.

I don't blame her. It was a tough afternoon. Dad dropped us off late, and the car ride ended in tears and bickering—Eva had no time to plan, and her hair suffered for it. She wanted it down and curled, but now, her blonde hair is frizzy and pulled into a bun that she swears is slightly lopsided—it isn't.

"This is a disaster."

I agree but instead say, "We'll be fine."

Eva is naturally a better socializer than I am when she isn't feeling out of sorts.

"No. I haven't eaten. I'm so nervous. We're probably going to get split up."

And hungry. I know the signs of an Eva panic attack when I see one, but I've come prepared. I rummage in my suitcase sitting at my feet, moving past my ballet shoes and silk pajamas.

"I have some crackers in my bag. Want some?" I ask.

She nods swiftly and snatches the crackers from me as soon as I dig them out of hiding. Same as me, she likes to plan and have order. Only, I *like* those things and she *needs* them. As she eats the crackers and bits of crumbs pepper her uniform, she stops swaying and bumping into my shoulder. One crisis averted.

Behind her, I notice the attention of almost all the new students as they pass us to get their room assignment. Long-lingering stares, and some stop to gawk. If Eva notices, she'll start hyperventilating.

"Emma, hurry up!" I call.

I adjust the skirt of my uniform and tug at the socks. I should have opted for the longer skirt option. Black is the only allowed color for orientation, and that includes sweaters and shirts too. Emma and Eva weren't thrilled, considering everything they typically wear is in a lighter color palette.

Doxlothia University's orientation *begins* at sundown. There are two moons in Vviveren. I used to love staring up at them back home, but I could never get a full view through the trees. Now I have a complete, unrestricted view of the periwinkle sky as a contrasting blue crescent hangs overhead next to a full pink moon. The campus is brimming with lofty brick and stone buildings and elegant iron streetlamps. All are draped in strings of fairy lights and lanterns in different house colors, which are directly linked to the dorm assignments. It's easy to identify the new students by their lack of color. The established pass by sporting one of the four house colors—purple, pink, blue, or green—on either their ties, slacks, accessories, skirts, or blazers.

"Got it!" Emma appears with her phone, her shoulder-length bob curling at her neck. She pulls up a picture, and we dodge the other students who don't mind moving us out of their way.

With eyes sparking in excitement, she zooms in on the list:

Emma Osborne – Luxxia House

Evangeline Osborne – Stelliea House

"I told you." Eva's fingernails dig into my forearm.

"Maybe Olivia is in your house," Emma says, jutting out her chin toward me.

It's not-so-subtle sister code for "be encouraging." And I am, but I'm not going to lie to Eva to make her feel better.

Before attending Doxlothia, we had to take a test. They made us come to the campus and tour before locking us in a room for two hours. The test was filled with *what would you do* questions. Students are sorted based on their compatibility and "ability to work together." It's not so much about like-mindedness as it is getting students to unify through differences. Doxlothia is Vviveren's leading university in interspecies connection, so its classifying system was hardly a surprise.

I love my sisters, but it's time for us to get a little distance. Twenty-one years of sharing a room is enough for me.

As soon as I think of the words, I spot my name a few lines down.

Olivia Osborne – Noxx House

My heart stutters. *Mom's House.*

My house knowledge is limited, but I know the most about my mom's old house. I remember her old violet skirts hanging in her closet that she'd worn for uniforms. Noxx House boasts some of the most prestigious alumni to make up the Vviveren cabinet—the ones who run the country. It's best known for its strategic thinkers, perfectionists, and highly regarded leaders, varying from celebrity athletes to CEOs in the city.

"Eva. Breathe. It's going to be okay," Emma says, now supporting Eva from the other side.

"Okay, we're going to get settled into our houses, then we can meet back in the courtyard. It's not a big deal."

"What if I can't find it?" Eva says, and they both look at me.

"You have the map, remember?"

While they continue to exchange worried questions, I dig through my suitcase again, realizing I will be sacrificing my map.

We're surrounded by cheers and howls as those around us celebrate their houses. Hordes of students in their respective house colors wave their flags and posters. They're lining the circular courtyard in waiting, shuffling around us to scream directly in our faces with their house pride. Eva's eyes stay wide like they're yelling *at* her for doing something wrong.

My father taught me houses at Doxlothia were a big deal. They each create legacy students, have their own traditions and history. But as I stare at the young adults around me screaming, running, and scaring my sisters, I can't help but wonder if it's more bullshit my dad peddled. Only time will tell.

I adjust the collar of my shirt and straighten my shoulders. We're still being gawked at. Perhaps I'm not used to the attention. We grew up in a secluded area and were homeschooled all but two years in our teen years, and even then, the school was mostly human.

I never thought I'd get to attend university, let alone start the same year as my sisters. I'm not complaining, us starting together makes this change easier, but it's not like we had any choice when Dad refused to let us out of his sight for more than a few hours.

Just like your mother, you and your sisters have special blood. I have to protect you. I don't need you to like me. I just need to keep you safe.

My dad's words ring in my head. Humans, werewolves, and vampires all live together peacefully, all the interspecies fighting ended centuries ago, and Doxlothia was founded shortly after. Seeing the campus for the first time proves it; there are booths for humans, donors, vampires, and werewolves alike. Most public schools are combined and with little issue from what I can tell. The Donor Program doesn't allow anyone under the age of twenty to join, and university doesn't start for the majority until twenty-one.

But Doxlothia is known as the safe haven for all, even humans who choose not to be donors like my sisters and me. Upon entrance to the courtyard, an iron gate holds a slate with the words "*a bridge between worlds*" carved deep into the stone.

"According to the map, our houses are on the left side of the river," Emma says to Eva, then looks at me. "Yours is on the far east side of the campus."

I look over my shoulder to the dimly lit path leading into the trees. "Right. So we'll settle in, and orientation is in a few hours at the front of the castle."

"Plenty of time," Emma says.

Eva's eyes are dull from the redness.

"Maybe call Jared. Tell him about the campus on your way," I say. I almost feel guilty for not having the same house assignment. Perhaps I should have prepared her better.

Jared is Evangeline's boyfriend. He's a human she met at the flower shop in our hometown, Groveshire. A safe match, but she'd never admit that. She says, "*He's nice*" when asked. He came for dinner once, and Emma and I interrogated him so viscously he never came again.

"Good idea." Eva grabs another cracker and chews.

"I'll meet up with you in a bit."

I sling my bag over my shoulder and head for the open path teeming with students. The ground is covered in colored cobblestones. Many are painted in various whimsical murals that resemble the constellations, with arrows and lettering that lead you to the various halls and houses. It's hard to see the full scope of the campus as the sun fades from the sky, but I'd memorized the map. All classes reside in the castle, along with the academic clubs. The other buildings are designated for arts and other extracurriculars. I am thinking about taking a detour to find the dance studio but second-guess it after worrying how long I might keep my sisters waiting.

The cobblestone bridge that leads to Noxx House is bathed in blue lights. I stop to gawk at the trickling water with lights lining the edges as the river bends into the trees. Noxx House looms above in a clearing with worn stone, a gabled roof, and a tower on the far right. The windows next to the front entrance are stained purple, and growing up the side onto the roof are branches of moon nightingales—a periwinkle flower that glows at night. I only know that because of Eva and her not-so-subtle flower obsession. The building isn't as massive and breathtaking as the castle but still as big as my former school with at least three stories. The lawn that wraps around Noxx House stretches far beyond what I can see, and there's another path leading out of sight. The sounds of celebration echo in the air from all sides, including a pack howling in the distance.

Gathered around the porch are various groups of older students already sporting their Noxx House purple, which varies in shades ranging from a deep-bluish plum to a light shade of lavender. They stop their conversations and stare for a moment as I pass. *It can't be helped.* As soon as my feet hit the hardwood of the porch, my shoulders drop.

I open the door and the foyer is in chaos. Some men bicker back and forth before disappearing into the common room on the right. There's a large arched opening on the left—

I stop, nearly toppling into someone because I'm staring at the tall ceilings and the stained-glass lights.

"Hi, Welcome to Noxx Hall. My name is Cherry," a woman with pure plum eyes greets me. Her hair is raven black on top and runs into long blue tendrils. I'm a little jealous. Ballet companies prefer neutral colors, so I've had dark-brown hair my entire life. Emma almost convinces me to dye a little strip under my hair for my birthday every year, but I refuse because it's too risky. A ballet dancer from my old school had to dye their natural-blue hair to black since before they were ten.

"You must be Olivia."

"How did you know?"

"It's my job to know all of the students assigned to Noxx House this semester, including identification."

It's not hard to identify me. Heterochromia isn't uncommon, but I've never seen anyone with a similar gold and violet pairing like me. Plus, it's normally seen in Weres. Mom used to say it was like I'd gotten the best parts of her love. Dad's golden eyes and her violet ones that her mother had. *It's pure magic,*" she'd said. She loved the unknowns of magic and potions.

"Here's the number for your dorm assignment, among other things you may need."

I finger the thick parchment between my fingers. Hidden between schedules is another map, a detailed list of the buildings on campus, and a pamphlet for The Donor Program.

I scoff, surprised she didn't give me the speech. There are commercials, presentations, and carefully curated campaigns dedicated to getting humans and werewolves to join since before we can talk. I'd already passed a few humans with badges, clinging to their lanyards. For many, being in The Donor Program is a sign of pride. It does have its perks. Better job opportunities, easier access to loans, and first dibs on housing in the city. But not everyone wants to be a donor or can be. Those who can't for medical reasons can file exemptions and still get access to the perks, but having blood that's more desirable doesn't fall under any type of exemption.

"Anything catch your eye?"

"The dance department."

"Oh, yes, I remember you were selected for auditions. You'll find the booth at orientation if you want to meet the program director. I will warn you, not many first-years get accepted in the company, but we encourage you to apply anyway."

"I'll get accepted." I tuck the pamphlet into my bag, then look up when I realize I might have offended her. Sometimes, people take my confidence as rudeness.

She doesn't though. Instead, her eyes spark with excitement. "That's the spirit we like to see in Noxx House."

There isn't much to unpack, so I decide to leave it. Other than a few old pictures of Mom and my sisters and some blankets from home, my suitcase is at least eighty percent ballet clothes. The room isn't that big, but the ceilings are high, which helps it appear more spacious. I want to scrub the whole place—the crevices in the stone walls, the tile floors with star patterns that lead to a small hearth, the arched windows—but I'll save that for tonight when I likely won't be able to sleep.

I run my fingers over the warm wood of my bed frame. The wood accents make the whole place feel less cold. My sisters and I had all summer to prepare for our move to Doxlothia University, but much of the history and traditions are hidden from the public, even with the constant stream of press at the school. My dad, who used to be a professor here, became extremely protective after my mom died, and my sisters and I weren't allowed to leave Groveshire unless he came along. That all changed when our acceptance letters came.

"Are you okay?"

Emma had screamed so loud I ran into our bedroom.

Tears streamed down her face, and she shakily held up an envelope. *"Look."*

The words were scrawled with a black pen. *Urgent: Doxlothia University.*

"Well, what does it say?" I asked.

"I'm in. I got accepted."

"When did you apply?"

"Are you kidding? I didn't! But here, look—you and Eva have one."

I grabbed the envelope and wasted no time opening it. There at the top confirmed my greatest want in a matter of seconds.

"I got in too." Without another word, I opened Eva's. She was at work and would yell at me for it, but I had to know.

"We've all been accepted."

"Why?"

I only knew one person with the power to do that. But why?

My father had changed his mind, and just like that, my dream school was at my fingertips. But the mystery of his reasoning haunts me as I remember his warning to bring my first aid with me everywhere I go on campus. I leave mine at the foot of the bed. Following my father's wishes is a habit I stopped long ago.

With a hand on the sapphire doorknob, I open the door to move into the chaos of the hallway. I brace myself for the man running by with a box in his hand while another chases after him at a speed I can't comprehend.

My body stops before my brain registers it, then I'm staring at the man coming from the door directly across from mine.

We close our doors at the same time. They click closed, and we halt.

A tall man with broad shoulders towers over me just a few feet away, wearing a mask—something you'd see in a horror movie. His shirt is nonexistent, and my eyes catch on the jagged scars across his chest.

My heart beats in my ears. Strange. A hot flash rings up my spine, and my throat dries when I open my mouth to exchange words. What words? Any. All. Something is better than nothing. You'd think I'd never seen a male with his shirt off before.

He twirls his fingers at me in a casual wave, and my senses snap back into place. I rest a hand on my chest and saunter down the hallway, my heart drumming hard against my ribcage. I'm just jumpy because of all the changes.

My phone chimes as I make my way onto the porch.

Em: *Haunted maze before orientation!!!*

I sigh. That was mentioned in the pamphlet. They turn the path that leads to the castle into a maze. *Doxlothia and their traditions.*

CHAPTER TWO

PARKER

"My chest kinda burns." I rub my sternum while devouring a burrito. They must have added extra hot peppers.

"Those burritos kill me," Zant says from next to me, wiping his hands. He's already consumed his.

The tree branch we're sitting on quakes under the weight of the two of us. His short, disheveled hair is being crushed by the mask dangling half on and half off his head.

"Worth it," I say, deciding any burrito from the culinary club is worth the heartburn.

Below us, a crowd of new students funnels through the haunted maze—a Doxlothia tradition since it first started. This year, I get to be the one doing the scaring and not the one walking alone in the maze, which is a path that runs through a wooded area and leads to the castle.   They set it up every year with artificial fog and obstacles you can't see around. I wasn't scared my first year, but it wasn't exactly a fun experience. Everyone else already had friends, packs, or even siblings to walk with. Zant is a year older than me and scouted me out in the maze. I almost killed him in the process of him trying to scare me last year.

Zant and I have been best friends since our early school years in the city. Long story short, our dads are business men who like to put their kids in private school. Only, my dad did it because he wanted to see me less and Zant's dad put him in because he actually loves him and cares about his future. I call him a daddy's boy, and he tells me to eat shit, but he smiles when he says it.

When I got Noxx House and couldn't join Zant in Solexxa, I was bummed, considering we'd gone to a private boarding school together and shared a room for years. But he said I'd be bored there, and he was probably right. Solexxa houses some of the smartest people on campus and produces the country's brightest scientist, lawyers, and several of Vviveren's famous botanists. Zant isn't interested in any of that, but he is smart. He says Noxx House is Solexxa's more energetic older brother that throws better parties.

I finish my burrito, thinking I want another. Just as I do, Zant pulls one from his bag and hands it to me.

"Don't say I never do anything for you."

"Why did you hide it?" I smile and snag it from him.

"I knew you'd find it and inhale it in a breath. I worry your stomach will burst."

I focus back on the crowd, eating my burrito, and Zant watches in disgusted horror as I devour it in four bites. Just when I'm about to get an earful, my spine straightens. Like a beacon, her steps call to me. There's no real reason for it—all the girls are permitted to wear the same shoes, but I still find her.

The girl from across the hall. I'd been such a dumbstruck asshole I didn't say a word to her then. I was afraid I'd scare her. A few of my packmates jump from the bushes, and she doesn't flinch but holds one of the girls while another one clings to her back. She looks tired and a little annoyed by the way she's shushing them every five seconds. Probably her sisters, if I had to guess. That type of annoyance is reserved for siblings.

Her dark hair frames her face, and her eyes stand out even in the dark. One golden and the other violet. I noticed them in the hall when her eyes widened, and my heart pounded at the sight of her.

"Who is that?" I ask.

Zant is on the council, which means he knows everything about everyone, and not just because they get the full list of incoming students.

"You haven't heard? Mighty Alpha didn't debrief you today?" Zant teases. Vampires don't understand pack dynamics. Just like they'd never understand the sensation of shifting under a full moon. There is nothing for them to compare it to. If you're not in a pack, you're a lone wolf, and that's for a select few. Being a lone wolf is the last thing I want to be. It's a lonely life, and if I'm packless, then as an alpha myself, it becomes nearly impossible to hide. All the ones I've known never had any family to begin with or were estranged from their pack for other reasons. It's all fucking depressing.

"I was in practice all day," I say, still staring.

"Uh-huh, is that why you're hiding here with me and not your precious packmates?"

I'm not hiding. My pack leader, Gavin, is on the council too, which means he and the other students on the council lead the orientation along with the dean.

"You're one to talk, shouldn't you be on your way to orientation right now?"

"I'm killing time. Someone's gotta keep you company. I can't believe none of them asked you to go scare with them."

I didn't expect them to. Being a stray alpha in Gavin's pack doesn't get me any fuzzy feelings from the rest of the pack. Still, it's better than the alternative. But none of that matters if I don't pick a mate this year. I sigh at the familiar twist of tension in my chest.

When I don't answer, Zant says, "The whole campus has been buzzing about them. Take a whiff."

They smell like a collection of floral perfume, spice, and baked goods, but it's not anything abnormal. "They smell human."

"You gotta tune into it. Pure vampire instinct. Focus on one of them. Think about her blood and the wetness of it on your tongue. Her heartbeat. The surge of blood when you drink directly from the vein."

Being a hybrid has its perks but also drawbacks. It makes everything fucking hard. Tuning into the werewolf instinct versus the vampire is different, and I have to concentrate real hard to do either.

Trying to humor him, I focus on the dark-haired girl I can't seem to stop watching anyway. I imagine standing in front of her, her eyes widening as I sweep the hair from her collarbone and run my lips over the warmth of her neck. Her blood pumping below the surface of her porcelain skin when I sink my teeth into the pulsing vein in her neck. The euphoria and the harmonious flutter of her blood as it surges into my mouth.

I take another long breath, and the hairs on my arm rise with the scent filling my head, and the rush carries heat from my skull to my toes. *So sweet.*

I almost never think about blood, but I'm thinking of her blood a lot now and how to get to it.

"Shit. That's different," I say. The burning in my chest is more intense, and now it's in my throat too.

"They've got something special. Those three sisters are all anyone is talking about, including the council."

Mention of the council snaps me out of my daze.

"I take it your stance hasn't changed this year?"

"I don't want a council seat."

He nudges me. "We need more people like you. We've got too many assholes and not enough golden boys like the great Parker Owens."

Zant has been asking me to join the council since before I went to Doxlothia. He called me the first year he got in and said, "*Dude, you gotta do this.*"

He loves the politics of it all, the power, but more importantly, the gossip.

"Don't fucking call me that." I try to wrestle him off the branch, and the bark snaps and cracks with our weight threatening to buckle it.

"You'd be an instant vote-in. All the girls screaming your name and holding up your posters. '*Oh, Parker. Mark me. Please!*'"

I tackle him again, and we fight until the tree cracks and sags a few inches lower.

"Truce," we say at the same time.

Noxx House has housed more people on the council than any other house. Zant says it's a sign. He thinks everything is a sign. His mom is really intuitive and into that stuff.

"I'm just saying it could solve just about every one of your problems this year."

The air's filled with all sorts of smells, but my eyesight improves in the dark, making the girl from the hallway easy to find again. She's getting closer, only a few feet away. Both the wolf and the vampire in me like watching her from above in the shadow of the treetop.

"It's too much pressure," I say before my attention is completely elsewhere.

"And Captain Owens can't handle pressure?"

"That's different. I'm good at sports. It comes naturally."

The last thing I need is to draw more attention to myself and make trouble for Gavin. No matter where I am, assholes seem to follow. One reason I joined

Gavin's pack was to lay low and stay out of trouble. Other alphas might consider it humiliating to submit in another alpha's pack, but I call it vacation. No one bothers me or asks me about the future. Why must I always *do* and be something?

It leaves me open to focus on being a good captain and getting onto a pro team. What more do I need?

"You're a *natural* leader." He taps me. "It's in your blood, I hear."

"Don't remind me."

Zant continues talking about all the things in my blood and the fact he believes in me. Blah, blah, blah, but I tune out his caring words like I normally do and find the girl from the hallway again. They haven't made much progress. Mostly, her sisters prevent her from moving more than a few inches at a time before they scream and use her as a human shield.

I need to know her name.

"Are you even paying attention?" Zant hits me on the shoulder, then follows my line of sight to the girls. "Fine, you closed-off bastard."

"She's got the eye thing," I say.

"Like Cane." He finishes the part of the sentence I don't want to say.

Different-colored eyes are usually associated with old werewolf bloodlines. She smells human though, so it must be distant.

"Do you know her name?" I ask.

"Uh, no, I skimmed the list. Let's go say hi. See if we can get her name. Ten bucks says I'll get her to tell me first."

I smile and tug my mask over my face. "Deal."

The girls scream as we drop from the trees and cut off their path while the dirt plumes around us.

The girl from the hallway doesn't though. Her eyes instantly shoot to me, and I have to stop myself from getting closer. Her heart stutters as I tilt my head and observe her. There in the buzzing lights lining the path, I take in her full image. The dark-brown hair that flows past her shoulders, and her bright eyes, uniquely beautiful, but it's her lips I halt on—soft and pale pink.

"Hi, ladies." Zant saunters closer to them. "Welcome to Doxlothia. Are we having fun?"

His mask is on and pieces of his black hair are curled next to his ears as he stands in front of her. Something foreign twists in my stomach and zips up my spine. I don't want him near her. Zant's a natural with women. I guess I am too, but I've never wanted to keep one from him. *Weird reaction, but okay.*

"No. I don't get this," the little blonde one with pink-tipped hair says.

"The haunted maze is a cherished tradition passed down from the inception of this school. It symbolizes the founders and their journey to finding this spot for Doxlothia in the mountains. Now we just scare newcomers."

"Seems cruel," the taller blonde says from behind the others.

I said the same thing last year. If I ever do make council, that's got to be one of the first things to change.

Zant moves closer, but the girl from the hallway keeps her eyes on me. It makes my skin itch—in a good way. My inner wolf rushes forward, and I step toward her till there's only a foot or two between us. *Closer.*

Her lips don't move, but it's like I can hear a voice. Likely all me and my growing desire to know what her skin feels like.

As a hybrid, it takes more effort for me to get a read on the emotions of others. Well, at least for me. Gavin introduced me to a hybrid upperclassman who wasn't even an alpha but just really good at everything. Smell. Blood drinking. I was a little jealous, but he had his dad to help him. And mine's a professional dick, so that was always out of the question.

"When you're a second-year, you get the secret code to bypass the maze, or you can become a scarer. Plus, no harm will come to you here. Name's Zant. I'm on the council, and I'm one of the nice ones."

The shorter blonde with pink hair rolls her eyes.

"I told you my name. Will you tell me yours?" Zant asks, moving closer to her and twirling a piece of her hair.

"My name is Emma. Evangeline is the oldest—" She's pointing to the other taller blonde one beside her when *my* girl stops her.

"You don't need to tell him, Em."

I swallow at the sound of her voice. *What is wrong with me?*

Zant smirks, and I feel his gaze but can't stop looking at her.

The longer I stand next to her, the more I sense. Unlike the other two who are filling the air with anxiety and fear, the girl from the hallway isn't scared. Even when I inch forward, something in her scent leaps. It's different. New. A sensation I don't think I've identified before. That's not uncommon for me, but this is desire.

She wants me closer. It's humming under my skin, urging me to please her. My heart kicks my ribs so hard I ball my hands into fists.

"I will if you will." *Oh, stars above, her voice.*

She's talking to me. She's actually talking to me. Wait, what was the question? Oh. Name. Right, I need her name.

"You first." I aim to keep my tone level.

Her heartbeat speeds when I speak, and a flush of pink spreads beneath her skin. She takes a step back, and her eyes taunt me. *Closer. Get closer.*

Now I'm imagining touching her again. Just her hand is enough or maybe her cheek. The need to know what her skin feels like pressed against mine has me licking my lips.

"What's the council?" Evangeline asks, brows furrowed.

"Oh, you'll see. The council is how this school is run. There are three ruling factors here—the board of directors, the dean, and the council that's entirely student run. The dean oversees the university and makes sure everyone is playing nice, but the council is what decides which programs get the most funding, events, rules—"

"So if you're on the council, that means you'll help escort us out of the maze." Evangeline perks up. "Right?"

"I'll give you ten seconds to run, and I promise I'll chase you till you reach the end of your destination."

I'm glad Zant is doing what he's best at—talking. For once, it's useful.

"You coming?" Zant shrugs at me before moving back to my girl.

"In a minute," I say.

Emma runs first, and Zant trains his eyes on Evangeline, who is still hiding behind her sister.

"You should run," I say, staring into her violet and gold eyes.

She doesn't flinch, and I wonder if she is waiting for the same thing I am. One brief touch. That's all I want.

"Come on!" Evangeline grabs her arm, but my girl stays still.

Zant tears after Evangeline with playful laughter and a chant that echoes in the trees.

Then it's just me and the girl from the hallway in the silent chaos surrounding us. Screams and laughter flutter through the air.

"What's your name?" I inch closer until her back is against a tree.

Her scent calms when we're alone, and I can't take it anymore. I test her reaction with a brush of my fingers against her arm. We tense together but melt in the next breath.

What is this? I've never felt this type of yearning before. There isn't a word for it.

Closer. Please. I swear her voice is calling to me, but I can't hear her. Her pupils dilate, and the hairs raise on her arms. She's trapped against a tree, and I still have this ridiculous mask on.

"You're not scared?" I ask.

Her heart hums in a cadence that feels oddly familiar. The entirety of her is familiar, though I know I've never met her before.

I cup her cheek, and she tenses, then leans into me ever so slightly. Excitement bubbles in my stomach at the warmth of her skin.

"No," she spits back.

"Then tell me your name."

"I don't give my name to random masked men."

"But you'll let them touch you?"

We're leaning into one another like we aren't strangers. Like touching our lips together right here, right now wouldn't be insane. Her blood pumping beneath her skin is so sweet, but there's another scent settling in my chest. It's the warm comfort of safety. I toy with a strand of her hair and drag my fingers lower, barely grazing her skin at the hem of her sweater. Her breath hitches.

My long breaths mirror hers, so I close the remaining distance till we're hip to hip and my hands move up beneath her sweater. And she's letting me, like we're the only two people who exist. As her eyes shut, I come to one troubling conclusion: I want to mark her.

I've never felt the urge, but now the need to sink my teeth into her is unbearable.

This girl *has* to be mine.

A scream rings through the air. It must be one of her sisters because she becomes lucid and shoves me away.

I'm dazed as she disappears from view.

Well, shit.

Chapter Three

Olivia

I tear through the clearing of trees along the lit path, passing a few groups of students till there are none, with the light from the moons casting a glow over the cobblestone.

"Eva! Emma!"

Nothing.

I run till my heeled shoes rub the back of my ankles raw and I heave for breath. Stopping in a dim clearing in the trees, I take in my reality.

I'm alone. The chiming laughter and cheers that were once close have dissipated. There's music just beyond the trees, but I haven't run into any new scarers jumping from the trees or lingering first-years. My stomach sours, and I dust off my skirt to get my bearings and catch my breath.

In the dense wood, a twig snaps.

Doxlothia is safe. There's nothing to be afraid of.

As I turn to the path forward, a shadowed figure strolls in. They're slender and wearing a blazer, with hands in their pockets.

If Doxlothia isn't safe, that unfortunately means my dad was right, and I'm not about to come to that conclusion so easily. So I keep my feet firmly planted.

"Well, hello there." A man with silver hair emerges wearing a plum blazer and slacks, brushing off his shoes as he comes to stand in front of me. He's ghostly pale.

"Ugh, filthy business. I was hoping to catch you here before the festivities."

He was waiting for me. My brain isn't working nearly fast enough to form a plan of action, but my body steps back a few feet all on its own.

He sniffs the air. "I see you've met Owens. Sweet guy."

"And you're ...?"

"Darien. Apologies. But you see, I'm not here for anything pleasant, I'm afraid."

I take another step back, but there's nowhere to run. One glance toward the path tells me I'm alone. The masked guy didn't follow me. I don't know why I think he'd be helpful. It's not like I know him, but as the silence spreads between Darien and me, I long for that feeling again—the safety and calm his touch brought me.

I blink, then Darien is in front of me, and before I can move, he grabs my wrist and slams a hand over my mouth. Yanking my arm away gives little wiggle room.

"I know. I know. But trust me. Of your options tonight, this is the better one. Plus ..." He leans into my neck, and I freeze. "I get to have all the fun."

I groan, trying to weasel away from his grasp, but his fingers dig into my skin so hard I think they might draw blood.

"Your heart is drumming like a scared rabbit. You're not used to this, are you? If you were in The Donor Program, this would be an easy act of submission. Didn't your mother teach you?"

Fire singes through my veins, and I bite one of his fingers, and he loosens his grip just enough.

"Fuck you," I spit.

Then I'm on the ground faster than I can comprehend. I've met vampires, but none of them were like this. My mom's donees were nice. One she'd donated to for years was her best friend in her ballet company. She'd bring me cookies.

This is evidently nothing like that. The ground is cold as I thrash around while Darien pins my hips with his knees with very little effort.

"You know it's been a while since I've gotten to experience this kind of thrill when drinking. It's a pity it has to end."

He leans in, and his teeth sink into my neck. My screams are muffled behind his grasp. A searing pain flushes through me, awakening the adrenaline lingering in my body, and I wrestle past the pain.

Every second, my muscles weaken, but I don't stop. I can't. I manage enough room to shove a knee in his groin, and I'm up on my feet so fast I don't register where I'm going.

Somewhere else. Somewhere safe.

CHAPTER FOUR

Parker

The hairs on my arms rise and my muscles tighten with the need to chase her. The wolf inside me begs me to follow her as she disappears along the path. I crane my neck, ready to run, but a high-pitched whine stills me. A few seconds later, I hear a cry for help.

I'm following the sound before my brain registers the movement, and I step into the brush. Seconds later, a man barrels into me with dirt and blood smeared in his hair and on his face. He's in all black, so he has to be a new student. His scent is heavy in a way I instantly identify him as a Were. Weres have stronger, richer scents.

"What's going on?"

"There's someone. He's—"

"Hello, Parker." Cane steps through the maze. His green and yellow eyes glow as he leans against a tree. His suit is pristine. I can smell the curiosity from others watching just out of sight. "I was just greeting ..."

"Finn," Finn says, wiping his cheek.

"You know how it is for first-years. Just seeing who might be interested in my pack. Finn says the lone wolf life is for him. Pity. I know you know what that's like."

A growl rips through my teeth, and Cane deadpans while straightening the blazer of his uniform. I've lost count of the years I've had to know this asshole and that stupid cropped haircut he's had since we were kids. He looks just like his father, who I've met and can confirm is also a jackass. Cane's entire family is known for their white hair and green and yellow eye coloring.

His attention lingers on my hand, and his nostrils flare.

He can smell her.

The thought snaps my rigid muscles into play. I need to find her. Now.

"You were looking for her," I say. His jaw tenses, but his mouth stays tightly shut.

Of course. Cane has connections on campus. He'd known she was coming. There's no way she knows the danger she's in. With eyes like that, the werewolves have likely already made plans for her, and they won't leave her alone. It shouldn't be my problem, but it is. Because if she needs help, there aren't many people here who will.

I say nothing to Cane before leaving. He knows my threats by now. It's implied, and he's not a fighter.

"You're fine, Finn. Fuck Cane."

"What about school?" he says as we walk back toward the path.

"If he does anything, tell me and I'll handle it."

"Is everyone here like that?"

"No, not everyone."

When we walk into the light, his eyes widen upon me shedding my mask. "You're Parker Owens."

I smile. "Yep."

He opens his mouth, and I suspect a string of pleasantries and compliments, but I don't have time.

I pat him on the back. "See you around."

Moving to track her scent, I smell my fingers where her sweetness lingers and let it marinate till my head is full of elation. There's no safe place for anyone who smells like that, but especially not at a place like Doxlothia where the most prestigious families send their vampire and werewolf sons and daughters. Blood like that is valuable. And anything of value here can be exploited. Throughout history, sweeter blood is sought after by vampires and werewolves alike. Now in modern day, you need to be careful till you're in The Donor Program.

Surely, she and her sisters are in The Donor Program, and I'm worried for nothing. Still, I need to check—werewolves are natural protectors of humans.

My heart is pounding so hard, nausea takes over when I smell blood. Why am I so worried? There are no chances of murder at Doxlothia. The smell of blood is normal here. She'll be fine. But the thought of anyone touching her is enough to make my skin tingle like I'm going to shift. *It would be faster.* My tracking skills are better in that form, but the loss of clothes during a school event could be a problem.

The sweet scent of blood gets stronger. *Fresh.*

I find her in the clearing, stumbling forward, and jet toward her. She buries her head into my chest when her legs give out. With one arm, I hold her up.

"It's okay. I'm here. You're safe. I won't hurt you."

For some reason, she believes me, and she leans into me so long I think she's smelling me.

"Let me look at you."

She blinks a few times as I move the hair from her face. Touching her is like being electrocuted. There's a bite on her neck with smeared blood. Vampires have so much practice biting humans they don't typically leave blood trails. She must've run.

"My ... sisters ... I have to ..."

I don't like how cold she is.

"Don't worry. I'll fix you up." I hoist her over my shoulder and head toward the entrance of the maze. It's not much farther if I run.

The Central Lawn is buzzing with activity and students, but no one pays us any attention as I move so she can sit on the grass. The glow from the lawn lanterns highlight the gold and lilac in her eyes. She's beautiful.

Surveying her again, I smell her to see if I can figure out who did this.

I have a guess, but it can wait.

"My sisters," she says, with more strength this time.

"I didn't see them, and I don't smell more blood, so I think they made it out." If Zant chased them out, they'll be fine. He is likely showing them around. He can be an ass, but he'd never hurt them. "They're safe with Zant."

She grumbles as I hold her upright.

"You're not going to like this." I lift her chin, and she doesn't flinch when I move my lips to her neck to lick the bite mark clean. I tune strictly into my inner wolf, holding my breath. Thinking about her blood and how good it tastes is the last thing I need to do while trying to heal her.

She groans again and shrinks away from me, but her fingers stay wrapped around my forearm.

"I know it's gross. But it's a Were thing. It closes your wound. Someone just took a lot of blood from you, but you'll be okay." Needing to warm her, I draw her to me, and a faint whimper leaps from her throat, as her fingers curl into my forearm. "I'll get you some Quik-Recover."

The fact she's been attacked is proof she isn't a donor. Donor Program rules are strict, and there are laws on harming anyone in the program. I'm not in the program because hybrid blood is the least sought after. But as an over six-foot male, I don't need to worry about people jumping out of the bushes to bite me.

I grab my bag from the utility lockers, and in less than a minute, I'm next to her again. I shake the little carton in front of her face before I punch the straw through. She takes it with one hand and reaches for me with the other. Happy to be her support, I scoot in closer so she doesn't need to work so hard to stay upright. Quik-Recover is an emergency aid for when someone sucks the life out of you. She'll likely still need a transfusion though.

"It's safe. It will help." I move the straw to her lips. As she drinks, the color springs into her cheeks and all that anxious energy making my skin itch dissipates.

"Why am I so cold?" she asks.

"Have you never gotten bitten before? Never donated?"

She shakes her head. *That explains a lot.*

"It's normal. Here." I put my arm around her.

The chill of the night doesn't help. I bring her hands closer to my stomach so she can warm them, and her fingers trail along my abs and work up my chest. Though her skin is cold, everywhere she touches me burns. It's oddly exhilarating. *Head in the game, Parker.*

"Still feel dizzy?"

She nods and leans into me, so I let her rest on me.

"It takes a few minutes to work."

She struggles to keep her head up, so I hold onto her face, rubbing her cheek with my thumb. There's something so natural about having her in my arms. The world around us fades away as I tend to her. I don't think about any of the stares or the fact that orientation has started—I just enjoy her presence.

"It will be okay. Don't worry. I won't let anything happen to you."

The words pour from me without warning. They're true, sure, but do I really need to tell this random girl that *out loud*? I need to get a grip. She might be finding this creepy while not being able to move as she's cradled by some guy in the grass.

I'm about to loosen my grip on her, but she lets out a lengthy breath and leans into me with one arm wrapping around my torso. Her heartbeat, once rapid, is slowing. It's the only cue I needed to stay holding her close. She lays her head against my chest, and I lick the sweetness of her blood lingering on my lips. I can't help but think of the asshole who sank their teeth into her, and the thought sends my brain to places that involve me starting fights. Bad idea.

"We'll sit here for a few minutes, and then we'll go to the nurses' station."

"And your name is …?"

"Parker Owens. Sorry, I got a little carried away back there."

"I'm Olivia Osborne." Her voice is soft, but her eyebrows are drawn together like she's studying me. The more she recovers, the more her hold loosens. *Olivia*.

"I have to find my sisters."

"They made it out of the maze. I'm sure—Ow!"

Something hard whacks me in the head from behind, and the edges of my vision blur.

"Stay away from my sister!"

With the large branch inches from my face, I snatch it out of the air.

"Ow?" I say, still confused on how I let some little blonde human clock me so hard in the head.

"Eva. He's fine." Olivia finally pulls away from me as the Quik-Recover works its magic. It has actual magical properties. I briefly remember the lesson I had on it in my early years of school, something about temporarily accelerating the production of blood cells.

"Please don't press charges." Evangeline's eyes widen.

I throw the branch, rubbing the back of my head, and it lands with a hollow thud.

"It's fine."

"Ah!" Then the shorter blonde leaps from the trees also holding a large branch like a baseball bat.

"Emma, he's fine! He helped," Evangeline says. Our brief interaction in the maze starts to come back. I wasn't really paying attention to anyone but Olivia.

"Are you sure? He looks sketchy." Emma drops her weapon and hauls Olivia from my grasp. "Are you okay?"

Evangeline clutches her chest in horror, her breath spreading up.

"I'm fine," Olivia says.

"She needs blood. I was going to take her to the nurses' station."

The three of them look up at me as I stand and brush the dirt off my pants. Unfortunately, I'm still shirtless, so I'm giving off douchebag energy. Their fearful eyes turn into careful surveillance. They definitely aren't buying it.

"We can take her," Evangeline says, cleaning up her sister with a cloth from her jacket.

I don't love that thought. Three helpless humans dragging their sweet scent—that is now out in the open and drying into the fabric of Olivia's sweater—all across campus.

"Why don't we all go? I can carry her. It will get her there faster."

"I guess we don't exactly know where it is. We're new here," Emma says.

She says it as if the fact they aren't in their house colors yet isn't a dead giveaway.

"I can see that. Where are you from?"

"The woods."

"In general, the woods?"

"Groveshire," Olivia says.

"Mom moved us there after we were born," Emma chimes in, and Olivia shakes her head.

"Oh, I've never heard of it."

"Most people haven't," Evangeline says. She's watching me the closest, and I'm happy they have at least a sliver of self-preservation. I bend to help Olivia off the ground, surveying her one more time. No open cuts allowed.

"Are you a medic or something?" Evangeline says.

"No, it's standard, especially for pack members to have medical supplies on them."

"So you're a werewolf," Emma says.

"I'm a hybrid. Vampire and werewolf. You do know that's a thing, right?"

"Of course we do."

Now they're all giving me some form of a glare. Emma rolls her eyes, Evangeline's eyes squint like I've just insulted her, and Olivia is giving me that endearing *shove it up your ass* expression.

"Doxlothia isn't generally dangerous. It's safer to be part of The Donor Program, for sure. There are still people here that will take a bite out of you if you're not careful."

I wrap my arm around Olivia to lift her over my shoulder but stop when Darien moves into our circle.

"Oh, I see you've caught my leftovers. But oh, two new little rabbits have come into play."

A growl leaps from my throat. I knew it was him. Darien smells like money. He only wears expensive cologne, and because he's on the council with Zant, I've unfortunately memorized the smell of it. That and the smell of his hair gel. They're under a magnifying glass and always have to look their best. Zant says he hates it, but I think that's bullshit.

Darien stops a few feet away—he knows better than to piss me off.

"Fuck off. You can't claim them. They are not part of The Donor Program."

"Oh, I know. And that's what makes it fun. Free game."

I grit my teeth. "Do they look like free game to you?"

The girls huddle around Olivia, and I'm in front, blocking them from Darien. The edge of my vision blurs and my hands tremble. I love the feeling of my inner wolf just below the surface, and I'd love to let it out.

But I also know better than to get into a fist fight with a member of the council.

Darien's smile fades as I step closer. Protection on behalf of others is a gray area.

"I expected nothing less from Parker Owens. Say, I hear you're going for the open council spot this year," Darien says with a taunting smile.

"Who told you that?"

As I say it, Zant saunters in, putting himself between Darien and me.

"Really?"

"Come on, gentlemen. Not in front of the new students. It makes us look bad," Zant says.

"Stay away from them," I say to Darien.

"You're going to have a tough semester ahead if you're keen on protecting these three ... without the help of the majority council."

"Worry about yourself," I say through gritted teeth.

Darien chuckles to himself and disappears through the crowd gathering for orientation.

"Sorry about that." I turn to the girls. "Don't worry about him. Here, let me get you to the nurses' station."

I go to hoist Olivia over my shoulder.

"Wait!" Evangeline sheds her cardigan and ties it around Olivia's waist.

I motion for Zant to follow me so I can give him an earful for spinning yarns about me to the council. Olivia's breasts are pressed into my shoulder, and the sweet scent of her blood floods my senses.

Oh, fuck. I'm in trouble.

CHAPTER FIVE

Olivia

The room spins as I sway on Parker's shoulder. Being upside down doesn't help, and I'm tired of having a man's hand on my ass.

"You can put me down now."

My head swirls when he does, but I'm stuck staring at the scars peppering his stomach. The fair skin of his chest makes them stand out in long jagged lines that span to his arms, with smaller scratches up his forearms. His chocolate-brown hair is shaved short on the sides, and the top falls onto his forehead.

He notices me noticing him, and his worried expression turns into a grin showcasing his canines.

We're at the main entrance of the castle, and the double doors are propped open to let in the draft of the night. The trickling of the water fountains outside greets us. Light from the candles lining the walls flickers with each gust, and the orientation is mostly contained on the Central Lawn, but there are a few groups of students lingering in the main entrance. The stone walls tower above us, and a double staircase takes up the center of the room. I've never seen a building so vast, and even though I toured the castle this summer, it still strikes me with awe.

"Here. It's this way." Parker stays next to me, ushering me with a hand on my back.

He escorts us to the left, through a windowed partition and down a hallway. There's no hesitation when he opens the door to a small lobby. It has the same ambiance as the rest of the castle, but there's a fireplace going as we all gather on a patterned rug. The castle is filled with intricately placed tiles that shimmer like moonstone in the crevices. The pamphlet said each was individually painted.

"Parker, what are you doing here? Don't tell me you already got into a scuffle." An older woman appears behind the desk.

"No. Olivia needs help." He swallows after saying my name. "I gave her some Quik-Recover. Someone bit her in the maze."

"Oh dear, come here."

She smells of firewood and antiseptic, leading me toward an open hallway. "The rest of you need to get back to orientation."

"Can't we stay?" Eva asks. "We're her sisters."

"Your sister will be fine here. It's best you don't miss anything as a first-year."

"I can stay," Parker says. "Since I've technically been. *Zant* can escort Emma and Evangeline. As a grand member of the council, he'll be a good guide."

Zant is standing next to my sisters, towering over them with his hands in his pockets. His frame is slender but muscular. Parker and Zant are still shirtless and they both have scars across their chests and arms. Only Zant's are lighter and less pronounced.

There's a look between them, but Zant says, "I'd be honored."

"Yes, yes. That would be lovely. Thank you, Zant." She obviously doesn't detect the sarcasm in his voice.

"I'll meet up with you after," I tell my sisters, who're being escorted away by Zant.

Orientation is crowded, so any worries I have of my sisters being attacked dissipates. I may not trust Zant, but I don't have much of a choice but to trust Parker who could have left me in the maze if he wanted. As she steers me to a bed, I try again to pinpoint what his game might be. Perhaps he's decided he wants my blood all to himself, so he's gaining my trust to drain me later. Or maybe he's going to use me in some deal for the council. Though, in his defense, he didn't seem too friendly with Darien.

I'm too exhausted to keep thinking, so I stop.

The infirmary is a wide room with tall windows lining the walls on either side. It almost looks like our greenhouse back home, but the stonework looks expensive. I'm taken to one of the beds in the back, and she instructs me to hold out my arm, then runs a handheld beeping scanner over my wrist.

"Quik-Recover is working beautifully. But let's get you a transfusion so you can be on your way. You'll be tired, but we don't want you to miss anything."

I've never been in a hospital before. The most I've ever encountered is a bad cold, but the medicine my parents brought home was quick to knock it out. Where I'm from, the medicine is mostly human invention, but there is clearly a more advanced way of doing things at Doxlothia.

Heeled steps click on the smooth, cream stone flooring, echoing around us. A tall woman with dusty-blue hair demands all the attention in the room. She, like the other staff, is dressed in a long, structured skirt and blazer top with the school logo.

"Hello, Mrs. Abrams." Parker straightens in her presence. His blue eyes are bright when he turns to me. "This is the dean of Doxlothia University."

"I know." I smile at her. "I'd shake your hand, but I'm a little dizzy."

"Oh, no need. I was just about to go out and start the address when I heard one of you girls was in the infirmary. Terrible. Stop by the front office and fill out a report. We'll investigate. I assure you we don't allow that type of behavior here."

"Actually, I know—"

Parker shakes his head swiftly.

"Parker ..."

"I would be happy to show her how to fill out that report." He flashes her a toothy smile. The weight of his gaze is heavier, so I decide to let it go for now.

"Perfect. I'm so glad you're showing her the grounds. I can't think of anyone better." She turns to me. "I've been anticipating your arrival all summer. Your father called me a number of times to talk about the accommodations. I was happy to hear you were attending ..."

Her brow furrows like she wants to say more, then my brain connects the dots and fills in the likely category.

"Have you given any thought to joining The Donor Program?"

That's the only real way the university can assure our safety. Donor Program participants are federally protected by strict laws. I know that. That's what my mother did and how she was able to attend Doxlothia in peace. I doubt anyone, including my father, anticipated one of us getting bitten on the first night here.

The dean is probably worried I'll tell my father, but he's looking for a reason to bring me home. There's no way I'll tell him this.

"I know you were selected for the company audition. I wish you luck on your dancing endeavors. You know we sure do miss your father here on staff."

Her words are a knife in the gut. At least someone misses my father's company. He was a professor for Interspecies Communication. I faintly remember the tapes my mother would show of his presentations. She was his biggest fan. Without my father's connections, we'd have never been able to pay for the tuition. It was a shock to me when I learned what he'd done. I wasn't sure what shocked me more, the fact I'd been able to attend the school I'd been dreaming about all my life after spending years coming to terms with the knowledge my dad would never let us out of his sight, or the fact that he'd changed his mind.

I still don't know why. Emma and Eva never press him on whys, and when I do, I'm the bad guy, so I didn't and packed up my stuff early summer and laid low in case he changed his mind.

"I do hope he's taking care of himself."

"He's fine." I can't hide the flatness in my voice.

She must sense it because she changes the subject. "I see you've already met our star Rage captain."

"Rage?" I'm trying to recall which sport that is through hazy memories of knowledge on supernatural sports teams. I didn't watch a lot of news or TV in Groveshire. Especially not any sports, and especially not anything humans can't play.

"It's where we pass around a puck on the ice and fight each other." Parker smiles.

"Like hockey?"

"Yeah, but not. It's rougher. The humans got it from us."

"It's a way for many packs to blow off all that energy and gently settle disputes. Here at Doxlothia, we founded Vviveren's first combined species team with Weres and vampires. We take a lot of pride in our players," Mrs. Abrams adds.

The memory of Parker's scarred body comes to mind.

"Parker is this year's Rage captain. The youngest we've ever had."

"Wow." I try to hide the sarcasm.

"I had a good captain last year," he says.

The nurse is busy hooking me up to a blood bag, and there's no pain to it. She mumbles to me about how far they've come in pain management.

Parker stays for the duration of my visit, and I'm thankful for his small talk with the nurse. It helps as the sickness slowly leaves my body until I'm able to function again.

It takes an hour, and I missed the welcome speech, but I don't mind it.

"Why did you stop me earlier?" I ask, as Parker and I make it out onto the lawn. The night air is brimming with glowing bugs that disappear with the light from the orientation stage coming into view.

"Things work differently here. If you tell the dean that Darien attacked you, he's going to make your life difficult."

"More difficult than he's already made it?"

"Darien is mostly harmless, but his family is on the board of directors, and that, you should be afraid of. He's on the council. If you do anything to mess with their ability to go to school here, they will find a way to get you sent out of here first."

"I'm not afraid."

I've dealt with difficult people before. Ballet is full of all types of people. Some are rigid and domineering and will do anything to get to the top.

"It's not about being afraid. There are just better ways to use your time here than picking fights."

"You're one to talk. Sounds like you end up in the infirmary a lot."

"I do." He straightens his shoulders and leans in. Then I'm back to thinking about the warmth his skin admits. "Listen, Olivia, Doxlothia is an amazing place. You like to dance?"

"I more than *like* dance. It's all I've ever wanted."

"Then trust me, you can't get to the top by picking fights with the council."

"So I'm just supposed to let them do what? Drain me any time they feel like?"

"No. I can help with that. I'll talk to my pack and see if there's anything we can do to get you protection for the semester at least."

"Are werewolves like bodyguards or something?"

"No, it's more about status. Werewolves hold the most prestigious alliances in our school, and a lot of them grow up with those alliances and take them into the government or their jobs. My pack leader is very respected here. Even the council will honor that respect."

"Why do you care?" It's harsh, but I need to know. If Doxlothia is a place where alliances are formed and the council rules, what's Parker doing helping me?

"I know what it's like to be alone and needing a little help getting the hang of things here."

We're standing too close as strangers. A few more inches and we'll be right where we left off in the forest. I turn my head and look up at him.

"Fine. Thank you." That's the best I can manage to a stranger I can't trust yet.

Parker's smile is back and brimming over with bright enthusiasm. "Great. I guess, welcome to Doxlothia."

CHAPTER SIX

PARKER

"I'm here," I whisper into her thigh.

My lips graze warm skin, and her faint whimpers fill my head like a song.

"Oh, Parker. I need you." She moans.

"Olivia, I'm here. I'm not going anywhere. I've been looking for you."

I wake with Olivia on my mind, but I have no idea why. Suddenly, helping her and her sisters is the first thing on my to-do list. We caught the tail end of orientation, and Olivia was exhausted after her transfusion she didn't want to do much, aside from visit the dance department booth.

My room is dark as I throw on my school uniform and grab my gym bag by the door. I'm careful not to slam it before slowly making my way into the dimness of the hall. It's early morning and not many students are up.

"Are you stalking me?" Olivia's pointed whisper is feet from me, so I spin to face her.

"Stalking? No. I have practice in the morning. I should be asking you that. *I* do this every morning. Why are you up so early?"

"The studio is open, and I have to dance consistently to stay in shape."

She's dressed in a leotard and tights with a bag slung over her shoulder and her hair pulled into a bun. It's so—

Fuck. Parker, stop it. We're just pretending we didn't almost kiss yesterday and my hands weren't under her shirt. Like that was a completely normal way for strangers to say hello.

"Ballet, right?"

She nods and starts down the hall, and I naturally follow.

"Let me walk you. Just in case. I'd rather not worry about you walking around campus in the dark."

The need to protect her is still very prevalent, and the tension in my chest disintegrates when she accepts my offer.

She says nothing else, but every few seconds, I spy her looking over at me as she picks at her nail polish. When we reach the studio, her momentum stops, and she opens her mouth to speak. Her room key falls from her hand and lands with a clink on the floor, and we both reach to grab it. When I step closer, her eyes shoot up to me.

Our hands touch as I relinquish it to her, then it's just me looking down at her. Again. Something charged moves between us in the silence.

"I'll check in later?" I offer her an out and step back.

She shakes her head, then hurries away from me like I've just confessed my undying love for her or something, and I resolve to let it go. *Weirdo.*

"Gavin, come on."

The ice rink is one of the worst places to have this conversation because it's so fucking loud, but I ask him to meet me there after practice since it's important. Also, it takes me a good thirty minutes to clean up and towel off all the blood before I hit the showers.

"No. And at least try to address me as Alpha in public."

"You can't be fucking serious," I spit.

Gavin leans against the wooden post while I shrug off my gear on the player's bench and my team exits the ice. His voice burns my skin, like my blood knows I'm taking orders from another alpha. It's an involuntary thing. "*A natural rejection of the bond,*" he'd said. I'm lucky he let me join his pack, but it's painfully obvious I can't stay even if I wanted to. I try not to think about it.

"Rules are rules. I can't break tradition for just any girl you want to protect. I don't let the others do it, so I can't let you."

As a legacy pack leader, Gavin doesn't make the rules in his pack. He just follows what's been laid out before him by his father and grandfather. I understand it even if it is infuriating. But still—

"They need help. I'm supposed to just watch them get torn apart this year? I thought we protected humans."

"We do. But we're loyal to ourselves first. We can't protect random humans that have no connection to our pack."

My stick splinters and cracks in my hand, and Gavin solemnly takes a seat next to me.

"I'm sorry, Parker. I wish I could help. But I can't play favorites."

It's not Gavin's fault. He's done nothing but risk getting his ass chewed by his father for me since we met. Alphas taking in other alphas is more than a little frowned upon.

I met Gavin and his pack my first day at Doxlothia. They'd set up a booth at orientation looking for new pack members. All of the packs on campus do it, but none of them wanted anything to do with me. Gavin was the only one who greeted me with a smile. I didn't ask if I could join, he asked *me* if I wanted to. Back then, I knew very little about what I wanted, but I did know I didn't want to be a lone wolf anymore. My pack is gone, so I knew the only way I'd get even a sliver of that closeness again was to join someone else's pack or create my own.

I'd heard him on the phone with his dad when he said it made their entire pack and his legacy look like a joke. He'd disgraced his family name sticking his neck out for me.

"Maybe you can look out for them another way? I know you'll figure it out."

Gavin is used to me doing this. Sticking my nose into other people's business. I had to make a stop to see Finn earlier to ensure no one was giving him a hard time.

"Okay," I start to say the word, but it hurts to get out. "Okay, Alpha."

Gavin flashes his perfect white teeth at me. He almost hates hearing me call him Alpha because he can feel my hesitation and rejection. I try to mean it, I really do.

"And I know this is a shit time to mention this, but now that you're a second-year ... finding a mate should be high on your priority list."

"I know."

All packs are different; some have old traditions, and some don't uphold any traditions at all. It depends on the family who founded the pack. Gavin's family is strict in the mating realm where it's mandatory for everyone in their pack to find a mate by the end of their schooling term. Gavin is one of the many in a line of his elders who has gone to Doxlothia, and all of them were mated before their third year. Gavin found his year one.

"Maybe you'll join The Hunt this year?"

"No," I say.

The Hunt is a werewolf exclusive ceremony. Weres come from all over to pick their mates from a pool of volunteers.

"You're not even trying."

"Practice keeps me busy."

He doesn't argue. He doesn't need to. Gavin agreed I could stay in his pack as long as I needed to, but that meant I had to follow all their rules.

"You've got enough shit to stress about. Don't worry about me. I'll figure it out," I say.

Gavin rubs the stubble on his chin. He keeps his beard and his hair buzzed during school, but he grew it out over the summer we spent together.

"You've got your pick of the whole school. I don't get what the issue is."

I don't either. "None of them feel right. It's like I don't feel what I'm supposed to feel."

My mom used to say meeting my dad was like finding out the sky was purple when you'd been told it was blue your entire life. It was like discovering a fact that had always been true but not seeing it before, and when she did, she couldn't stop staring in awe at the thing she found.

She'd tell me their love story over and over again when I was a child. How she was meant to marry someone else. Her father arranged her marriage. That's pretty common for werewolves. But when she'd met my father at Doxlothia, the world stopped and she never thought about another man again. Her dad wasn't happy, but she created her own pack and married my father. They both went on to do work in the Werewolf Council. It wasn't easy for him to get in as a vampire, but they were such an unstoppable force. That's what Mom said—she exaggerated a lot.

I haven't felt it yet.

"I get it. You'll find your purple sky," he jests, nudging me in the ribs.

I smile. He's the only one I've ever told that story to.

Forcing my attention back to the ice, I remind myself why I'm here. It's never been about girls for me. The Rage team is all I have as far as a future. It's that or my dad dragging me to work with him on the Werewolf Council, and that's my last resort. I need to stay focused.

But there's this strange itch in the back of my skull that makes me wonder what Olivia is doing right now.

CHAPTER SEVEN

OLIVIA

"Parker." His name slips off my lips as he lowers his to my abdomen.

"Yes?"

"You feel so ... you make me feel so good." I gasp at the pleasure.

"Let me show you how good I can make you feel, Olivia."

I can't remember the last time I had a dream so vivid. It's all still there when I meet my sisters for breakfast. The warmth of his breath at my ear, his fingertips digging into my thigh. The wetness of his lips ghosting over my skin. The tightening in my lower belly grows with each deliberate touch.

"What are you thinking about?"

Emma's voice snaps me from my daze, and the roar of the dining hall greets me along with the saturated smell of lingering food. The clinking of glasses and laughter echo into the rafters. Everything in the castle is carved stone except for the ceiling, which is a giant window. There are colorful murals painted in the vaults of the arches. At the edges are large weeping pots of florals and vines hanging from the walls.

"Nothing. Just a dream I had." I regret the words as soon as they leave my mouth. There's never been a day in Emma's life that she hasn't pried.

"What about?" she says, dividing her egg quiche into little bites with her fork. Next to us, Eva's attention is elsewhere. She's on her phone, likely texting her boyfriend.

"Nothing interesting."

I hear his laughter before I see him. My attention catches on his brown hair as he moves into the dining hall with Zant and a few other guys, who I guess are either part of his pack or his team. I wonder what the difference is. How many friends does he have?

"Was it about Parker?" Emma's eyes grow wide.

"No." It's a little scary how accurate she is. If I don't entertain her, she'll drop it.

"Liar. What was it about?"

"Nothing."

"Doesn't sound like nothing."

"It wasn't that interesting," I say a little too loud. Parker's head shoots up from across the room, and he winks at me. Then my face grows hot.

"You're blushing. You had a sex dream."

I grab her hand and squeeze. "Be quiet. Everyone can hear you."

"What's happening?" Eva cuts in, dropping her phone on the table and grabbing a biscuit.

Emma leans in to whisper to her. I hate them.

I think about moving to a different table, but who else will entertain me for the morning? I focus on eating. Classes don't start till Monday, and we have the majority of the day to walk around and get our bearings before the house round table starts. I don't think I've been less excited for anything.

Social gatherings aren't a source of energy for me like they are for my sisters. Luckily, the women at the dance studio told me it was free to use in the mornings. I went this morning, but I'm plotting another spot in my day where I can sneak away and dance. That's the only thing getting me through the mountain of stress that being the target of the whole campus has piled on me. From what I can tell, as long as we stay in populated areas, we're safe for now. At least safe enough to find a way to defend ourselves.

I should have believed my father's warnings, but I'm not ready to admit I was wrong yet. I'll admit it once I find a solution to keeping my sisters safe.

"It's not a big deal. I don't blame you. He had his hands all over you. You should have seen the way he was looking at you," Emma concludes, then takes a bite of her quiche. "Did it at least ... end well?"

"She's right. It's not weird. I have dreams about Jared all the time." Too much information, but I appreciate Eva's offer in the conversation. Maybe I do love my sisters. "I never get to the end of them though."

"It was ..."

Let me show you how good I can make you feel, Olivia.

"It was fine."

Emma and Eva snicker about it to themselves. Despite being the oldest and the youngest, they've always got on really well. They flock together in most cases. I'm used to it by now. Being the odd one out, the first call during a crisis but the last when something exciting happens and having to hear it in passing. It used to bother me when I was young, but now I enjoy the break from the collective chaos. I have my own things, and they have theirs.

The dining hall resides in the center of the castle. I doubted the student body would gather in the mornings, but that seems to be the case. The entire room is a sea of house colors. There's no division among us, but I do see patterns. The girls in my hall are gathered in a collective purple blob across the room, and like myself, the majority of us in Noxx House seem to choose the darker color palette. Emma mentions her housemates are really chatty, typically eat together, and that she might ditch Eva and me to eat with them sometimes. I don't mind. I was shocked when she sat with us this morning. In school, she never ate with us because she ran with her own crowd.

Evangeline, sporting Stelliea pink with a large ribbon in her hair, shrieks when her drink dribbles on her skirt, so Emma helps her wipe the spill with her sweater sleeve while talking about dying the ends of her hair blue to match the Luxxia colors.

As I eat, I study the framed posters on the walls with letters to the student body signed in red *from the desk of the council*. Many of them are rules, some of them are proposed plans for campus expansion and upkeep, and some are events.

A group of students moves through the hall, the room settles at their presence, and a few people snap pictures. I count the heads, and when Zant breaks away from Parker's table to eat with them, it confirms my suspicion.

The council take their seats at their own table, and Zant's smile fades into a more calm, calculated smirk. There doesn't appear to be a single leader. It's ten students taking turns talking, and some have brought notepads and pens.

"Good morning!" A girl dressed in Luxxia blue sits in front of us. "I'd love to interview you girls for the university paper."

"Why?" I say.

Emma elbows me. "That sounds great! What do we need to do?"

"Just answer a few questions. The whole school has been abuzz." She's scrolling through her phone as a reference.

"What is that?"

"Oh, this is a chat forum. Mostly gossip. It's not connected to the university paper, but we use it to find fresh content people are interested in. You're all over it."

She holds up her phone and scrolls through rows of comments.

Who are they?

Dibs.

They smell so fucking good.

Why is Parker Owens there?

That bitch better stay away from him.

There's a picture of Parker and me at orientation. He's looking down at me with subdued, contemplative eyes while I talk to the women in the dance department booth.

"Oh no," I say.

"Why do people care about us?" Eva asks.

"Have you smelled you?" she says.

My sisters and I share a collective beat of contemplation and marinate in the fact there is a place the entire student body has been discussing our arrival. There was no school paper in Groveshire. No online chat forums. Our school's graduating class had twenty-five people. This is new territory.

"Sorry, I've gotten a little ahead of myself. I'm Autumn. I'm a vampire, so I smelled you three right away."

Autumn has tight shoulder-length curls, light brown skin, and her pearl nails gleam as she opens a note on her phone to start typing.

"It's Olivia, right?" She points to me, and I nod. Then she moves to the right. "Emma and then Evangeline. Do you go by Eva?"

"Only my sisters call me that," Eva says. "Do we really need to do an interview? That seems a little—"

"Excessive," I say.

"Oh, after coming from Groveshire, this place must be a lot to take in."

"How do you know that?"

"Your father was on the staff. A simple search pulls up your hometown. I imagine the smell of your blood is the reason you three have led such a secluded life. Is that true?"

"I ... I guess so," Emma says. "Our father was very protective of us growing up."

"Then why aren't the three of you in The Donor Program? Surely, he'd have wanted to assure you with the protection it brings."

"Our father let us decide," I say.

"Will you join the program this semester, you think?"

"Well ..." Eva looks at Emma. Emma looks at me.

"It's no one's business what we do with our blood or why we aren't in the program."

She types it as I say it.

"Even if it's safer?"

"No. We're not joining."

I hear the vibration of her fingertips on the screen even with the roaring of students in the dining hall.

"Autumn, I appreciate your work. But we won't answer any more questions about our father. Or what we're doing with our blood."

Someone has to say it, and Emma will tell her everything, and Eva is easily swayed.

She smiles, and I'm relieved when she isn't offended, so I don't have to dig my heel in further.

"I appreciate your honesty, Olivia." Her eyes are gold and sparkle with what I regard as sincerity. "Would you like to answer any questions about Parker Owens?"

I open my mouth to protest, but as I do, a shadow looms over us.

It's Darien and two others—all council, and unfortunately, all male—blocking the sun from the window and souring my morning further. *No break this morning apparently.*

"What a pleasure. The Osborne sisters all wrangled up in one place," Darien says. His silver hair is tame, and he's wearing Noxx House purple. *Joy.* My skin crawls with the memory of his hands in my hair and the pit of hopelessness as his teeth tore into my neck.

Emma moves to gather her plate, and I grab her arm to keep her from running.

"They can't do anything to us here," I say, taking a bite of my muffin. I'm stuffed but need a second to gather myself and decide what to do next.

I have no idea who these people are, but they're looking at me like I should know. Autumn scoots her phone to the middle of the table, and I glance while I chew:

Silver hair – Darien – vamp/plays well with all

Tall and grumpy – Barrett – Were/Rich

Scowling with red hair – Aster – Were/Very rich

I give a thankful nod, but it still doesn't answer why they're gathering in front of my sisters and me.

"Are you going to tell me what you want, or do I wait as you all stare at me all day?" I glare at Darien and throw my napkin on my plate. "You won't get any more blood from me, if that's why you're here."

"We wanted to invite you to our table," Aster says. His voice is smooth and cold, and they're blocking my view of the dining hall. Aster's hair is clean cut on the sides with straight, bright red hair brushing his forehead.

"We're not interested." I stand and motion for Eva and Emma to follow me before we're blocked again.

I may not know much about Doxlothia or the social hierarchy, but I know this is bad. It's bad to have piqued their interest. It's bad to deny their request. And it's bad to have the entire dining hall watching our conversation.

"We insist." Barrett goes to put his arm around Eva's shoulder, then I'm done with my civil approach and pull her next to me.

"Maybe we should ..." Emma tugs at the hair resting on her collarbone.

"The council is very interested in you. We just want to talk," Darien states, like that's going to make me more likely to trust them.

"Not interested in you or them. Now stop blocking our way."

I will likely regret the hard approach. I have no cards to play, yet I have to play anyway.

"Maybe I want something in return," Barrett says. His sharp canine teeth peek out when he speaks.

"*We'll* discuss what we want … together." Aster gives him a charged expression, and I'm lost.

"I don't know what you want with me and my sisters but—"

"You're all lovely but … it's something we want from you," Aster corrects.

What could two Weres possibly want to ask me?

"There you are, beautiful." Parker's voice accompanies a large hulking arm around my shoulders. "Sorry, I had to run the team through some stuff."

"Parker Owens. Pleasure." Aster's scowl doesn't budge.

Something happens between them, then Aster and Barrett shrink away from him. They turn as if they want to face him head-on. Their spines straighten, and the attention is solely on Parker.

There's that sensation again. The safety Parker brings, soothing me.

"Is it? Is there anything in particular you're grilling my girlfriend about because we have somewhere to be."

"Girlfriend?" they say at the same time I do. Darien smiles widely.

"You're joking," Barrett says.

"Olivia is *mine*. I'm taking her as my mate." Parker's eyes flicker to me, then back to them. "Tell your friends she and her sisters are protected by Gavin's pack. Steer clear."

We go to leave, and Aster's voice echoes through the dining hall. "And you'd be willing to be challenged for her, then?"

I don't understand what's being implied.

"Time and place and I'm there." Parker's the only one without rigid shoulders and a hardened jaw. He grins. "I didn't know you had that much time to practice shifting with all the time you spend learning daddy's empire."

Parker leads us away before they can protest, and the dining hall erupts in lively chatter and clambering glasses. He leads us to the Central Lawn, and I feel ten pounds lighter with the distance.

"What are you doing?"

"Trust me, you want them to think we're dating. Aster and Barrett are the top of the pack food chain here. The thing they really want to talk to you about is you being their mate, and they aren't the type to take a simple 'no.'"

"Mate? Why? And why me?"

"Your eyes. Heterochromia signifies Were lineage, and its common among the strongest pack leaders in history. I'm guessing they didn't teach you that in Groveshire."

My father didn't exactly explain it like that. Parker keeps going when I don't smile.

"If anything, they'll take it as a symbol of good luck. That and your blood would be a great benefit to them. I tried to tell you. You and your sisters will be magnets to all the assholes in here."

"But since you're dating Olivia, it's different?" Emma asks.

"We're not dating," I say.

"I'm in Gavin's pack, and his pack is revered. They'll leave you alone if they think I'm going to claim you as a mate."

"Didn't sound like that."

"Aster can challenge me. He won't win and he knows it." Parker smirks as he says it but steps closer to me. "Think about this for a second. You're not part of The Donor Program for some reason, and you and your sisters are walking around with some of the sweetest blood in this place. Everyone in the council has eyes on you and your sisters right now. You need protection, and Gavin won't unless you're connected to the pack in some way. This way, he'll have to say yes."

"What's in it for you?"

"Other than seeing your pretty face more often? I have to have a mate, or I can't be in Gavin's pack. He's been on my ass about it, and this way I can have at least a moment's peace from worrying about being kicked out. This satisfies us both."

"I think we should listen to Parker," Eva says. "Seems safer."

Eva is too trusting.

"I agree. Plus, this sounds kind of fun. You two running around pretending to be boyfriend and girlfriend." Emma smiles at me. I regret mentioning the dream. In fact, I regret waking up this morning.

She *would* think me becoming some type of werewolf bride was a fun, exciting new development.

I sigh. "Parker—"

The tips of Parker's ears pink, and he leans in. "Yes?"

Warmth trickles into my face as he bats his eyelashes at me.

"I appreciate you trying to help, but no. The last thing I need right now is to be dating the captain of the Rage team and drawing more attention to myself."

All this is an annoying distraction, but there has to be some other way to remedy this and get protection for my sisters and me that doesn't involve me having to be seen as someone else's mate. Where would I find the time to fake date Parker?

This isn't how I imagined my time at university. I imagined hours and hours spent in the ballet studio where no one bothered me. A place that was truly dedicated to ballet, and ballet alone.

"We'll figure it out." Meaning *I* will figure it out.

Emma is whispering to Eva again, and somehow, I know it's about that stupid dream.

To my surprise, Parker's carefree grin doesn't falter. "Well, if you change your mind, I'm all yours. And you know where to find me."

We exchange numbers, and I'm empty again when he leaves. A strange hollow sensation that I decide to blame on indigestion. I remind myself and my sisters that Parker is a stranger, and no amount of safety he brings is going to convince me to trust him that easily.

"She definitely likes him." Emma is a loud whisperer.

News spreads like wildfire. By the time the campus clocktowers chime for noon and we arrive at the house round table, I've been asked about Parker three times. Twice while in the nearly silent library.

The first was when I was combing the stacks and a Stelliea girl, shorter than me, stopped me.

"You're dating Parker Owens." Her mouth was agape.

"No. We're not dating. He was—"

When I tried to walk past her, she grabbed my shoulders. *"Tell me. What cologne does he wear? Please."*

I'm able to dodge her and find what I'm after: *The Imperial Index of Protective Charms and Crystals.* I thought getting them might prove difficult, considering these types of crystal are listed as forbidden according to the Doxlothia handbook. It turns out, getting access to forbidden items is not hard in Noxx House, but Solexxa was going to be my next guess. A girl in my hall pointed me to a third-year student who was eager to sell to me, only because he'd already heard I was dating Parker, and apparently, Parker is loved by virtually everyone.

"You're sure we won't need to enter The Donor Program? I mean, either way, I'm scared, but I'm more scared of being attacked or ambushed in my hall when I get up to use the restroom at night or something," Emma says.

Eva is biting her nails. "I don't want to. Dad said it isn't safe. Plus, he'd be so disappointed."

Mom's death was an accident. It was no one's fault, but the result of a continual strain on her heart brought on by a previous illness and her participation in The Donor Program. They didn't catch it. She joined the program as soon as she turned of age because of her sweet blood and the fear that someday someone might use her blood for their advantage or worse. She'd told me it was the best decision she'd ever made.

Dad says people like us shouldn't be in the program because people get greedy when they taste good blood. I can't tell whether he's right or if I want him to be wrong. But the thought of me or any of my sisters being drained to near death is enough to make me want to avoid being forced into anything we're not prepared for.

"No one has to do anything we don't want to do." I drop a rectangular dusty-blue crystal in each of their hands. "This is Veratala. I hear it stings like a bitch and prevents Weres from shifting for at least five minutes. And this one is Loxeth. It's to be ingested only in emergencies. It will make your blood smell repulsive and taste poisonous. But it will also make you sick."

It's a soft, pink petite stone. I double-check they both place them in their skirt pockets; Emma is notoriously forgetful.

"This won't work," Emma says.

"Any better ideas?"

"Yeah, the hot hybrid staring at you from across the lawn."

I glance in the direction she's looking and see the massive outline that is Parker Owens.

"You volunteering?"

"I'm pretty sure he's only interested in you. He's *staring*. Hard."

I sigh. Ballet somewhere else would have been easier. Quieter. Less hassle. I wouldn't have minded the alone time or the separation from my family either. But Doxlothia is the only way to the top. The Doxlothia company is a small university-funded and managed company that is directly tied to the International Ballet Company of Excellence. My mother had been in that company before leaving to settle down with my father. When he stayed on as a professor at Doxlothia, she went on to join the IBCE.

Doxlothia is unique in how it's tied to the most sought-after ballet company in the world. Getting accepted to the company in Doxlothia means I'll be guaranteed an apprenticeship in the International Ballet Company of Excellence, something I've been dreaming of all my life. It's what my mother did. It's what I will do.

I just have to keep my head on straight. Especially around Parker.

CHAPTER EIGHT

PARKER

The house round table is the crux of house collaboration. Basically, it's just everyone gathering on the Central Lawn to play games. While other schools have house competitions, Doxlothia encourages us to collaborate with other houses all the time.

Last year, I spent it getting drunk, but this year, I need to masquerade as a guy who has his shit together.

"Staying out of trouble?" I say to Olivia, who stole my attention when she walked onto the lawn.

The sun is high overhead, so I use my body to block the direct rays from her eyes. Her sisters whisper among themselves.

"Moderately," she says. "I got these."

I hide the fact I'm impressed she seamlessly found the fully illegal source for them that quickly.

"That's perfect." I fiddle with the blue one. I forget its name but know just by the shape of it. "For this one, you really want to try to get it as close to the heart as possible. It will hurt literally anyone you jab with it. With the little pink one, you have a good ten minutes of use before you start throwing up. Stab them with the blue, swallow the pink one, and run."

"Where did you learn that?"

"I had to swallow one of these when I was eleven. It was part of the self-defense curriculum. Nothing like that in Groveshire?"

Olivia gives me an exasperated twitch of her eyebrows.

I've never been to an all-human town or city, but nondonors typically flock there, and that leaves vampires no reason to go. All vampires are required to enlist in The Donor Program to receive blood when they turn of age, but that doesn't mean people don't find exceptions to that rule, legal or not.

That's why being in The Donor Program is taught as good for all of society. It's the safest option because it comes with strict governmental laws and regular doctor check-ins to ensure no one is abusing the system.

There must be a reason they're not in The Donor Program, but Olivia looks uncomfortable enough, so I don't ask.

There's a quick flurry of cameras and chatter as a man is being escorted off the lawn toward the gate. I sigh.

"Who is that?"

"Oh, Finn. He, uh ... had a run-in with Cane before orientation. I heard he was talking to a professor about it. This morning, they got a tip about him bringing illegal potions to school. Cane is friends with a lot of the Weres on the council, so I kinda saw that coming."

"You weren't kidding. They work fast," Olivia says.

"How did that investigation report turn out, by the way?"

She shakes her head. "I didn't get the feeling that I'd be hearing much about it. When I went to check on it, she couldn't find it. Do you think the dean is in on this?"

"I don't think there's any way she doesn't know about it."

"If my father knew, he'd flip."

"Are you going to tell him?"

"No way."

She's got daddy issues too. *Noted.*

"Well, it would be my pleasure to walk you ladies around and show you the ropes. The house round table is designed to get all the houses working together. You'll each get assigned a partner from a different house and run through all the games with them."

I usher them out to the lawn where two houses are setting up for tug-of-war.

"Each house has their activity of choice. Stelliea and Noxx House care the most about tradition so we've each had the exact same activity since the school was founded. Noxx House hosts the capture the flag tournament at sundown, and Stelliea hosts croquet. Looks like Luxxia decided on tug-of-war this year and Solexxa went all out with a full-on obstacle course."

"We don't get to pick our partners?" Evangeline asks.

"No, it's a random lottery system that pairs you with someone in another house."

We line up, and I watch the girls get their assignments. The council has set up their booth in front of the castle, and Aster and Barrett stand out against the gray stone. Aster in violet, and Barrett in green. They must smell me as soon as I walk up because they take a break from their conversation to glare at me. I wish Gavin was here, but he's prepping for capture the flag.

"How's Operation: Damsel in Distress going?" Zant's voice steadies me.

I don't take my eyes off Olivia and her sisters.

"I'm busy right now. If you're going to make fun of me, go do it behind my back."

"What? I think it's nice you care about those three little humans so much. And, surprise, asshole, I am being helpful. I obviously couldn't get you paired with Olivia because she's in the same house, but I did put you with one of her sisters. The little one. Name starts with an E."

"Really?"

"Yep, and because I knew you'd worry, Olivia got paired with Chase in Stelliea, and her other sister is with Ryker in Solexxa."

My rigid muscles loosen. Ryker and Chase are both familiar faces and new additions to the Rage team this year.

I'm just about to sing his praises when I notice Aster and Barrett bickering. The hairs on my arms stand on end with the heated air between two Weres. The crowd parts for Barrett making his way toward Olivia.

My blood is hot. Council members don't participate in the games.

"Why is Barrett going over to Olivia?"

My skin burns at the itch of shifting, and her eyes widen at his presence.

"Oh, fuck this. He did this on purpose. He must have had the same idea I did," Zant says.

What was his plan? To get her alone? To mark her? I have to do something. She's got the crystals, but it might not be enough.

"I have to stop this."

Barrett has his arms around Olivia, leading her to start the Solexxa obstacle course. Our eyes meet in the crowd, and the panic in her gaze seers into me as he steers her away.

"I think I'm going to kill him."

"Come on. Let's follow them!" Emma runs into me, grabbing and ushering me toward the obstacle course. "I'm a little competitive. Fair warning."

"Me too." Though, I don't really give a shit about the house round table when Barrett instructs Olivia to put her arm around his waist while they wait for their legs to be tied together.

I turn to Zant. "Can you watch Evangeline? Make sure Aster doesn't have any rogue plans?"

"On it."

Emma and I are close enough behind Olivia and Barrett that I can still see her. There are various obstacles to move around, and you must do it tied to your partner. Most of it is out on the lawn, but up ahead, the teams disappear through the trees, laughing and falling into each other. We tag team it in minutes and the course zigzags into the trees, where a neon string leads us along.

Emma is way shorter than me, so we're uneven when we walk forward through the obstacle course into the forest. There is axe throwing, but I sneak Emma past so we can skip it. We're slow moving because I don't want to hurt her, but I need to find Olivia. Once we're in the trees, I lose sight of her, and adrenaline pushes my muscles to work faster. Barrett is trying to get her alone.

"I don't see her," Emma says.

I scent her fear to the west, and it sends the itch of my skin into overdrive, so I snap the rope on our ankles.

"What are you going to do?" Emma asks.

I briefly mull over what I'll do if I find him with his teeth in her skin while she cries in pain. Nope. Not going to happen. The need to shift draws through me from my heels to my scalp. *Not yet.*

"I'll challenge him."

Because in the end, none of the confusing feelings I have for Olivia matter. She's mine to protect either way, and if they're going to try to hurt her, I'm going to fuck them up.

CHAPTER NINE

OLIVIA

I think Doxlothia is trying to kill me.

Barrett is taking me farther into the forest, where the tree branches prick at my skin. The scrapes burn, and he's moving us so fast the blisters on my feet from ballet rub relentlessly. I haven't seen another student in minutes, and their laughter is growing farther away by the second. I dodge branches while Barrett barrels us forward. My ankle aches with each step. I have no choice but to hold onto his waist, or I risk slipping.

"I know about your arrangement with Owens."

"There's no arrangement."

"Talk only when I ask you a question."

Oh, so that's how this is going to be. I wince at the pain from the rope rubbing against my skin.

"I know the arrangement between you and Owens is fake. Am I wrong?"

Barrett isn't messing around, and I doubt he wants to know the type of cologne Parker wears. His eyes are the same emerald as his blazer, and he keeps them fixed forward like there's a destination he has in mind.

"You're wrong."

"Don't lie."

"Don't ask me stupid questions."

He grits his teeth. I'm afraid if I stop moving, I'll sprain something.

"What will it take? What has he promised you? I can give you more. A car. Money. I'll give you anything you want. A spot in the IBCE, you've got it."

I'm already pissed off, so that brings bile into my throat.

"Is that how you got what you have? Your family gave it to you?"

He yanks me forward, and I gasp at the pressure in my leg. I can't risk injury. Not with my audition days away. Maybe I should scream.

"I'm told your mother was in the company. My father is friends with the artistic director. Be my bride and you'll get anything you could ever want."

"Don't talk about my mother." I open my mouth to scream, but he stops so abruptly I fall into the dirt.

"My patience is wearing thin with you."

"If you think that now, imagine if we were wed."

He picks me up with one arm, and I yank away to stare him directly in the eyes.

"This isn't about me, is it? There has to be another reason you're willing to take me as a wife to get me away from Parker."

His pupils dilate when I mention Parker. I'm right. This isn't just about me. It's about Parker having me to himself. Parker having anything he doesn't.

"You're threatened by him."

"You know nothing, human." He spins so fast, slamming his fist beside my head into the tree. "I'm trying to make this painless for you."

I scoff. "Says the man trying to bribe me to be his bride. This is about Parker. You're afraid of him—"

He pins me to the tree, leaving little room to wiggle. If I needed proof Parker feels different and I hadn't hallucinated it, Barrett's breath in my face is enough.

I shrink away from him. My heart is hammering in a desperate, nervous cadence. His body pressed against mine is suffocating and painful, and a branch is digging into my back.

"You can get scared, huh?"

He leans into my neck to smell me. I'm rigid. Defenseless. I swallow. I do have the crystal in my pocket, but getting it out without him noticing won't be easy.

"Maybe threatening you should have been my first approach. Wed me. Everyone wins. If not, your life can get harder, and so can Parker's."

"Fuck you."

"Maybe I won't give you a choice. Maybe I'll mark you right now. It will hurt, but I don't think that will be much of a problem for me."

My stomach flips. The thought is terrifying. I don't know much about marking, but I do know it involves another painful bite. I wriggle, but there is no way I'll make it past him.

"You really are a charming fellow." Darien's voice cuts the air, and he leans against the tree next to me.

"Parker is making his way this way, and he's bound to shift instantly if he sees you trying to mark his *girlfriend* up against a tree," Darien says, pulling a dead leaf from my hair. Barrett's grip on my wrist is so tight I know it will bruise.

I'm not relieved to see him, but I am relieved to not be alone with Barrett any longer.

"Don't tell me you believe their little tirade."

Darien's eyes stay on me, and he shrugs. "They're more than friends. That's for sure."

Okay, I am a little thankful for Darien. He buys me enough time to grab the crystal from my pocket and shove it into Barrett's sternum as hard as I can. He falters back and howls in pain.

Darien bites back the laughter as I brush off my skirt and remove the tie from our ankles.

"Stay away from me."

"Olivia." Parker walks through the trees with my little sister in tow, and I'm instantly lighter. Relief. Safety. All is back within my reach.

"Parker." I walk to him and pull Emma toward me.

His eyes are yellow when he glares at Barrett and Darien.

"What happened?"

"He ... he was going to mark me."

The light leaves Parker's eyes—no blue, no yellow, just flared pupils taking up all that space—before pinning Barrett to the tree by the throat. His fingers lengthen to claws and dig into Barrett's skin while brown fur coats his hand and forearm.

It's so quick. So effortless.

Emma squeals, and I squeeze her to keep quiet.

"Challenge me. Let's do it right now."

Barrett spits on the ground, still hunched over rubbing the spot on his chest.

"You can't, can you?" Parker continues, digging his heels in.

"Parker, let's just go," I say. I'm not sure he's thinking clearly, and I have the strangest urge to keep him out of trouble.

"Come on. We can make it a huge thing. Your dad and his friends can watch. I'm ready, right now." Parker's shaking but smiling, and his voice is tinged with excitement.

"What does that mean?" Emma whispers to me.

"Weres have fighting traditions that can be recognized by the Werewolf Council if held in an appropriate manner and venue." Darien is beside us, lingering over my left shoulder like a dark fairy.

Barrett is still in pain from the crystal, but his eyes are deadly. His pupils grow. He wants to shift. Would he take the challenge?

"Unless you want to be embarrassed, I suggest you stay the fuck away from her." Parker shoves him into the tree. Barrett is larger than him and taller, but Parker throws him around like a rag doll.

"Parker. Come on," I say.

"Of course, baby. After I make sure he understands that you're mine." Parker's claws leave a trail of blood trickling down his neck. "And trying to mark what's mine puts me in a bad mood."

Barrett finally agrees, and Parker drops him into the dirt.

"So the rumors are true, then?" Darien says.

"Stay away from them. Or don't and accept my challenge. I'm good with either," Parker spits before ushering me and Emma back toward the lawn where everyone else looks to be having an amazing time. I spot Eva roped to a guy in an emerald blazer. Her eyes widen when they get to the axe throwing and he makes it right in the center on the first try.

"Come here." Parker's touch is gentle on my arm as he steers us away from the crowd.

It stills the drumming heartbeat in my head. My nerves instantly calm. His pupils are still dilated, and his normally blue irises are a muddy shade of green.

"Did he hurt you?"

"I—no ... not really."

"Hand." He holds his palm open, waiting for the hand I have tucked behind my back. I'd shoved the crystal into Barrett's chest hard enough to break the skin on my palm.

There's blood smeared there, and his jaw sets at the sight of it. He brings my hand to his lips and licks. The cut mends in an instant. I almost said no, but I couldn't get my mouth to form the words with his touch dissipating all the fear I'm trying hard to hide for Emma's sake.

My face burns when he continues to survey my arm for any more cuts. Emma's mouth falls open, but she recovers her composure quickly.

With a stuttering breath, I still at Parker leaning into my chest and sniffing at the top of my head and shoulder.

"Um, do I need to give you two a minute?" Emma pops her lip gloss from her pocket, beaming while she smothers her lips.

"I'm just checking her scent. Making sure it's right."

"Tell me what this fake dating entails."

I can't imagine another run-in with Barrett, let alone any of the others. If I can guarantee my sisters' safety now, I'm going to do it.

Parker sniffs me, not saying anything.

"It can't be that hard, right? We just need to be seen together ... like at the Noxx House party on Sunday. Can you guarantee your pack leader, Gavin, can help protect us?"

He nods, and with every second that passes, more of the cool blue returns to his eyes. "Yes, as long as we can convince him we're a couple."

"I don't think that will be a problem." Emma smiles from ear to ear. This is her being tame. As soon as Parker leaves, she's going to shriek into my ear about this, and I won't get a moment of peace for the rest of the day.

"I think we should. I mean ... if you still want to," I say.

Parker is staring a hole through me, moving my hair from my shoulders to survey me.

"Parker, what?"

"I won't let that happen again. I promise. I'll protect you and your sisters. I mean it."

He reaches like he wants to touch my cheek but drops his hand. The tendons in his neck are tight as his jaw hardens.

Maybe it's too soon to trust Parker, but he's shown more than once he's someone who's willing to fight for me. The anger in his eyes and the spilling of blood a few minutes earlier aren't things that would be easy to fake, and I trust that more than I care about the length of time. Parker isn't eloquent with his words, but his actions speak for themselves. This is who he is.

"I believe you."

CHAPTER TEN

PARKER

I didn't expect Barrett to accept my challenge, but that didn't keep me from being disappointed when he didn't.

There's no way Barrett would risk losing status in a challenge. Maybe that will be enough to get them to leave Olivia alone for good. After the house round table, I spent the rest of the weekend showing her and her sisters the campus. Since the fake dating is new, me physically going everywhere they go is the only way I know they're safe. Emma and Eva were both mortified when Olivia and I escorted them to their rooms.

But that's all going to change tonight. It has to or I'm going to spend our first week of classes running around the campus accompanying them everywhere. Coach would not be happy.

"How do you want to handle PDA?" I lean to whisper in Olivia's ear as we enter the common room.

Noxx House is alive with movement. It's Bonding Night. In Noxx House, that means all of us argue till we agree on an activity both the introverts and the extroverts like. Last year, the introverts settled on watching and judging the extroverts from the sideline as we played rugby out on the lawn. It oddly worked for me; they only praised wins they thought were worthy, then degraded us the other half. It was pretty great.

Olivia has her eyes locked on Darien and isn't listening. I don't blame her. Darien is an asshole, but he's small fish compared to the rest of them. Zant and Darien are two of the four vampires on the council, and Zant tells me he is a selfish lover of chaos but not inherently corrupt like some of the others.

With a hand on her shoulder, I bring her to my hip and away from him and his friends. He's not the only annoying asshole in Noxx House. There are plenty to go around. Cane and Aster are here too with their buddies, sitting on a couch by the far fireplace. When we walk in, their scowls disappear into the violet lights. Our common room stays dimly lit most of the time due to the stained-glass windows.

"You're safe next to me. Now back to the PDA talk."

She sighs. "Is it necessary?"

Yep. She probably thinks I'm being a creep.

"No one is going to believe I'm going to take you as my mate if we look like acquaintances. We don't need to kiss, just look friendly. We already have the quick timing working against us here."

Her eyes glaze over as she analyzes the room. Noxx House has the largest common room. There is an area for chess, two fireplaces, and a large glass room that overlooks the lawn and the trees. It's set up for the painters and sculptors in our house. It pales in comparison to Luxxia's common room that has an area for every creative endeavor you could think of.

"Just kiss me. It's fine." Her eyes snap to me.

"Wow, so eager. Have you been dreaming about this moment?"

It's a joke, but her face drops in horror. "Did Emma tell you? I'm going to kill her."

I take a beat, letting it sink in. *Oh, shit.*

"Uh, no. It was a complete shot in the dark. Have you had a dream about me?"

Her heart stutters. "No."

Oh fuck, she did. "Go on. Tell me what it was about."

I can't hide the grin spanning my face. She shakes her head, refusing to answer, and I think that can only mean one thing.

"Did you have a sex dream about me?" I'm having fun already.

"Would you just shut up and kiss me so we can get on with the night?"

"Like right now?"

She nods.

"I don't know, I want to hear more about the dream."

"Don't be a baby about it, just kiss me."

Her brows furrow and she places her hand on her hip like I'm the one being exhausting.

"Alright." I grab her forearm and bring her into the heart of the common room where I can ensure more people will see.

Leaning down, I breathe in her scent. I'm in her air, and she stumbles. Grabbing her hand, I bring her a step closer so our chests are almost touching. She's so nervous; it's cute. I wonder if she's ever kissed anyone before. Her gaze is trained on my lips as I cup her cheek with my palm. She flinches at first, but I run my thumb up her jaw and stare into her eyes. *Relax.*

One quick glance around the room tells me everyone is definitely watching.

Wasting no more time, I tug her by the waist toward me and lift her chin so her lips meet mine. *One quick kiss for the party.*

Pure electricity seers through me when our lips touch. Hot. Like an electric wire on the skin. She hesitates, then deepens the moment with another kiss. Then another. I squeeze her, needing her against me. Every swipe of her tongue takes me further from reality. I can't get enough of her. The softness of her lips. Her heart rate skyrocketing. I need her. *No one else can have her.*

We realize it at the same time, and our eyes open.

I see her for the first time. Olivia is the type of beautiful you see in actresses you dream about as a kid. That, I saw very clearly the day we met, but something has shifted.

She *feels* like mine.

She tastes like mine too.

That's a little much for a man she just met. I'll need to drown out that revelation with liquor immediately.

We're both dumbfounded, staring still.

"You, uh, want me to get us drinks?" I say.

Her lips are wet with my saliva. It's hot. That calm outer exterior has cracked just enough to see the embarrassment peeking through in the pink of her cheeks.

"Yeah, let's do that."

"I'm on it."

A flash blinds me on my right.

"What a cute couple. Has Parker Owens found a mate?" Cherry is the only one in Noxx House who works for the school newspaper. I was hoping she'd be here.

"Yeah, I have." I kiss Olivia's cheek for good measure, and she looks at me with a lethal stare.

"Will you give me a quote for the paper?"

"Do I have to? I already gave an interview," Olivia says, and I quietly back up and leave her there to grab our drinks.

With a little distance and air, it's better. I just got carried away for a second. That's all it is. The alpha blood is messing with my head again. Is this why I couldn't "mind my fucking business and eat my food" like Zant had so lovingly put it that day I'd told him about what happened in the dining hall?

I'd been eavesdropping, staring a little, but everyone noticed when Aster and Barrett walked over to Olivia and her sisters. Her expression stayed calm, but her heart was hammering, screaming for help. She needed someone in her corner, and even if I didn't understand why, I wanted to be that person.

"Parker." Gavin steps beside me as I pour some alcohol into a cup. *Oh, shit.*

"Hello, Alpha." I sip my drink and meet his glare.

"I know your game."

"There is no game."

"Tell me right now. That's an order."

I grit my teeth. "I'm taking Olivia as my mate."

"I don't believe you. We just talked about this—"

"Things changed. This thing with Olivia is real."

"This has nothing to do with what happened in the dining hall a few days ago?" His brow furrows as he takes another drink.

"Nope."

I don't like lying to Gavin. I shouldn't be able to, technically. Once you're linked in a pack, doing anything to oppose the Alpha is supposed to be nearly impossible. I still have a hard time sensing anything pack related even while bonded to Gavin. For packmates, it's visceral. When the Alpha feels something, they all do internally in some way. Since I have alpha blood, the most I can sense is a mildly uncomfortable stomachache.

"Hope I'm not interrupting." The thud of Cane's thick-soled shoes accompanies his voice.

"No," Gavin says.

"Aster is wanting to talk with you, Gavin."

"I wonder what about."

I pretend not to notice Gavin's tone.

"Have to get back to the Mrs. anyway. Catch up later?"

I don't look in Cane's direction. The last thing I want is to make more problems for Gavin, but I don't have many other options. Aster and Barrett respect Gavin, or at the very least, they're willing to be civil and settle disputes without fights or antics.

It still feels like the right thing to do. It's not fair Olivia's father sent them here with no protection, thinking he was sending them to some type of safe haven. They need me more than I care about ruffling feathers on campus. Aster and Barrett have never liked me anyway.

Olivia is hiding in a corner, nearly blending into the curtains when I find her.

"You weren't supposed to kiss me like that." Olivia looks really cute when she's pissed off at me. There's a trickling of rain hitting the stained-glass window as she leans against it.

"You're the one who shoved your tongue in my mouth," I say, handing her a drink.

"You're saying that was all me?"

"No. I don't know what that was."

My answer doesn't satisfy her even though it's the truth. It just happened. And if she lets me, I'd like to do it again.

She draws her arms to her chest and huffs. "New rule. Don't touch me."

"We really need to make a show here if you want anyone to believe this."

"Fine. After this, you don't touch me."

She's going to be stubborn about this, but as a human, she has no idea how much I can sense, and that kiss wasn't forced. Every stroke of her tongue was deliberate and needy. And ... *Fuck, I have to stay focused*.

I sip my drink and savor the burn of the alcohol. "Okay, I won't touch you unless you ask."

"I won't ask."

I shrug. "You might. And it's okay to change your mind."

"I don't want to be known as just Parker Owens's mate. That's not why I came here."

"You came here to make a name for yourself?" I ask.

"Yes ... and no. I just want to be known for ballet."

"And you will be."

"Tell that to the girl who ambushed me in the library for the name of your cologne."

"This is all temporary until ... we figure out a better solution to our problems."

I use "our" a little too easily, but Olivia doesn't seem to mind. Her shoulders drop from her ears, and the scowl on her face softens.

"Here." I wrap my arm around her waist and haul her onto the couch in the center of the room. She tries to take the spot next to me, but I shift her to sit on my lap. "You'll sit here."

She adjusts with her hand on my knee. If I wasn't so intent on watching the crowd, I'd have to adjust myself. Olivia smells really good, so I have to fight the urge to bury my face in her hair. I shake that thought out as quickly as it comes and take another drink. *Don't know what is wrong with me today.*

I can't stop staring at her. She watches people like she has to memorize every article of clothing for a quiz and guess the person's most likely hobbies. It seems to calm her because she relaxes into me more with each passing second, and I keep reminding her to sip on her drink.

"Having fun?" I ask. Noxx House has still not figured out our preferred activity for the night. I voted for mud sports outside in the rain. No one liked the idea.

"No."

"What would make it more fun for you?"

"Not sitting with my ass on your leg." She shifts her hips.

I move her till she's fully in my lap. "Is that better?"

A smile dances on her lips. At least she finds me amusing. Gavin moves across the room, typing into his phone. I feel his stare, and seconds later, my phone vibrates. *Shit.*

This arrangement can work, but I do need to make a show.

"I'm not being attentive enough to my girlfriend." I brush the hair from Olivia's shoulder so I can gain better access to her neck. It's a vampire thing. There's nothing better than that soft, thin part of the neck where the heartbeat thrums. "Let's talk about you."

I wet my lips and run them over her pulse, burying my face into her hair. Her back straightens, and goose bumps prickle her arm, then my mind wanders back to the fact that she's digging into my lap.

"What about me?"

"You're a ballerina. Tell me about your audition. I bet you're going to kill it."

"Not going to tell me how hard it is to get into the company like everyone else?"

"You look mighty capable to me. Getting into any of the clubs or sports here is not easy. You got an audition. That's more than most get. Plus, that's what they said when I showed up."

Her head hangs, then she turns to look at me. "Thanks. I'm ... really excited to audition. I've been dreaming about it since I was little."

We're both competitive and driven. Not surprising, most people in Noxx House are.

"All my life, it's the only thing I've ever wanted to do."

She's genuinely smiling now.

"One day, when you're famous, I'll tell everyone *the* Olivia Osborne sat in my lap."

We talk back and forth about her dancing. She tells me about what they wear and why, then moves onto the shoes and when she started pointe earlier than most at nine. I never knew so much work went into dance, but as she gets more comfortable, her words get faster till they're pouring out of her quicker than her mouth can keep up with.

"What about you? Will I get to watch you practice?" she asks. "I've never seen it played."

"Definitely. And I want you at all my games when the season starts. Right now, you can come and watch us all get the shit kicked out of us while I try to get the team in shape."

The hairs on my arm stand on end at the danger wafting in the air.

Cane is closer and watching Olivia. Were instincts are pretty much the best thing ever. It's like having a sixth sense. He whispers to Aster, and I *know* they're talking about her. I lick my teeth to prevent from clenching my jaw.

"Parker?"

"Yes, baby," I whisper in her ear, and the small of her back lifts as she sits upright.

She likes it.

"Mind wandering a bit?"

"Can you blame me? I've got the most beautiful girl in the room with her ass in my lap." As I say it, I catch the eyeline of Cane. His green and yellow eyes rake over Olivia, so I squeeze her tighter. *What a fucking prick.* "I can't keep myself from thinking about what I'm going to do when I get you in my room."

I kiss her shoulder and drag my bottom lip down the soft skin of her arm, so close to using my teeth. *Stay the fuck back.*

Cane smirks. All the other Weres are looking, including Gavin and Aster. Good. Cane and his buddies stalk about on my left and to my right, and Darien and the other vampires are closing in too. I fight the urge to scratch as my skin burns with the itch to shift.

"What's wrong?"

I clutch her waist as a warning and draw her impossibly closer. They are too close to her, and she doesn't smell enough like me. I need to take her somewhere and *make* her smell like me. I'm so fucking itchy.

I could hoist her over my shoulder and take her to my bed. Then she'll *really* smell like me. I have to get my scent on her, inside her, everywhere. Because she's mine and no one else can touch her.

I kiss her arm again and lick my teeth. This time because my mouth is salivating at the thought. The urge to mark her grows, and if they step any closer, I will. *Yeah, good fucking logic, Parker.*

"Tell me." She squeezes my hand. "You're looking very wolfy."

"Meaning?"

"Your eyes."

"Everyone is looking at you. I don't like it. It makes me want to take you to my room and scent you. So they get the picture loud and clear." I'm clearly not thinking straight.

Why else would I tell her that? What am I doing? Olivia may be my fake girlfriend, but no way am I contemplating marking her. I've never wanted to mark a girl before, not even the ones I actually dated. But it's the same urge as before, luring me into the scent of her skin.

Every second feels drawn out, and I ache when I think of not being able to mark her like I want to. I can't have someone else's teeth on her, let alone their hands. I need to think of something else. Anything else before I snap. So I turn to the first thing on my mind.

"What do you want to do tonight? I was thinking we could explore that mask kink you have." I move closer to her neck, needing to be closer to her pulse. "Is that what your dream was about?"

She squeezes my knee, and her nails hurt. *Fuck.*

"I don't know what you're talking about."

"I don't know many girls that would let me pull them against a tree."

That makes her laugh, and it snaps me out of my possessive dissociation for a split second.

"You know plenty."

"You were into it." I keep pushing, more interested in her reaction than anything else going on. "I could tell. What would you have let me do if we'd been completely alone then?"

The fresh scent of her arousal floods my senses. It's faint. Quick and unexpected but sweet and enticing. *Well, there goes my self-restraint.*

"I think you might have let me strip you ..."

"No." She takes a breath and lets it out with a sigh. I need to stop. My dick is already hard thinking about it. But it's all hypothetical. I mean, in fake-boyfriend land anything is possible. If she were my girlfriend, I'd want her to think about me touching her.

"You're right. You wouldn't until I chased you. You know you don't need to dream about it, baby. I can make it happen whenever you want. Just say the words."

"Parker," she warns, but the sweet scent grows stronger, and I can't quite help myself.

"You've thought about it. Me running after you in the forest, finding you ... slipping off your skirt and leaving it at your ankles—"

Without warning, she leans back and squeezes the hair at the nape of my neck.

"*Dear*, we're in public, remember?" She glares into my eyes. I like the way she's hurting me and the bite in her voice. I swear I hear her whisper the words to me, but her mouth stays closed. *Get a hold of yourself.*

"You're right. Sorry, I ... I'm being ... I don't know." I shake my head. "I don't know what the what the fuck I'm saying."

"Who is Cane to you?" she asks, fully wrapping her arm around my neck. It's intimate, but I won't complain.

"How do you know about him?"

"You were glaring at him more than the others earlier. I asked Cherry."

"Cane is the biggest asshole I've met. We grew up together. Me, Zant, Cane, and a few other guys here I don't talk to all went to the same school in the city. All our dads work for the Werewolf Council."

"Why does he look at you like that?"

I huff. "I don't know. He hates me. I don't know what his father fills his head with, but my father told me his dad is an egomaniac. My dad is his second-in-command and gets ordered around all the time, and for some reason, Cane has taken that as an invitation to hate me."

I take another drink.

"I'm getting the impression you have daddy issues."

"Uh, yeah, same as you, I guess, and I don't like to talk about mine either."

"Fine. What other history is there with Cane? There has to be more."

"Loads. More than I can tell you in a night, but I can give you a recent hint. I found him in *my* bed with my girlfriend. See that girl over there, staring at us and him."

I point at Mia. She is staring and fidgeting with a piece of red hair between her fingers.

Olivia's eyes widen. "Yeah ..."

"That's one of his mates. Different packs have their own rules, and Cane's frequently takes multiple mates. He already had two and decided he'd set his sights on my girlfriend for a trophy."

"That must have been terrible."

"Yeah, finding them in my bed together was a bad day. But I got over her quickly." I'm a shit boyfriend. Pretty sure my most spoken words to her were *"Sorry, I've got practice."*

"She doesn't look happy."

I smirk. "Yeah, I don't think he has much to do with his mates after he bonds with them. She asked me to fuck her once. Showed up at my door at one in the morning."

Olivia's face drops, but she recovers so quickly I almost didn't catch it.

"I told her to leave." I lean next to her ear. "In case you're curious. She's avoided me since."

I can't tell if she finds me amusing or annoying. Probably both, but she doesn't leave my lap, so I relish in the warmth of her body twisted on mine and trace circles on the small of her back.

Suddenly, I know it's going to be a loss when she separates from me, and she says, "I need to go to the bathroom."

"I'll walk you."

"You need to follow me?"

"With the amount of assholes in here, yes."

I leave her at the door and make my way back over to the drink table for a refill.

"I have to say, I thought you were lying," Gavin says, taking a cup from the table and pouring himself a drink.

"I know." I shrug.

"I mean, we had that conversation and suddenly you tell me Olivia is your mate, but after seeing you two tonight ... it's obvious."

"Obvious, huh?" *Fuck yes.* We got them so good.

"Yeah, I'm just glad I don't have to worry about you the rest of the semester."

It's going to be an interesting semester, that's for certain. I can't wait to tell Olivia how convincing we were.

"I've never seen you act that way before either."

"I don't know what you mean." I sip my drink.

"Oh, so you weren't thinking about marking Olivia in the public common room?"

"No. Definitely not. I have class."

Marking someone in public is the equivalent of having sex with them, and I don't want to be one of *those* people. But I also need everyone else to keep their teeth away from my girl friend. A girl who's a friend that I also weirdly want to mark. Nothing I need to think that hard about tonight anyway.

"Uh-huh." I eye the door to the bathroom, scanning for Cane and Aster's friends lingering nearby.

"Well, you don't need to worry. Her and her sisters are under our protection. I already have things settled with Aster and Barrett."

"Perfect."

CHAPTER ELEVEN

Olivia

"Checkmate." I suppress a grin, staring at the chessboard.

Darien's smirk falters on the other side of the board. His sleeves are pulled up and his hair is out of place, where he's raked his hand through a couple times over the last hour.

The entire common room erupts in cheers.

It took another hour, but Noxx House finally agreed on a group activity. Battling Darien in chess. When he offered the suggestion to the room, I immediately accepted. The alcohol might have aided that rash decision, but Parker's encouragement was the only protection I needed.

Parker squeezes my shoulder, and his lips touch my ear. "You are brilliant."

"Let's go again," Darien says.

"She beat you. Take the loss."

Parker shoots me a rakish grin, and it charges me in a way I don't expect. We're both athletes, so we must share the competitive draw. I'd almost like to go again to show him I can beat him more than once, but the lateness of the night is creeping into my sore muscles and tired eyes.

"Cherry, make sure you get this in the paper." Gavin, whom Parker introduced to me before the game, is smiling ear to ear.

"No need for theatrics." Darien's expression sours as he leans back in his chair. "I need a drink."

"I think theatrics are in order. It's been months since anyone has challenged you."

"You should join the chess team." A girl tugs on my arm.

I don't have the heart to tell her I don't have time to play chess and do ballet. There's only enough room in my brain for the perfection of one hobby. The rest of the house is prepping for the next game while Parker escorts me to the drink table.

"Where did you learn to play like that?" Parker asks.

"Will you crucify me if I tell you it was my father?"

"Before the fall out."

"Yeah. Before." *Before my mother died.* I don't say the words lingering in my mind. It's something I'd rather keep to myself. Talking about her brings up questions. People ask because they feel obligated, and I answer because if I don't, I look like I'm not handling it well and people worry. I like to talk about her when I want to or when someone genuinely wants to hear.

"Give me two minutes! Then I'm all yours." Parker disappears into the common room when one of his packmates calls. I met a few of them. They mostly poked fun at Parker about finally finding a mate, and Parker took it all on the chin with a smile. He relaxes when they're around and so do I.

I move into the comfort of the hall, away from the noise to decompress, and text Eva and Emma to see how their house parties are. Emma sent a message about Luxxia's slideshow night where they all convince each other to watch their favorite movies, and Eva sent a picture of a row of easels and canvases for a paint night in Stelliea. She painted a bouquet of flowers.

It's getting late, and my body aches for sleep.

"Sorry, I just wanted to tell you how impressive that was." Gavin has a booming voice that echoes but a presence about him that's calming.

"Thank you." A beat passes between us. "I'm glad I got to finally meet Parker's pack leader. I'm sorry I don't really know much about pack dynamics. This thing with him is ... unexpected. We have this connection I don't understand."

I hope that's enough to explain the timing. Gavin is so stoic I think he'll catch a lie, so being vague is my best bet.

"How much has he told you?"

"Just that he got to integrate with your pack and he's happy there."

Gavin smirks. "He's a rotten liar. But sweet."

"What do you mean?"

"Parker isn't happy. He can't be under me. He knows it. I know it. He tries really hard, but he's stalling I think."

"Why can't he be happy?"

His brow bends, likely wondering why Parker hasn't mentioned it. "Parker is a natural-born alpha. Alphas can't be led by other alphas. More than that, he's got dominance. It rivals even the greatest leaders on campus." He must see the vacant look on my face. "Dominance is a trait you're born with that other Weres can sense. It means nothing if you can't back it up, but Parker can rival the top packs because he shifts regularly, and he can fight. They see that when he plays Rage. Plus he's a natural leader, very caring. His friendliness and confidence intimidates people. He'll be a good match for them when he finally accepts his blood and creates his own pack."

"Even you?"

Gavin is one of the largest males I've ever seen. He's tall and wide, and his forearms are the size of my head.

"Ha, yeah, but I won't let him have the satisfaction of my admission."

"So why didn't you hate him when you first saw him? If you felt his ... dominance."

Gavin smiles. "The first time I saw Parker was his first day at Doxlothia. We were running our pack booth. That's something a lot of packs do to feel for new recruits. Suddenly everyone goes deadly still. I felt him close. I thought it was Aster or Barrett. My pack growled, and seconds later, Parker strolled up with this huge corn dog in his hand and said, '*Hi, I'm Parker*.'"

Gavin's laughter is infectious. I can tell he's told the story many times. "He had no idea my entire pack was ready to attack him if he got any closer. It was confusing at first because the energy coming off him was so ... pure. So raw. Powerful. But then he explained how he didn't have a pack, how his mom was born an alpha but his dad raised him. He was clearly lost and had no compass for Were etiquette, and he didn't know how to feel it."

"You have a soft spot for him."

Gavin doesn't look at Parker like the others do. Their interactions remind me more of me and my sisters than anything. A combination of annoyance, love, and complete acceptance.

"Parker is a good guy. He'll accept his alpha blood. He just needs to stop getting in his own way."

"You said his mom is an alpha." My attention catches on that bit. Had his mother left when he was young, so that's why he was raised by his father?

"Was. She died when he was a child."

"Oh." I don't know why I'm shocked. We have a lot of things in common. And the dead mom club isn't reserved for me and my misery. But I didn't think we had *that* in common.

"Shit. I've had too much to drink. I should not have said that. Parker doesn't really talk about his mother, so please let him tell you when he's ready."

I force a smile. "I won't say anything. Thank you for everything. Protecting my sisters won't be an easy task."

"You guys talking about me?" Parker strolls in. He's undone his shirt, so the top of his chest is exposed, and his tie is hanging off his neck haphazardly.

"Just that you should listen to your Alpha more." Gavin grins at me.

"If I did, I'd be unstoppable. Top student and model citizen even my father could love." Parker hangs an arm over my shoulder. "Too depressing?"

"I'll leave you two to your night." Gavin grins at me and leaves Parker with a pat on the back.

"Olivia." Parker's voice is in my ear as he leads me farther into the hall. "Can I ask you something?"

"I think you're going to ask either way, so get it over with."

He waits until after another student passes by to lean forward, placing a hand over my head to pin me to the wall.

"Can I touch you now?" he says in a low, sultry voice.

My chest is instantly heavy. Parker's flirting should not work on me, but his eyes sear me into submission, and I stay comfortably still with my shoulder blades to the wallpaper.

"Touch me ... how?"

His lips brush my neck, and I nearly gasp.

"Like this."

"I ..." I can't think with the heat from his body centimeters from my cheek. "Why?"

I squirm to make sure no one is watching us. He smells like the liquor we were consuming, and he had more than me.

"Is it yes if there's a reason?"

His skin touching me burns. It's so soft it almost hurts. It's barely there, yet he's moving like he *knows* where he wants his lips to go. He's everywhere, like he's seeping through the fabric of my clothes, and it's almost like what I need—

He backs away, then I'm empty and hollow. There's a loss there I don't understand and don't like.

"Yes," I choke out. "Yes, if there's a reason. A good one."

"Oh, there's a good reason."

His lips tease mine, then he moves to my jaw. It's like we're picking off where we left off in the maze, conveniently forgetting everything else. *This is good for our cover.* That's why I let him continue.

It has nothing to do with how hot he is on my cool skin. Or how when he's near, the part of my brain that's constantly working overtime just flips off.

Yearning simmers under my skin and hollows out my abdomen, and it's amplified by Parker's breath. He understands it all, and every breath I forfeit, he's there to fill with his own, teasing me at my hairline and ear.

His kiss hits my jaw, then he tilts my chin to gain access to my neck. He's testing my reaction. First, it's a kiss. Then he uses his tongue.

I breathe out a strangled whisper. But it's not a no. Not a protest.

Warm and wet, his tongue caresses toward my ear, and my breathing becomes shallow and my fingernails dig into his arm.

"Relax," he whispers. "You're always so tense."

My shoulders fall from my ears, and I let him lead. The throbbing of my heart travels down my thighs when he groans hungrily.

I wonder his reason. I wonder my own. This doesn't make sense. Maybe this is about the dream. I have one sex dream about Parker, then he gives me a little attention, and I cave. I like the simplicity of that explanation even if it's embarrassing.

Parker kisses my lips, and my mind goes blank. His tongue slips in my mouth, and he licks my teeth. I grip his shirt, suddenly desperate to give him a little more.

I shouldn't be kissing him while no one is around. Because if I'm not kissing him for our cover, it just means I'm kissing him. Still, I let it last, savoring each stroke of his tongue and the smell of his hair when he's pressed up against me.

I'm floating in the heady air between us when I lay my head back against the wall.

"Stay in my room tonight." He presses his forehead against mine, and his eyes are glowing yellow in the dim flickering lights of the hallway.

"Are you serious?"

"Yes. Don't make me beg. You don't smell enough like me. It's making me crazy."

"I'll think about it." It's a terrible idea. I can't trust myself with him, and this is more than enough proof for me. I don't allow myself to think about being in his bed. I need actual sleep. It's been such a long day and—

"I've got snacks. Warm bed. Clean sheets. Can we go now? Please?"

"Are you begging me?" I tease.

"You like that idea, don't you? Me getting on my knees for you."

He leans back to look at me. Heat pools in my gut, and I swallow. I need to go before my resolve crumbles.

"I have to get up early," I say, peering down the hall. He doesn't care; his lips are at my throat again. I should tell him to stop, but I like the way it feels when his lips move to my ear, so much so, I let my head fall back. I like the way he smells, the way his fingers dig into my hips. When I don't answer, he moves lower on my collarbone, and I let him. I don't know why, but I do know I shouldn't be in his bed, brushing up against him. There's a variable I'm missing that comes into play every time he touches me. It changes everything.

My body jolts when his tongue reaches my collarbone and his kiss turns to a light suction. It's good. It's so good.

"Please, Olivia." He nuzzles into the hollow of my neck. The yearning in his voice makes my heart hammer. "If you're in my bed all night, you'll smell like me. That's the easiest way."

I sigh, pushing him off me and finally gaining back my sanity. I don't need to know the other ways. I need to get in my own bed.

"I've thought about it. No."

He pulls back and chuckles in defeat. "Fine, but I'm giving you one of my blazers to wear around campus."

"It will swallow me."

"It will be so hot. Please."

My cheeks heat and I sigh. "Fine."

He shrugs off his blazer, places it over my shoulders, and walks me to my room. And even long after he leaves me, I still feel him all over me.

CHAPTER TWELVE

OLIVIA

My hand reaches for the surface as my lungs burn with water. I'm drowning.
Help me.
Someone, please save me.
I can't breathe, but I reach. Hoping. Pleading.

Thunder wakes me, and I shoot up in bed. Lightning cracks, and I rush to the window to draw the curtains. Another rumble of thunder vibrates through me as I sit on the edge of my bed in the dark.

It wasn't supposed to storm, just rain. I swear it wasn't. Otherwise, I would have prepared.

With trembling fingers, I go for my phone and check the weather. There's a storm warning for the next two hours. I dig through my closet for my headphones, but I must have left them in the studio when I dropped off my ballet stuff in one of the lockers. It's fine.

I dial Eva's number first, my leg bouncing. Nothing. I try Emma next. She isn't good at comfort, but it's better than nothing.

She doesn't answer.

No. No. No. The thunder snaps again, so I put my hands over my ears.

No, this is fine too. I don't need help. I've dealt with this before; I can do it again. It's been so long since I've been alone during a storm. My sisters and I always shared a room, and having them there made a difference.

It's the emptiness of it I don't like. The lack of calm. That's why I always have headphones. How could I forget my headphones? I listen to ballet ballads all night, and my mind drifts back to variation. There's certainty there, imagining myself dancing alone in the music.

Without music, I'm alone.

My brain is half asleep, churning out spirals of thought faster than I can keep up with. The rumble shakes the room, and I put my hand over my heart and breathe in for four counts and out for five. I stand to warm myself at the hearth, but my fingers won't warm.

She's never coming back.

It's always like this. The combination of thunder and the memory of that haunting truth. She's the only being who would make this better. She always knew what to do and what to say, no matter how panicked or scared I felt in the night. *She should be here.*

Wobbly and lightheaded, I stumble into the hall and another crack of thunder booms and lightning illuminates the dark hallway. *She would answer the phone.*

Moving always helps. Anything is better than being alone in my bed. The common room is my first thought, but I find myself staring at Parker's door.

It looks just like mine. Same sapphire handle and wooden design fixed with gemstones and pained filigree. But there's one word lingering in my head at the sight of it.

Home. He did say he wanted me to stay with him. Would he care if I woke him up?

I'm still half asleep, not thinking clearly, but I remember the feeling of his touch and the safety in it. I shouldn't. What am I expecting him to do?

Shivering in the dark hallway, I stiffen as thunder shakes the floor again, then I bang on his door. The worst he can do is turn me away, and if he does, I'll go sit in the common room with my humiliation. It wouldn't be my first time being embarrassed in front of him.

The door opens to a shirtless Parker with his pajama pants falling below his hip bones. He sleepily moves the hair from his eyes. "Olivia?"

"Can I ... stay in your room?"

He cocks an eyebrow. "Change your mind?"

My fingers bend around the doorframe as the thunder shakes the building again. "Please."

I just need to get somewhere quiet. Safe.

His eyes soften. "Ah. Got it. Yeah, come on."

I'm shaking till I attempt to settle onto his bed. Should I just sit on the floor? He's likely annoyed. He should be. I think about going back seconds before the thunder grumbles again. I'm not afraid of much, not really. I'm not afraid of the dark. I almost drowned once as a child, but I'm not even afraid of water or swimming. I don't mind snakes or spiders, but thunderstorms have always accompanied my worst nightmares as a kid, and that's only been amplified in my mother's absence.

"Do you need anything? Water?"

"No ... I just can't sleep like this." I'm raw and open. It's paralyzing.

"You're afraid of the thunder." His voice is gentle.

I nod. It's embarrassing to be afraid of thunder and storms. It's a child's fear that my parents were confident I'd grow out of ... until my mother died.

"Well, you're safe. Here." He turns to rummage in his drawer and pulls out some headphones to cover my ears.

"Thank you." I place them firmly over my ears. The muffled noise is welcomed. It takes away the sting of the thunder. Parker's room has no windows, so I'm safe from the lightning too. I stay sitting, content to sit up in his bed when he hooks me by my waist and hauls me into him.

We're spooning, with his body hot against my back and his arm around my stomach. I've never been held like this before by anyone. He's smothering me, but it's not suffocating.

My mind races with thoughts of my childhood. When it stormed, my mom would lie in my bed or stay up with me. I'd sit in her lap, and we'd play with puzzles till the sun came up and the thunder died. Once she was gone, I'd wandered into my dad's room during a storm, but he'd tell me to go back to my room.

I wish she was here. I wish I could call her.

"Better?" I can barely hear his muffled voice.

"Yes," I say, letting my hips sink into him, and a singular tear falls to my cheek. It's relief leaking from my eyes as the threat dissipates but also the familiar ache of grief.

"I'm sorry." My muffled words come out of nowhere.

Sorry this is too much.

Sorry I'm being embarrassing.

A burden.

Inconvenient.

I'm in the way. I shouldn't have forgotten my headphones. I should have checked the weather and not made this anyone else's problem. He shouldn't have to share a bed with a grown woman who's afraid of thunder.

"Don't." He rubs my arm. "It's okay."

When I sniffle, his grip tightens around me and he rests his chin on my head.

He doesn't think I'm a burden.

He isn't mad.

I let go of the fear, and our breaths sync with each exhale. It's as good as I'd hoped it would be. All-consuming comfort. So warm.

"You're safe." He repeats it until my muscles stop spasming and the tears stop staining his pillow. His hand runs up my forearm to my shoulder, and with my eyes closed, the thunder fades.

There's just him. The sheets smell of fresh linen and his shampoo. Every breath is a gentle lullaby lulling me toward sleep.

He tugs on my leg to open my legs farther so his leg can slide between my thighs. I let him. Because it's safe. I sense it in his touch. All of this is natural. How things should be. All the puzzle pieces fit together. *We* fit.

Parker feels like someone I've known all my life.

It's impossible. I'm too tired. Sleep is taking me.

But I know him.

I swear I do.

Chapter Thirteen

Parker

There's a hand in the water, reaching toward the sky.
I fall to my knees, grasp it, and pull with all I have.
You have to live.
You have to keep going. Please don't leave me here alone.

I wake with Olivia lying across my chest. My leg rests between her thighs, and one of her legs is draped over my lower half. Her scent greets me, and I don't want to move. She looks so peaceful even though the headphones I gave her have fallen off.

I close my eyes to fall back asleep, but the remnants of my dream stir in my mind. I don't remember my dreams. Except this one. It's always the same one. The dream I've had since I was a boy—a frozen lake spans before me with a break in the ice, a hand stretched to the sky, and the shadowed outline of someone beneath the frigid water. I fall to my knees and grab the hand that's sinking into the depths, desperately pulling to save them while screaming for help.

They never come up. I never see the conclusion, always waking in a panic.

But not today with a beautiful girl lying on my chest. The echoing of student laughter and movement in the hallway startles her.

She shoots up. "I'm going to be late."

I turn on my lamp and check the time on my nightstand. "Relax, it's only six thirty."

There are no windows in my room, so it's basically a dungeon if there's no light on.

"That's late. I should have gotten up to dance. I still have to—"

I drag her back down to my chest. "Let's take a few more minutes before all chaos breaks out, okay? I need some time to wake up first."

She settles into me with a hand over my heart, and I bring it into the light. I want a little more time to inspect her and hold her in my arms. And now she is relaxed, fully open in the safety of my room. She's different when she isn't intimidating every man with that sullen stare. Everything is softer: her eyes, her skin. We should be separating, but instead, we choose connection.

"Did you sleep all right?" I ask.

"Yeah. I didn't wake up at all. Normally, I will even with headphones."

"Is this a pretty normal occurrence for you?"

I was shocked to see her perched in my doorway last night. When she jumped at the thunder, it was obvious.

"You mean knocking on a man's door and asking to sleep in his bed? No. I'm usually more prepared or my sisters help me. When I was little, they let me sleep in their beds, now I just use headphones. We all slept in the same room anyway. I called them last night, but they didn't answer. They're probably blowing up my phone."

She doesn't make a move to get up, so I run my hands through her hair. It's like we're in a bubble. The kind where we aren't just friends enjoying the sensation of each other's skin. Olivia feels familiar. Her skin. Her scent. Her hair. When I stroke her and squeeze her next to me, it's like I've done it before a hundred times.

It's never been like this for me, and I know once that door opens, it's over. She chose me last night, and I'm happier about that than I expected.

"Have you always been afraid of thunderstorms?"

"Yeah ... since I can remember. It's embarrassing."

"No it's not."

"It's a child's fear most people grow out of. Sometimes, it sends me into a panic attack if I'm caught off guard. I was going to go to the common room if you didn't answer."

"You mean with the huge windows where you can see the lightning and hear the rain hitting the grass in unison with the thunder?"

"I didn't have anywhere else to go."

"That's okay." I rub her arm. "You can lay in my bed with me whenever you want, and I'll hold you."

She's quiet and averts her gaze to my chest. Probably too forward, but I don't regret saying it. The memory of her trembling in tears while lying in my arms is still fresh.

"You wouldn't tell anyone?"

"Our secret. No questions asked."

She smiles and sits up to run her hands through her hair. It's a tangled mess, but I don't mention it. "Will this help with the smell?"

"I have a little confession. I started to scent you in the hallway last night. I should have told you, but I was tipsy and needed to scent you before I let you walk anywhere else on the campus alone. But scenting is ... more effective if I can lick places other than just your neck."

She wipes her eyes. "Are you asking me ... if you can lick me?"

My phone dings, and as much as I want to ignore it, I need to check if it's Gavin.

It's not. I've been sent a picture in the Rage team group chat:

This you, Cap?

It's a screenshot from the forum, a picture of Olivia and me in the Noxx House hallway with her head against the wall, and my lips on her collarbone. My skin itches when I see how into it she looks. The caption reads: *Heated Hallway Rendezvous*. There are already four hundred likes and a hundred comments, and it was only posted thirty minutes ago.

"This is perfect," I say. "We want these people to believe we're heated lovers in the hallway."

"You knew someone was going to take this picture."

"Well, no, not really. I just got caught up in how I wanted to make you smell like me, but it's not enough ... Could I ... scent you again? Like right now?"

"You do want to lick me."

"It's not as gross as it sounds. If you encounter any other Weres on campus, especially Aster and Barrett, I want it to be obvious you're mine."

She stares at the hearth I don't use—Weres are hot enough—and my pile of Rage gear on the floor. I got put in one of the smaller rooms this year, but I don't miss the light from the window. I'm hardly in my room anyway. Olivia fingers the knit blanket at the foot of the bed—the baby blanket my mother made me. I don't advertise that, but I'll tell her about it if she asks.

"I don't know," she concludes.

"Do you trust me?"

"We just met." She huffs. "I trust that you're decent enough to help me ... three times, but those things didn't involve you licking me."

"Technically, two of them did. But you're right. Trust is earned. I'll show you. Nothing happens that you don't want to happen. You're in control."

"I don't want to have sex with you."

I can't help but smile at the way she says it. Like she'd accidentally stumble upon us doing it. "I didn't think that was on the table, but it's noted. No sex. Just licking occasionally. All for the cause."

She bites the edge of her cheek. "Okay."

"Lay down."

"Why do I need to be lying down?"

"It's easier. I need access to you. Under your clothes."

She sighs but complies. The scent of her arousal flutters into our space. I'm about to be tested. I want to make a smart-ass comment about how good she's being at listening, but I need to stop flirting with her while my lips are on her body. The less talking we do, the better. It will be quick and—

"W-what are you doing?" she asks as I move the hem of her shirt up and reveal her stomach.

"Trying to get the hardest part done first. It can't just be your neck. I need to scent you everywhere."

"Hurry up."

I lean over her and move lower, lifting her shirt higher. "Yes, ma'am."

Testing a patch of skin by her hips, my lips brush against her, and she flinches.

The skin on her stomach is hot. There's a brief, aching satisfaction that comes from knowing it's because she was lying on top of me.

"It's okay. Relax."

Her heart races as I kiss her stomach and caress her hip with my tongue, then when I reach the bone, I suck and creep up with deliberate light flicks of my tongue. She's so warm. She tastes so sweet. I linger longer than I should, but once I taste her, I want more.

It's just us. Our scents mingling in my sheets. The sound of my wet kisses as I lick skin, and hushed breaths.

Her fingers twist in the sheets by my head while her breath catches in her chest. There's not much room for us both. The higher I go, the more my broad frame pins her to the bed. She holds her breath when my lips meet her ribs. I think I'm making her uncomfortable, but her arousal is growing with each pass of my tongue on her stomach.

"It's okay to like this, you know? A man kissing your body. Running his tongue over you. There are no cameras here. No one is watching. It's just me."

I kiss her again. Then another taste. It's so fucking good. "You can make noise."

I remember her words from before. There was a specific reason she used them. I hope she'll tell me one day, but right now, it's about trust.

"I won't tell anyone."

She doesn't speak as I move up her abdomen, but her hands unwind from the sheets and twist in my hair instead. The first breathy exhale accompanies my lips on her stomach, and her back arches.

I should have kept my mouth shut. Because *what the fuck*.

I'm starved for her in a way I don't understand.

One tiny motion, and I want to map her body with my tongue. I want to explore all her curves as if I've waited a lifetime to kiss her stomach and taste her skin. Like I've missed her—someone I've just met. My hand supports her lower back as I drag her into me. I could make this faster, but every soaring beat of her heart fastens itself to me. I want to give her more, to make her feel good.

My pace slows, then I stop just below her breast and lick. Her fingers clench in my hair, and a satisfied hum vibrates in my throat. She melts into me, her legs spreading farther, her breath rushing from her lungs. She likes this. *I* like this. It should be awkward. We're practically strangers, but there's something natural about touching her.

There's no ignoring where all my blood has rushed to. I fight the ache of my cock and drive my hips into the bed. My own carnal urges bubble up, but I beat them down. I'm thinking of blood and claiming. Marking. Biting. Sex.

I run the bridge of my nose down her abdomen and stop just below her belly button.

For a split second, I let my mind run wild with fantasies of scenting her the proper way. A way she won't be able to wash off in the shower. The possessive need to fill her is excruciating. The urge boils over in my blood till I need it so bad I run my teeth over the skin there. Lower and lower. All of this is mine. I'm never going to let another person taste her.

"Parker."

It's the first time I've heard my name on her lips like that. Sultry and needy. I just want to give her what she wants. More. Less. *Anything.*

"Yes?" I have the best angle of her bare stomach and the underside of her breasts.

"You feel so ..." *So, what, Olivia?*

I tug at the hem of her pants, and her fingers tighten in my hair. Her cheeks are flush, and her eyes are filled with desire.

"Trust me," I say, and I wait for a nod of approval before I drag her pajamas past her ankles. I can't believe she's letting me. *Shit.*

The scent of her arousal ruins my resolve, so I run my hand over her thigh to not startle her. I know where I want to touch her. But I don't. I won't, even if every instinct in me is screaming to.

She gasps when my lips meet her thigh.

"You were saying ..." I say as I go to work scenting her thighs and running my tongue across her smooth skin.

Another kiss ... and she lets out another breathy noise. "You make me feel so good."

Let me show you how good I can make you feel, Olivia. The words are on the edge of my tongue. It's more than wanting to satisfy my own aching cock and possessive carnal desire. I want to show her good things and give generously. I'm the only one who can. The only person allowed to touch her this way.

She rocks her hips slightly, desperate for friction, and it hurts not to give it to her. I may not touch her like I want to, but I'm thinking about it. Slipping her underwear to the side and filling her the way she craves. The moans she'll make with her body trembling around my fingers. Her bad night would be just a terrible memory.

For my own sanity, I shift my attention back to the way her skin tastes.

Every kiss is like a brand. *Mine.* Another kiss. *Parker's.* And another. *Only.*

I need everyone to know. I need her to know.

"You wear tights to ballet, right?"

"Yes, why?" Her words are a breathy exhale.

"Good." I suck at the skin of her thigh. She gasps, gripping my hair again. The exhale morphs into a faint moan. "I needed to leave a mark on you, but I don't want you to get in trouble."

The fresh red bruise of blood pooling beneath the skin on her thigh satisfies me enough to stop touching her for now.

Her breath calms and a strange sense of peace lingers between us as I pull away and help her with her clothes. It's too easy. We should be awkwardly fumbling through it, but it's like our bodies recognize each other.

I don't know what's happening between us, but I like it.

Chapter Fourteen

Olivia

Parker Owens is just a man. I have to keep reminding myself of that as we share the common bathroom, staring at each other in the mirror and brushing our teeth. He spits his toothpaste in the sink, then goes back to brushing and winks at me. It's disgusting, so I'm not looking at his bare chest or thinking about those lips covered in toothpaste and how mere minutes before they were pressed to my lower thigh. No, because he's just a man. Nothing more.

Parker is so many things, and I've seen him scarf down an entire plate of food at orientation in seconds and now brush his teeth, so I can confidently say he is gross. But he's kind. And his hands are sure, and I know what his tongue feels like pressed to the underside of my breast. I spit my toothpaste in the sink, gazing over the veins in his forearms and hands as they grip the edge of the sink, and I remember the tenderness of them digging into my back. How soft, careful, and deliberate his touch was.

It's just lust because of that dream. It's nothing more than that. Though, I guess it wasn't lust that drew me into his bed and had him happily hold me all night long. And he could have kept touching me. I could have asked him to. I wanted him to. More importantly, he could have asked me but didn't.

We spit the last of our toothpaste out and rinse in sync. It's early enough that it's just the two of us in the coed bathroom. Apart from someone in the showers. The steam lingers in the air and billows up into the arched ceiling while the warmth creeps in as condensation at the edge of the mirror. It's large and elaborate like everything else at Doxlothia and has silver inlay with filigree lining all edges.

Parker smiles, tousling his hair with his fingers. I make quick work of wetting my brush and tugging my hair into a bun for ballet. I should have started warming up for auditions earlier, but when he turns to look down at me and our chests nearly touch, I can't bring myself to regret it entirely.

"Wow." He looks me up and down. "Hot."

"Move." I finish pinning my hair and drag my warmers up over my tights. "I take it you don't know many ballerinas."

"You're the first." His teeth are perfect, with his blue eyes sparkling. It's distracting.

Parker is beautiful. To deny it would make me a liar.

"What made you want to become a ballerina?"

I pause, take a breath, and focus on the mirror. I have two answers to that question. Both involve the truth, but only one involves mentioning my mother. I'd been roped into too many awkward conversations about her, so I developed a way around the madness that makes everyone comfortable. But Gavin's words are still fresh in my mind. Parker lost his mother too. He can take the real answer.

"My mother was a ballerina."

"Was?"

"Was." That's all I care to offer. I'll let him make up any assumption he desires. "She had a lead role in her company. I practiced nearly every day with her. She's the one who taught me."

I try not to think of her. Not in Noxx House. A place she once roamed. Had she pinned her hair in this very mirror? Was she ever late because she was lying in some man's bed all night? Surely not. My mother would never.

Parker smiles from ear to ear. It's so distracting I forget we're still standing in the bathroom.

"What?"

"You just lit up a little." He leans with his back against the sink counter. "Keep talking. Tell me more about her."

"Her name was Olive. She named me specifically after her while my sisters got our dad's family traditional names that start with an E. Ballet was her entire life, and she was a legacy. Noxx House was her house too. I knew when I filled out the test I'd get into the same house. Just a feeling."

"So you're like a miniature version of her?"

My cheeks heat and my heart stutters. It feels like a compliment.

"Yeah ... that's how I like to view it."

"She sounds amazing," he says it with a big tight-lipped smile that seems too genuine for me to find any faults with.

"I came to audition."

There's a blue-haired girl with a pixie cut blocking the entrance to the dance studio. Her pointed glare and black nails clicking on the stone next to my face have my bitchiness dialed up a couple notches. I let it show only through the disinterest plastered on my face and the way I try to weasel past her in the door.

Ballet is a competitive art, so I've grown up learning to deal with competitive people. It's a reflex at this point but requires a level of confidence if you want them to back off. Even if you don't believe it, you have to show it; they smell fear.

"You can't."

"This says sign-ups right here." I motion gracefully to the piece of paper pinned to the door.

"Humans almost never make the Doxlothia company." She sniffs the air, and I have no idea if she's Were or vampire.

Maybe there are subtle signs I should have learned. Yet another thing to graciously thank my father for when I see him again.

"You're Parker Owens's mate, aren't you?"

Guess the scenting worked. My mind flashes to the long sniff Parker took of me before he left me for the ice rink. His ears reddened and he beamed.

I sigh, trying to emphasize how bored I am. "Can you move? I need to warm up for the audition."

"There's no point. I'm saving you the trouble."

I'm contemplating how hard this girl can punch versus starting my warm-up outside when another girl strolls up.

She's got straight, shiny cinnamon-colored hair, and freckles peppered across her cream skin. She is in head-to-toe pastel pink and puts an arm around me like we're friends.

"Don't listen to her. The company takes anyone with talent. Don't think having boosted strength and extended stamina will gain you a spot alone. They take all things into account, including technique and artistry and those who work hard."

"Who are you?" I ask.

"I'm sorry. I'm Octavia Vix." She holds out her hand in a greeting as if she hadn't already welcomed me by drawing me toward her and her floral perfume. Her nails are also pink. I think Emma would squeal. And then I remember Emma *did* squeal. When Octavia entered the dining hall with the other members of the council.

"You're on the council." I inhale. "I'm Olivia."

"I know. Your name has come up quite a lot lately at breakfast. I'm one of two other humans on the council, the daughter of the director, and a second-year if you really want to get specific." She turns her attention back to the blue-haired girl. "Fia, move."

And then promptly thanks her as she lets me inside.

"You're the daughter of Mrs. Vix?" I ask.

"Yes! You'll love her. I help her out in the studio with things like organizing her calendar and setting up the room. I might have seen your video submission." Octavia fluffs her hair, like she's testing my reaction. "I'm in charge of handling emails for her. Your fouettés were so clean. I could never."

"I'd be happy to run through them together sometime. I'm here a lot."

"Really?" Her eyes sparkle, and she grabs my forearm.

"Of course."

I miss being in ballet school for that reason, to mingle with people who understand it and crave it. The satisfaction of helping each other work through weak spots. I wasn't always good at fouettés till an older girl helped me practice and refine them after class. You learn so much from watching others.

"I'd love that. I'll meet you here! I've heard you've been practicing early."

"Yeah, I had a routine back at home. I've been trying to stick to it."

My sisters tease me for being unnecessarily rigid in my schedule, but that's what my mother taught me. Early mornings are my time to be alone with my thoughts and ballet.

The ballet studio is a wide room with mirrors fixed on the front and back walls. Only one is solid stone, and the other has three large windows that overlook the Central Lawn. It's a vaulted barrel ceiling that makes the entire room feel large. And judging by the amount of people auditioning, they need the space.

I take a spot at the barre next to another girl who is stretching her leg at a perfect vertical. When we make eye contact, she stretches farther to make a slight bend. There are others watching me too with their back bends and extended splits.

I put on my headphones and get to work. Like those who enjoy the routine of curating a perfect cup of coffee, I enjoy perfecting my warm-up routine. They have foam rollers to the side, so I take the time to roll out my legs and body. I plop on my warming booties and move to stretching my legs and ankles, listening to the playlist I've curated with the perfect amount of songs that hit at just the right intervals if I stay on task. I finish with my more extreme stretches, examining the room as I do.

Maybe it's due to Parker's scent, but no one is paying attention to me, so I breathe a sigh of relief and study all the men and women I'll be auditioning with. Octavia has set up chairs on the other side of the room for the director and anyone else in leadership who's coming to watch.

My head says to manage my expectations, but my heart is pumping in my ears at the thought of the opportunity. I'd almost given up on that dream at ten years old when my mother died. My father pulled me out of ballet for four years, till at fourteen I begged him to reconsider. Even though I'd continued to train on my own during those years, I feared they held me back, and I'd given up on my father ever letting me go to Doxlothia and auditioning for the company. The only way I'd ever be able to get in was as a legacy, and for that, I needed his blessing. That's what made it all the more shocking when he did come around.

The nagging why of it all lingers, but I wring it all out while warming up. His reasoning stopped mattering years ago. I can't depend on that for any comfort or knowledge. The only thing I can depend on is my ability to execute what I've practiced my whole life for and what I know I can do.

After forty-five minutes, it's time for auditions to start, and my time slot isn't one of the firsts.

A woman in a long dress walks up with her arms crossed over her slender frame. Her sleeves fluff and fall as she muses. "Welcome all! My name is Charlotte Vix. If you have made it to this stage, you were selected for an audition spot. I don't think I need to tell you what an accomplishment that is."

I recognize her along with the others who file into the room. The program and artistic directors are head of the IBCE. My stomach falls, and I have to remind myself to take a breath.

I'd had to submit photos and a video to be considered for the dance program in general. Those who aren't selected for company are put in the student-run classes and are still able to learn. They can graduate from Doxlothia and get a job at another company, but I'm not interested in that option.

Unlike my other auditions and competitions, there isn't a number attached to me.

"Olivia." Mrs. Vix looks me up and down. "Your photos were beautiful. You looked like a spitting image of your mother."

My throat dries, and I have to push out the words in a peppy tone that doesn't sound like me. "You remember my mother?"

"I do. I remember talent." The wrinkles by her eyes crease into her blue eye shadow with her smile. "Looking forward to your audition."

As I await my time slot, I don't focus on the other dancers. My mind disappears to a time when my mother roamed these halls and touched these floors. The sound of pointe shoes on the hard floor is the sound of her shoes. The music playing and the variation is hers. When I dance, it's almost like she's there. In a way, my path seems like a continuation of her dream of being principal in the IBCE before she gave it all up for my father.

He never protected her dreams. She dropped out as a soloist, and though she became principal in another company, she'd told me she wished she'd stayed a few more years before deciding to settle down. Her dream was just out of reach.

When it's time for me to take the floor, I'm so in the zone the entire thing is a blur. I disappear into the variation and the music. I don't feel my feet hit the floor or the burn in my calves during my fouettés.

I don't think about what happens after.

I don't think about anything but ballet.

Fluid arms and light feet. Lines. Perfection.

Ballet is the definition of perfection. There's always something to improve. I can be better if I practice and push a little harder. That's why I love it no matter the outcome; I will still be doing the same thing the next day and the next. Dancing. Perfecting. Pruning. Shaping myself into someone more graceful, more poised.

Something better.

Someone better.

I'm not fully lucid when I finish my variation and thank them, then receive my next-step instructions and exit the building. The sound of students passing and the echoing of laughter in the trees doesn't hit my ears again till my cell phone buzzes.

My dad finds the worst times to call me. I've already ignored it twice. Once on the first night, and the other during the Noxx House party.

I sigh and bring the phone to my ear. "Hi, Dad."

"Hey, honey, sorry to bother you again. I hadn't heard from you. Your sisters told me you were auditioning today. I wanted to see how you were adjusting."

"I just got finished. It was good."

There's a shuffling on the other end. "You ... uh ... felt good, then? Do you think you'll get in?"

Annoyance creeps into my chest. "I don't know. I hope so."

He already knows how much I want it. Somehow having to speak those words out loud makes my chest tight. It feels like work.

"How are you settling in? Any new people?"

Parker is the only person who comes to mind, but I'm unwilling to take questions about him, so I say, "Yeah ... I got into Noxx House."

He pauses for a second, then clears his throat. "That's great, kid."

It's not that my father is a terrible person. It's that he's decided to start being a good father out of the blue. And that's great for him, for whatever hurdles he had to climb to get there. I'm happy for him, really.

But my mom died more than ten years ago, and all those years, he'd pulled away from us and ripped us away from everyone else. Grief took over his life, and he gave up the career he loved. He ran away from work and his children and retreated into vacant solitude. There physically but not mentally. Absent for dinners and performances and only offering his input to say no it's too dangerous or that we couldn't go somewhere. For years, I was alone. I had no support other than my sisters, and they needed me while I needed him, but he was always locked in his room.

That doesn't just go away. Not even when he sat us down to tell us he was sorry and he'd put in our applications for Doxlothia. It was his bridge, but I'd already had the gasoline in one hand and the lighter flickering in the other.

"I've got to go, but ... thanks for calling, Dad. It's good to hear your voice."

No one has disappointed me more than my father, yet inflicting pain on him only leaves me with a guilty pit in my stomach. I do for him what he couldn't find the courage to do for me. Give empathy. And I don't know when or if I can ever forgive him for that.

Chapter Fifteen

Parker

I can't stop thinking about her in my bed. Her attraction to me is based solely on the fact that I'd pinned her down and used my tongue to scent her. She'd think that about any man who'd done the same. That's a good thing, right? That's what I want. Because I don't have time for a girlfriend. Even though I've willingly agreed to be her fake boyfriend in this scenario to help her. But that's totally different. All I need do is protect her, and scenting her is a huge part of that.

I guess I didn't need to lick her thighs. Was it my fault her thighs were so lickable and enticing? And leaving that mark on her thigh was for ... me. Okay, fuck, it was for me, but that doesn't need to mean anything. As it stands now, we're friends and everyone thinks she's my girlfriend, so that forbids any other guy from leaving marks on her thighs, and that's a good thing. I think. Now I'm back to where I started: in practice thinking about Olivia under me, in my bed, panting and saying my name.

I'm nearly tackled to the ice as a teammate flies by.

"Head in the game, Captain!"

Right. I speed past Zant on my right to maneuver for the puck. The game rules are pretty simple to follow. I'd started playing young, and thankfully—because it could be lucrative—my dad had no problems paying for gear for all my games. Not that he stayed for any of them. But I'd learned easily enough. One, unlike hockey, you can only touch the puck with your stick with no exceptions, and that can be *really hard* when the puck is rigged to move around and bounce all over the ice. Bumping the puck with any other part of your body will get you a deduction. The other stuff is pretty standard. There are eight people on the ice at a time, and we don't have standard offense and defense positions like in hockey. Except for the goalie, we do have one of those. You need to get the puck through the net for a goal. Only, how you get those goals is the fun part. Shifting, hitting, and bleeding are all permitted.

It's versatile. Some teams choose to forgo the fighting unless necessary. Rage champions are known for the different ways they play the game—some are great fighters, others quick and strategic.

As team captain, I have to be able to do it all.

This is a practice scrimmage, so we're split into teams. I clip an opposing teammate, knocking him to the ground, but my focus is on Zant. It's the last drill of the day, and I'm trying to trigger a riot play.

"Come on, big boy." Zant taunts me.

I growl and plunge my blades into the ice. The ice is an irritating nuisance but necessary for evening the playing field. The great thing about Rage is that werewolves and vampires can play together. It was the first game of its kind, and it all started at Doxlothia. Soon after, a lot of the other sports followed suit with combination teams.

I slap the puck to Chase, hoping he blocks it even though he's on the opposing side. He's our new goalie and he needs the practice.

He dives onto the ice, missing the block completely but it's fine, we're working on it.

"Chase, what the fuck are you doing?"

"Sorry, Cap!" He stumbles to his feet with a wave.

I swoop in for the puck again and look for someone to pass to. Anyone. Anyone at all, but all these fuckers want to do is fight each other on the ice. This year, no one wants to listen to strategy. They all want to fight, and it's hard to be mad at them because that's my favorite part too.

I fight the frustration and decide to take it myself, but then I see Ryker is wide open and ready. He's a new transfer student and one of the only ones who listens.

He's quick with it and hits the puck between two other teammates and passes them on the left, taking it right to the goal.

Finally.

I'm about to go get it when Zant blocks me.

"Didn't we talk about this?" I say.

I give him one more second to move out of my way. Threaten a man with an ass kicking and that should be enough.

"We're tied now. Gotta do what I gotta do."

"Bad move." I grit my teeth and rush him till his skates lose contact with the ice and we're crawling and fighting for leverage.

Meeting your match on the ice is tough. When someone knocks you onto the ice, you have twenty seconds to get up. If the person who tackles you is able to keep you down, well—

The whistle blows, and the coach points to center ice. "Parker and Zant, in the circle."

I wink at Zant and yank him back to his feet, knowing I'm about to kick his ass. When the score is tied and you can keep your opponent down for more than twenty seconds, it triggers a riot play. A play I'm always trying to trigger because it ends the game early.

Whoever challenges and wins, will end the tie and the game.

I strip my gloves, and my skin itches with the coming shift. Weres are only permitted to shift up to fifty percent during games unless there's a riot play against another Were opponent. That keeps things equal. Also, werewolves have trouble with traction on the ice in shifted form. I tried it once and laughed with my teammates on how ridiculous it looked on video.

Zant sighs. "I didn't want to spend all my time in recovery today, but here we go."

We've been doing this dance since we were kids. Zant is one of the first people who ever saw me shift. It's only fitting he helps me train while I kick his ass every day in practice.

Because of Rage, shifting is as natural as breathing. My fingers shift into claws, and hair coats my arms. Our bodies collide in a final riot play, and every strike counts.

Last year, I was elected captain at the end of the year when our previous captain graduated. Zant was ecstatic. He'd seen it coming, but I didn't. I have the

C on my uniform, but it's like I'm wearing a costume. Our team this year is at a disadvantage. For one, there are no pack affiliations. All the previous successful teams at Doxlothia were stacked teams, where the majority of the players were part of the same pack or part of two coworking packs. Now it's just me, a few lone wolves, and a few vampires like Zant.

Zant is bad at scrap work with Weres, which is exactly why I needed to trigger the play so he can practice.

I'm left-handed and so I leave my right side open for him to make it an easy blind spot. But he's too slow. I clock him with a claw to the face and lunge to tackle him to the ice. We trade a few blows, and he clocks me in the jaw.

"Enough. Parker's game," Coach Zepheus calls. "Honestly, boys. What was that? I've never seen you guys less cohesive. You need to communicate more. Owens, come see me."

I stand and leave my arm out to help Zant up, and he slips on his own blood. "Aw, buddy. I went easy on ya."

"Shut the fuck up, Owens." He winces.

"It's Captain here, bud."

He flips me off. Gotta say, I enjoy the one and only time I've ever had any authority over him.

I skate over to Coach with my tail between my legs because I already know what he's going to say. Practice was a shitshow. Coach Zepheus is a big, burly Were with a two-year-old daughter who comes to visit him nearly every day. She's practically our mascot at this point. I kinda wish she was here right now because he's less inclined to rip me a new one when she's tugging on his leg.

"What's up, Coach?"

"You saw what I saw out there. You tell me."

"There's a lot of new guys on the team this year. We're still learning how to work together."

"You're right, and it's up to you to lead them. Your predecessor believed you could do this."

That, he did. At least someone did. My dad had barely bothered to change his tone when I told him I'd been picked as the team captain.

"Are you sure you want to do this?" It was loud on the other line, and I could barely hear him.

"Uh, yeah. This is huge."

"I know. I meant, you're certain you can handle that?"

"Yeah, I've been working hard, practicing every day—"

"It takes more than that to be a team captain. We're talking about real leadership here."

"I know. I can do it."

"Good then, son. Congratulations."

He'd have a heart attack on the spot if he ever uttered the words "I'm proud of you."

"Things will be different this year. You're playing a completely different game. Being a leader is more than being a good player."

"Yes, sir. I know, Coach."

Last year, Doxlothia had a record-book year. Our team was solid from front to back. It will be hard to follow up.

He uncrosses his arms. "I know you do. You're more than capable. I'm just waiting to see it."

Him and me both. I'm starting to think I've tricked everyone who's ever met me. Somehow, I made it on the most successful Rage team, we won the tournament, and then I was chosen for team captain. It felt like a dream at the time, and now I'm still in the dream but not waking up. And the dream is gradually getting harder and morphing into a nightmare. How am I supposed to get the team ready for the season, let alone continue our streak at the tournament?

And if I do mess up, my chances of going pro are basically nothing.

"I can do it, Coach." Hollow words for an undercover fuckup.

I'm secretly a choker, and no one has figured it out yet. But only because the ripe time for my misery hasn't shown itself; the universe is waiting for me to show my ass to the world. What I wouldn't give for just one phone call with my mom to talk to her about it all. Her pep talks were the cure for everything.

"You're ready, Parker. You gotta believe in yourself a little more. Your team needs you. I know you got your hands full this season, but we'll get things in shape."

After a few more minutes of lecture, I leave him to go check on Zant who is bellyaching and wiping blood off his face with a towel.

I move to sit next to him on the bench.

"You know ... I told you we needed to work on your groundwork."

He glares first, then hits me in the shoulders. "Would you get me some blood, you asshole?"

"Already got it," Chase says.

Chase whips around us and throws us a blood bag. We're only allotted a certain number for injury, so we need to use them sparingly. His jersey is the only one without blood on it. He told me the reason he wanted to be goalie was to avoid fighting.

"Thanks, Chase. Everyone else besides Zant, let's burn them out. Rapid fire. Sudden death."

The guys groan in unison. Sudden death is the complete obliteration of the remaining strength in our muscles by passing the puck around till we literally can't move. That's how my captain taught me.

I sit next to Zant to ensure he doesn't pass out. I'm going to have to finish sudden death regardless, might as well procrastinate.

"Worried about me?"

"Just making sure you participate in sudden death." I wrap my arm around him, and he shrugs me off.

"You say I need practice, but you're the one daydreaming on the ice."

"I'm a model leader. I would never."

"Uh-huh." He wipes the bit of blood from his chin. "It has nothing to do with a certain Noxx House girl?"

"No." I shrug. "We're casual. Just for show."

"Yeah, sure. That's why you're scenting her in the hallway."

"Scenting her is part of it."

Zant knows me. I don't even fuck girls for the fun of it. "Stop fucking lying to me."

"I'm not. She's ..." Just a woman? I can't say that because I don't invite women in my room to sleep and cuddle all night. I didn't tell him about Olivia staying in my room even when he could smell her immediately. "Under my protection."

Not a lie.

"Okay Mr. Noble. Good thing because she's going to need it. The council is on one lately. Everything is on fire. They're announcing funding cuts today. Some programs are getting cut entirely. Olivia is lucky Octavia holds a council seat and her mother is on the board for the dance department. It's only going to get worse. The Weres are going to back a nomination for Cane."

"Oh, fuck no."

I'm starting to think I'll never be rid of that parasite. Cane will continue to latch on to anything close to me and gradually find ways to suck the joy from my life.

"Yep, and everyone here loves him, so he's probably gonna get it. If only there was someone we knew who would be a good rival … Maybe the beloved Rage captain? If you'd just campaign, I can help you."

"You know I don't want to. I can't be on the council. I have my hands full with all of this. You saw the practice. I can't even—" I sigh and run my hands through my hair. "I don't know what you think I'd be able to do."

"You gotta get Mr. Owens's voice out of your head." Zant's smile is gone, and he's staring out into the rink where the rest of the team is struggling. Chase and Ryker are bickering back and forth because Chase wants to fuck around and do goalie shit, and it's interfering with Ryker's shots.

"What's that supposed to mean?"

"The worst part about being your friend for so long is knowing how long you've let him fuck with your head. I wouldn't bring it up if I thought you couldn't do it. One day, you'll stop fighting it."

Zant's encouraged me to accept my alpha blood since we were kids. When we were younger, it was probably because he wanted me to beat up Cane and put him in his place, but when we were teens, he started telling me I was wasting my potential. But how? Rage is my thing. It's the only thing that's ever made sense and brought me a real sense of purpose. Why do I have to have more than one thing? Why do I need to make my own pack when my mother's rejected me after she died? They had their reasons. Can't I have mine?

I used to want to accept it and take over her pack. I dreamed of the leader I'd be when I became of age, but when she died, she took all that confidence with her.

If Cane gets the council seat, Gavin and his family are going to have trouble. Cane's pack would get stronger. Then Aster and Barrett will go unchecked with the majority of Were packs in the school.

Fuck.

Parker Owens: The Golden Boy is in all the papers, but I'm an average player who knows how to win Rage matches, awaiting the moment someone else will come in to show the others I'm not that special. Not pro material. I'm just Parker. A lone wolf at heart.

Chapter Sixteen

Parker

"How much longer?" she asks.

"Soon," I whisper into her hairline. I'm not in a hurry. I've waited a long time for this.

The sun beats down on me as I make my way back toward the castle for class. Doxlothia's academics work differently than other universities, and those who play sports or who are in special programs spend the majority of their time perfecting those talents. However, there are a few classes we're all required to take. I don't mind. They're interesting subjects that aren't available at other schools like the History of Interspecies Cooperation, and Potions and Elixirs for Healing Modalities.

My gaze lingers on the dance hall. I haven't talked to Olivia since this morning, and it feels like too long. We've spent the whole week together and I'm getting used to her in my routine. I pull out my phone to text her, then spot a familiar head of blonde curls across the path, and her sweet scent makes her a decent beacon. Olivia's sister Evangeline is sitting on a bench with her head in her hands, sobbing.

I hurry to plop down next to her, slow and quiet.

"Hey." I start small.

I have a little sister, though she's way younger than I am. Evangeline is likely my age. I've learned to be calm and offer my sister *anything* she asks for in a crisis.

She startles, moving her hands from her face, revealing red eyes and smeared makeup. I halfheartedly offer her a dry towel from my bag as a way of telling her. She says nothing and breaks into another sob.

"Evangeline, right?" Olivia mentioned only her sisters call her Eva. "I know you don't know me very well, but ... uh ... you know, I'm a brother ... so like, I get it ... well ... I don't get it. But I could. I mean. Fuck. Do you want to talk about it?"

A slight wave of protectiveness has me wanting to hide her from everyone walking by whispering, then typing into their phones. Anything could be bothering her. What if it's a girl thing? Oh, I'm in way over my head. I should probably just call Olivia. Or do I just want to hear her voice again?

"My boyfriend hates me."

Okay, now we got something to work with.

"Boyfriend, huh? Why would he hate you?"

"He hates that I came here. I don't even know why I'm here. I'm not good at anything. You've seen Olivia and Emma. *They're* good at things. Olivia has ballet, and Emma can cook and bake. And I have nothing. There's no reason for me to be here. I don't know why they even accepted me other than my father and mother being legacies."

"That's how everyone gets in here. Don't worry."

"But most of them have talent! Something to show that required hard work and practice."

She's pouring her soul as if we've had more than just passing casual conversation. I lean in.

"You feel like a fraud?"

"Yes! I'm a fraud, and my boyfriend knows it. Everyone knows it. This is just so ..."

"Terrible."

"It is terrible." Her rant is concluded as she wipes her eyes.

"You know ... I feel like that all the time."

She opens her mouth to protest.

"Hold it. Let me finish. Even people like Emma, Olivia ... me. We don't feel like we belong here. And everyone is trying to convince the world they do. So what? Your boyfriend is kinda mean"—*Fuck him*— "and you haven't found that thing you like doing yet, it doesn't matter. You're in the perfect place to find it. Give it time." I shrug, not entirely certain I'm being helpful, but she doesn't start crying again. She simply nods as if she's processing it and the fact she's sitting on a bench where everyone is staring at us.

"If anything, do you want me to escort you back to your house? You know, where there are less people."

"Ugh, I don't care. My life is terrible anyway, who cares what everyone else thinks."

"That's that Osborne spunk I'm coming to know and love."

She smiles and blows her nose into my towel, then wipes her eyes with the clean side.

"You can keep that," I say.

"I'm sorry. I'm such a mess. Everything I touch turns to ash. Sometimes literally."

"You sound like my brother."

"You have a brother?"

"Yeah, my older stepbrother. We don't get along that well because he's really moody."

And a vampire. And an asshole. Still love him though, I guess.

She laughs. I'm happy I'm able to help a little.

"There's a reason you're here. You'll figure it out in time. And your boyfriend ... Well, do you want me to beat him up? Because I will. That's about the only thing I'm able to help with there."

"No. No. We'll work it out. It's fine. Thank you." Evangeline's nose is red, and she sniffles, but a little bit of her smile is back.

"Eva!" Emma comes running toward us. "Is Jared making you cry again? Get up, woman."

She hauls her from the bench, wiping her skirt and plucking rouge petals from her sleeves. Doxlothia has a plethora of trees with different flowers that bloom almost all times of year except winter. Right now, there is a mix of purple and red.

Her momentum stops as if I had been some invisible pole that suddenly smacked her upside the head. Or a branch.

"Parker."

"I was just going. I've got Potions in like two minutes."

"You're all ... bloody." Her nose crinkles as she eyes the closed gash on my forehead that Zant so lovingly gave me as payback for earlier this week. I hadn't had time to clean off the dried blood.

"You'll get used to that here."

CHAPTER SEVENTEEN

Olivia

"I don't want you to go. I'll miss you," he says, while my head rests on his bare chest.

I trace circles with my fingers, savoring every beat of his heart. I don't want to wake up.

"There's assigned seating." Someone in the official Doxlothia staff uniform motions to the door. Too young to be a teacher, must be some type of professor's assistant.

I read the chart, which appears to be hand drawn, and once again, I'm curious as to what the school spends its money on. Once I'm settled into a seat, I skim the book on my desk. *Enchantments and Elixirs for the Curious.* There's nothing like this in Groveshire.

Groveshire is primarily a human town. That's why my dad wanted us to stay. Humans have a habit of sticking to what they know. Many still opt to be magic and elixir free. Just like there's still a whole range of people who take hormonal birth control to prevent pregnancy even though there's an elixir that's one hundred percent effective. There are still humans out there who don't want to be part of the program and don't trust it in its entirety. That's why they flock to secluded places and primarily human towns get formed. Vampires stay close to the city where the pool of donors stays large.

Goose bumps rise on my arm seconds before Parker walks through the door with his bag slung over his shoulder and blood smeared on his forehead. He lights up when he spots me. After a quick wink, he eyes the chart, then his smile widens. I watch till he disappears behind me. A chair screeches against the hard floor as he drags it from his desk.

"Hey, baby." His breath is on my neck.

What are the chances he'd be seated right next to me in the same class?

I've never had a nickname. I don't even let my sisters shorten my name.

"Quick kiss?"

I scoff. "There's barely anyone in here."

"Oh, right." His fingers play with the ends of my hair.

"You can't distract me. I know nothing about this stuff, and I want to learn."

"Are you that easily distracted by me?"

I sigh, watching the others take their seats. The class is divided into thick wooden desks that each have an old iron sink and a drain in the pebble floor. There is a windowed ceiling with green vines spread out and flourishing in the sun. It's breathtaking and rich with history. Along the stone walls are pictures of professors from many years before. The sun hits the colored stone and casts a soft rainbow in the air.

"How did ballet go today? I wanted to drop by to watch, but we're prepping for the moon festival. It's an offseason tournament. A bunch of other schools are coming to play, and my team is *not* ready."

"You'd want to watch me?"

"Yeah, definitely. Is that not a thing? Will it embarrass you to have your *boyfriend* there?" Parker leans in close to my face.

My cheeks heat. "No. I just didn't think you'd want to."

Since my mom died, no one in my family watches me dance unless it's for a big performance. I can't blame them. It brings up memories.

"If I get in, then I'll probably be in the studio late. You could come then."

I say it casually like not getting accepted wouldn't be the biggest blow to my ego and leave me in shambles. Ballet is the only thing that filled my time in Groveshire, but everything was low stakes there. My ballet school wasn't prestigious, and before Doxlothia, I'd prepared myself to audition for a smaller, lesser-known company.

"You'll get in," Parker says, nonchalantly.

The professor greets the class, and I try my best to pay attention while Parker's calloused fingers linger in my hair. Every time he brushes the skin on the back of my neck, I have to refocus.

"Everyone, take a look at your table. We have the supplies set up that we will be going over step-by-step. Your table mate will also be your partner for the semester. Go ahead and mingle with them for a minute."

Parker lightly bites my shoulder.

"Hi, partner."

I'm not sure Parker is my type. I haven't put much thought into what my type is, but the only person I've ever dated was serious, calculated, and possibly even more ambitious than me. And that's saying something.

I think Parker is ambitious too, but in a different way. You don't become captain of the top Rage team without the skill or drive. I know that after observing Doxlothia. It's not about money, though that's important. Everyone here is the best of the best or wants to be. It's all about talent, strength, and status.

"Will you take this seriously?"

"Oh, I live seriously. I know a lot more about potions than you. I'll be a great teacher. Can you handle that? Someone telling you what to do?"

My cheeks warm. His eyes rake over me, slowly, deliberately. *This is all part of an act, Olivia. Get it together.* You can't let a flirty man get under your skin this easily. It's embarrassing.

"I won't take orders from you."

"You sure?"

He's looking at my lips, and I shift my attention to the veins in his forearms. Again.

"Now, your first assignment and the elixir we will be constructing is Nexum Adoratia."

The students groan, and I scribble it in my notebook. I know a handful of the most common elixirs, but they're all medical related.

"I know, I know, but it's the base level elixir for a number of others we're going to cover this semester and the number one most asked about. I like to knock it out quickly. We'll be running through as many social potions and elixirs as we can, and then we'll move on to medical."

"What does it do?" I ask Parker.

"It basically just makes you more open. It gives you that feeling when you drink alcohol and the wall comes down and you suddenly don't care what people think of you."

"You've had it before?"

"Oh, yeah, I made one with my friends when I was like fifteen. Some people call it a love potion because of how many people have fallen in love because they were under the influence of it."

The groans of protest make sense.

"Will you try it?" Parker bats his lashes at me. "Open yourself up a little?"

I'm glad the elixir takes weeks to cure.

"Don't hold your breath."

The professor explains the ingredients one by one. And then it's time for the demonstration. We're allowed to work among ourselves or follow along.

"Okay, so we're using the wolfstone cauldron, do you know why?" Parker says.

"Are you going to tell me?"

He places a hand on top of mine, guiding it into the cauldron. With two fingers, he presses mine into the stone. Liquid heat runs through me and up to my ears. His fingers curl into mine, and the pads of my fingers run over the rough, cool surface.

"Feel that?" he asks.

I nod and untuck my hair from behind my ear in case my flush is obvious.

"It's thicker, and the little indentations in the stone make it a good heat conductor. You need really high heat to make Nexum Adoratia."

"Aren't you knowledgeable," I jest.

"I'm more than a pretty face." He chuckles. "Potions are kinda my favorite. My coach is an expert."

"Now." He removes my hand and turns it over. His tongue wets his bottom lip, and he smiles like he's holding in a joke. After opening a glass container named *Betwitched Milk Clay*, he scoops out a dusty-blue bead of paste with flecks of gold. "This clay reacts with the oils on your skin."

I inhale while he spreads it across my palm with his thick thumb. He pads over my pulse and up to my fingertips, and the clay folds and smooths.

"I can do it," I say.

"You're right, I should be having you do this on my palm."

We scrape the clay into the cauldron, and he has me open a vial with a cork stopper and pour in the liquid. Then we take the wings off a dead Lucaria Moth with a pair of tweezers and drop it in.

"Do you know how to mix it?" he asks.

"I'm sure the professor will tell me."

I tune back into her teaching, but she's still a few steps behind and helping another group.

Parker grins and leans back in his chair to watch me. "Ask me nicely."

"Show me."

He waits, his gaze floating on my lips, then up to my brow, which is bent from annoyance at his stalling.

"Please, show me."

"Oh, baby, I'll show you whatever you want me to."

I roll my eyes and wait while he grabs the stick and stirs it like you would anything else.

"See, simple."

He leans back in his chair, and I square my shoulders.

"You're exhausting."

"Oh, you haven't seen anything yet."

CHAPTER EIGHTEEN

OLIVIA

"You're so beautiful." A thumb traces my lips.

He pushes inside me, and I gasp.

"You're mine." His words stitch me together.

Aching pleasure runs through my abdomen, and I cry out.

"I'm here," he whispers in my ear, thrusting into me, and my hips buck into his. "Good, just like that."

I'm caught in the feeling of him inside me. It's perfect. It fills every ache and desire.

I'm whole.

"That's it. Ride me, Olivia."

I wake alone, tangled in the sheets. The memory of my dream is enough to get me to my feet to warm my hands at the hearth. I brush my finger over my lips as it replays over and over.

I've had that dream before. More than once.

The first time proceeded a night I'd rather forget. The last time I let myself get entangled with a man, I'd given him what he wanted and then he left before returning the favor. I never even got undressed. I believed it was my fault, but he'd been my dance partner for four years and a constant in my life, never let me fall, and we pushed each other. He supported my dreams. Dance is passionate, and we shared that passion growing up until we were adults and those close performances and variations became more. Those lingering touches turned to kisses in the dressing room and then a date and then another.

Then it ended the first night we were truly intimate.

I'd cried myself to sleep only to dream of a man making his way into my bed. Typically a thing of nightmares, but I knew this man. I reached for him and his safety and welcomed his warmth and his hands caressing my body as he sank into my sheets. There was comfort in him wiping my tears and filling me till I couldn't speak. Despite how well I remember that dream, I can't see his face, but I remember his grip and the euphoria of him satisfying me till the pressure in me shatters and pleasure spreads through my body like wildfire.

His voice.

There's no denying it's the same. It's the same words. The same everything, except this time, I identify those hands, those lips, that voice—it's Parker.

It was Parker's warm hands holding me close and cradling my head. Has it always been him? I chuckle out loud at the thought and press my forehead to the cold stained glass. That's absurd. My subconscious must have inserted him into what has to be a random dream sequence.

"That's it. Ride me, Olivia."

My mouth dries and I swallow. The infliction of my name has always been specific. The way his words roll off his tongue, and the way he speaks my name like a whisper of praise. It can't be. I'm remembering it wrong.

Parker became an addition to the dream because of our recent encounter. Were we considering that sexual? He probably didn't, so I shouldn't since we've decided to have this whole fake relationship, which means nothing is technically real. But it felt real, and the ache between my thighs had been consuming me alive. All those kisses. His hushed warm breath against my skin sent my head into wild fantasies. It didn't mean anything to him, but obviously, my subconscious made a different choice. That's all it is.

My shoulders fall from my ears as I let out a breath. With that decision, I make my way to my dresser to get a start on the day. There's no way I'll be able to sleep again.

It's been a full week since the audition. After I finish my morning class, I get a notification that the results will be posted this afternoon. Which means I'll be totally useless until then. The sun is up, and I haven't seen or heard from Parker yet. We almost always walk out of our doors at the same time. If not, he texts me as soon as he gets up without fail with a little smiley face and some type of flirtatious good morning, and I respond with a quick hello and head to the dining hall to eat breakfast with my sisters.

I'm already used to him walking with me, and there's a strange emptiness as I do all the things he usually does with me, like chatting to the lunch staff while he hands me a plate. He holds them for a few seconds first because they're hot right out of the wash, while I gather the napkins. So today, I burned my hand on the plate and I skipped the napkins because there were too many people.

As I eat my egg and cheese bagel, I check my phone again. I think I'm hiding the disappointment well until Eva leans over my right shoulder and says, "Oh, you like him."

Emma chuckles on my left. "She does."

"I don't."

"You've just checked your phone at least three times in fifteen minutes." Eva isn't wrong.

"I'm checking about the audition."

"Right. I knew this relationship wasn't going to be fake." Emma butters her scone and crinkles her nose after taking a large bite. "They're overmixing these. Too dry."

"You only say that because you have your head in the clouds."

Emma is a romantic, and up until recently, I've avoided her and her rom-coms and romance books, but as we get older, we have more in common. Now she's roped me into her and Eva's monthly book club. I had to tell her I needed a break from romances centered around vampires. I couldn't take another Donor Program love story.

"I like my head in the clouds, and up here, I can see you very clearly." She takes another bite and adds more clotted cream to her apparently dry scone. "It's okay to like him, you know. The world won't end if you decide to trust another man and—" She gasps. "Find him attractive."

"I wouldn't consider 'what's his name' a man," Eva says, but she knows his name. We just never say it anymore. My sisters were the ones who convinced me the situation was a lot more embarrassing for him than it was for me. And they'd been the only ones I could turn to when he'd told all my ballet friends I was inexperienced, so he broke it off. What I never understood was the cruelness of it. What did I do wrong to deserve that?

I was mortified. I still am. My skin crawls when I think of it.

"I don't need the distraction." And Parker is the definition of distraction.

"Whatever you say. I did see that picture of you in the hallway." Emma giggles. "I had to sign up for the blog so I can keep tabs on my sister, who is apparently getting neck kisses from her fake boyfriend."

I note the ends of her hair that she dyed a Luxxia blue. Blue suits her.

"He has to scent me … for things."

"For the record, I'm protesting the blog." Eva smiles sweetly. Not surprising—she hates drama.

"Just saying, you looked *pretty* into it. I'm sure it was terrible for you to have some hulking man kissing on your neck," Emma concludes, now finished with her scone and scrolling the blog.

I try to remember any part of it being unpleasant but come up with nothing of use. My attention returns to Parker's usual spot in the dining hall, but he doesn't appear next to his team, and Gavin and his pack aren't there either. A few members of his team see me looking and playfully wave. *He's fine. Eat your food, Olivia.*

Emma's gasp and her hand hitting the table echo in the roar of the dining hall.

"What?"

"This isn't fair."

She's staring at a hole in the table.

"What is it?" I grab her phone and read the headline: *Culinary and Baking Clubs Will Not Accept Any New Students This Year as Set by the New Council Rule.*

"Some asshole named Dacre decided to close off the culinary and baking clubs this year. This is ridiculous, I swear. I already signed up for the cookoff."

It's only seconds before her hands are shaking and tears are running down her face. I hand her a napkin.

"I'm sorry," I say, knowing it's hollow in the face of her disappointment. Emma and I share a common trait of ambition. I'd almost say she's a tiny bit more ambitious than me, but I think we have different reasons. Emma wants to be great and so do I, but I want to finish Mom's dream, and Emma wants her name in lights.

"What about classes?" Eva asks.

"Classes aren't—you know it's not the same. The clubs are what get you noticed and get you the best jobs. It's not fair. This is the whole reason I wanted to come to Doxlothia!"

"Dacre is an asshole." None of us saw Zant take a seat across from us. "Unfortunately, the council is being overrun with a lot of them. I don't have to tell you all that, now, do I?"

He's wearing a lighter green blazer than he normally does that compliments his olive complexion.

"What are you doing here?" My tone is harsher than I intend. Zant may be Parker's best friend, but he isn't mine. He's still a wild card in my book, and being connected to the council doesn't help.

His smile widens. "I'm extremely loyal to your boyfriend. I've been told to keep my eyes on the lot of you, and I heard tears. Good thing is, I think I can help a little."

Parker only told Zant about our arrangement, and I don't like it, but he deserves to have someone to talk with about it who isn't my sisters or me.

Zant has kind eyes. "I do have access to the culinary club's main lounge. I could take you. Would that cheer you up?"

Emma sniffles, but her eyes light up. "Can we go now?"

"Yeah, let's go. The whole Osborne clan can come if you want."

"I have class," I say, putting the trash from the table onto my plate. "But have you heard from Parker? I haven't seen him."

"You know I haven't." Zant continues with that smile, plucking an apple from the table. He knows exactly where he is. "You should definitely go check on him in his room."

When my sisters and Zant leave, there's still no message, and my next class is Potions. Parker is my lab partner, so I need him to be there. That's why I make the walk all the way back to Noxx House to check on him. Definitely not because I'm worried. And the fact I've packed him a plate from the dining hall is a common courtesy.

Chapter Nineteen

"I'm scared," she says. Her bare feet swirl in dirt as the wooden swing she's on creaks. We're in our secret place. A place among the trees where the forest floor is covered in moon nightingales. I never need to look for her because I know where to find her.

"Why?" I take the spot next to her.

"I'm scared of everything."

I place my hand on hers. "I'll protect you."

A light knock wakes me, assaulting me with chills and a splitting headache. It's not worse than the hollow sadness lingering in my chest. It's a loss when I wake up, and I don't know why. Like when I wake up, it's dragging me from somewhere else I'd rather be.

"Parker?" There's a hard knock at the door. "It's Olivia."

"Come in." My attempt to sit up results in the room spinning, so I lay my head back on my pillow.

Seeing her walk through my door almost cures me. Because even in the dim light, I see she's got half her hair pinned and she's opted for one of the shorter uniform skirts.

I have the most breathtaking fake girlfriend.

"Are you all right?"

Internally, I'm giddy she sounds worried, but on the outside, I'm on death's door. I don't think Olivia thinks much of anyone outside her circle, so the fact she's here means I'm in her head.

"What are you doing here?"

She drops her school bag and moves to the hearth to bring in some light, almost tripping on a pile of clothes on the floor. The fire light leaves us in a soft-yellow haze, and she flips on my bedside lamp.

I grab her forearm to bring her to sit, and her skin is cool against mine. I want her in my bed.

"Are you sick?"

"A little. There's a full moon today."

"Don't werewolves get supercharged then?

"They do. But hybrids without blood get weak. Gavin usually brings me some blood from the infirmary after his classes, then I'll feel better by tonight."

Not all hybrids need blood, so we aren't required to sign up for The Donor Program, but sometimes, that makes getting blood harder when you need it. It's easier to get blood when you're younger because you're only allowed to drink from blood bags until you enter The Donor Program, but because I don't need blood that often, I don't think it's worth it. Now I have to rely on private sources.

"I was looking for you. I didn't see you at breakfast."

I laugh at the serious dent in her forehead, then reach up to poke her there. "I'm sorry. I should have told you."

"What can I do? Can I get you medicine? Blood?"

"Medicine won't help. And they won't give you any blood at the infirmary. They don't just hand out blood, especially to humans. Gavin's preapproved because of his dad."

"So you just lay here all day, and skip class?"

"Usually. And nobody misses me when I do." I grip my pillow tighter to my chest.

"I'm heading to Potions, and I ... wanted to ... bring you a muffin."

I smell the mountain high plate of food on my nightstand. It's more than a muffin.

I grin. "A muffin? Are you saying you missed me?"

This beautiful woman smuggled a plate out of the dining hall to bring to me, and even cuter, she's lying about it.

"We live across the hall from each other. I don't have time to miss you. But ... are you really not coming to class?"

Why does it feel like she wants me there ... that she needs me there? Something about that gets the blood pounding in my head, which sends the ache in my skull down my spine.

Her eyes sparkle in the dim light of the hearth. It looks different in each one as it mixes it with the different colors.

I lean back on the pillow. "I want to, trust me. But I'm too exhausted. My head is killing me."

"They don't have a better way to get blood for hybrids?"

"Hybrids don't need to be in The Donor Program. There's no use in me joining when I don't need blood that often. I just get by."

"What if you take my blood?"

I blink a few times and lift my head. "Did you just offer to let me bite you?"

"Yes. People in The Donor Program give blood all the time. I've seen it."

I fully sit up and run my hands through my hair until the world stops wobbling. I've never had someone offer their blood to me before. Not even my previous girlfriends. Most of them were in The Donor Program, and there are strict rules and appointments in the program. They donate, so often they can't spare any blood. They also take special supplements to aid in increased blood cell production. It's a normal thing to see someone drinking from their source. Not suggestive, really, unless it's a couple making out in the bathroom and tapping a neck vein. Mostly, it's a simple wrist bite. Some opt to donate through blood bags only.

"I've never drank from a human before," I admit.

"Do you have that Quik-Recover? I still have some variations I want to practice, and we need to be in class in thirty minutes."

"I do, but ..." I stare into her eyes. "Just like that? You're not even scared?"

"I gave more than enough blood to Darien, and that was without my consent. Giving you some to carry out your day isn't any different."

"Yeah, but there are rules. Regulations."

"I didn't think you of all people would care about rules."

"I don't, but I've been drinking from blood bags all my life. I don't know what to expect."

"Are you saying no?"

She's set and doesn't look the least bit nervous. Now my beautiful fake girlfriend is offering me her blood? Is she a dream? It's almost like she's been crafted for me, then found her way into my bed. The smell of her blood is engrained in my mind, and remembering our time in the maze has me focusing on the pumping of her blood just below the surface. Her heart is fluttering, and her scent has me licking my teeth.

"No. Take off your shoes," I say.

I draw her toward me.

"My shoes?"

"Yeah, I don't like shoes on my bed."

"It's not like I'll be rolling around in your bed."

I laugh. "You might."

She undoes the straps on her heeled sandals, and I stare at her legs between her skirt and her socks. Once she moves to sit next to me, she calmly places her wrist in my lap.

"Don't take too much."

She does trust me. I swear the pain in my skull dissipates a little. I lift her wrist to my lips and savor the pulse there. "I won't hurt you. Tell me to stop if it's too much."

Her heart hammers, and she shakes her head. Something charged moves through the air. The little switch in my brain has me forgetting all about the ache in my body.

There's only Olivia and her sweet blood, ready for me to take.

A flash of euphoria zings through my veins when my teeth enter her skin. Her blood is hot on my tongue, and a soft whimper escapes her throat. I almost stop, thinking I've hurt her, till the fingers of her other hand grip my thigh and the smell of her arousal hits me. *Fuck*.

Heat spreads through me. Her heat. Her blood. And I drink deeper. The taste is indescribable. It's better than anything I could have imagined fresh blood tasting like. And it's even better because it's Olivia's blood.

I don't realize I'm hauling her into my lap till she's there. Skin on skin.

She's willingly giving herself. The thought draws a groan from my throat, and she leans into me, her breaths slowing.

This blood is mine. I won't let anyone else taste her like this again. Her muscles loosen while mine get stronger. She's emptying herself for me, allowing me to take all I need. I have to protect her.

I lap at the wound on her wrist with my tongue. Savoring. Tasting. Her cheeks are flushed while she watches me. This turns her on like it does me.

Oh, this girl. *My* girl.

She gasps when I grab her by the waist and seat her so she's straddling me. My hips dig into hers, and her eyes widen. She can feel how hard I am.

Threading my fingers in her hair, I bring her neck to my teeth and sink into her again. A strangled whimper leaves her throat as I drink, satisfaction thrumming through my brain. This is the best fucking day of my life. It's more than the taste. It's her on my tongue. It's her wanting me. It's Olivia on top of me.

"Parker." My name comes out of her mouth more like a moan, and her hips buck into me.

I lean back. "I know, baby. But just a little more, okay?"

She nods desperately, and her warm blood floods my mouth one last time before I retreat and lick her neck.

"Feel okay?"

Her heart is hammering, but her breath is slow. All the ache in my body is gone, like it never existed. We keep doing this, falling back into this natural rhythm, and something about it feels so good.

"I feel … really good," she whispers. It's an admission to more. My length throbs.

Those glossy eyes confirm it. She wants me.

"You like this," I say.

Her breaths are uneven, and our noses almost touch while I take in a long drag of her scent and nearly shake from the rolling need lingering there.

"I can smell how much you want me." I brush the hair from her neck, waiting to see if she protests, but there's nothing but another needy swell of her chest as I kiss and lick at the skin just below her ear. She adjusts her hips to get more friction, and I help, moving my hand to her lower back and pressing. "Have you ever been touched like this before?"

My lips move to her jaw, and I'm hyperaware of how intimate this is and how this is supposed to be fake. But there's nothing fake about the way I want her.

"I've only been bitten once before."

"You know that's not what I mean ... I can feel how much you want me. How your heart picks up when I press into you."

Her heart responds in a pleasing flicker, and I take a long sniff of her hair.

"You smell like you need me."

She gasps when my cock throbs between her thighs, followed by a soft groan.

"When I did this before, it wasn't like this ... All of this is different."

For me too. There's no thinking of other girls with Olivia on top of me. I've never had anything that compares to what's happening here.

I stop moving, tearing myself from her scent. "Do you want me to stop?"

Her trust is the most important thing to me. Even if I sense how much she wants me, maybe she isn't ready. Maybe she doesn't want me to be the one who gives her everything her body is screaming for. I want it to be me. I hope it's me.

"No. Don't stop."

"Good. Let me do something nice for you." I grin and squeeze her tighter.

"Something nice?"

"Yeah, you helped me. I'll help you. Then we'll be even." I lift my hips into hers so she understands exactly what I want to help with.

"I ... I don't want to have sex."

"No sex, underwear stays on." I don't need her naked to make her come, and that challenge excites me more.

"Okay." She nods and I wait. "Yes."

Once she utters that word, I'm sucking at the skin on her collarbone. She's given so much, and the urge to fill her is excruciating. With the rolling of my hips, I rub against her, placing my hardness between her legs, and she breathes in relief.

She's letting me lead. Trusting me to keep that promise. My hands move up her bare thighs and under her skirt till I've got both on her ass and I'm rocking into her.

"We probably shouldn't do this," she says right before she moans, and it's so satisfyingly loud.

Olivia wants some guarantee this isn't going to change everything. I'm not sure if it will, but nothing will change that she can trust me. That I'll protect her and her body. That I'll never hurt her.

"Let me make you feel good."

I'm rolling her into me, and her arousal grows thicker. My skin itches like shifting is on the edge. I take a deep breath to calm myself, but the pressure of her is already making the urge to bite her louder. I think of stripping her. Filling her. Biting her as I take her from behind. My fantasies only make me squeeze her tighter to me so she can use me just like she wants.

"Y-you can't tell anyone." Her voice is shaky.

"We're supposed to be dating, remember?"

I grind into her again. She's close. The sweet scent of her orgasm grows, and I'll do anything to drag it from her. Our bodies meld together in the sheets. She's panting. Softly pleading under her breath ...

Then her scent shifts. Fear.

Her grip on me loosens, and she pulls away.

I stop, cupping her cheek. "What's wrong?"

There's something she doesn't want to say. I wonder if I've scared her somehow. Maybe I squeezed her too tight. Maybe she's dizzy from blood loss.

"Did I hurt you?"

She shakes her head, our faces still close. There's that little dent in her forehead again.

"What are you afraid of?"

"Everything." She places a hand on my chest. "This was a bad idea last time I did this. I don't want to repeat my mistakes."

She looks away when she's sad. She did it when talking about her mom. Then again when she mentioned her dad. Whatever she's referencing must have hurt, because she's staring at the lint on my shirt and running her finger over it.

"I'll never hurt you." I rub the back of her head. Maybe this is too much. We're crossing a line, and she's not ready yet, and that's okay. "Let's stop. We don't have to do anything."

The air between us calms, and what's left is my hand in her hair and my thumb on her cheek. I can stay like this all day. Holding her while her breathing calms, staring into her eyes.

"You always say that."

"Say what?"

"You say 'I won't hurt you.' The first time you said it I thought it was just a throw-away thing. Something all men say. But you say it like a mantra. You repeat it on purpose."

I grit my teeth. She would notice that.

"It's one of those really shitty childhood things. I ... uh ... once, I lost control as a kid. It's common for Were children. I hurt someone I really care about." I contemplate telling her, I don't usually tell this story. "My mom. I felt so guilty and then I didn't want to shift anymore. I was scared I'd just lose control and hurt everyone. She taught me to say those words and learn to mean them. It's a reflex. I don't say it unless I mean it."

That memory haunts me even now. My mom's bloody arm. My dad yelling and threatening me. He never forgave me for that. He says he did, but he still loves to bring it up when he has a little too much to drink. That was the first day I'd seen the face he greets me with now every time we get together.

A moment passes between Olivia and me. I keep rubbing the back of her head because her heart rate is now a calm pulsing beat, and she stays with her cheek pressed to my palm. I won't rush her. Her lashes flutter, and she runs her tongue over her bottom lip. We share a brief, low breath, and I move away and—

She kisses me.

One peck, then her tongue enters my mouth.

I draw back an inch, then deepen the kiss, guiding her with my hand on the back of her head.

Oh, fuck.

There's no hesitancy in the way she's moving on me. She wants me.

Blood rushes through me. I lick her teeth and bite at her jaw.

"You're so beautiful," I whisper before I pin her underneath me. An easy motion. She looks like a dream with her skirt hitched and her legs flush. My whole body is itchy again.

I cover her lips with another kiss. It's smoldering and hungry. I need her to have less clothes. She doesn't protest when I strip off her sweater, and she shivers when I run my fingers down her stomach and breathe in the sweet scent of her arousal.

Her scent is so loud. Like she's begging me. Screaming. *Can a scent say things?*

I hear the words in my head like she's saying them. *Parker, please touch me.*

I lift her skirt. The less between us, the better. When I press into her again, she stops me.

"I need more ... Will you?"

I know what she means somehow.

"Yeah." Then my pants are off.

In the shuffle, I see the underwear she's chosen. A black lacy thong. I hook my finger around them at her hip bone. "Did you wear these thinking of me?"

I know it like I watched her pick them out at her dresser. I'm moving around where she wants me to touch, and her hips buck.

"Yes."

I groan, grazing her stomach with my nose. *I knew it.*

"Parker." Her voice cuts me. It's pleading. Demanding.

I keep my grip on her underwear and slip them lower. She writhes against me, my lips just inches below her belly button. Her legs are shaking, and I suck on her hip bone.

"You wanted me to touch you like this."

"Yes."

I can't get enough of her. Wishing. Clawing.

She offers, so I do too. "I wanted to touch you too. So bad, Olivia."

I stare into her eyes and place myself between her thighs so she can feel me throbbing for her. "Do you want to come?"

She nods. And I kiss her forehead. "Hold on to me."

We're so close. And even with thin layers between us, she's warm. So warm. And I'm hard. She shudders when I grind into her. It's good for me too, but I don't think of myself. I adjust till I get her rhythm.

"Oh, Parker. Please."

Pleading on her lips is enough. It's all I want.

"I'm here."

She's moving on her own. Using me. That's good. *Feel it out, baby.*

"Good, just like that."

Her fingers dig into my shoulder, but she keeps a steady pace. She's close. So close.

"I ... I'm going to ..."

"That's it. Ride me, Olivia."

I kiss her as the orgasm rolls through her, then she collapses in my arms.

CHAPTER TWENTY

OLIVIA

I can't tell anyone about this, especially not my sisters.

There's an explanation for why Parker just whispered the words from my dream. There has to be one. One that's perfectly reasonable and not magical. It's a simple case of déjà vu. Yeah, one of my classes talked about that. That some things in the universe sync at the same time, and it seems like you've experienced the moment before.

This probably happens to everyone and I'm worrying for nothing.

"You are going to smell like me ... you could shower, but I like it. And it's good for our cover."

I'm having a mental breakdown, and Parker is worried about the way I smell.

He hands me a Quik-Recover box. The taste is sweet and a little like lemon. Every drag of liquid through the straw brings light back into the room. I can't believe I did this.

"This was a *bad* idea," I say.

"Why? It doesn't have to mean anything."

Have to? Meaning it could. Did he want it to? Did I want it to? I just met him. It's too early. Too much. I'm stripped down to my underwear and so is Parker. I frantically start the search for my sweater, and Parker hands it to me from the floor.

"I can see you mentally crashing and burning before my eyes. It's not code for anything. We're friends. That's it. I could tell you … needed help just like I did. We helped. Who cares?"

"But I just told you … all of these things."

"That you think about me while you pick out underwear? We're attracted to each other. It's not a big deal. It actually makes this easier."

"But …"

I moaned his name. I begged for him. It shouldn't mean anything, but …

The bed shifts with his weight, and he sweeps the hair from my ear. "What are you afraid of? That … I'm going to embarrass you with this newfound information? Use it against you somehow?" He bats his eye lashes, but he's frowning. There's a softness about him when he's serious. His gaze is intense, but I don't mind it because I know he's listening.

"No, that's not it. I trust you, or I wouldn't have done it."

I really do, and maybe that's the terrifying part. This is so unlike me. Coming to university and getting in bed with a man this soon is something I'd have never predicted for myself. Parker wasn't on my bingo card.

"Good. I like touching you. And you like it when I do. It's casual."

He's right. I'm thinking about this too hard.

I can work with casual. Connected dreams with a man? No. Off the table. I promised myself no distractions if I ever got to go to Doxlothia, and now that I'm here, my entire life is nothing but distractions.

Parker stands in his boxers, and I see him in a new light. His thighs are large and chiseled with muscle, and his broad shoulders contrast his tapered waist. I get a good look at those scars covering his muscular back as he rummages through his wardrobe.

"Is this … a regular thing?" I ask.

"It could be. If you ever want me to help you again. I definitely want to ask you to let me bite you again."

I'd expected the bite to hurt like when Darien's teeth tore my flesh, but Parker's bite was warm from the moment his lips touched my skin, and once he started drinking, the burning desire in my body became unbearable and all I could think about was never wanting him drinking from me to end.

He smirks, and I think he's looking at my lips. Probably just making sure I finish my drink.

"What was it like?"

"Like ... everyone else has been eating the most delicious chocolate cake and I've been chomping on carrots my whole life. It's so fucking good. It's like warm and ... there's this feeling when it slides down your throat—"

He stops, as if he's just now registering that I'm human and he's talking about consuming my blood. "It's good. And I'm really happy you're not in The Donor Program because I don't want anyone else biting you."

Oh, what would my mother think? No. It's fine. This isn't much different from being in the actual program. That thought sends my heart pumping. It is different because I'm not contractually obligated to do anything for the rest of my life.

The contract was the problem. The contract is what killed her.

"Is that a protective werewolf thing?"

"No, I think this is more of the vampire side kicking in. Vampires get very possessive when they find someone with good blood. And yours is top shelf. You never told me why you and your sisters aren't in The Donor Program."

There's a silence between us as we get into our school uniforms. The whole interaction is fluid. We stand in front of each other and finish at the same time. Without asking, he helps me adjust my hair, and I help him with his. It's too natural. Like a well-worn path, but we haven't walked this before.

"My dad hates it. My mom was in, and she ... died. It was an accident. She was already weak from a lingering illness, and the stress on her heart was too much."

"I'm sorry."

I hate the pity that comes from telling someone my mom died, but Parker's sorry doesn't feel like pity.

He knows.

I shrug. "My dad gave up his job and all his research, started joining these anti–Donor Program support groups. All it did was instill fear in my sisters. I wouldn't join, but ... I don't hate it as he does. I hate him more for being so useless and not doing anything but scaring them with his stories."

He shakes his head like he understands, and I know he does.

"I think my mom would be disappointed. She would understand his resentment, but ... she believed in The Donor Program. My mom was naturally a believer in things bigger than herself."

A memory sparks in my mind. It's a glimmer.

My mom smiles at me and holds her Donor Program badge in my face.

"You see this? This means I help the people in Vviveren."

"What about your dad issues you mentioned?" I ask.

"He's a dick to pretty much everyone except my stepmom who has never liked hearing about my mom. I think it's because she knows their love was different. After my mom died, he met her. She brought her son to live with us and then my dad ended up having a daughter with her. He treats her like a princess, so that's good."

"Your mom ... died too?"

"Yeah, her name was Lucy." His brows shoot up like he's shocked he said it, then he softens. "She got sick. She wasn't in The Donor Program, even though my dad is a vampire. She was the Alpha of her pack, and it's typically frowned upon for pack leaders to be donors. My dad wasn't interested in doing anything with me after she died. I think I reminded him too much of my mom. Which is good. She deserves to live on."

Parker's staring at my lips, and as I finish my drink. There's a little scar below his bottom lip, and his upper one is cut as if a claw nicked him. For a brief moment, I imagine those lips on mine again in a messy upper-lip kiss.

I clear my throat and lean away. "If you feel better. Then hold up your half of our deal and get ready for class."

"Yes ma'am."

He shovels the food into his mouth I smuggled from the dining hall.

"So about earlier. Would you let me ... bite you again?" He says it between chews. I'm reminded I should be disgusted, but I'm not.

"You got blood on my sweater."

"You're right, I should have had better control."

There are about a million reasons I should say no to letting Parker bite me again, but oddly, even with the audition results coming today, I don't have the usual anxious nausea in my stomach.

"I'm not saying no."

He grins. "Friends with benefits is going to be so fun."

"What if I get attached?" I tease. "What if I show up at your doorstep begging for you?"

"I wouldn't show up on my doorstep looking for sex if I were you."

"Why?"

"Because ... I'd pull you inside, lock the door, and take you up on that offer."

"You're kidding." My heart kicks.

"Am I?"

"I don't know."

"Just saying ... you're a different story. And if you're ever feeling that itch, my door is open."

I swallow, warmth growing in my face again.

"Well, I don't plan on showing up at your doorstep in the middle of the night anymore, so don't wait for me."

"We'll see about that."

I excuse myself to the restroom to fix my hair before we head out. My eyeliner is holding on by a thread, and despite Parker's attempts to help, my hair needs to be repinned.

"I expected to find a certain hybrid lingering about. Imagine my surprise when I see a beautiful woman bent over the counter fixing her makeup."

My stomach flips at Darien's words, but I continue wiping my eyeliner and reapplying without saying a word.

"Oh, come on, that quick to write me off?"

"Tell me what you want or leave me alone. Or try to bite me again. I'm sure Parker would love the opportunity to tear into you."

"No doubt. Though, it's not advised to drink from a human who's already donated for the day."

He wants to get under my skin. I pull out my lip pencil, continuing to ignore him. How does he know? It has to be the smell of the blood on my sweater.

"Not that anyone would dare to bite Parker Owens's *mate*."

He drags out the last word, and our eyes meet in the mirror. Parker said he was going to take me as his mate. But that was for show. I don't know what mating means with werewolves.

"Have you ever thought about how much you two have in common? Such a coincidence that your boyfriend shares the same love of competition as you. You're both in Noxx House. You just happen to have rooms that mirror each other. Remarkable. Do you have any other things in common?"

"What's your point?"

"I just wonder if you think about it." He plucks lint from his uniform jacket.

"You think too much about me."

"That's true." He flashes his teeth, and I turn to leave. "Just think about it, Olivia."

As I move to the hallway, I vow to not think about it out of spite. At least not today. Audition results are today, and that's the most important thing. Everything else is a distraction. Parker shuts his door behind him, with my bag in hand, his smile warm and bright.

A beautiful distraction.

Chapter Twenty-One

Parker

Shit. This is real. I honestly thought giving her an orgasm would fix this link between us, but it's worse. I just spent the last hour in class trying to fight the urge to sniff a lock of her hair.

I've never been this possessive with a girl before. I'm going to have to mark her. I haven't told her that yet, but it's a bit of an intense question to ask a girl you've known for a week and a half. *"Yes, it's completely necessary that you have my mark on your neck because it's a visual reminder to everyone that you belong to me. You'll have my scent on you twenty-four seven, and it will scratch this possessive itch in my brain. Did I mention you won't be able to cover it up?"*

She'll love that, I'm sure.

I'd beamed as I kissed the top of Olivia's hair when I led her through Noxx House and we passed Aster and Cane and their buddies.

She smells so deliciously like me now, so it's hard to focus on anything else.

I also want to bite her again. Blood wise. Which is strange because I've never had the urge to bite anyone. I guess when you do nothing but drink cold blood bags, you don't know what you're missing. Now I know I was missing her heartbeat, her warm delicious blood in my throat, and bringing her to the edge of orgasm, and I kinda want to do it again. Like right now.

I briefly broke away from Olivia to catch the last few minutes of practice, and I make it just in time to watch them doing their final runs on the ice.

"Our captain has returned from death's door!" Zant shouts.

"Just in time for sudden death." Chase is in his goalie gear, motioning to the ice. His blonde hair is dripping with sweat from underneath his helmet.

He's always been a little shit.

"Let's not kill him today," Ryker says. "Maybe tomorrow, though? Double sudden death."

"Love that you're all harboring murderous feelings for me," I say, stopping at the edge of the ice to observe them.

The other guys spout a string of loving insults my way as they finish out practice, including the triplets, who throw darts at my picture they have pinned up in one of their dorms. Zant showed me the picture and almost choked at dinner laughing at it.

Sudden death tomorrow will be hell, but no way I'm missing going with Olivia to hear her audition results. She told me she was nervous, so I offered, expecting her to say no, but she immediately told me to meet her outside the studio at a certain time.

Zant drags me into the corner of the locker room once they're done. They've done a shit job of keeping it tidy on my one day off. Punishment can wait till tomorrow.

I swipe someone's sweaty T-shirt onto the floor so I can sit.

"Wait, so tell me again. The whole set up from start to finish." Zant shakes the water out of his hair and towels it dry.

"She comes in to check on me. I tell her I'm sick as shit and I'm bedridden for the day and then she offers her blood ... so I drink it and ... yeah."

"Uh-huh. That's it?"

I nod, and he sniffs the air. "Sure, that's why your hair smells like women's hairspray. I dated a dancer once. I know the smell."

"You can't call your one-night stands dating."

He once slept with Octavia when they got too drunk after a council meeting. She let him down easy after, and he pretends he doesn't care. He talks about her a lot, though.

"Beside the point. What did her blood taste like? I'm curious."

"Like … I don't even know how to describe it to you. Does it always feel like you don't want to stop and just keep drinking forever?"

"Sometimes. Depends on a lot of things. Having the hots for your source definitely adds to the experience."

I've had the hots for girls before, and this isn't comparable.

"So is she your source now?" That whole sentence is foreign.

"Yeah … I think so."

"At least you won't miss practice anymore."

We arrive at the ballet studio, and a group of women and men are all standing around swaying anxiously. Everyone is dressed in leotards and tights, and I stick out, but no one cares because they're all mumbling their worries to each other. Olivia's got that determined look in her eyes. She's in a light-blue leotard and leg warmers, with some see-through fabric covering her shoulders, and I think it may be the best thing I've ever seen her in. *Okay, fuck.*

Now that we are actively crossing boundaries, it would probably help for me not to think about her like that. I need to keep my urges in check. And today is all about Olivia.

I try not to be happy about giving her an orgasm on what is likely the most stressful day of her life. But I am. I love helping.

The director comes out with Octavia beside her, and I give Olivia a comforting squeeze. Zant was right about the smell of hairspray. The whole room is enveloped with it. Everything I know about Octavia is what Zant has told me, but she's mirroring the director's updo today, down to the little pieces by her face.

"Okay, everyone. I've got the list here. Please be aware, if you are not accepted into the company, you are still free to use the studio and attend our weekly all-open classes."

She starts down the list on her clipboard, and Olivia's heart drums erratically. She's bouncing, so I place my hand on her head to steady her.

The minutes tick by and the room stays at a low whisper. I'm taking in the amount of mirrors and the muted orchestra music playing in the background when I hear it.

"Olivia Osborne."

She reaches for me with a staggered breath.

"That's good, yeah? You're in."

She's nodding, her eyes wide and glossy. There are more names, but she's still holding on to me.

"Alright. That's all for now. We will decide on our first performance by voting this afternoon."

The whole room erupts into chatter and excitement. I keep a protective field around Olivia while they push around.

"I did it."

"You did it!"

She wraps her arms around me, and I smother her, then she stands back with her eyes sparkling as she wipes the wetness from them.

"Hey, Olivia." A lanky man with fluffy brown hair comes up to her and waves. "Congratulations."

"You too."

"Oh, hi, Parker." He turns to me with a smile.

"Hey, congratulations, man." I extend my hand, and he awkwardly shakes it.

"Thanks ..."

Shit. I'm not blending into her world. Is shaking hands not a cool congratulation thing? In Rage, it's a little formal but widely accepted, and this is much more formal than my sport.

"I'm going to go talk to Octavia real quick, I'll be right back," Olivia says.

There's a silence between this guy and me, and his unease is lingering in the air.

"So, uh, so it's likely I'll be one of her partners ..."

"Oh, cool. What was your name?"

"Theo. I just want you to know it won't be weird. I'm not trying to date your girlfriend ... or mate."

"Oh." I'm surprised he even cares enough to bring it up. "Good."

"The last thing I need is Parker Owens barreling in here to beat me up for touching her waist."

I chuckle. "I wouldn't ... but I might if you drop her."

He swallows.

"Just give it your best and make her famous. I'll be happy."

I stay watching Olivia talk with Octavia across the room. They're arm in arm, already looking friendly for having just met. I guess the same can be said for Olivia and me. The entire room is roaring with sound and movement, but she's easy to see. Her eyes are bright, and her smile stretches all the way across her face. I'll do anything to keep her smiling like that.

Chapter
Twenty-Two

Parker

"You're going to give up on me," she says.
The swing creaks, and she's refusing to look at me.
"Never."
"You don't know that. I ruin things."
"I do know. I'm not leaving."

Part of being in Gavin's pack involves meetings. A lot of the time, we have to get dressed up and take the train to the city where we greet his dad, who scowls at me, and show general support while Gavin gives speeches on things concerning Were policy. The only downside is I have to see my dad there. He loves Gavin.

Thankfully, today we don't have to go to the city, but I do have to attend every student assembly. I'm wearing a blue suit. Navy blue is Gavin's family color, and during assemblies are the only times we're allowed to wear anything other than a school uniform with our house colors. Werewolf packs are all about respect and tradition. Even though I despise school assemblies, supporting Gavin is important.

We stand in a crowd surrounding the tall stone podium that sits right in front of Languid Lake. Black birds dive in and out of the trees, and the afternoon sun hangs overhead. Some of the leaves have started to change with the semester stretching on. A few yellow leaves fall and fade into the depths of the dark-turquoise water.

I pull at my collar as the sweat beads at my neck.

"Did you tell your sisters about the audition?" I lean down to Olivia's ear.

It's been an almost two weeks since, and she's spent most of her time dancing or with me. Which I'm not complaining about, but she hasn't mentioned her sisters once.

"No. Emma is still upset about not getting into the culinary club. She's been shutting herself in her room. And Eva ..."

"Eva has guy issues."

I told her about the day I'd found Evangeline crying in the courtyard.

"Her boyfriend has been upsetting her every day. I tell her to break it off, and she won't, then suddenly I'm the bad guy. She's not any help with talking to Emma right now, so it's all falling on me. I'm not sure what I'm doing wrong."

I don't think she realizes how much she does that. She thinks any problem can be solved by something, and when it's not, she finds a way to make it her fault.

"But ... they didn't ask you how it went?" I tuck the hair blowing in her face behind her ear, which shifts the frown on her lips.

"They're just distracted. I'll tell them. I convinced them to come today. Maybe a little fresh air will help."

After a few minutes, she excuses herself to meet them in the crowd.

Aria Hillard takes the stage to read the recent rule amendments after all the packs have finished their speeches. Aria is one of the human council members and often serves as the voice of the entire council for important events.

"It's time to announce our council member nominees for the school year. As you know, we have a vacant seat, and we take filling that seat in earnest so we may continue to serve this school and be the bridge between worlds. We will announce the nominees and hold an election where we encourage all students to participate."

I shift my feet and stuff my hands in my pockets. The nominee list is always long, and knowing Cane is going to be on the list makes the whole thing obsolete. The packs will rally around him, and he'll sweep the election. A lot of people are nominated, but whoever is backed by a member of the council will get in. That's how Zant explained it to me.

Zant is sitting next to the podium with his hips shifted forward and a bored expression on his face. I subtly flip him off, and he crosses his arm, hiding the middle finger he's flipped to me. His rise to the council was easy. The vampire world of politics is different than Weres'. Weres are pack-minded, and vampires just have to be charismatic and calculated thinkers. Both things Zant excels in.

"Cane Archibald," Aria calls, and the pack members howl in unison. Cane is standing somewhere to my left, waving and bowing. He's so full of shit.

"Dashing, Owens. Where's your other half?" Gavin moves to stand next to me.

"She's getting her sisters." I nudge his shoulder. "Great speech, as always."

"Yeah, I saw you whispering in Olivia's ear during. I half expected you to take off."

"Never. I would not embarrass you with such blatant disrespect."

He smirks. "I get it. Mates are different. And you and Olivia … it's obvious."

"What's obvious—"

"Parker Owens." My name echoes through the speakers.

The crowd vibrates with color as they shift to look at me.

"Uh, what?" I say, but the crowd is so loud the only person that hears me is Gavin.

The students are whispering words of encouragement and praise, but my world is a blur.

What the fuck? How did I get a nomination?

All official nominations must be registered by someone in the council.

Zant.

I'm going to kill him.

"I didn't know you were running this year?" Gavin's voice is low. Hurt. He thinks I've planned this without telling him. I open my mouth to speak, but *I'm itchy.* Why would someone do this to me?

I move to push my way to the podium, and Gavin stops me with a hand firmly on my chest.

"Whoa, you good?"

"No. I didn't do this. Someone nominated me. And I think I know who."

"Don't do anything you'll regret. Stay here."

"I have to find Zant and kick his ass."

"No, you'll stay and calm down. That's an order."

I grit my teeth so hard I think they're going to break. The tug in our bond urges me to comply, and instead of giving into it, I spit on the ground. *Yes, Alpha* is the only reasonable response to his command, but I can't get myself to say it. A part of me wants to, but that part isn't strong enough.

"I know you're trying to help." I start and stop, clenching my fist and taking a steadying breath.

He's patient and waits. "It's okay, take your time."

"I want to be respectful here, but respectfully, I need to find my best friend and beat him within an inch of his life."

"As if you could." Zant's smiling as he makes his way through the crowd.

Nominee announcements have concluded, and students are breaking from the huddle.

I step forward and roll my shoulders.

"Whoa, whoa, what's happening?" Zant puts up his hands in surrender.

"You nominated me for council? We've talked about this about a thousand fucking times."

"Wait, what? I didn't do it. I was coming to ask you why you didn't tell me."

"Bullshit!" I move forward and Gavin grabs me. "You're on the council. You know something."

"It wasn't me! You know me. I wouldn't do that without asking you."

"If it wasn't you, who else would it be?"

"I don't know."

My phone chimes, but I ignore it. The whispering and shouts are muffled by the roar of blood in my head.

"You weren't on the nomination list I saw at the start of the week. Someone must have recently added you."

I'm not letting him off that easily.

"Parker, you'll want to read this."

Gavin nudges me with his phone.

"Not now."

"Look."

I squint to see past the glare on his phone, and the headline on the latest blog forum reads: *The Osborne Sisters: Three Little Liars.*

Underneath are four lines:

These sisters have secrets. Who do you believe and who can you trust?

Fake relationship.

Little thief.

Cheater.

"Shit." All the anger runs out of me.

There's a stirring of emotion in the pack. Gavin's nostrils flare, and I feel the faint flicker of it in my chest. He wants to ask me if I'm lying. I can't worry about it now. I have to find her.

"Sorry, both of you, for being a dick. Really. But I ... I have to go. Olivia needs me. Can we reconvene?"

They nod, but I'm already backing into the crowd, searching for her in the wash of house colors. I'm swimming in the movement and the heightened emotion of everyone around.

Her fear is like a siren in my head that leads me right to her within a sea of people.

"This isn't happening." For the first time, Olivia's voice breaks from the calm, calculated smoothness.

"I know. It's okay. We're going to figure this out."

"No, how did this happen? How did they figure it out? We—" She spins around, and I grab her shoulders to stop her from being pushed away in the crowd. It was dispersing, but now they're gathering around us. "Emma ran and Eva followed. But I had to find you. I ... I ..."

I grab her hand and spin her to face me. "We'll figure it out."

"What's going on? Who nominated you for council?"

Her words cool the heat in my chest. I didn't need to tell her. She already knew.

"I don't know."

"Everyone is giving me dirty looks."

When she faces the crowd, she's calm, but when I look into her eyes, I see them glimmering and touch her cheek. "I'll protect you."

Camera flashes blind us from both sides.

Autumn from the newspaper has her phone out, ready to take notes.

"Olivia, do you want to make a statement for the paper? Is this fake relationship referring to you and Parker?"

Olivia glances at me.

"It's not true," I say. "It's not fake. Olivia is my girlfriend."

"Do you want to comment more on the rumors?" Autumn asks.

I press my lips to Olivia's, with my thumb on her chin, and she responds with a desperate parting of her lips. My tongue slips in her mouth, and I lick the taste of her off my lower lip when I lean back.

"That's what I think."

"Oh. Okay. Noted." Autumn smiles and types something into her phone.

I wrap an arm around Olivia and lead her through the crowd, growling at the men lingering too close to her. My teammates are the only exception when they come up to congratulate me on the nomination. The damage control of that can wait till we find her sisters.

Scenting for them leads us into the boat house. An older building on campus, with crafted moss stone and a rotting wood door. I run my fingers over the iron door handle and breathe in the scent. Inside, there are two heartbeats and soft sobs.

"They're in here."

"It's me, Olivia. And ... Parker is here too." Olivia opens the door, and the sunlight shines on the girls hiding at the back of the room. They're nestled between the boat slips next to a broken rowboat and a couple of oars.

She runs to them, and they collapse into the deck. I stay at the door, deciding protecting the boat house is the best way to help.

I turn my attention back to the lake to give them privacy. The water is shimmering, and the rowers are out practicing and grunting.

Evangeline is crying inconsolably, and Emma's voice is a whisper. "It was just a notepad from the lounge. That's all. That's all I took. I promise."

"It doesn't matter."

"All my friends are texting me and asking. But I just ... I want to go home."

I glance, and they're both crying into Olivia's shoulders. She doesn't say anything but moves her hands through their hair and hums like a mother would.

That's when I see her. How tired she looks. How she's the only one who isn't crying. I know it's not the only time she's done that. How many nights has she spent awake being the comforter? Her sisters need her, and despite her world falling, she's holding it all up, along with them.

Sometimes, we have roles we don't want to take but we're born into. And she's proof of that. Only, she doesn't fight it.

I think of the nomination, and what it means—opposing the two strongest pack leaders on campus. Aster and Barrett will fight to ensure Cane gets that seat.

And even if I don't want it, that seat means power.

Someone has to stick up for people like Olivia and her sisters. If protecting them means stepping up, I'll do it. I'll sit on the council. I'll do whatever it takes to protect her.

CHAPTER
TWENTY-THREE

OLIVIA

A boy with brown hair sits on a swing surrounded by moon nightingales.

This place is familiar, with my feet fitting each outline in the worn path through the flowers. I've been here before. My feet created this pathway.

I don't see his face, but he's waiting for me. I know that. He's always waiting for me.

There are too many things going on in my brain.

I'm staring at a diagram of a fully transformed werewolf in my textbook. I've seen pictures before, but this book is so detailed I can't tear my eyes away. Standing on its hind legs, its yellow eyes stare through the paper. With coal-colored fur, giant claws, and large teeth peeking through the snarl on its lips. I imagine Parker's Were form, and the images of my dream flutter through my mind. The book is filled with things I've not learned. It explains the different effects of various moon phases, and there's the mention of heterochromia over the years. I flip through the pages, skimming ahead while the professor lays out our next assignment.

Mates. The word catches my attention, and I stop.

It's only three pages and mostly about history and reproduction.

Linked Mates: a bond since birth.

My skin flushes as I read on: *Linked mate pairs have been observed throughout the centuries and appear in clusters as the result of a catalyst. One mated pair will spawn many others in this rare phenomenon.*

The bell tolls, snapping my gaze from my textbook. It hums through the walls and echoes into the stone ceiling. Gathering my materials, I fight the heaviness that's weaved its way between my ribs. Darien's words flicker in my mind like the lit flames of the oil lamps on the walls. Tugging at the collar of my uniform, I pull out my phone.

Parker's the first message at the top:

Parker: *Hi, pretty.*

I'm stopping by right after practice.

Let's do something fun tonight.

A few minutes later.

Parker: *You're either ignoring me or paying too much attention in class.*

I like it when hot girls ignore me.

But you won't be doing that tonight ;)

About thirty minutes later he sent another.

Parker: *Zant's asking me to ask you if Octavia ever mentions him.*

Emma's is after that.

Em: *I hate it here. Someone in the culinary club took my panna cotta out of the fridge and left it on the counter all night.*

The conversation I'd had with my sisters is still in the front of my mind, though disaster is at my door. Literally—someone wrote *Liar* over my locker in the dance studio. It doesn't bother me much, or at least it bothers me the least between my sisters, so I try not to complain. There's nothing that can be done about it, so it's useless to worry about. They don't understand that we just need to wait it out, and mentioning anything related to that gets me an eyeroll.

The night after the post was the worst. I sat across from Emma who clutched her legs to her chest while she shivered on my bed. The hearth in my room had a rolling fire going all night long.

"I want to go home," Emma had said.

"Who cares what these people think?"

"I do!"

Emma turned to Eva, who had barely spoken a word since the post went live. *"Why aren't you saying anything? I thought you'd be the first to want to leave."*

Eva shook her head. *"I don't want to go back to Groveshire. I just don't understand why we're being targeted. Everyone in my hall has turned on me. They think I'm either the cheat or the thief. I don't think they even know why. Doesn't matter. This blog is all they listen to."*

"The blog is meaningless. We can't go home. We can't let them win," I'd said, but it took all night to convince Emma to stay. She had to return the notebook, which she said she'd only taken as a dare to get back at Dacre—the council asshat who deserves to stub his toe every morning; her words, not mine.

Emma leaned in and looped our pinkies. *"I promise, though, I just wanted to see the legacy recipes. Yes, I was peer pressured to steal, but for me, it came from a good place."*

I don't think I was the one she was trying to convince.

Whether Emma stole the notebook for recipes doesn't matter when it's clear my inner circle has a target on its back. Over the last few days, icy stares from the Weres on the council have turned into an inferno of pure disdain.

Luckily, Gavin's pack protection has held up, and I'm reminded of that when I see Eva barreling toward me with a Were trailing behind her. He's tall and lingers for a few seconds before moving out of view. They aren't bodyguards or anything, but I notice a lot of them from a distance. They must scent for us and linger enough to ensure their duty to Gavin is fulfilled. We've all had dinner in the dining hall a few times, and to say it was awkward is being generous. It's the way they eye Parker that I don't like. Like he's a foreign agent and they're awaiting the moment he turns on them. There's no way Parker doesn't see it or feel it, but his big wide smile never leaves his face when he's around them.

"I need to talk to you."

"Can it wait? I need to talk to Parker."

"No. Come on."

She grabs my forearm as our steps echo on the mosaic stone tile that lines the halls, and I let her guide me through the castle till we reach the observatory. Without a word, we climb the spiral staircase in the cramped corridor, and I glance at the painted mural lining the walls. There are star-shaped windows carved into the stone that let in the sun.

We don't stop until it's just us alone with the treetops and the baby-blue sky.

"I didn't cheat."

She says it like an oath.

"Okay? I didn't think you did."

"I didn't cheat but ... I can see how someone might think I did." It's only then I notice Eva isn't wearing her pink lip gloss or bow in her unkempt hair. "Ugh! I didn't want to say this, but it's eating me alive not to tell anyone. Jared and I broke up."

"Oh."

When she mentioned cheating, I'd assumed academics.

"Yeah, we broke up and then I might have ... slept with someone that same night. But I'm telling you we were broken up, but whoever made this whole smear campaign obviously doesn't know that. Or they do and are just trying to make me look bad."

Her words are like viscous honey in my brain.

"Wait. Who did you sleep with?"

She shakes her head like it's unimportant. "Just a man in my hall. We were just friends, I swear. We still are ... It was just one night."

"What happened with Jared?"

"He proposed."

"Then you broke up with him?"

"Don't judge me."

"I'm not, I just ... I thought you'd want to be married."

"I thought so too, and then he asked me and I ... said no. I'm not sure who was more shocked, me or him."

"Is this a good thing or a bad thing?"

She's not crying. Not even a sniffle. There are missed lunches or sales that have prompted more tears. Maybe she's in shock.

"I don't know yet."

I contemplate what her admission means. Did the person who made that blog post know that? How would they know Eva slept with someone in the first place? It could be anyone in this school, but I have two werewolf council members at the top of my shit list. But that might be too obvious even for them, and that doesn't explain Parker's council nomination.

I need to talk to Parker, but it will need to wait till after ballet. *Focus, Olivia.*

Ballet is why I'm here.

Ballet is the only thing that matters.

"Olivia – Giselle."

There must be a mistake.

I settled on Willis as a role I could be happy with at the very least. I hadn't let myself think of Giselle as a possibility. I'd blocked the dream from my brain, knowing it was unlikely, to save myself the despair of not receiving it.

There's a dissatisfied echo in the ballet studio.

"Do you know the ballet?" Theo, one of the male dancers, asks from next to me. He's the only one who will talk to me today, aside from Octavia.

Do I know it? I've practiced that exact variation in my room since before I was on pointe. I know the variation. I could literally do it with my eyes closed. *Giselle* is my favorite ballet, and the role of Giselle is the lead.

"Yes," I say. I want to scream. I want to cheer, to tell someone. My sisters come to mind first, but I can't tell them while the world is ending. But I'm going to burst from happiness.

I listen to the rest of the character assignments. There are two casts, one for years three and four, and another for years one and two. Fia squeals when they announce her as a lead role as an upperclassman.

My head is down as I tape my feet, and I nearly knock over Octavia as she scrambles to tidy up the room.

"Oh, Olivia, I wanted to let you know I had them clean up your locker. All of that stuff will clear up soon. I don't ever believe half the stuff on there."

"Thank you. I'm not used to all of this. So many people seem to know who I am here."

"Well, get used to that. The dance world is already abuzz with the performance news. Congratulations on the lead. You might just be the youngest first-year to take that spot."

That means all of Vviveren will know and see my name in the papers.

I don't thaw from the shock of it till Parker saunters through the door with wet hair and sweats—not school uniform appropriate—and leans down to kiss me.

Fake kisses are supposed to be quick, but the seconds tick by as I kiss him back. We're both enjoying this. I know it. He knows it. Only, neither of us have spoken a word about it. We're just moving around each other like planets in a natural cadence.

"Someone's happy."

"I got Giselle. It's the lead."

He picks me up and twirls me around. "Ah, I'm so fucking proud. I don't know who that is. But let's celebrate so you can tell me. We can go tell your sisters—"

"No. Not right now. We need to talk first."

I wait till everyone has funneled out of the studio, and gently wave at Octavia as she winks and closes the door behind her.

"Breaking up with me?" He smiles, pushing closer, and I walk backward until my shoulders hit the mirror. The magnetism of him hits me again, and I have to take a breath to focus.

"We do need to set ground rules."

"Like?"

"Like maybe we shouldn't kiss in here unless ..."

"Unless there's a reason? It feels so good to kiss you." He leans forward till his lips rest near my forehead. "If you need more reasons, I've got plenty."

I have to work hard to draw myself out of the rhythm of him against me. I know why we shouldn't. The nagging thoughts I've tried to push out are back at the forefront of my mind.

"What do you know about mates?"

His brow lowers. "Like werewolf mates?"

I nod.

"Werewolves take mates by marking them with a bite ..." His thumb grazes my neck. "Once that person accepts the bond, then they're mated. Anyone can be marked as a mate. Vampires and humans included."

"So it's all by choice? There's not more than that?"

"Yeah, it's voluntary. I mean there are linked mates, but—"

"What's that?"

"Werewolves can be linked. They don't choose it, and they pretty much always end up together."

My heartbeat is in my ears. "And what's that like? Are there … dreams or anything?"

He flashes his canine teeth in a smirk. "Are you still having dreams about me?"

I straighten my spine, ignoring his question. "You don't dream?"

"It's rare I remember a dream."

Those blue eyes pan over my face till they're fixed on my lips. It's as if he's seconds from letting go and placing his lips on my neck. "Are you afraid we're linked mates? Is that why your heart is beating so fast?"

"I don't know. I was curious."

"You don't need to worry. You're human and I'm half vampire. All linked mates have been full-blooded werewolves."

I let out a relieved breath. Darien was messing with me, just trying to get in my head. I don't know why I entertained anything he said.

"Too much commitment for you?" Parker's tone is playful.

"I don't think I'd be a good mate."

"It's funny you say that because I was just about to ask you something." His fingers rub over that spot on my neck again, and he leans in to kiss me and run his teeth over my skin.

"Let me mark you."

Heat gathers and sinks like a stone in my stomach.

"I don't want anyone to *think* about touching you. I need all of you all to myself. And the mark is just for display. You don't need to accept. They fade over time."

"What about when this arrangement is over? What then?" I say.

He leans back to deliver his next line, with his eyes locked on mine.

"I'll propose to you by then."

That draws a trickling of laughter from my lips. He's got to be joking.

"And you're certain I'll say yes. I have no plans to be married."

"Oh, I'm sure. All your commitment issues don't scare me."

After a few more seconds, the weight of his gaze leaves me, and he retreats. I don't scare him. There's relief in those words. I'm not sure if he's being serious or if I want him to be.

I'll wait to tell him about what I learned from Eva. The electricity of the excitement is still lingering, and all I want to do is dance.

"I want to stay here and practice the variation. Is that okay?"

"Yeah, I'll go get us some food and come back and watch. Sound good?"

I hesitate for a moment.

"You want to spend your night watching me dance? Don't you have more important places to be?"

"This is at the top of my important list." He grins from ear to ear. "I think my girlfriend is overdue for a date."

Girlfriend. My heart flutters. There's no one here to watch that admission.

Once Parker is gone, he takes all my confusing thoughts with him.

Then it's just me and Giselle.

Chapter Twenty-Four

Parker

"What's wrong?" Her hand lands on mine.

Neither of us are on the swing. We're together but younger, sitting in the flowers.

I wipe the wetness from my face. "She's gone."

I don't tell her who. She just knows like she always knows and wraps her arms around me, and I cry in her lap.

I've gotten used to waking up to Olivia in my bed over the last week. There's no sex involved, but that doesn't stop her from trying to sneak out in the morning like I'm a one-night stand. Since she got her role in the Doxlothia company, she's gotten up even earlier than before.

"Will you at least call me later?" I joke as she puts her things into her bag in the dim light coming from underneath my door.

She smiles. "I'll see you later."

I sit up on my elbows, wiping the sleep from my eyes. "You need to sleep more."

"You're telling me?"

"Yeah, I'm telling. You're not going to show up at my doorstep at one a.m., and then sleep till five a.m. again. You're coming over early, and we're going to bed together so you can get a full night of sleep."

Every night like clockwork, she appears at my door looking groggy and telling me she can't sleep. I've started to wait for her. My bed is small, but I miss her when she isn't there pushing me off the side and stealing the blanket.

"Okay."

I had no idea it would be that easy.

"Good. I'll see you later, then."

Once she leaves in the morning, I can't sleep anymore, so I go to the rink to practice. The stars above know I need it, anyway. Olivia is the best thing I have going in my life, and everything else continues to be a shitshow, including getting the team ready for the season.

That's not the worst part.

There's still the issue of the council. It's been over a week since the nomination and we still aren't sure who put my name in. None of the werewolves on the council were happy with the announcement, except for Gavin, who got more excited at the thought of me joining the more we talked about it. Luckily, Gavin didn't take much convincing about the smear campaign with Olivia's sisters being bullshit. Man doesn't really care about rumors. He's used to it because of his father's work, and he was a big help in keeping the packs calm with the politics of it all. He told me what to say if any of the news people ask.

I've been dodging dirty looks from Cane my whole life, but now things are on another level with the nomination. Regardless of who did it, I still have to deal with the consequences. That's why after practice I put my suit on and stand among at least ten people trying to talk to me at the same time.

"Don't you clean up well," Zant says, and I straighten my tie. "Big smile for the camera."

He motions to the row of people with cameras. Some are from the newspaper, and others are a few journalists from the city. Doxlothia news is the Vviveren's news, considering it houses the kids of the biggest leaders in the world.

"Mr. Owens, with your new step toward leadership, do you think you'll participate in this year's Hunt?"

"No." I have no intentions of leaving Gavin's pack, and I'm still trying to convince Olivia to let me mark her.

"What do you think your mom would think about your nomination for the council?" a blonde reporter asks me.

I expect questions about her, but my chest tightens at the mention.

"She'd be proud, I think." Just as proud as when I brought her mud pies.

It's really sunny, so I have to shield my eyes. Sunny days remind me of her, and we used to sit outside all day long when I was a kid, but now is a bad time to think about it.

"What are your plans for your path into leadership? Do you have any thoughts on starting your own pack or continuing your mother's work?" Autumn, from the university newspaper, is holding a recorder to my mouth.

The flash blinds me, and I open my mouth to speak, but my throat is dry.

My mother was a Doxlothia legacy and a mate advocate. She's the reason for at least twenty percent of the laws we have around protecting mated couples, and she did a lot of casework too. Matchmaking. That was her favorite part. Working with real people.

"That's enough questions for today. We will present a full list of initiatives by Monday morning," Zant says, wrapping an arm around me and moving me to a quiet place on the Central Lawn.

"You did great," he says.

My relief is short-lived.

"We're going to be late to team practice."

I've already gone for the day, but I have energy left to burn. I roll my shoulders to loosen the stress knot gathering there. I can't be late to practice. The team needs me to be one hundred percent. Things have only slightly improved in our practices, and any absence from me is sure to set us back.

"We'll make it. Stop stressing."

"Easy for you to say. I've got a lot of things in my brain right now, and this council stuff is just adding weight."

"You mean Olivia."

"Yeah, she's part of it."

"You're so fucked." Zant chuckles.

"You're supposed to be my encourager."

"I encourage you to stop messing around and ask Olivia to be your girlfriend for real before she decides she's done and wants someone else to hold her at night."

I didn't tell him, he just knew as soon as I walked up. Olivia was in my bed again last night. Zant grinned as soon as he saw me and raised his eyebrows. It was her smell. Sleeping in the same bed saturates me with her scent. The only downside is her scent lingers in my sheets after and makes me miss her. It's a habit for us that's working its way into a well-worn path.

"She barely wants me to, let alone some other guy."

"Really? You don't see her wanting to fuck her dance partner or, I don't know, any of the other monster dicks in this place? You're not the only one strong enough to protect her."

"Okay, now you're actually making me mad." I breathe through my flared nostrils and try to get that image out of my head. I can't think of it without my skin itching.

"That's the point. I worry for you. If Olivia goes rogue on your plan, I'm afraid you might *actually* kill someone at this point, and I hate to tell you this, but my dad won't let me be seen visiting you in prison. He loves you, but it's bad for my image."

"Comforting."

"I'm serious. You like her. You don't want anyone else touching her. You need to ask her for real."

He's right. I just hate it when he's right. Zant loves thinking he's helping me by telling me obvious things out loud. I do want to ask her, but there's this nagging little voice reminding me she might say no. And that reminds me that there might be a day when she won't want to sleep in my bed. Then all of this will be for nothing, and I'll, what? Find a different mate so I can stay in Gavin's pack?

I'm the one who just had to make the point that this is casual.

"I am serious about her. I'm ... fucking obsessed with her."

"Tell me something I don't know, brother."

Aster brings a drove of photographers onto the lawn. His scowl and bored expression are nowhere to be seen. He finally matches his smiling face on the posters in the hall, fluffing his red hair, flirting, and laughing through his questions.

"Just the guy I wanted to see," I say.

It's a split decision that feels right. My body moves on its own.

"What are you doing?" Zant says slowly.

"Playing the game."

I'm already across the lawn when I hear Zant cry out.

"Wait—"

"Hi!" I put an arm around Aster's wide frame.

He smells like danger and blood as he bites his tongue, but he smiles.

"Owens."

"Are you two friends?" a reporter asks.

"Definitely," I say. "He's graciously decided to back my nomination."

"I thought he was backing Cane Archibald for the nomination?" another asks.

"That was before he knew I wanted to join. We go way back. Right?"

"Of course. What an honor to support Doxlothia's Rage captain in his endeavor for success." There's no hesitation in Aster's words as they roll off his tongue. "Could you all give us one moment?"

Aster maintains his smile until we're out of hearing range, and his fingers turn to claws as he fists my arm.

"What the fuck are you doing?" he hisses through clenched teeth.

"Sending a message. I know you're fucking with Olivia and her sisters. Now my image is your image."

"You think I wrote that blog post?"

"If it wasn't you, I can only think of one other person."

He scoffs, dusting off his pants and fixing his hair. "Or maybe you're wrong. Maybe ... the same person that got you nominated is the one who ran the Osborne sisters' names in the dirt. Or maybe they just got what they deserved."

"Careful."

"Fine. You want to play the game. We'll play. Careful what you wish for." He spits on the ground before walking headfirst back into the swarm of paparazzi with a smile.

I nod. My blood sings with that challenge. The natural fight of his inner wolf against mine.

Chapter Twenty-Five

OLIVIA

"It's you," he says, with no trace of doubt. "It's always been you, Olivia."
I'm full. Infinite. Safe. Home.

It's not my fault. It's just one day, sleeping became impossible without being next to Parker. It makes no sense. But his scent and warmth are a calm to my senses, and everything in my brain turns off almost instantly. He's right, though, I can't keep working my body like this with no sleep.

I feel sluggish after my warm-up, so I turn on my music.

It's just me and Giselle. And that's how it's supposed to be. It's the whole reason I'm here. I move from one variation to the next. It's simple at first. Fluid and easy. Then I forget a step and stumble in my recovery.

My body is slow, but I've been eating enough. I know the variation. It should be perfect by now. But I'm stumbling, clunky. A step behind, and my arms are too rigid.

When I watch myself in the mirror, I look like I don't know anything. There's a child somewhere with better talent and shiny promise making me look like a fool.

It's good but not great.

My ankle slips and I stumble back, attempting to find my rhythm again. But my form is sloppy.

I do know the steps. I do. Fast feet. Balance. Balance. Balance.

My right pinky toe rubs raw in my shoe. It's no excuse for why I can't complete the variation all the way through.

Why did I get picked for this role?

I'm going to blow my chance.

I'm going to choke as an ultimate failure.

Fear floods my brain, and I slip. A tear of frustration runs down my cheek, streaking the mascara stinging my eyes.

I know better than to wear nonwaterproof mascara to ballet. I'm better than all of this. Maybe my talent has run its course. Or maybe it was never there at all. I abandon my variation to sit on the floor with my head on my knees to catch my breath.

What would my mother say? Or worse, my father or sisters.

Everyone would try to comfort me and offer their full acceptable lengths of condolences to the end of my career. My gut twists. They'd be sad for me. They'd pity me. It would be a big deal. Earth shattering for them and me.

"Whoa, what's with the tears?" Parker's voice echoes in the studio.

"I keep messing up. This is it for me. I suck."

He sits next to me, wipes the tear from my cheek, and sets down a plate of food.

"You're being too hard on yourself and working your body too hard."

"But what if I can't do it? What if ... it just crumbles. What if I fail? What if I'm not as good as I thought I was? I can already imagine what everyone will say when it's over: 'It's fine, Olivia. You'll be fine.' But it doesn't make it better. Everyone knows me as a dancer. If I fail ... I have to face all the pity. The disappointment. Everyone will worry about me. I can't even think of the press."

"Okay. Say it crumbles ... You get to the performance of your lifetime, and then fall apart on stage. I'll pick you up and wait for you to get changed. We'll get some food and then ... I'll take you somewhere alone. Whether that's our rooms or if you want to take the train to the city, we'll figure out the next step. Ride out whatever wave of press follows, and then ... you'll dance again."

"That's it?"

"That's it. The world doesn't explode."

"What would you think of me?"

"That you had a shitty night, and it doesn't touch the talent you have. Olivia, I love that you dance. I love that it makes you happy, and I love that you're carrying on your mother's passion ... but ballet is the least interesting thing about you."

I sit with that, first slightly offended. Ballet is who I am. It's an extension of myself. It's all I work toward. It's all I've ever wanted. Who would I be without ballet?

"To me, you're the same whether you dance or not. Whether you become the most famous ballerina in the world or you don't, won't affect the way I feel about you. You're just Olivia to me, and you're my favorite person to be around."

I don't know who just Olivia is. I replay Parker's scenario again. Making a fool of myself on stage, and then ... running into hiding. Would it be so bad?

I move my hand to his, and he rubs my knuckles. What Olivia could he be talking about? My life without ballet is just me eating and sleeping and attending classes. I have no other hobbies. I've never wanted anything else.

"Why am I your favorite person, then?"

Shouldn't it be someone like Zant who's funny? Or Gavin, who I'm sure has many interesting things going on. It's probably my blood or my smell ...

"I think waking up next to you and watching you brush your hair is interesting, the little comments you make about the weather, or when you tell me what you're learning in class, or eating dinner with you."

"Those things sound boring."

"It's not with you. I just like you. I like the way your brain works and the cute way you get embarrassed when you open up about something. The competitiveness you try to hide, but I know how good it felt for you to beat Darien in chess. And you listen to me ... and that's nice because ... for a long time, not many people did. I had Zant and Gavin, but it's not the same thing. I like ... that you look for me. That you definitely don't need me but you get excited to see me like you do."

"You just like me," I repeat his words.

There's nothing to do about that. He says it like it's a fact I can't deny. There's no way I can run away from it or make it better. My baseline of existing is good enough.

My shoulders fall from my ears as I surrender to the sense of relief it brings. I lay my head on his shoulder, then tilt my head to kiss him on the cheek.

He beams, taking a monster bite of his burrito before setting it aside.

"Now, that being said, let's get you up and try again."

"Maybe I should just stop for tonight."

"No, don't end practice on a bad note. Can I help?" He hauls me from the ground and helps me brush off my practice tutu.

"Well, you could hold my waist while I practice the second act."

"Got it. Tell me what to do."

I run him through it all. It's clumsy, but I'm more sure. I do know this ballet. And all that practice comes back. The heat of his hands through my leotard accompanies our lifts. He has no trouble lifting me, but we laugh through his lack of grace.

"My feet are trashed." I groan, moving to take off my pointe shoes.

"Come on, I'll take you to the ice tub." In seconds, his arms are around me and I'm being cradled as he ushers me down the hallway. His heavy steps sound on the wooden floor.

He walks me into a large room, where a hexagon stone tub sits in the center. Arched windows surround the tub, with the tops of the trees outside scratching at the glass.

He starts the ice bath while I sit on the edge, then he kneels at my feet.

"Let me do it." He motions to my shoes.

"No way. I don't let anyone see my feet."

"I'm not afraid of feet. I share a locker room with a bunch of men that regularly tear into each other's flesh for fun. I'm not easily disgusted."

I shake my head, mortified. "No, seriously I've had these on for hours, and I have a bruised toenail."

He taps my thigh. "It's okay. Come on. Give me your foot."

I cringe at letting him grab my calf and watch him remove the elastics. I can't look at his face. There's real fear pumping through my veins at the thought of his disgust.

"Oh. Wow," he says.

"Parker."

"I'm kidding. I promise."

I peek at him. His brow is bent as he surveys my feet, but it's not in disgust. He looks … worried.

"It won't hurt if I take this off?"

He's pulling at the tape on my toes like a sticker he's afraid to destroy.

"No, I'm used to the pain."

I guess ballet wear and tear is similar to his sport in that way: continued pain over time that your senses eventually start to ignore.

He carefully removes the tape on both of my feet. It's disgusting. It's terrible. I'm mortified and feel like dying, but he's not reacting. His large hand squeezes my heel, and I groan from the relief.

"Feet in the tub," he orders, and I don't protest. The ice water on my swollen feet draws a yelp from my lips, but as the seconds tick by, my muscles loosen.

After a few minutes, he towels them off. One of my toenails is black on my right side, and I have open sores at the top. My pinky toe might lose its nail soon.

I gasp as his thumb moves to the arch of my foot.

"Did I hurt you?"

"No, it … That feels so good."

"I'm going to try to avoid your blisters."

He uses a dab of healing balm to massage my feet. There's a level of shock I have to work through. A man is massaging my mangled feet, and it's kind of nice.

And better than that … he wanted to. I didn't need to ask.

I think I'm staring at him too much, so I close my eyes, relishing in the sensation of his fingers bending into my skin. He grabs more healing balm and works it into my calf and back down to my arch. Heat trickles down my spine. I have to breathe through some of it. The intensity of the relief he's providing is blinding.

He stretches my foot ninety degrees, and I wince. He stops, lessening the pressure, and eases back into it.

"You're doing great."

His praise singes through my veins, and I breathe out as he tries again. He breathes out with me. My heartbeat responds, and I feel it everywhere. My head. My chest. Between my legs.

"Does that feel better?"

I nod, watching his hands and the way his veins pop as he continues. I need to change the subject. Focus on something else.

"I'm surprised you didn't run. My dad used to say my feet looked like a man's ... He was joking, I think."

"Not very funny." Parker is focused on his task, oddly taking working the soreness from my muscles very seriously.

"My dad was clueless after my mom died. He didn't know how to take care of his girls. Eva and Emma think he tried his best, but ... I think he just fell apart. He gave up on his life's work. He didn't go out anymore and didn't let us either. I was restricted to my town's ballet classes because he wouldn't let me go to any of the ballet schools in the city. It's like he thought sheltering us would save us from the world, and now I think my sisters and I could have benefited from not being so isolated. One blog post and suddenly the world is ending."

"Yeah, death is ... strange, what it does to people. After my mom died, I think my father hated looking at me. He got enough reminders of her at work, and then he'd come home and want a break. That's why it's Rage or nothing for me. I can't go back home."

That, I understand.

"Ooo." I exhale as he concentrates his thumb in the arch of my foot.

"Deep breaths."

"Your mom ... What was she like?" I want to imagine her. Did she have the same blue eyes as Parker? The same hair?

"She was tall and warm. Always hugging me. Worked on the Werewolf Council. Really in-your-face bubbly. Straight, dark hair, but her eyes were bright blue like mine. It was how people identified her pack because her eyes stayed blue in shifted form."

"What happened to her pack ... after she died?"

He presses three fingers down the length of my calf. It burns in a soothing way. "They wanted to preserve all of her work in the Werewolf Council and instead of passing that work to me, they exiled me. She hadn't specified that she wanted me to take over in her will ... She got sick suddenly ... and so they appointed a new Alpha, and yeah ..."

"Is that why you don't want to accept your alpha blood and make your own pack?"

"Forming my own pack isn't as simple as just having a group of people to hang out with. Suddenly, I have to ask myself, what do I want to do for the world? Do I want to carry on a path like my mother? Form my own? Then I'm responsible for this whole group of people who form their lives around me, and I don't know if I feel ... good enough for that."

Parker doesn't think he's good enough? How is that possible? Everything about him is perfect, and it's not an act. I see it in the way he treats others, and I've seen him on the ice. It's in his touch and how he makes me feel ... important.

I think any mother would be proud of a man like that.

"What would your mother say?"

He pauses to look at me. "Probably that whatever I choose to do will turn out just fine. She was so ... relaxed. An easygoing leader who never panicked. My mom was my hero."

"My mom was my hero too." Heat rises to my cheeks, and I bite back the emotion building in my throat.

"Moms are cool like that." He smiles and drops my feet.

I like the ease in which he says it. Like they're still here.

The chime on my phone cuts my focus. It's Emma sending me a link to a blog post.

Aster Supports Parker Owens in Surprise Backing for Council.

"What did you do?" I hold up the phone. "This has your name written all over it."

"I wish I could say it was a long story, but I kinda made an impulsive decision that may or may not come back to bite me in the ass. Tell you about it in my room?"

"No ... not yours. Mine this time."

He licks his lips and smiles.

Chapter Twenty-Six

Parker

"This is the last night we're apart."

"How do you know?"

"I can feel it. Something is changing." I kiss her cheek, then her neck.

The other Rage teams have arrived on campus for training. It's one of many leading up to the moon festival, an offseason tournament that doesn't affect the school ranking but still weighs heavily on me and my team. There are a lot more Weres on campus than usual, and they're all staying in the guest houses by the lake for a big party in the guest common room. I've spent the majority of the day meeting captains and coaches.

The buildings next to the lake are all crafted and carved wood inside, each room decorated according to one of the houses in Doxlothia. The main room has all four colors incorporated but oddly doesn't make you want to throw up. It is muted and murky, like Languid Lake that sits still in the dim light outside.

There's a slight pull on my pant leg, and a head of dark curls is all I see before I'm bitten on my knee.

"Trying to bite my leg off?"

Coach's daughter giggles and runs back to him.

"Mia," Coach Zepheus scolds his daughter, "we don't bite."

He runs a hand through his wiry salt-and-pepper hair and sighs.

"She's going through a biting phase."

Biting phases for Weres are the worst. Even worse than vampire children, I hear.

"Tsk. Tsk. You're going to be fully gray by next year, Coach."

"You did good work today. Gonna have some fun?" Coach Zepheus hauls his daughter into his arms and pats me on the shoulder while giving me a sympathetic smile. It helps ease the constant knot of tension in my chest.

The diplomatic part of the day is over, which means the wildest party on campus is about to begin. It's an exclusive party to the athletes from other schools participating in the tournament, but you can bring a date. And mine is almost here.

"Going to try," I say under my breath.

It's my team's first test, and if we lose in the offseason, it won't go unnoticed. I can already see the headlines: *Owens Leads Championship Team to Ruin.*

My dad would scoff at that, no doubt. Tell me to quit the team and deal with the damage control, put on a suit, and join him in the Werewolf Council. I'd rather do anything else than to have to go somewhere I'll be reminded of my mom's absence every single day.

I say hi to a few more people and check my team is behaving. She should be here any second now—

"Hey, Captain." Ryker walks up sipping a beer, nervously eyeing the place Coach just left. "Can I talk to you?"

He's hanging his head, barely meeting my eyeline. Oh yeah, it's terrible, all right.

"Yeah. What's up?"

"I ... know this isn't the best place, but I had some shit happen today, and I ..."

He stops like he's really holding back the last part, like it hurts to say.

"I think I should quit the team."

"What? Why? What happened?"

He flexes his jaw, drawing his arms in. This is one of those rare times I see his tattoos on the tan skin of his forearms. They're always covered by his jersey.

"It's not a good time for me."

"Bullshit. What's the real reason?"

"I don't want to make trouble for you, man."

I push his shoulder. "I get myself in trouble. There isn't much you can do to damage my reputation that I haven't already done. Just tell me."

"Truthfully, I just think I'll end up weighing down the team. My dad and my uncle are making some trouble for me and a lot of other people. It's better I just let this go, I think."

I don't know much about Ryker himself, but I've heard of his family. He is one of the few who didn't come here as a legacy. There was a lot of suspicion surrounding his entry into the school, including that his father just got out of jail and paid his tuition for all four years in cash.

"I'm not letting you quit. We need you."

"No you don't. I'm washed up anyway. I sucked this week in practice." He chugs his drink and sets it down with a hard crack on a nearby table. "You'll be better off without me."

The rest of my team are lining the drink table on the far end of the room. From this angle, we're starting to look like we have it together. Compared to the other teams that have almost full functioning packs.

I need to keep mine together.

"Let's go to the ice and work out some drills. I've got energy to burn and can go till my fingers bleed. Get all that shit out of your head and just enjoy the game."

I can see it in his face when we're playing—even when he's getting his teeth kicked in—that he loves it. Anyone willing to play such a painful sport does.

"I need the distraction anyway," I say.

"Tonight?"

"Yeah, just give me—"

Olivia walks in with Octavia; in a violet dress that's all sparkle. Short. Her legs are covered with wide-net stockings. My heart stutters. There's never been a more beautiful woman in the history of Vviveren.

"Maybe ... after. Yeah?" Ryker smiles, following my line of sight.

"Yeah. I'll be there. Give me an hour ..." I focus on her ass in that dress while Octavia ushers her toward the drink table. Both are invited guests, but I'm not sure who Octavia is here with. "Maybe two."

Our eyes shift to one another, like she can sense me, and a satisfying spark runs down my spine.

"Have fun. I'm going to go find Chase ...You won't tell anyone about this?"

"About what?"

His smug smirk is back. All is well in Vviveren.

That's one crisis averted. We really do need Ryker. He's one of the most levelheaded strategizers we have on the team. Honestly, the best part of being captain is getting to lead. That, I'll miss on a pro team.

"Have you heard anything from Aster?"

I hate that prick's name in her mouth. Olivia's lips are wet from alcohol, and her eyes are heavy while she stares at me with her back pressed against the wall.

She rubs her leg against mine. Teasing. Playful.

"Just this morning when he told me he hoped I'd drop dead after his speech to the school about what a great addition to the council I'll be."

"Do you think things are shifting? You'll become friends and then the threat is gone." She's playing with my fingers, tracing the tips of each one. "Then this will be over."

I swallow the lump in my throat, choosing instead to focus on how her fingers move up my arm. Even with the music blasting behind me, it just feels like me and her.

"Is that what you want?"

She stops, biting her lip. "I don't like pretending."

She's going to break my heart. *Fuck*. Can't I have this just a little longer?

"So maybe you should mark me."

The words *mark me* on Olivia's lips send my blood south. Especially when she's looking up at me like that. Her hands have moved to the inside of my blazer, her eyes soft and anticipating. She only gives me that look. I think. I've kept careful watch on her with other guys, and it's never the same. This is just for show, but she's very convincing. Ballet does require acting skills, I've learned, but this is different. Or do I just want it to be? It has to be the alcohol.

"Uh, come again?"

"Maybe ... you should mark me. There's no arguing with that. It's real."

"You believe in Were mating rituals now?"

"If I choose it, yeah."

I cup her cheek and run my thumb over her lips. Her eyes widen. Does she really mean what I think she does?

"What about after? You know that means you'll be bearing my mark on your skin, right? Even in your leotards."

"I won't be able to cover it with makeup?"

I chuckle while leaning into her neck to smell her. My mind is alive with the thought of that. My teeth sinking into her skin while I fully take what's mine.

"No way. I love the enthusiasm, but marking is ... well, it's easy to put a mark on someone, but until they accept, it affects people in different ways. It can hurt, make you crazy with lust, all sorts of things. I want you to understand what you're getting into."

"How would I accept?"

"Uh ... sex. That's the only way to solidify the bond. And you have to bite me."

"Oh."

She looks down, thinking. She hasn't told me about the dream, but I'm certain she's had at least one sex dream about me. I wish I remembered my dreams and could say the same.

"You wouldn't need to accept. We'd just have to ride out the effects until it fades."

"I just wear your mark until we're out of here? Easy."

"Like end of year?"

"End of school."

I bite my cheek to hide my excitement.

"You really want to do this? You're not drunk?"

She shakes her empty cup. "This is water. I've heard Octavia does heavy pours, and I want to practice tonight."

That means she's been flirting with me for real. I grip her wrist, and she tilts her head as I wrap another around her waist so we're hip to hip.

"Okay ... then I will. Let's do it this weekend. The sooner, the better."

I can't keep myself from smiling as I lean into her lips. My body hums with the satisfaction of how easy it is. How it's never quick, and the way need drips from her tongue and scent. She can't fake that.

I should ask her to be my girlfriend for real. I open my mouth but stop. This isn't the right place or time.

Plus, what if I'm misreading this. Maybe she doesn't like me, she just likes me touching her. That's a thing. Then if I tell her, it might freak her out, and she'll never talk to me again.

No. Parker, don't be a fucking coward. I need to be a man and ask her. Tonight.

She snaps me out of my spiral when she says, "I don't think it's about me, anyway. I think it's about you. Aster and Barrett obviously see you as a threat."

"Other Weres have always treated me like a threat because of the alpha thing. Gavin told me ... that he thinks I'm going to be something big and that one of the greatest pack leaders that ever lived four hundred years ago was a hybrid. I don't know what he sees in me."

"You don't think you'd be a good pack leader?"

"I kinda thought I'd stay a lone wolf after my mom died."

"Well, maybe ... all the other lone wolves thought that too. Maybe they're still waiting for their Alpha. For you."

I can only manage a half smile. "I'm not sure I've got what it takes."

"You're a good leader. People look up to you. I've seen it ... really, you're the kindest, most generous man I've ever met."

My chest warms with her compliment. It's so nice I don't even ruin it with a joke.

"Come on." I lead her into the crowd, where there are other Weres with their girlfriends and mates. It's almost time for me to meet Ryker on the ice, but I can't resist one dance.

Savoring the beat of the music, I tug her closer till her ass is brushing against me. I have to lean down to put my lips next to her neck.

"Comfortable?"

She nods, and I tug on her hips. I love how she lets me. Now that she's said the words, my brain won't let the thought out. The thought of marking Olivia. Then I can't stop imaging biting her and how this urge I have for her is never going to stop. Even if I do mark her and I'm lucky enough she accepts the bond one day, I want to claim my territory with her over and over again. And that's just one part of it. I tune into the sweet scent of her blood again, and my mouth waters at the thought of fresh warm blood touching my tongue. I need something. I need her.

The air shifts as Aster and Barrett funnel into the party with their packs, and the room erupts in praise. Those fuckers would plot their way into the only free moment I have with Olivia.

"Parker ..."

She must notice my eyes, because I'm itchy and *wolfy*, as she puts it.

I guide her through the crowd, and we slip into the bathroom. It's dimly lit, with stone sinks lining the wall of mirrors. Sturdy.

"What are you doing?"

I smile and prop her up on the counter.

"It's good for our cover," I say.

"Uh-huh. Sure."

"I think I'm starting to crave blood." *Your blood.*

"It wasn't like that before?"

I shake my head, moving closer till our lips brush. I thought drinking fresh blood would make me feel ... detached, but it doesn't. With her blood pumping in my veins, I'm stronger than ever.

"You want to bite me here?"

I fall to my knees while holding her gaze. Her breath hitches and her eyes widen.

"Maybe."

I move my hand over the netting on her legs, and her breaths are already faster.

"Parker, the door."

I reach up her dress and grab the edge of her tights to draw them down around her ankles, and my lips meet the skin of her leg.

"You're letting me undress you so easily."

"W-what are you doing?"

"Drinking." I kiss her upper thigh before sinking my teeth into the warmth of her skin. Her fingers twist in my hair, and I groan as the blood rushes to my tongue.

I can't drink for long, but it doesn't matter. A little of her is enough. Even if her whimpers make me feel like stripping her right here.

Footsteps sound outside the door.

Lifting her, I bring her into the stall behind us. Thankfully, the stall door goes all the way to the floor. The heavy bathroom door smacks against the wall and echoes into the ceiling. A group of girls funnel in with laughter.

The stall is big enough to press her to the wall to the left of the toilet. The smell of her arousal is making me insane.

"If you're quiet, I won't stop," I say next to her ear. "Would you like that?"

Her fingers tug at my shirt, and she nods. I hold a finger to my lips and kneel to the floor. She stifles a gasp when I disappear underneath the hem of her skirt. My tongue finds the vein in her leg, then I sink my teeth in. This is so fucking hot. Her tights are still around her ankles. She's turned on, and I love the taste of her skin when I lick her thigh to close her wound.

A soft breathless sound leaves her lips, and I bite lightly at her inner thigh. A silent reminder to be quiet. The girls in the restroom are conversing while they wash their hands. I'm too consumed with the taste of her on my lips to pay attention.

Olivia fists my hair and moves me closer while my fingers find the wetness between her thighs. Her hips buck as I kiss her leg. Higher and higher. She's so desperate for my touch. I could do so many things she'd like. I tug at her underwear, waiting to see if she protests, but she's gripping me tighter, moving my head between her thighs.

Of course I'll do what I'm told. I press my tongue to her center in one long lick to taste her. Wet, sweet, and perfect.

I've been a starved man. One taste, then I'm pressing her into the wall. Licking. Sucking. Her legs shake as I dip my tongue inside her.

I have every intention of making her come, but she's not doing a great job at being quiet. Her breaths are getting louder and louder, and her fingernails are digging into my shoulder. I slow down, pressing my tongue to her clit and savoring the wetness pooling.

When the door closes, I stand to press my hips to hers. There's something in her eyes. Wild desire and pleading. *Oh, baby.*

I nuzzle my chin against her hair, taking in the smell of how much she needs me. My fingers meet the wetness between her thighs, and I stifle a groan. It's just our ragged breaths and the heat of her pressed beneath me. Thankfully, any smells of blood and sex are concealed till we open the stall.

"Is this what you want?" I swipe my fingers through her wetness again.

She nods and buries her head into my chest. My lips caress her forehead. I wish I could capture this and bottle it up. The way she's panting. She wants me inside her.

The door opens again, and her head falls back, and her eyes widen in desperation.

With one hand, I cover her mouth, and with the other, I push a finger inside her.

Her whimpers are muffled by my hand as I pump inside her, and her fingers wrap around my forearm.

More? I mouth, and she shakes her head up and down swiftly.

Tears of pleasure gather in her eyes as I strum my fingers inside her. I can't stop watching her eyes. Those gold and violet pools drip with tears of pleasure. The silent pleading for more of me. Her body is calling to me, begging me to please her, and I want to. I will. Whatever she wants, for however long.

When the door closes again, she keeps her grip on my forearm.

I smile. "You don't want me to stop?"

With flushed cheeks, she shakes her head. *Fuck.* I've never wanted a girl this badly.

"You smell like you need me all the time, Olivia. It's like you're screaming for me."

My cock is hard as I press into her; and she shudders when I trace her bottom lip with my thumb and open her mouth slightly. The image of her getting on her knees in front of me is now at the front of my brain, and my entire body tingles. I wonder if she would or if she wants to please me as much as I want to please her.

I pull my fingers out, and she groans.

"You need me," I say, licking the skin on her neck.

"Yes," she breathes.

My fingers slip back inside her one at a time.

"*Parker*. Please."

"Tell me. Say the words, baby."

"I need you." Her voice is a whimper.

"You need me ... where?"

"Inside me."

"You want more than my fingers, don't you?"

She nods, tears of pleasure break free and roll down her cheeks. Her scent is stronger the longer we stay this close. Her heart is frantic, but there's no hint of fear or worry. This is full trust, and with every glorious stroke inside her, she lets go a little more.

"You're so beautiful." I lean in with a groan and breathe hard into her neck before I lick the tear from her cheek. "We'll get there."

It's not a matter of if, it's when. Her admission should be shocking, but it's not.

Our bodies are both screaming for the connection. Getting inside her will be a religious experience, and I'm ready, but she's not, so I can wait.

I remove my fingers.

"W-when?" She swallows.

I raise a brow. I can't believe we're having this conversation. Is this still casual for her? Maybe the bigger question is, could I be casual after that? Watch her give another guy attention without the urge to kill him?

I'll give her whatever she wants. Even if it guts me after, when she decides it's over.

I have her now. That has to be enough. But I should ask her. I will ... tonight.

"When you ask me to."

CHAPTER TWENTY-SEVEN

OLIVIA

I don't want to know what I look like. A mess, probably. Dazed expression. Open. Vulnerable.

My chest is tight, but Parker helps me with my clothes before planting a kiss on my forehead, and that makes any uncertainty dissolve. We're still close, chest to chest in the bathroom stall.

"I promise to return the favor for letting me drink."

"But ..."

He moves his lips to the tip of my ear and hushes his voice till it's barely audible. "I want to take my time with you and make sure you're relaxed. I can't ensure that here."

When he pulls back to face me, his pupils are large and his presence is all-consuming. I shrink under his gaze and lean into him ever so slightly. The thundering heartbeat in his chest thrums steadily beneath my fingertips.

"I also don't know if I can trust you to be quiet. I'll finish what I started. My room tonight?"

"I ..." I find the full strength of my voice. "I was going to practice late tonight with Octavia."

"Perfect. I can help you wind down after. Would you like that?"

There's something deathly charming about Parker. The way he smiles with those perfect canine teeth. It's the smile of a confident man who knows he has me exactly where he wants me. This is usually where I run. Hide. Anything, really, to find a reason not to bind myself any further to a man who is looking at me like he has three little words dancing on his lips. But I don't feel the urge. I'm trying harder to hide my disappointment that we have to separate. The remnants of my dreams dance in the foothills of my mind. I have a dream nearly every night about him, and none of them involve clothes.

Are Parker and I going to have sex tonight? And if we do ... does it mean something to him ... to me?

I accept his invitation.

Parker is hesitant to leave me with Octavia, even after she assures him she's drinking her last drink, then we're heading to the studio. We're one and the same dancing wise, and she never turns down an opportunity to practice when I ask.

"Your future mate is safe here. No one will touch her." Octavia giggles. I've never heard her giggle before. She's typically an intimidating athletic machine in the studio, but here, she's bubbly and flirty. I even see her eyeing Barrett across the room who is not being subtle in that he notices. There must be a story there. They are on the council together, so it makes sense they are friendly since they meet for breakfast, but the thought of it makes my stomach turn.

Parker kisses me long and hard before saying his goodbyes, then leaves the party with Ryker. I'm proud of him. He told me about helping Ryker practice and convincing him not to quit. I'd seen them practice a few times, and during that time, I saw the same worry lines of stress scrunched on Parker's forehead that I see staring back at me in the dance studio mirrors. The look of someone who has something to prove and a lot to lose.

"You smell like sex and Parker." Octavia tugs me by the arm to the corner of the room.

There are so many people here it's hard to see anything. She effortlessly waves away the males lingering on the bay window overlooking the lake so we can sit. The seat cushion beneath my fingertips is plush.

"I have ... nothing to say about that," I say.

"No, tell me something. Parker has been a girl magnet ever since he showed up. The masses are jealous of how quickly he picked you. You must be special to him."

There it is again. That strange sensation loitering in my gut about Parker. From the moment we saw each other, there was a spark. I'm not a believer in love at first sight, no matter how many times I've read it in the novels Emma suggests. Love can never be that easy.

"He's very attentive," I say, only then realizing I'm thinking of Parker and the word "love" at the same time.

Her eyes widen. "Go on."

"There's just this feeling around him. Since I met him. It's like knowing someone you've known your whole life. Have you felt that?"

She shakes her head. Her hair is up in a ballet bun and doesn't move a centimeter. "No, but I want to. I'm surprised he hasn't marked you yet."

"We just agreed on that actually. I wanted to ask you if you've ever—"

"No. But a few of my friends have." She chugs the last of what's in her cup and twirls a finger at someone saying her name from across the room.

"Anything you can say to help me prepare?"

"You don't have anything to worry about. When your connection is close, I've heard it's euphoric."

My cheeks warm at the thought. Who am I kidding? The fact I'm even considering having sex with Parker is a testament that I care about him. How can it not be with the ache I feel at his absence? I promised myself I wouldn't get attached to someone like this again. Especially not now that I'm so close to achieving everything I want.

We don't talk about Parker for long. While standing at the bay window watching the crowd, I pick her brain about her previous performances and anything ballet related I can draw out of her. Her favorite ballet is *Swan Lake*, one I've not practiced before. She is the first person I've known since ballet school that gets it—the unbridled yearning for success, performance, and perfection that's plagued me since I was a child. It plagues her too. She never tires of talking about ballet, and I don't either.

After thirty minutes, I'm brimming with excitement to get my pointe shoes on and practice variations. We've been asked if we wanted drinks at least ten times, and none of them were water.

Octavia abruptly stops talking, and her chin juts out. "Leave her alone."

I glance behind me to see who she's talking to. Barrett and Aster are there towering over me.

"Why the hostility, Love Bug?" Aster lands on the couch next to me, nearly falling with his head in Barrett's lap when he sits too.

I raise a brow, silently locking eyes with Octavia and mocking her nickname. She shrugs sheepishly.

"We could get you a stronger drink," Barrett booms from next to me.

"I've had plenty. Thanks."

Aster and Barrett share a look.

"I'm serious. Leave Olivia alone. I know that's why you're here. I won't tolerate you pestering her."

"We would never." Aster laughs a loose, throaty laugh like he must be on his second or third drink himself.

"Let's have a drink together," Barrett says.

"We're about to go to the studio," Octavia says.

"Come on. Just one." Aster places two fingers into his mouth and whistles.

A few seconds pass, the end table in front of us has a platter filled with glasses filled to the brim.

"I'm not drinking with you," I say.

"What if I can offer fun?"

I scoff, turning to Octavia and motioning for the door.

"For your little sister, Etta." Aster's words catch my attention.

"Emma," I correct.

"Right. I hear she's devastated about not getting into the culinary club. I could help with that. Me and Dacre are quite close. There's a trip to the city coming up, and while I can't get her into the club, I can get her on the roster for that trip."

Emma would flip. She's been in a spiral for weeks. Plus, she deserves to go on that trip.

"What makes you think I'd trust you to keep that kind of promise?"

"That got her attention," Barrett says, leaning back after plucking a drink from the table.

"Octavia can vouch for me. Right, Love Bug?" Aster says.

She rolls her eyes. "Yeah. I could make sure they keep their promise."

"Fine. One drink."

I take a drink from the platter. They're all the same. A milky blue adorned with fruit on a toothpick. It's surprisingly good and tastes nothing like the alcohol Emma would sneak us into our old room—Dad despises alcohol.

"Should we all share a truth? Make things fun like the girls do?" Aster snickers, his eyes shifting from Octavia to me. "Come on, no dares."

"I'm too old for old games," I say, taking another drink.

"Then no game. We each say a truth, get to know each other."

Aster *is* drunk. His cheeks are flushed, and Barrett is visually annoyed with his antics. I do have one card to play, and I'd love to see their reaction.

"Fine. I have one," I say.

"You have to sip first."

I take another drink, hopefully satisfying that oath.

"Barrett tried to mark me. Did you know that?"

"You what?" Octavia isn't smiling anymore. She lowers her drink.

There's a thick unease tainting the air and adding weight between each of us. My words stick.

"You wanted a truth." I sip my drink. "He told me he was going to mark me against my will at the house round table."

"You don't understand what you've done." Barrett readies himself to stand, and Aster yanks him back into the couch. He didn't know. A shocking yet oddly satisfying revelation.

"I'm fine with my decisions. He had a lot of interesting things to say when he forced me to be alone with him in the woods. Something about bribing me to be his fiancée in exchange for—"

"Quiet." Barrett chugs his drink before slamming it down. "No more games."

Aster is up on his feet following Barrett's retreating form. "Hold on. What the fuck was that? We agreed ..."

His voice dissipates into the roar of the crowd.

"Are you okay?" Octavia's mouth hasn't closed since she heard the news. "I didn't think he'd do something like that. If I'd have known, I ... I would have done something. Barrett and Aster, they're friends of mine, but we're not that close."

"It's fine. I'm okay. Parker found me."

"You're so calm. I'd be freaking out." She sips her drink, and her fingers fumble with the rim of the glass. "My mom tells me that's why I'm not ready for a lead. I wanted to be your alternate, but she says I underperform under pressure."

"What? Really? Is your mother quite ... severe?"

Straightforward is how I'd seen it. But I never knew she was like that with her own daughter.

"*Olivia.* Please. You've seen her. She loves perfection. Raw talent. I'm good, but I'm not sure I'll ever be great. Sure, I try, but ... I don't know if I can break into natural talent."

"You *can.* Are you kidding? I've seen you dance. I've learned things from you already."

She chugs the rest of her drink and smiles. "You know, you're really nice."

"Am I not supposed to be?"

"My mother was excited for you to come because she knew your mother. I didn't know what to expect."

"Let's go practice. We can mess around and do some variations for *Swan Lake.*"

"That would be amazing. I've been so forgetful lately and haven't been setting my alarm for practice as early as I normally do. I'll get us some water."

When she walks away, I quickly text Emma, informing her I am in fact the best sister and she owes me. Hopefully, my sacrifice will cheer her up.

My phone chimes, so I check.

An anonymous text reads:

Enjoying the party?

I scan the room. No one in my direct eyeline is watching.

"Octavia, said to give you this." Someone sits a water bottle on the table beside me.

"Thanks."

I check my phone again and type:

Who is this?

There's no answer for a few minutes, so I continue sipping on my water. There's nothing I can detect on anyone's faces nearby. No one is paying me the slightest bit of attention. Most of the men have shifted away from me, and there is nothing but groups of women with wide smiles and laughter near. Probably Parker's doing.

Unknown number: *You look beautiful tonight, Rabbit.*

A feeling unease nestles itself in my stomach like a loose screw rattling around in a metal machine. Rabbits are easy prey. Someone has to be watching me.

I sip nervously and watch the crowd. This has to be Aster or Barrett. One of them has my number and is trying to threaten me. I don't see them. Only Darien laughing with someone in the corner. He must have snuck in when I wasn't paying attention. I guess rules don't apply to the council.

"Your heart is beating like a scared rabbit." His words echo in my mind.

Warmth creeps under my skin. I check again.

Unknown number: *Things are about to get really interesting for you.*

I try to stand, but my body is heavy. I tug at my dress to bring air to my skin where sweat is forming. Every second that ticks by, the sickness grows.

I blink once.

Then another. It's slow. Unsettling.

My vision blurs into a shadowy haze.

Knees shaking, I force myself onto my feet. The water bottle falls from my hand and spills over my shoes, seeping into my socks. I'm at the mercy of it. Watching. Unable to move. My limbs feel like I'm underwater, and when I step, I fall into the wall, knocking into a group. There's talk. Laughter. Flashing of lights.

My senses are fleeting. There's only a vague sense of what's going on lingering in my mind, like half my brain has been turned off.

I open my mouth to tell them I need help. There's something wrong. Terribly wrong.

A shrill ring cuts the air, and I'm being moved. Fast. I'm outside alone before the others, far enough from the door I can clutch onto a tree. The windows are flashing with a bright light while the crowd funnels outdoors in a panic. Whoever moved me is gone. Or was it me and I don't remember moving?

The air should bring coolness to my skin, but I'm burning. My skin is on fire, and my heart is pounding hard against my ribs.

I scramble for my phone.

A drumming fills my skull, and white-hot heat courses through my limbs. I stumble, dropping my phone into the dirt.

I'm almost too scared to think of the words.

Someone drugged me.

A gnawing desire curdles in my stomach and runs between my legs. My entire body throbs with a need I've never felt before. I grip the tree again while it washes over me from head to toe. I need it to end.

It's blinding.

It burns.

But I need something to make the desire stop. I need so much I can't think.

My normal processing is gone. There's just desire and the need to satiate it. I put one foot in front of the other and kick off my shoes when they make me wobble on the path.

I know exactly where I should go.

Chapter
Twenty-Eight

PARKER

If I am going to win the election and the tournament, I have to work harder. That means, as much as I wanted to stay with Olivia and stare at her in that dress all night, I had to step up as captain.

Ryker huffs as I hit the puck and it barrels toward him. He slapshots it right into the net.

"And you said you were washed up." I'm out of breath too.

I'm glad I didn't let him give up. He does have talent. He just needs someone to give him a chance.

I skate around the rink to hit another puck his way.

"P-Parker." Olivia's voice cuts through the air.

She's on the other side of the rink, walking barefoot on the ice, stumbling toward me. Like a mirage in the dim light, her purple dress sparkles in the haze. Her feet are covered in dirt, and she slips, but I'm there in seconds to hold her up and keep her from falling into the ice.

"What's going on?"

Anger rips through my throat. She's hurt. There's no other explanation for her to be walking around without her shoes. I smell the smallest tinge of blood from the scrapes on the bottoms of her feet. The thought of her bare feet on the ice makes me cringe, so I scoop her up and out of the rink.

"What's wrong?"

Ryker skates behind me but quickly places a hand over his mouth and nose and backs away.

I still don't get it. Her cheeks are red and her eyes are glossy while the skin on her arms is warm. Warmer than it should be if she just came from outside.

"I-I need you," she says.

"What?"

She grabs my face and kisses me. It's so desperate it shocks me.

Then I smell it.

The scent coming off her sets the hair on my arms straight. I *need* her. My entire body eases forward to take her and satiate the need rolling off her in waves. Her scent has changed, amplified over a thousand times, making what is normally manageable, borderline intolerable.

I'm suddenly sixteen again, going through a rut for the first time. It's that bad.

It's unnatural. All-consuming torture.

"I need you. Please help me."

My blood runs cold, and I search her arms and neck. "Did someone mark you?"

It's the only reasonable explanation. She's acting like she's in heat, which is impossible because she's human. But her scent—

I really need to fuck her. I push the thought out and hold my breath to bring my focus back to her. What happened to her at the party?

"Make this stop," she begs.

"Who did this?"

"I was at the party and ..."

I sniff at her neck, focusing harder. I have to know if someone else touched her. But her scent is clean, apart from the aroma filling the air and making me dizzy with desire. I linger there with my lips at her neck, licking my teeth. My head is swimming too.

I'm overly aware of Ryker, who is now on the other side of the rink, which still feels too close to her for my liking. I haul her into my arms and sling her over my shoulder.

"We're going back to the dorm. Come here."

"What's happening? Do I need to call someone?" Ryker yells.

"I'm taking her to my room. Can you get a hold of Octavia Vix? Let her know I have Olivia, and check to see if she's okay."

He nods, and I grip Olivia while she squirms. My shoulders are back, and I'm ready to protect her from whoever might try to take her.

Someone did this to her on purpose, and I will find out who.

As soon as I shut the door, she's on me, pulling at the buckle on my pants. She still smells like euphoria in a bottle, and every few seconds, I'm blocking out the image of me bending her over the side of my bed.

"Hey, we're not doing this."

"But why? You said if I asked." She tries to strip my jersey off, but I stop her. There's pain in her eyes from my rejection.

"Please, Parker. I hate this."

Weres experience their first rut in adolescence, and it was one of the worst experiences in my life. I remember locking my door and counting the minutes till it ended.

"Baby, I know. But it will pass."

"No. Make it end. I'll feel better if you touch me … if you're inside me. I want it to be you."

I kiss her forehead and smooth down her hair. "I can't. I'm going to leave"—*lock*—"you in here and go figure out which one of them did this and how to fix this." I omit the part about leaving the scene so gory the dean will scream in horror, but I need those fuckers to pay for this. I need to rip someone's throat out with my teeth.

"No! Don't leave." She's looking at me like that's the most horrible, shocking thing I could have suggested. I move to press a hand to her cheek, and, in the next breath, she breaks into a sob and all that alpha energy runs out of me. Any thought I have about leaving dissolves.

"You can't go."

"I won't leave. Come here."

I drag her into my bed with her squirming. She keeps trying to kiss me, touch me. I've never been so uncomfortable while holding a beautiful woman. The need to mark her jumbles around in my head like worms in my skull. Every time I push it out, the thought comes back. It's maddening. But stars above, I need her to be *mine*. I need her to smell like me so bad it's all I can think about. It's obvious, isn't it? That I've wanted to since the day I met her, but when she smells like that, it's so permanent. It's a fact I've been able to hide from, but now it's branded in my skin.

I rummage for my phone, then struggle to find the number in my call list. This is a potion. It has to be. And *mypotions.net* pulled up nothing, which means whatever the fuck it is, it's forbidden.

And only one person can help me with that. Thankfully, he picks up on the first ring.

"Hey Coach."

Olivia is running her hands over the inside of my waistband.

"Owens?"

"Yeah I … need your help with something."

"It's nearly midnight. It better be good." His daughter is crying in the background.

Olivia's hands are under my shirt, running over the scars on my chest. She smells so fucking good.

"I know. You're just the best at potions, and uh … I have a friend … in the city who just called me, and we think she's been drugged. She's not a Were, but is experiencing heat-like symptoms and—"

"Is she safe?"

"Yeah, her, uh, boyfriend is on the other line trying to figure out what to do."

"Is it having an effect on him? Is he Were?"

"Yes. I couldn't find it on the web—"

I grab Olivia's hand to stop her from undoing my pants, and she moves to kiss my chest.

"Adentium Colseum. It's an ancient potion that doesn't exist anymore. Or shouldn't. It's been scrubbed from most sources. It's illegal to post the recipe on any website."

"The one they used in the old mating rituals?"

My brain isn't conjuring the source of that brief remembered information. Not while Olivia's breath is by my neck. Just the remembrance of old stories I'd heard in my younger years of school.

"Yes. Well, that's why it's forbidden. The only way to stop it is to be marked."

"Got it. Thanks. Fill you in with how it goes."

"Parker—"

I drop my phone on the bed and steady Olivia with both hands. Someone drugged her so they could mark her, and still, she ended up in my arms. I'm angry. I'm relieved. I'm still so turned on by her but mostly just happy she's safe with me and I can fix this.

"Don't you want me?" I hate the sadness in her voice. She sniffles and her lip quivers.

"Oh, baby. I want you. But not like this ... I know how shitty it feels."

I haul her onto my bed and into my arms.

"But I want you ... just you. I mean it. I want you to be my first."

Her first? Fuck. *Fuck.* I squeeze her and keep my eyes on the door. The safest place for her on campus is in my arms. Even if someone smells her and comes for her, they won't get her.

"And we will. But not right now."

"But it ... it means something to me. It does. You have to know that." She sniffles.

I move the hair from her face, smoothing the lines in her forehead. "Okay, I hear you. It means something. It does for me too. That's one reason out of a very long list that we can't tonight."

She groans and buries her head into my chest. I have to think of anything other than her smell. I imagine watching her dance. Something neutral and awe-striking. It's enough to dislodge the surging in my brain that tells me to strip her. Keeping her safe tonight is the most important thing.

"I won't hurt you," I say, rubbing the warm skin of her cheek and kissing it.

"Parker ... you smell ... you smell like ..."

Like an alpha. Like she needs me to fuck her, but I won't. As a human, finding the words would be nearly impossible, I imagine.

"It's *so* good."

"I'm going to fix this. I promise it won't hurt."

Her heartbeat is calmer now as I lay her down and move the hair from her neck.

This isn't the way I wanted to mark her. This is far from how I wanted the night to go, but I can give her relief and that's all I want.

Her fingers grip tighter and tighter in my hair as she tugs me toward her for a kiss, so I kiss her cheek and stroke her hair before running my lips across her neck.

I let go of my vampire instinct and focus only on my inner wolf, and it's ready. Already on edge, waiting for me to sink my teeth into her. I'm not thinking of the taste of her when her blood hits my tongue.

The bite jolts me like a live wire in my veins.

My world snaps in two.

Gavin prepared me about the bond of it, but as soon as I feel the tug, I know it's different. Nothing like what he described.

Oh, fuck. Olivia is …

She starts to relax. Her tight muscles loosen and her breaths calm. Her eyes grow heavier and heavier.

I'm still rigid as the mark dissolves under her skin.

She's … I can't believe she's—

"Don't leave," she says, pulling me.

I'm not even the least bit tired as I bring her onto my chest.

"Never."

Olivia is my mate. My linked mate. The fucking sky is purple.

Chapter
Twenty-Nine

Olivia

"I found you," he whispers in my ear. "Finally."

A large set of arms is squeezing my head when I open my eyes. Parker's scent surrounds me. I recognize the coolness of his sheets, and it all comes back—the burning in my body. A filmy haze lingers over my memory, and I'm missing fragments. I attempt to move, and Parker squeezes me, so I crane my head toward the light to see him. His eyes are closed, but he's holding me hostage in his arms.

"Parker ..."

His eyes shoot open, and he breathes deeply through his nose. "Hey, feel okay?"

"I feel better. I think."

He releases me, with very little room to wiggle free, and his pupils are blown as he sniffs at my hair.

I assess myself more thoroughly. Nothing hurts. Clothes are on.

"Tell me I didn't strip for you." I'm half teasing, but Parker is still smelling me. Only, it's more subtle. There are bags under his eyes, and the whites are bloodshot. His hair is a disheveled mess, and when I move my head over his chest, I realize he never changed out of his jersey.

"No. Clothes stayed on," he says.

"You look ..." Tired. His eyes are a weird in-between shade of his normal blue and the Were yellow, leaving them a murky green.

"I had to protect you. Someone drugged you. Do you remember?"

"Yeah, most of it. We need to ..." Parker isn't letting go of me. "What?"

"I'm sorry ... you just smell different. Do you feel different?"

Then it comes back, the memory of Parker's teeth in my neck. The burning and aching in me instantly calmed, then I was unable to stay awake for another second.

"You marked me."

"I know. I'm sorry. It was the only way to stop the potion."

"No ... it's okay. I mean, it's not exactly like we planned, but this works too. I just don't feel any different."

He's staring at me with a soft, worried expression. It's strangely docile. My thoughts race, then I remember what I said ... what I admitted to.

"This is good. I was hoping it would be the same. That way nothing would change."

I don't want the way he feels about me to change because of the mark. I want Parker to still want me in the same way. Just Olivia.

"Yeah. Right." His eyes stay that weird in-between color, and he turns his head from me.

"Can you see it?"

He moves the hair from my neck. It's so tender. Tentative. Like he's afraid too much pressure will hurt me.

"No. It doesn't show up right away. You'll start to see it come through tonight, and it will gradually darken."

I wait for his smile. That confidence to peek through. The elation that even though something terrible happened he kept me safe. Or the cockiness from him marking me, and that I'll smell just as he intended. But there's pain behind his enlarged pupils.

"What?"

His eyes dart to mine. "Hmm?"

"You're looking at me ... strange."

He shakes his head. "Don't worry about me."

"Do you feel different?" I ask.

"I …" His nostrils flare, and a muscle feathers in his jaw. "It might change as it develops."

Before I tell him that doesn't answer my question, there's a knock on his door and we separate.

My feet have dirtied Parker's sheets, and there's no sign of my shoes or phone.

"Where is our sister?!" Emma's high-pitched voice pierces the air.

Parker opens the door to let them in, his shoulders falling.

"I knew she'd be in here." Eva's eyes widen when she sees me, and she flutters in, huffing in panic. "I was so worried when some random person called me this morning saying they found your phone on the ground."

Eva is listed at the top of my contact list under *Eva–ICE: pls state type of emergency immediately.*

"I was wondering why you weren't texting me any details about the trip. Then when Eva called me, I was certain you'd been killed!" Emma says.

"I'm fine." I assure them; they're making me anxious now with their worry.

I fill them in from beginning to end, starting with the messages I received, to the terror when I realized I'd been drugged … and Parker is *staring*. I try not to notice the heaviness of his gaze, but it's hard. There's an intensity to it like a bright light after a night alone in the dark.

He only speaks up to mention his findings on the potion.

"So the point was to get Olivia marked by another werewolf? That's what the potion does?"

He nods.

"Thank the stars above Parker found you first," Eva says.

"Yeah, Mom was looking out." Emma grips my hand, and my heart skips.

How would she react to such a thing? Especially now that I've been marked.

We skip the marking part. Well, I skip it, so Parker skips it too. It's a silent pact to keep that to ourselves for the day. This is the last day it's a secret. The last few hours before the news breaks and everyone sees me as Parker's mate.

That's not the part I'm worried about. I'm sure my sisters will understand, but I'm too groggy to explain today—and I'm more concerned with why Parker won't stop staring at me like that.

"Someone is targeting you. And I'm going to figure out who," Parker growls.

CHAPTER THIRTY

PARKER

"You found me." Her words feather my neck.

Olivia is my *mate.*

I can't think of anything else.

Nothing else matters.

"Is there no way you can stay in your room today? Say you're sick?" I ask, seconds before she goes for the door.

Her sisters have just left, and I've got my last moment with her alone.

"Why?"

"Because ..."

The thought of another male looking at you will send me into a blind rage, and I will hurt people. It's all I can do not to shake. My skin is crawling with an itch that is not going away. I could run for hours. I *need* to shift. Just to take the edge off.

"You smell so different. And I ... I'm having a hard time thinking about anyone else being around you right now. Especially when I know you're being targeted."

I want to say it. I need to tell her, but not right now. I have to go talk to Gavin and Zant, and figure out what the hell happened last night. I've already missed practice this morning, and Coach has called me ten times.

Plus, she doesn't remember. I was hoping she would remember something. Any of the dreams. Did she have the same dreams I did? The ones where we met on the swing surrounded by the flowers?

When I woke up, I remembered them all. Every dream I've ever had about her came rushing back into my brain like they had always been there. Only, the girl in them is fully visible now and I awoke with her lying in my arms.

I've been looking for Olivia my whole life and didn't realize it.

She's the girl from under the ice.

The girl on the swing.

I know her. I've missed her. I've yearned for her and met her in my dreams every single night, then felt the loss each morning in her absence.

"Does it hurt?" Her face falls. "You seem in pain."

"No ... it's ... just taking an adjustment."

Who am I kidding? She won't stay locked in her room. I can't hide her away forever. There is no going back to the way things were before.

But the bond is too fresh, and the thought of any of those assholes seeing her today makes my entire body itch. I lied. It does fucking hurt. She could get hurt. She wants casual and for things to stay the same, but they're always going to be different now.

I don't know how to say it. It's like I'm running a fever, and I'm hyperaware of the steps in the hallway near my door. My thoughts are moving so fast I can barely catch them.

Why doesn't she remember? I'm so fucked. I'm going to take out the first guy who looks her way in Noxx House and kill him. She'll freak out. I'll freak out. It's going to be a total shitshow.

"Okay," she says.

"You will?" I try not to sound too excited.

"I don't want to, but ... if it helps you, I can take one day off. Just one. I have schoolwork I can work on. Plus, I'm tired after last night."

"Do you need anything right now? Feel sick? Hungry?"

"I'll have my sisters bring me some food from the dining hall. Don't worry."

I sigh in relief and tug her to my chest. She has my mark on her, and I sense it when our skin touches. Like a magnet clicking together, it's a perfect fit. I have to pull away after a few seconds. Touching her is going to make me shift. My wolf recognizes her. It's agonizing. It's euphoric. It's terrifying.

"Are you okay? You're still acting strange," she asks.

"Yeah. I'll be okay." *After I do what I'm about to do.* "You're the one I'm worried about."

"For being drugged, I feel fine."

I smooth down the wiry bits of her hair.

"Tonight, though ... I want to take you somewhere."

"Where?"

"It's a secret."

"Okay ... my smell won't ... hurt you?"

"It's the opposite, actually."

She grips at my blazer and tilts her chin up to kiss me. *Oh?*

Her smell is alive now. It tells me she wants comfort. She's worried. Curious. Calm. I swear I black out for a second when our lips touch. She shudders when my tongue enters her mouth, and I chase out all that want building inside her.

She draws back, licking her bottom lip. Can she sense it too? Is she in denial?

"Tonight." I assure her.

She's got a finger pressed to her bottom lip like I've shocked her.

I only hope it will help her remember.

The morning was a clusterfuck from beginning to end, and as I lie in wait in the bushes, breathing in the calm of being in my shifted form, I replay the talk I had after summoning an emergency meeting with the two people I trust the most.

Gavin and Zant have stayed acquaintances despite my best efforts, but they both agreed to meet me at the edge of the Lost Lake Woods.

Gavin and Zant stared at me. Not saying a word.

"You're telling me ... you're linked mates? You're sure?" Gavin looked the most surprised.

"Do you know of any other way I've been dreaming of her my entire life?"

He reminded me of how there hasn't been talk of a linked mated pair for more than a century and they're all full-blooded Weres. Like I needed the reminder.

"I know that, but it's true. And now everything fucking sucks. My skin is on fire. I'm so worried about her I can't think of anything else—"

"Parker."

"I've felt like I'm going to shift from the moment I woke up."

"Parker. Your alpha blood is awakening."

"What? No, I haven't accepted."

"I don't know if you have a choice. Look at your hands. You ... smell different. Marking Olivia was what you're meant to do. She's your catalyst. Your body is changing to protect her."

My fingers sharpened to claws.

"Fuck!"

"Did you tell her?" Zant asked, way too amused by my apparent suffering. I expected nothing less.

"No."

Their eyes widened in a what-the-fuck expression.

"I wasn't sure! I don't exactly have luck with my own Were instincts. I'm going to tell her tonight ... bring her somewhere special."

"You being linked mates is going to change everything," Gavin said.

"I know. That's why I needed to talk to you and ask you both to ensure I don't do anything stupid when I confront Aster and Barrett."

"You can't just go up to them accusing them of drugging someone," Gavin said.

"He's right. You need evidence," Zant said.

I couldn't confront them in public. Fine. No one said anything about ambushing them on their run. The only time they're together and not surrounded by their packs, and I know that because Zant complained about them being late to council meetings when they ran too long. The woods are supposed to be off-limits to students, but asshole Weres who have money can do just about anything they want, and a forbidden wood all to themselves is mighty tempting.

I have to admit, I enjoy it too.

They don't see me stalking them. I've tracked them for miles, and they haven't stopped to look around once. That's because they're never the prey. Bunch of assholes at the top of the food chain with no one to challenge them.

The words from Olivia's text set my blood ablaze. *Rabbit.*

Now they're going to see how it feels to be hunted.

Barrett's the bigger Were with black and silver hair. He's my first target. Aster's warm reddish fur makes him easy game and doesn't camouflage well, but he's faster than Barrett, so he's a few yards ahead.

I charge through the trees, the dirt flying in a haze. In seconds, I'm feet away, and a howl rips through Barrett's throat as I tackle him to the ground and my teeth rip into his shoulder. He's big, but he's slow when he reaches up to swipe me with a claw.

Aster's close. Three. Two. One.

I dodge his ambush from the back and pin him to the ground with my claws in his neck.

I want to rip into him. Make him bleed.

Aster wiggles free in a flurry of dirt, yelping, and they circle me.

"*Owens*," Barrett snarls inside my head. It's faint. I have to concentrate really hard to hear it.

Packmates can communicate in each other's minds with ease when in wolf form, but enemies take a little effort. We'll have to keep the sentences short.

"*Surprised to see me on your date?*"

They both snarl. I prefer communicating in wolf form. It's easier. Natural. No games.

"*Let me guess, you're here about a girl*," Aster says.

Barrett snaps his teeth. "*Rabbit.*"

A switch flips, and a deep rumbling growl rips through my teeth as I take a step forward. It's like I'm in control of every muscle. Ready to fight if they give me the chance.

They shrink back, then reposition, holding their ground.

I'm not afraid.

I can take both of them now. It would be a difficult, bloody fight, but I'm more than willing to take that challenge.

Olivia's face flickers to the front of my mind, and the shiny thread of our bond flickers, reminding me I'm here for a reason.

"*Took a tumble on the forums last I heard*," Barrett says.

He's talking about the photo. The one someone took of her while she stumbled around seconds after she was drugged. Emma showed us while they were all piled in my room.

This was their plan. For her to make a fool of herself at the party. Get marked by someone else under the guise of her drinking too much.

The image is seared in my brain. Olivia falling into someone in a blurry shuffle.

"I'd choose your next words carefully."

"Maybe she should be careful how much she drinks. She'll embarrass you."

It's like my skin is peeling off my body. It's physically painful not to act on the instinct running through me.

But I need proof. I need something.

"So it was you."

They're still circling.

"Prove it," Barrett says.

"You wanted to play," Aster says.

Olivia was right. This is about me. They're playing this game with real people as their pawns. My people.

They don't know yet that she's my linked mate. That *I* marked her.

What will they do when they know? It just makes her a bigger target for them.

"Maybe you should keep a closer eye on her."

I lunge. Teeth bared and claws out. I'm going for his throat but get his face. A long, deep gash sprays dark red across the dirt. My teeth stay at his neck, and an intense growl shakes my whole body.

"Stay the fuck away from her."

They are denying it. It doesn't absolve them. I know it was them. I'll have to find my proof another way.

Their growls are accompanied by a deafening howl. Their packs will answer and be here in minutes.

That's a fight I wouldn't win.

"See you at the podium. Might want to cover that up," I say.

That gash won't heal easily, but it sends the right message. I'm finally starting to feel it. It has always been in my blood, but now it is singing to me.

Maybe I do want to be an Alpha. Bad news for them.

Chapter Thirty-One

OLIVIA

"This place is ..."

We stop at the entrance of an abandoned atrium. Parker wouldn't tell me where he was taking me, only that it was a surprise.

I stare at the last remaining support wall that's worn from the weather and elements. The glass is broken, but the towering stone arches stand high into the sky that's growing dim in the twilight. It's a part of the wood now. A silent sleeper that blends into the surrounding trees and growing vines and flowers threatening to cover the stone completely.

"This is familiar ..." I say, staring at the floor that is one with the woods.

It's a bed of moon nightingales that stretch all the way to the wall in a blanket of periwinkles. Some are darker, more violet, and others almost a full baby blue.

Parker and I stroll into the opening, and he waits patiently for me to get my bearings. I protested when he insisted we come into Lost Lake Woods. What was this place used for?

"How did you find this place?"

I slip off my shoes and socks to mingle in the clay and flowers.

"My mother brought me. Doxlothia has summer camps for kids. It was ... different. Not as wrecked. The school used to grow herbs and stuff before they cut off the woods for students. In the summers, we came and she'd let me play in the dirt and flowers."

"I can't put my finger on it, but it's like I was here in a dream." I chuckle, but Parker doesn't smile. He's still staring, with his eyes a hazy bluish green.

I stop when I see the tree branch stretched into the opening from the broken ceiling, and a swing sits on the far side next to a perfectly preserved window.

"Yeah, that's why I wanted to bring you."

"What do you mean?" I ask, spanning the gap between me and the swing. There's no path, but I move my feet into the grooves in the clay. Déjà vu casts over the scene in its familiar milky haze.

I've done this before. There's eerie excitement at the thought.

"Olivia. I—" He stops, ears reddening, and his eyebrows fly up and eyes soften. "Your mark ... my mark. I can see it."

I reach up to touch the skin there, but he's already caressing it.

"Does it look bad?"

"No. It's perfect." He leans down to kiss me there. "Oh, baby. This is—You have my mark. It's so ..."

He sucks at the skin of my neck, and I gasp at his lips on that specific spot sending an ache throughout my entire body. That suction turns into a plethora of kisses, and I laugh at his enthusiasm.

He's happy, and there's a calm in knowing I want to make him happy. Have I ever cared about making anyone else happy before? My father once, long ago. My sisters, sure, but that's different than this.

"Parker, I need to tell you something."

I can't keep pretending. I can't keep hiding from him.

"Wait. Let me tell you mine first," he says.

"Now?"

"Yeah, you might want to sit." He motions to the swing.

I do, mostly because I want to. I want to touch the frayed threads holding it together and the wood underneath me.

"I hoped you would remember if I brought you here."

"Remember?"

I don't think I've ever seen him nervous, but I'll never be able to say that again. Parker is fidgeting, his foot tapping, with worry lining his forehead.

Now my heart is pounding.

"You're my mate."

"I know, that's how you told me it works."

"Don't freak out." He brings his hands out to steady me like I'm a skittish foal about to bolt.

"What is happening?"

"I didn't think it was possible but ..." He's staring at me, unable to say the words.

"Parker, spit it out."

"We're linked mates. We've been linked since before we were born. I think I knew it, but I didn't let myself think it because I thought it wasn't possible. But it's so fucking obvious. We have so much in common."

"No. You said—"

"It's like trying to deny gravity exists. I can feel it in my blood. It's you. It's always been you."

Linked mates. Did I know it too? Denying it is easier than the truth. I did know. I've known for so long but didn't want to think about it.

Because I wanted this to be real. I didn't want that to be the reason for everything.

The reason he feels like a long-lost friend.

The reason I stopped to gawk at him the first time I saw him.

The reason the moment his skin touched me I knew that I'd been searching for him my whole life.

"You're the one on the swing. This swing. The one in my dreams. I was meant to tell you this, right here."

"You said you don't remember your dreams."

"I didn't. But after I marked you, I remembered them all. And there's so many ... We've been hanging out together here in our dreams and neither of us knew."

"You knew earlier today and you're just now saying something?"

That explains that look.

This is too much at once. Is that why we're here? The reason Parker held me at night and it felt so safe. The reason we got so close too fast. It's all ... a bond. Fabricated. Something told us we were meant to be together, so we fell into the pattern.

It's not real. My heart aches at the thought.

"I wanted to be certain because I knew you didn't want things to change."

I shake my head. "Maybe you're wrong ..."

"Baby, you don't get it. I *know* it's you. You almost drowned when you were a little girl, didn't you?"

I suck in a breath. "How ...?"

"I never remembered my dreams ... except for one. Someone drowning in the water."

"No." This isn't happening. Parker isn't—

"I reached for you and begged for you to live. I've had that dream over and over again since I was a kid, but I never saw who it was. I'd wake up in a panic not knowing if I saved them. It used to eat at me because I knew this dream meant something. But it was you. I know it was you because now I see you under the water."

They never saw who pulled me out. No one was paying attention that day by the lake. They said I just vanished one minute. Then the next, I was on the dock gasping for breath.

"Do you not feel it?"

Parker's voice breaks, and a lump gathers in my throat. I'm hurting him. Of course I am. This is why I should have kept him far away from me. I'm not cut out to be his mate.

He deserves more. Someone nicer. Better. Just better.

"How can I? I'm human and don't sense the same things." I wipe a tear.

I'll never feel the bond like Parker does. I don't remember the dreams. I'm standing now, staring at the swing and willing myself to remember more than a hint of familiarity. All that safety and sureness from Parker is evaporating because it was just the bond making him want me. It's not his fault, but it hurts.

"I need to go."

"Wait. Please."

"No. You're telling me that all of this ... this bond between us is because of some magic thing. It's not because ... it's not because of us. It's not a choice."

I sniffle, drawing my arms around my torso.

His eyes soften. "You think I don't care about you?"

"I think some magical bond told you that you should. I knew there was a reason I couldn't think straight when you were around and why I agreed to all these ridiculous things. And we never would have done any of this without that and—"

"Olivia, that's not true."

"You don't know that. I just need a minute to think. I need to be alone."

I wanted it to be real. I wanted him to choose me for me.

I'm moving back toward the opening when the flash from a camera stops us both.

"Linked mates, huh?" A man with a camera I don't recognize takes another succession of photos. "Beautiful mark, Parker."

Perfect. Absolutely perfect. I slip on my shoes and head for the cover of the trees, not caring what Parker plans to do with him.

I just need to run. It's familiar. Freeing.

"Olivia, wait!" Parker's voice is a far-off echo.

But I keep running.

Chapter Thirty-Two

I can't sleep without her. I keep staring at the place she should be. There's a gnawing in my skull that won't let me close my eyes. It's the bond urging me to go to her and patch this up, but not for me ... for her. Her sadness thickens in my lungs, making each breath more difficult, like a bruised rib.

It's past midnight when I finally will myself to get up and stand at her door.

"Olivia? Can we talk?"

There's rustling and whispering inside. The hall is dim, and all the noise is down in the common room. I've ignored all my mentions and texts. None of it matters without Olivia.

"I know ... today was a shitshow and I probably should have just told you when I woke up, but I was scared."

Scared of this exact thing. Her leaving. Rejecting me. My stomach is in knots, and I don't know if I can make myself get back into my bed alone.

"Please, just open the door."

There's more whispering, movement. I smell cinnamon. A signature Emma scent. Gavin is right. My alpha blood must be awakening because everything is getting easier. Even the scent of their blood is easier to identify now. I can sense it all in one long breath.

Nothing but silence follows, and I lean my head against the wood door.

I wish I could call my mom. She'd know exactly what to do.

It's not Olivia's fault. I know what it's like to not feel what I'm supposed to feel. She can't sense the bond at all. After going my whole life being the one who can't sense anything, it's almost ironic. If she could, she'd see that it's never been just the bond, it's her I'm in love with.

"Fuck the mating bond, okay? I just need you to talk to me."

I can't go back to my room and sit in the silence. I'm a groveling, pathetic man seconds from getting on my knees at her door, and I don't think I'd care if a whole host of photographers came to publish this moment on the front-page news.

"We'll figure it out. Don't shut me out. Not now … not after I just found you. We don't have to complete the bond. We'll reject it together, and it will be fine. Things can be the same. However you want them to be. I just need you."

There's more whispering, then seconds later, the door opens, and I catch a glimpse of Emma giving me a thumbs-up before Olivia comes through the door and shuts it behind her. Her slender fingers wrap around my shirt, and she buries herself into my chest. My body is on fire from her touch. It has to be different for humans. I wish she could understand how strong this thread is between us.

My hands are in her hair in seconds, and I rest my chin on top of her head. Finally, the burn is gone, like she's a healing balm to the terrified, anxious parts of me.

Without a word, she tugs me by my shirt toward my room.

"What part of what I said did you like?"

"We don't have to talk. I have to get up early tomorrow."

"Oh … okay."

When we're inside, she drops her pants to the floor and pulls me into bed.

Her scent calms all my senses when she lays her head on my chest, so I close my eyes. I'm not sure I've ever been so afraid of anything else. Her arms are tight around me, and she tangles her legs in mine. I'm losing her even while she is clinging to me.

I don't realize I'm shaking at first. There's so much moving through me. The bond is so intense. Fresh. Powerful. Unyielding. It's all I can think about. Never letting her out of my sight and knowing she will have to be.

Her rejection.

The fear of being separated.

She may decide this is the last night we do this.

It makes me think about my mother. When she got sick, I laid my head next to her bedside and begged her to stay. I hide the tears in my eyes when I rest my head over hers.

Her fingers press into my skin, and she traces the scars on my chest, soothing me, and I squeeze her as the lump builds in my throat. Tonight, she's holding me together.

Our heartbeats sync in rhythm as seconds tick by. Her existence is enough.

Chapter
Thirty-Three

Olivia

"Please don't leave me, baby," Parker begs over and over. He's sobbing, shaking me.
I'm so hot. My skin is burning.
I'm trying to stay.
Please, I don't want to go.

"You're being ridiculous."

Emma just finished giving me her fifth lecture on love for the day. According to her, I'm calloused, out of practice, and totally ruining my own life. We're currently sitting in the Stelliea House garden while Eva does her afternoon duties of weeding and picking produce. I'm helping. Emma is not. I've felt sick to my stomach all morning as the reminiscence of my dream lingers.

There are no shapes. Barely words remain, but the *feeling* of it stays in my gut like a heavy stone.

I'm sitting knees first in the dirt to stay off my tired feet. I snuck out early this morning to get my practice in before anyone else got into the studio.

I needed to clear my head. Just be Olivia, even while the entirety of Vviveren has imploded with the news. The first linked pair in more than a century. Emma showed me the feed on her phone that was flooded with pictures of me. They're pictures of Parker and me arguing while that asshole cameraman hid out of sight. Then a few blurry ones of me putting my hand to the camera and Parker pushing him. But clear as day, you can see the mark on my neck—an imprint of Parker's teeth, dark like a tattoo. I'm still too afraid to look at the ones of me at the party. Some things are too embarrassing for me to swallow.

Octavia called me in a panic this morning to check on me, and then brought me a coffee. Which I barely drank while she rattled off a plethora of questions I couldn't answer. It's my fault for responding to all her calls with texts after the party.

"The mark is hot," Emma says.

I spent nearly twenty minutes staring at it in the studio mirror.

I roll my eyes. Though, I'm thankful for their company.

Being Parker's linked mate isn't gaining me new friends; in fact, it's the opposite. A group of Were girls growled at me on the front lawn this morning. Emma says it's jealousy, but I know the true answer. They don't think I'm good enough for Parker. They see me as Olivia Osborne, a difficult, stubborn girl they think parties too much and is stuck up. I know because I'd read at least twenty comments saying that exact thing. They hate my hair. My eyes. The way I breathe, probably. I even overheard a rumor about how I'd ensnared Parker into some fake scheme that involves me using his notoriety and a fake linked mate bond to get a spot in the IBCE.

That one worries me the most. What if someone from the IBCE actually believes that? Would I get kicked out of the Doxlothia company? Never be let into the IBCE? Octavia told me it would be fine, but I don't know her well enough yet to know if she's just trying to cheer me up.

"I mean ... did you really think this thing with Parker was casual? That you were just friends?" Eva doesn't look up from her handful of weeds.

"I ..." It sounds silly to say it aloud, but being with Parker is so easy I didn't question it. Sure, we were playing a role to the outside, but when we were alone, falling into that rhythm never felt like it. It was real to me and like no one else existed. I didn't need to question it. Parker didn't need a different label, and neither did I. Plus, I was going to tell him how I felt ... or show him that night.

I saw that elation in his eyes when I mentioned marking and the possibility of things for our time at school. He wanted me. I never had to question the future because Parker never made me worry there would be a day he didn't. Maybe that was foolish ... Surely, this hasn't all been a Were thing. The bond *making* him want me. But what if it was? Maybe he did want to mark me ... to touch me because of the bond.

Would he have stayed and helped me out without it?

I already know my answer. He would because that's who he is.

"We never talked about exclusivity. He never seemed interested in anyone else. And you know I'm not."

"So what about now, if you saw Parker with another girl, you'd be cool with it? Your linked mate," Emma says.

I know what she's trying to draw out of me.

"I didn't say that."

"Okay, but what if? What if you reject the bond and he chooses someone else?"

I swallow, scooping up a pile of weeds and shoving them into a wicker basket. I don't think of it. I can't. My stomach hollows.

"You need to talk to him. That's all I'm saying," she says.

Eva's phone rings, thankfully saving me from more interrogation. She dusts her hands off on her apron and brings it to her ear.

"Hi Dad," she says, and I shift my attention back to the weeds.

"He called me too," Emma says. "You should talk to him."

"No."

"But he wants to talk about the linked mate thing."

"That's why I don't want to talk to him. Of all the things going on right now, Dad is the last person I want to talk to about this. Please ... tell him I'm fine."

Eva and Emma share an exasperated look. They don't get it. They think I'm being unreasonable, rude.

"I just think he's trying, and it would be nice ... to visit without that weird awkward silence between you two."

Spoken like the youngest child.

"You can't dictate my relationship with Dad."

"I know. But he's trying. And ... it's like, he lost her, and I guess I know what that feels like and why that might make him go a little crazy. I don't think Mom would want us to fight."

I glare. Emma pulls that card more than anyone, and it's not fair.

"Emma." Eva shakes her head.

Emma huffs. "Fine. I'll shut up. Keep being closed off. I will stop trying to get the family to stick together, then."

Emma and Eva continue to bicker back and forth. Maybe Emma is right ... I'm the only thing in the way of my family reuniting and being happy.

Suddenly, I have the urge to check my phone, but not to see if my dad called me. Which he did.

Parker hasn't texted me. He's giving me the distance I asked for so I can think. I try to be anything but miserable as I go back to picking weeds.

I decide to hide in the Noxx House library for the remainder of the day. There's a secret door that leads to a basement—Parker sat with me one afternoon while I figured out the puzzles to get the key—and there's never anyone down here. There's cushion floors and low lighting, like everywhere else in Noxx House, which makes it the perfect place to search for information on linked mates in peace.

Except for today.

Darien is sitting in the stacks with his fingers holding up the cracked, crumbling spine of the book in his hand.

"Olivia." He doesn't look up. "How did I know I'd find you here?"

"You're probably stalking me."

"No. Not me. I did pluck this for you, though. Saved you the trouble of combing around for it."

He holds up a book, and I reluctantly reach out to take it. With all the areas of danger, somehow Darien seems the least scary right now. I may not like him, but I'm picking up on his strategy. He's a sideline sitter; he holds his cards close to his chest. He won't outright attack me now that I'm Parker's mate.

Wow, that's the first time I've let it sink in.

The silver spine reads: *Linked Beyond Time*.

"That's the best book you'll find on the subject here."

"So you don't believe it's fake like the others?"

"Oh, I know it's not. You know everyone talked about Parker when he first arrived too. You two are really quite similar. When he took to you so quickly, I had an idea shortly after you arrived to look in your files, and you know what I found?"

"You're going to tell me."

"You and Parker share the same birthdate and time, down to the minute. You both have deceased mothers who died when you were ten, and both happened in the spring. And your mothers were friends, well, at the very least, acquaintances."

He hands me a picture of my mother. The blood drains from my face when I see those familiar violet eyes and dark hair. It's the dimpled smile I miss. One faint and the other clearly visible. She's laughing with another woman who's taller and has a wider smile. From her nose up, all I see is Parker. There's a cauldron in front of them. They were lab partners.

I squeeze the book to my chest to put something between us. Anything so his words aren't carving me open.

"Where did you find this?"

"Doxlothia yearbooks. You don't know anything about linked mates, do you?"

I shrug. I hate answering rhetorical questions.

"Linked mates' lives run parallel to each other until they diverge. But no matter what, accepted bond or not, they will remain linked till death. Perhaps beyond, who knows? So, say you do reject your bond with Parker, you find another man to marry you—very unlikely now, by the way—Parker would, too, marry. Say you have a baby girl with those beautiful eyes of yours. Parker will also have a girl. Then one day you decide to enroll that child in school, you might find they attend the same one. Your children would probably end up friends. Even if you traveled as far as you could away from him, you would always find your way back to each other somehow. It's quite fascinating."

"Again, I say you seem very interested in my life."

I take a step back toward the door to get Darien out of my space and my head so I can think. But when I blink, he's in front of me. This time, I'm not afraid of his teeth in my neck.

"Exactly, Olivia. Always remember that this is a game. And you of all people should know the way to win is to think a few steps ahead."

"Is that why you showed up when Barrett took me alone into the woods?"

"Of course. Can you imagine what would have happened if he'd actually marked you then? Parker would be front page for murder."

"And that would be bad for you."

The edges of his smile curl insidiously.

"Why would I want to remove the most interesting players off the board?"

He brushes my shoulder as he passes for the stairs. "Read your books. Cuddle with your mate. But remember the game."

I stop him when I hear the top step creak.

"Wait ..."

He's right. I should be focused on the game everyone here is apparently playing. But I'm still lingering on his words. My palms sweat as I grip the book close to my chest. The nagging question floats to my lips.

"Whose mother died first? His or mine?"

I know the answer. The knot of it grows in my throat. If we're linked, one of us must be the trigger for the other.

"Yours," he says before disappearing and leaving me in the study. "My condolences."

I'm the thorn in Parker's side. The thing that took and continues to take from him.

I'm left with the weight of it when I make my way back to my room. I linger, with the half-turned knob of my door, and lay my head on the wood. My head is full of the life Parker could've had if he wasn't linked to me—loved in his mother's arms, a father who was present ... another girl, someone better. Someone who could share in the bond with him.

A pack full of people who love him.

It's not fair. Everything that's happened to Parker is my fault.

I'm such a coward.

I let go of the knob and knock on Parker's door while the picture burns a hole in my pocket. He opens it and lets me in without a single word.

Chapter Thirty-Four

Parker

Olivia's feet dangle in the flowers as she swings.

I place a hand on her forehead, and she stops. "You're burning up."

"Something is coming." She frowns, staring out the window where the storm clouds gather.

I don't think I've ever been in so much pain in my life. This doesn't even compare to getting my shit rocked on the daily and my skin torn open for afternoon fun. No. This is infinitely worse.

Once I scented her, it was like a bomb went off. I've never smelled anything so fucking good. She's always smelled that way, but I wasn't able to sense it. But now I can't think about anything else.

It's sweet torture to have her scent linger on all my clothes. It's knives in the heart, a sick aching in my stomach, and yearning that has me stealing little pieces of her clothes and stuffing them in my gym bag to smell after practice like a creep. But I can't tell her any of that, or I'll add to her mounting pressure.

I have some weird ominous dream, and she sneaks out again in the early morning. That's my cue to get on the ice and subject myself to someone's ice blade in my thigh. It took no effort to take me down on the ice, and as I look up to the blinding lights, I contemplate never getting up again and letting the Zamboni bring sweet death. That or bleed out on the ice. Both sound good.

Zant helps me off the ice and tries to give me his form of a pep talk, then tells me about council bullshit. He doesn't understand how my biology won't let me focus on anything that isn't Olivia right now. Aster and Barrett have been oddly quiet since our talk in the woods, and that's probably because the bomb that's blown up the entire interweb says Olivia and I are linked mates. Who knows what they're plotting now?

I should care. I do care.

But I care a little more about what the hell Olivia is doing right now.

Eating a scone in the library? Taking a stroll on the lawn? Lying in bed thinking about me?

I need to see her. It's not stalking if it's friendly, right? Just a quick glance to see she's okay, then I'll be good to go about my day of agony.

Okay, maybe it's creepy either way, but I get a free pass to check on her once a day.

I don't find her in Noxx House, but it's a great way to trace her steps for the day. She's easy to track, solely because we're linked mates and her scent is so strong.

That term in my head is still taking some adjustment. Along with the fact that I remember all the dreams I missed out on. It's like a whole lifetime worth of memories dumped in my lap all at once. Even more than before, Olivia is everywhere.

I track her scent to the dance studio, not that I needed to track her to know that's where she went this morning, but she isn't there anymore, and it's nearly noon. Next, I follow the scent into the castle. It's a little all over the place in the lobby, but I follow it to the left and up the stairs to a hallway I'm pretty sure she doesn't have a class in. There are so many people muddying up her perfect scent.

There's a dark-haired girl in Noxx House purple standing in the common area. The sun from the arched windows lights up her hair. It's the wrong shade of brown, and this girl is taller, but why does she smell like Olivia?

I stand over her, leaning in to sniff her hair. It's so strong. I'm entranced by it, as I stumble forward into this random chick, and catch myself with my hands on her shoulders.

"Why the fuck do you have her shirt on?" It's harsh, but the alpha blood is kicking my ass on self-control. Did they steal this from her locker?

"Do you like it?" she says, eyes sparkling with excitement.

Pain shoots through the center of my chest like I'm getting rammed with a Rage stick right in the heart.

Then I smell her—my girl.

But it's fleeting, moving away.

"Move."

I brush past the girl and chase Olivia's scent through the crowd.

The pain is growing, and my face heats as I walk past door after door.

I stop at a door at the end of the hall. All my senses settle. She's close. There's a soft sniffling inside. She wants space, so I have to use my full willpower to stay outside. When she emerges, I'm both impressed and sad that she hides her tears so well. The only indicator is the redness in her cheeks.

"I sensed it. Through the bond," I say. "She had your shirt on. It wasn't ... it wasn't what it looked like."

"I know. I don't know what I'm doing or why I'm crying."

Olivia's eyes well with tears again, and I haul her into a hug while she sheds the rest of them into my shirt. We're getting looks, but I hide her face with my jacket.

"There's a lot going on," I murmur. "You don't have to know how you feel about it all at once. Have you eaten today?"

I plant a kiss on her forehead, and she wipes her cheek. We haven't talked at all. You don't need to talk to hold someone while they sleep.

"I did."

"At five this morning?"

She nods.

I take her to the dining hall immediately and fill a plate with a high-protein sandwich, fruit, and some fries. We sit in front of a window where it's warmer. She keeps rubbing her hands over her legs like she's cold, so I give her my blazer.

My worry dissipates when she takes a few bites of her sandwich.

"With everything going on, it makes my stomach hurt, so I haven't wanted to eat a lot. But I think that's making it worse."

"So that's why I feel like I want to puke every time I wake up?" I say, handing her a fry.

She nibbles it slowly. "Haven't you seen the latest about Olivia Osborne?"

"No. I try not to check that stuff."

She slides her phone in front of me, and the entire feed is filled with her or us. Some are just full threads dedicated to her. The others are weird theories about our relationship. I stop when I read a headline: *Olivia – The Master Manipulator.*

The stealing is starting to make sense.

"I should say something."

"No, that will just make it worse." She sighs. "I'll just let everyone at Doxlothia hate me right now."

"I don't hate you." I move the hair gathering close to her food and push it behind her ear.

Stupid. So stupid. Of course she knows I don't hate her. Now I look like an asshole who is pressuring her. I cringe internally at my own pathetic monologue.

The corner of her mouth twitches. "I know."

She likes it.

"Everyone only started to like me when I won Rage games. When I first came, I'd scroll through the forums looking at all the things people had to say about me. They thought I was going to tank the team because I didn't have a pack."

I still remember the sinking anxiety of scrolling through all the comments.

Packless.

No way he makes it through the season.

He'll never be pro.

Sometimes, those comments still pop into my brain.

"They always have an opinion. The minute the team tanks, they're all going to turn on me. It's just the way it is. I stopped looking at that shit."

"I'm sorry. I don't think I'm helping your reputation any."

"You don't have anything to be sorry for."

"Yes, I do. Everything is my fault. I make things harder for you."

What does that mean? How could she think she makes my life worse in any way? She's got to be referencing something specific, but there's no indication she's going to tell me what that is. I'll just have to show her she's wrong, and that takes time.

"Olivia, can I tell you something?"

She waits, eyebrows raised.

"Fair warning, everything that comes out of my mouth is going to sound like I love you, and I don't want to add any more pressure to you."

She stops eating, blinking suddenly. "Tell me anyway."

"You don't need to be jealous of another woman. Ever. Especially ones that steal your sweater. I don't think either you or I have even begun to process this. I mean, you could tell me to go away and leave you alone, and I'd have to stalk you wherever you went. Nonnegotiable. I'll drop out of university and follow you. They'll have to lock me away to stay away from you."

A trickling laughter comes out of her throat when she sees I'm serious.

"That's what makes you smile today? The image of me stalking you?"

"I'm imagining you peeking in my window and watching me sleep."

"Oh, you like that thought, huh?"

"Like I'm ever able to sleep without you anyway."

She leans toward me, and all the fear and worry that's been tainting her scent is gone. Her attention floats to my lips, and I lean in, desperate to taste her lips again. It tells me what I knew before the bond. This thing with Olivia is real.

A tall man in a dark-brown suit and a velvet tie catches my eyes as he stalks toward us in the dining hall.

That man is my father.

"Why the fuck is my dad here?" I say, reeling back.

Olivia's head shoots up as he nears. Accompanying him is a woman with her hair smoothed down in a sleek blonde ponytail. His dark hair hasn't started to gray yet. I'm a little shocked. I haven't seen him in months since I didn't go home for the summer.

"This is your father?" Olivia looks up as he stands over us.

"You must be Olivia." He nods, holding out his hand. "I'm Fredrick Owens."

She takes his hand in a firm handshake. I can tell because his brow raises like he's somewhat impressed.

"You look a lot like your mother."

She squints. "You remember her?"

"I remember her dancing. We attended Doxlothia at the same time."

Olivia blinks a few times like she's registering that, and I take that as my cue to cut in.

"What the fuck?" I say.

"You didn't expect me to see my son's name at the top of the Vviveren City Newspaper and not be the one to come and register him into the linked mates' registry."

"You could have called first."

"What registry?" Olivia asks.

The woman next to him—probably his assistant—speaks in a calm, chipper tone. "Linked mates need to register. There's testing to ensure it's a true match, and it protects you both in the event that you solidify the bond. Have you solidified it yet?"

"That feels intrusive," I say to my father, who is staring at Olivia.

His bushy, untamed brows are drawn together, as his calculating eyes fixate on her. Oh, hell no. He can treat me like shit, but I don't even want to give him the chance around her.

"It's protocol. And it's for the safety of your mate."

I should have expected the Werewolf Council to get involved, but my dad showing up is still a rare occurrence in my life. I wouldn't have taken that bet.

"We haven't," Olivia says.

"This sounds a little ..." *Like it might stress Olivia out.*

"It's okay. We can register. What do I have to do?" Olivia says.

"Give me your finger." The nurse holds a hand out for Olivia, with a needle in the other.

We're in the infirmary, and there's light coming from the windows, but the curtains are drawn with us all huddled together. I don't like the way they're closing in on Olivia.

A growl rumbles from my throat.

"It's just a tiny prick. She'll be fine," the nurse assures.

Olivia pats the bed next to her for me to sit, and her fingers slide over mine as they prick her finger, then mine.

Then they're close to her again, looking at the mark on her neck. I'm completely rigid and on edge with them poking at her. Every move she makes, I fight a muscle twitch. They're doing this to torture me, surely.

"We've already run a thorough check of your histories, and you both meet the criteria for linked mates. Now we're checking a sample of your blood after the marking."

My dad is watching us with his hands in his pockets. "Hundreds each year try to claim themselves as linked mate pairings. The council must test."

I wonder if he thinks we're bluffing. He never gives me the benefit of the doubt. I bet he wanted to come to do damage control for what he thinks is a fluke. Can't have his son being an embarrassment.

The nurse's scan is quick.

"Yep. Parker's blood matches with Olivia's. It can only be tested for once a mark has been placed. It changes your blood cells. You even become the same blood type. Looks like you're the first linked mate pair in more than a century."

Olivia's heart rate shoots up, and I wrap my fingers around hers to comfort her.

"I'll get the paperwork started. I will need your signatures."

There's a long rambling about paperwork. Court dates to attend. Lots of things I can barely keep straight because *fucking stars above, Olivia and I are linked mates*. It's still as permanent as it was when I marked her, but the registry makes it set in.

As a kid, I went through a phase where I found the idea of linked mates so fascinating. A lot of Were children do. Even though magic exists, linked mates' rarity makes it seem like some fairytale. And when one pops up, multiple will follow, and that's the phenomenon so many crave. Throughout history, it's often brought about peace—even back at the beginning before all interspecies decided to live peacefully, because linked mate pairs are associated with prosperity and connection. No one can predict it, and they're not even sure why it happens.

My dad's assistant opens a large book and motions toward Olivia and me. "This states your names, and date of birth into the official registry. Please sign."

There's another pinprick, and I use my bloody thumb to press into the cool paper next to my name. Olivia does the same. All signatures in Vviveren are in blood. It's seen as the highest oath.

"Feel okay?" I ask Olivia.

Her scent is calm, and that's making all of this easier.

"I'm fine." She motions to my father. "You don't have to watch over me."

"I would like to talk to you outside if I could." My father motions toward the door.

I don't want to leave Olivia, but telling my dad to fuck off right now seems like the wrong move, so I follow him out into the hall, where I can still easily see her. There's a little window cut out in the wooden door.

"You look good," he says. "A mate ... linked mates. This is great."

Great for him and the prestige it will bring to the family.

"Thanks ... Olivia is extraordinary. She's warm and talented. Wants to continue her mother's dream of being in the IBCE. You'd admire her work ethic."

"And have you met her father yet?"

"No, not yet."

Speaking of not knowing how we feel yet, Olivia's father is a whole new added stress to the mix. She obviously thinks he's a dick, so I'm inclined to agree with everything she says, but also ... he made her. My perfect person. So in a way, I already want him to like me. That's gonna be a killer on my daddy issues, considering I can't even get my father to have fun talking to me.

There's no small talk with my father. No *"How are your classes?"* or *"Rage team going okay?"*

He only asks about things he cares about.

"The offseason tournament is coming up." He checks his phone before looking up to me.

"Yeah, I know."

"You're prepared? It's a big time for you. If you're set on going pro, you need to win."

As if I could forget the stress of my future career sitting on my shoulders, while my life erupts into chaos.

"I know, Dad. You don't have anything to worry about."

He nods, never really making eye contact with me. I think he's got more wrinkles than when I last saw him. At least by the eyes.

"Well, it's good to see you."

"Yeah." I wave him off, and my feet stick to the floor.

The imprint of his fingers burns my shoulder after he goes to stand by Olivia while she inquires more about linked mates, but I stay with my back against the door. I don't like looking at my father for the same reason he doesn't like looking at me. He reminds me of Mom and a brief time when things were different and we were all happy. He doesn't seem the same type of happy as before. I guess I'm not either. Like there was a before and after Mom type of happy we just learned to deal with.

My father asks Olivia about ballet and offers her a brief condolence for her mother. There's this little chip in my armor even I don't think about unless he's here. I'm already counting down the minutes till he's gone.

"I'm sorry you've been paired with my son. I tried my best." He says it like a lighthearted joke, but I grit my teeth and let my head hit the door.

He's going to embarrass me. Tell her about how much I got in trouble in private school with Zant, which was nothing but harmless fun like skipping classes to run around the city or organizing a fighting club in the pool room at night.

"Parker is an amazing mate. You should be very proud of him," Olivia says with no hesitation.

My shoulders drop from my ears at the sincerity in her voice.

"That boy has been trouble most of his life."

"If you're not proud of Parker, you're not paying attention," Olivia says.

The room stays silent after.

Chapter Thirty-Five

Olivia

"You're my mate," he whispers. I think it's the most beautiful thing I've ever heard.

I don't stay off the forums. It's hard when Emma won't stop sending me things with my name in them—everything has my name in it. I'm sitting on the ballet floor, darning a set of my ballet shoes while scrolling through it all. My stomach is sick again. Only a handful of people in the company will talk to me, and unfortunately, Octavia is out today.

"Olivia, we need to work on your solo." The director slaps the barre pole, and it snaps me from my spiral.

"Right."

"You're properly warmed?"

"Yes." More or less. I shove my phone in my bag and tug off my leg warmers.

The music for Giselle starts, and I lift on my standing leg and lower my arms, focusing on keeping pretty lines. My first variation is perfect, but the second, I wobble, even with my partner. We aren't synced yet, and it's my fault. I'm the weak link. I've been distracted.

Keep it fluid on the top and balance. Balance. Balance. I'm a beat behind. My face slips for a second, and I'm dizzy because my breathwork sucks. I try to catch up. *Push. Push. Push.*

My foot slips and my balance falters till I'm falling so hard I don't have a choice but to put my arms down to catch myself.

A sharp pain rings through my wrist, and I pull my arm up to my chest and steady myself with my eyes closed.

I don't care because my ankle is throbbing.

"Are you all right?" Mrs. Vix asks.

"I'm fine." I let out a shaky breath. I don't know if I can stand, but I can't lose my spot.

Not standing is not an option.

"Then let's start again."

Snickering comes from the other girls as I go to stand.

Theo reaches to help me, and I shoo him. No one thinks I can do this. I can't show weakness here. I breathe through the throbbing, determined to push through.

If I lose my spot for the performance, I may not get another opportunity to prove myself. This is my only chance.

"Dear, be truthful, are you well?"

I place my wrist down and wince at the stinging pressure. Fia's satisfied smile mocks me in the mirror. *No. No. No. I'm not giving up my spot.*

"I can dance." I assure Mrs. Vix.

"Looks like she hurt her wrist," the room rumbles in a whisper.

Mrs. Vix goes to open her mouth again, but the hall bell rings, and she sighs. "One moment."

Making my way to my feet is difficult with one hand, and my fingers don't move when I attempt to bend them. Theo grabs me by the elbow and helps me to the other end of the room, and I'm too humiliated to protest. When Mrs. Vix comes in, her eyes beeline to me.

"I've got a linked mate dripping water and blood in my hallway."

When I reach the hallway, Parker's standing in his full uniform with no shoes, like he ripped his skates off and rushed here. His hair is wet with sweat and blood, and he's looking me up and down like he's worried I might die on the spot. There's a scratch on his cheek oozing blood but healing before my eyes.

"I'm fine," I say, to get that look off his face.

"Let me take you to the nurse." He almost knocks over a stone statue in the hall on his way to me.

"Splendid idea," Mrs. Vix says.

"No, I can dance," I say desperately. "Please don't give up my spot."

"Come back tomorrow, we'll reevaluate."

"But ..."

My voice is hollow as she almost shuts the door.

"I know how much you want this spot, Olivia. Rest up. We'll see."

Parker effortlessly lifts me into his arms bridal style and starts toward the nurse's office. With my arms wrapped around his neck, the heat emanating from him is blazing hot.

"It's just my wrist."

"I know your ankle hurts."

"How?"

He smiles. "I, uh ... felt your pain through the bond and got tackled to the ground. Then I just bolted for the studio."

"The physical pain?"

"Yeah, but mostly I could feel how upset you were."

I lay with my head on his shoulder and move my throbbing wrist to his chest. Our first performance is in a few weeks, and if let up now, I'll never get this momentum back. This had to happen at the worst time. I've lived with the fear of an injury taking me out of dance since I was a little girl.

Because what would I do?

"Don't worry and get yourself hurt," Dad would say.

It lingers like an itch at the back of my skull. Because what if? What if it crumbles? What if there is no ballet?

"I can't believe I slipped."

Parker's breaths are even and steady as I cling to him.

"It will be okay. You heard her, you'll be back to dancing tomorrow."

I hope he's right. Because what if? *What if?*

Chapter Thirty-Six

I pace the floor next to the fireplace while I wait. My socks catch on the rug, and I almost trip. Olivia is nauseous because she's nervous, and it pulses in and out of the bond as she gets checked out. I squeeze my fingers at the pain in my wrist, as they likely try to adjust her for x-rays.

They wouldn't let me go back with her. She's obviously a grown woman who doesn't need my help but ... what if she does need me? What if the nurses are shit and don't listen to her? What if they hurt her more?

The alpha blood is to blame. I'm so fucking worried I've asked the nurse five times how much longer. I look like a jackass, but I can't stop. We're linked, which means I'm made to protect her. It's basically woven into my DNA. That makes me relax a little after growling at the male nurse in the infirmary when he tried to take her back.

I stop pacing, and Olivia waddles out of the door with a nurse. She's barely hiding that limp. I knew she wasn't going to tell them.

"No breaks. Just a sprain. They suggest taking the day off and resting ... together. Since we're linked, they said your Were cells heal faster, and they think it will heal me quicker through the bond." She sighs and crosses her arms; her wrist is tightly wrapped for support. "Can we go to my room?"

"Done."

I squat, waiting for her to wrap her arms around my shoulders. There's no way she's walking on that ankle all the way back to Noxx House. She rolls her eyes and wraps an arm over my neck, finally giving in.

"Olivia, stop being a stubborn pain in the ass. We have to get off your shoes."

"No, we don't."

"Lay down," I tell her for the second time. She's staring at me from the edge of her bed. I started the hearth for her, and the glow reflects in her defiant eyes. I love her bed and all the overlapping fabrics of blankets she's brought from home. It kinda reminds me of how my mom used to decorate our home. Long dark curtains with various layers and frills.

I smirk when she finally does what I said and undo the ribbons on her legs. Starting with the good ankle, I take off her pointe shoe. The muscles in her calf tense as I do.

"Relax, I'm used to the smell of your feet by now."

"Shut up."

I rummage through her bag and pull out the bandages and fuzzy socks to tend to the few blisters on her foot before moving to the next. Her room is unusually messy, with piles of old clothes at the foot of her bed. She's locked in her head the entire time I tend to her foot and move onto the next one.

I squeeze light pressure at her heel to ground her.

"Okay, I'm going to be gentle. Tell me where it hurts."

"It doesn't hurt that much."

"Why didn't you have the doctor look at your ankle?"

"I just told you."

"I know it hurts, Olivia. I can feel it."

"I'll be fine. I can still dance."

"I know." I assure her, knowing that's all she cares about.

She winces as I remove her shoe, and her fingers claw at the sheets. I soften my touch and run it around the cool skin of her ankle.

"Does it hurt here?"

She shakes her head, and I slowly roll her ankle. Her brow dents while her teeth grind.

"Don't worry. I don't think it's that bad. I can get you some ice." I observe the blister on the top of her foot. "I'll need to rewrap this though."

"Then you'll stay?"

"Do you want me to?"

"I don't know. I'm sorry. I'm so ... so ..."

She catches the tear rolling down her cheek. "I'm overwhelmed. Too many things are going on. I don't know what to do. And it's Giselle, it's not just getting into the IBCE. This is my dream role, and it's slipping away."

My fingers work into her calf. "Relax. It's going to be okay. You'll keep your spot."

"You don't know that."

"I do."

"You definitely need to go back to practice. The tournament is coming up and—"

"Let me worry about practice." I drag my knuckles slowly down her leg and toward her ankle. Her heartbeat slows and she closes her eyes while I work on the tense knots in her muscles.

"Since werewolf saliva has amazing healing qualities, maybe I should just start licking your feet."

Her eyes fly open, and she lets out a worried laugh. "That's disgusting."

I chuckle and lick my lips before planting a kiss on her ankle. "Here, right?"

"Yeah ..."

I press my lips to her ankle bone and toward her heel.

When I drop her leg, she moves to sit up while I unwrap her wrist. I'd do anything to make her better, and the fact I can do this gets my heart pumping. I lick my lips again and kiss the center of her wrist.

"Where does it hurt?"

"It all hurts."

I plant kisses up and down her wrist until my lips are in the center of her palm again. Her skin is warm and delicious, and I'm pretty sure I could do this all day.

"Parker?"

"Yeah?"

"I don't want you to go back to practice. I want you to stay with me."

The way she's looking at me is doing things to me. There's something about when she strips it all away.

"I'll stay, baby." I stop myself. "Sorry, I probably shouldn't call you that now."

Things have changed, and I'm not sure what she'll choose. If she wants to just be friends, I'll make it happen. We've always been friends, and we can stay that way.

She grabs my jersey and tugs me toward her. "I like it."

This time her tongue enters my mouth first. Okay, we aren't friends.

It's torture she can't feel this, how my body identifies her and how it yearns to please—but I can wait for however long she needs to understand how much I care. I don't know how to make her believe me.

"Parker ... will you touch me, and we don't have to tell anyone?"

"We are literally the most talked about couple in Vviveren right now. People know."

"I just want you to touch me, and I don't want to care about anything else."

Her scent blooms with yearning while she grips at my jersey. I know what she's asking me.

"You're injured. Maybe you should rest." I move the hair from her forehead to kiss her there.

"I know you'll be gentle."

She looks up at me with desire brimming. I inhale, marinating in it. It's oddly calm. The aching from being apart is finally quiet, and it's like nothing else matters.

I rest a hand under her chin. "I'll touch you, and it's our secret for today ... it's just you and me."

Our lips meet in a slow, wet cadence. I kiss her cheek. Her neck. When my lips graze my mark on her skin, she moans.

"I want more than last time ... I want you," she says.

"Whatever you want, baby."

I'm already hard. I don't know how many times I've fantasized about this, but her touch is better than any dream.

This is different from anything we've done before, not that I want her any less. I didn't think it was possible to want her more, but this is a new kind of want. It's almost sacred. We won't be able to take this back. I feel it in our rapid heartbeats and the way her fingers dig into my skin.

She watches me strip. Then kisses my chest between me taking her clothes off. I'm careful to avoid her wrist.

"Wait." I stop just short of tugging off her shorts. "Tell me why."

Hovering over her, I drag a finger down the valley of her breasts, and her breaths melt into long sighs. Nothing has ever felt this good. Because she's *my mate*.

"Is it because you want to feel good and I'm the only one you trust to touch you?" I ask.

Her back arches into my touch when I bring my fingers below her belly button.

"Or is it because ... you think about me touching you, only me, and you want more ..."

Either way, I'm hers, but I need to know for my own sanity, that way I can pick up the little pieces of my heart enough to function.

"It's only you that I want." Her violet and golden eyes glisten in the dim light of the hearth.

Yep. Her pants are coming off. We're about to have sex. And we're in her room, which means ... Oh, shit—

"Fuck. I don't have any protection."

"Oh, I started taking the protection potion a couple weeks ago."

Those words send my skin ablaze with the itch of shifting, and I tower over her, pressing her hips into the mattress.

"You did that ... thinking about me?"

"Yes." Her gaze shifts uneasily. "I thought it might be a good idea so we didn't need to worry about anything when we ..."

"We?" I brush my fingers over her stomach. Still reeling from the fact that she thought about this. *Weeks ago.*

"When I asked you to have sex with me." She swallows, with her heart stuttering.

She's so fucking cute. Her cheeks are all red like she's embarrassed to admit it.

"Holy shit, Olivia. You're a dream. You're *my* dream."

"Will you?"

"Yeah, baby, I will."

She squirms while I strip off her underwear, then pin her by the elbows.

"Careful. Your only job today is to take what I give you and let me keep you from hurting yourself further. This is really your first time?"

She nods. "I almost did once with my dance partner. But he left before it happened."

Olivia opened up about her asshat dance partner over dinner once and the night he made her cry. *Fucker.* But his colossal loss is my momentous gain.

"That night I had a dream ... about you."

Oh, fuck yes. She left out that part. "Tell me more."

I lick between her breasts and take a nipple in my mouth, and she arches into my touch. Her perfect breasts I've been wanting to touch and taste. So many times, I've imagined this. Her breasts are full and supple. It's messy and wet as I suck, and we both moan. I want to savor it. Olivia is completely naked and firmly set in my arms.

"So you've been fantasizing about this for a long time, haven't you?"

I pick a spot on her collarbone to press my lips to. My mind runs wild with all the things I want to do. *Mine. Mine. Mine.*

"I didn't know it was you until after I met you."

"It's always been me, baby. I've been waiting for you for so long. Every night, I was with you."

My tongue runs over my mark, and she gasps.

"You can't—"

A hum runs through my throat at the way her body presses into mine when I lick there. Her fingernails dig into my shoulder. The whimper that leaves her throat when I suck at her skin brings the itch through my entire body.

"Wait. I'm going to ..."

"Just from my mark? Oh. That's so fucking hot."

My blood is boiling. Every second, I'm more excited to touch her, but she needs me to be gentle. I have to take care of her. I want to be inside her, but she needs to be relaxed and ready.

"In these fantasies, how long does it take you to start begging for me?"

I kiss each finger on her injured hand before safely placing it on the pillow next to her head and giving attention to her breasts. She squirms again when my tongue meets her nipple, and I nibble at the underside of her breast.

"I need you," she breathes into my hair.

"I know."

The mess on her thighs gives her away, with my fingers teasing her between her legs.

"Shit. There's no way you are already that wet for me."

I think of her eyes when I pinned her in the bathroom stall. She wanted me inside her because she'd imagined it. Over and over.

"Are you finally going to tell me about those dreams?"

There's so much I want to do with her, but for now, keeping her from using her hand and injured ankle is my priority. This time will be different, but still, it's everything I've wanted. I kiss her hand. Knowing as our skin touches, I'm healing her.

I don't want to break the connection.

"You snuck into my bed," she says.

"Oh? You mean like this?" I focus on her clit, moving in slow circles.

Her hips buck, and a strangled whimper leaps from her throat.

She's ready for me. I just want a few more minutes to look at her and revel in how she's completely naked, with wetness covering her thighs from me touching her. The only clothing left between us is my boxers. My mouth waters at the sight. I'm going to claim her, and everyone is going to know.

"Parker, please."

"What, baby?"

"I need you inside me."

"You're so pretty when you beg."

She really is. *My* girl is coming undone in front of me.

I reach my hand into my boxers to thumb over the precum on my cock, then press my fingers into her. Slow at first, then deeper until she's writhing and clenching around my hand. There needs to be more of me inside her. She needs to be full.

"Tell me more, go on."

She gasps as I curl my fingers to strum inside her.

"Yeah? Tell me about the dream," I ask, knowing she can't talk while she's coming apart on my fingers.

She doesn't understand the obsession. How I'm already thinking of how every drop of me inside her is going to make her smell like me. She has my mark and now ...

She's gasping when I pull out.

"You were in my bed, and you'd come every night to—" She catches her breath. "To strip me, and we would ... have sex. It felt so good—"

I can't go another second without being inside of her. My boxers are off before I pull the blankets on top of us so she's warm and comfortable.

"Was it like this?"

"Yes. Exactly like this."

My fingers graze her cheek. "I need you to know something ... if we do this, I'm not going to let anyone else have you, even if we reject the bond. I know that makes me an asshole, but I don't care. I need you to know how seriously I take this."

Even just once with Olivia will ruin me. Because she is *the* girl. I couldn't keep myself from her if I wanted to. Even if she married, I'd still be here watching her live her life and silently waiting for the day she comes back to me. And I think I could let her if we never have sex and connect like this, but I won't be able to afterward. I won't be able to see her with someone else without making it everyone's problem. It might even tear us apart, make it to where we couldn't go back to being friends, and I can't live without her.

"I don't want anyone else," she says.

"No. If you want another man to ever touch you like this, tell me right now. Because I'm not joking. If you've ever had any hopes of meeting another man when you're older or dating your dancing partner—"

"I only want you. I mean it."

That sentence is all I've ever wanted. I take in that last second. One final moment before we can't go back. The warmth of her skin and the smell of calm in her scent.

"You're so beautiful." I graze her bottom lip with my thumb and push into her, inch by inch. I kiss her forehead. Then her cheek. "You're mine."

The world stops when I'm completely inside her. I'm so scared of hurting her I can't let myself fully experience the pleasure of it yet.

"Feel, okay?"

She nods. "Parker ..."

"Yeah, baby?" Our noses are touching.

"I love you."

I was right. Being inside Olivia is the greatest fucking moment of my life. I thrust into her slowly. "I love you too."

Another thrust. "So."

Then another. "Fucking."

And another. "Much."

Nothing too hard, I'll know if I've hurt her because of the bond. There's only the swelling pleasure as she opens up further and further. She needs to feel this love and remember it, whether she chooses to bond with me or not, because she deserves it.

I'm so lost in her. Her pleasure runs through me as something tight builds inside me the more I grind into her. This is otherworldly pleasure. It's got to be our linked mate bond.

"Parker it's *so* much."

"I know." I soothe her, with my lips at her ear. "But I'm made for you, baby. You can take it."

I nudge her knee open, and she gasps as I fill her deeper. This is how it should be.

"See, we fit. It's perfect."

Those beautiful, perfect legs shake, and the imprints of my fingers on her thigh are the only place I'm willing to leave a mark on her today.

The only noise in the room is the sound of the bed frame creaking while I grind into her over and over. Her orgasm flush comes so quickly I almost come too.

She gasps my name in shock.

I stop. Letting her ride it out as she squeezes my cock and her pleasure floods my senses. I'm dizzy. Shaky. This is different. Of course, it is. We're linked in ways I hadn't realized.

I can't imagine what this would be like with the mating bond complete.

With one arm, I haul her on top of me, still careful of her wrist that I kiss a few more times for good measure. It was so fast. I can't last like this, so I have to make sure she's perfectly satisfied.

"I need you to come for me again."

Her eyes are glassy. "I don't know if I can."

"Don't be a quitter, Olivia."

Her eyes spark with defiance, and I wrap her hair around my hands, tugging and guiding her till I'm inside her again. She's so fucking wet. Her head falls back as her body shakes from the pleasure. The sight of her riding my cock is what I imagine it must be like for people who freak out over art. Because she looks like a painting created just for me. Her orgasm is blinding as we ride the wave again, with clenched fists and soft-spoken whispers. I have to bury my face into her hair to steady myself.

"I don't know how long I can last like this." I lick the sweat on her neck and nip at my mark. "Fuck. I can feel everything."

"Everything?" She rests her forehead on mine.

"Yeah. It's the bond I feel every sensation you feel."

We stay connected when I spin her and pin her to the bed. I'm not done running my lips over her skin. Anywhere I can reach.

Lifting her hip with one hand, I go deeper. "See that ... I know that you need me right ... there. And every time I hit that spot, it's like ... I can't think. It's ..."

We both moan, teetering on the edge. There aren't words for it. Her eyelids flutter as I demonstrate my point, driving deeper and hitting that spot over and over.

I run my finger over her nipples, licking my lips. "And when I touch you here, your body flushes with this ache, like you want me so bad you'll let me do anything."

"I will," she breathes.

Her nipple is in my mouth in seconds, and I thrust inside her. I suck on her breast, hitting that spot until we're both seconds from coming.

"You should ... finish inside me."

My heart stutters, and my inner wolf leaps into the driver's seat. I squeeze her, plunging deeper inside her. I've wanted it so bad I banned it from my thoughts because it physically hurt to think it might never happen.

"You'd like that?" I ask.

My muscles twitch with the itch of shifting when she whispers her acceptance. I leave her lying on the bed and lift her hips before placing a pillow under her lower back.

"I need you to smell like me as long as possible after this."

"Okay. Whatever you want." Her leg wraps around my waist, and her fingers twist in my hair. That injured hand is already feeling better.

I slip inside her again. She's so tight and wet. I lap at her neck where my mark is till that tension snaps, and it's only seconds of that aching till she's loose in my arms—spent and blissful. My release spills inside her, and I work to ensure all my thrusts fill her just how I want. The bed frame creaks when I grip the headboard on either side of her.

In the sobering seconds after, I track her scent for any fear, uncertainty, doubt, but she's relaxed. She just wants me to hold her.

It's minutes of me caressing her head before we separate. I wait for her breath to slow and her heart to calm, and show careful attention to every drop that spilled out of her, pushing it back in.

"Don't get up. Not for a few more minutes. I'll reserve you a bath down the hall."

"This changes things," she says, eyes trained on the ceiling.

Her hands rest on her chest over her heart, fingering the ends of her hair. She's right. Having casual sex with Olivia was never going to be an option.

"Yeah … it does." I lay my head on the pillow beside her. "You okay?"

She's smiling when she turns to me. "As long as you don't feel like bolting."

"Funny I was going to ask you the same thing."

"No urge."

"Good. Because I've got a hot date tonight, which includes watching you sleep."

CHAPTER THIRTY-SEVEN

OLIVIA

"Stay with me."
"Stay with me."
"Stay with me, please."
Parker won't stop crying.

I wake in the middle of the night in Parker's arms.

There's something eerie and uncomfortable in the air. A dream I need to remember lingers but won't take shape. It's right on the edge of my tongue, but as I blink in the darkness, it fades into nothing, never to be caught again.

All the pain I'd had the day before is completely gone. My wrist. My ankle. Both healed all by Parker's desire and meticulous work of his lips.

I sit up and he stirs, dragging me back down with him. There's claustrophobia in his arms, and a relentless racing of my thoughts.

He still doesn't know.

Parker doesn't understand how I truly feel, and it's my fault he doesn't. Maybe he still thinks I'm playing games with him, like I might string him along for my own pleasure. Contrary to what everyone else in the school thinks, I could never hurt Parker in that way. He's my best friend. He's ... my mate. Through my life, he was there, even if I couldn't sense it.

There's a lump in my throat when I hear his voice.

"Hey, baby."

"Parker ..."

I've never needed someone like this before. I've never needed love, but if I don't have his, I might burst. My heart will stop instantly. The dam inside me will burst and nothing can repair it.

But he doesn't know, and suddenly, all I want is to make him understand.

My lips meet his bare chest, and my body is on fire again. Like how it always feels when he touches me— I never want him to stop. It's a never-ending need embedded in my skin that wakes when he's here. He stirs, caressing my head while I kiss down his abdomen. His fingers tighten in my hair, sending a prickle of pleasure down my spine.

"What ... are you doing?" he asks.

"I want you. I need you."

"Wait, what's wrong?"

Of course he can tell. I can't hide from him. I'm absolutely bare despite the coverage of night. It's so uncomfortable.

"Just let me make you feel good." My lips don't meet his stomach again because he tugs on my arm.

"Come here."

He pulls me till we're face-to-face. The light from the hearth is dim in the corner, and his blue eyes are fully awake as a finger runs under my jaw.

"I know it's the bond that makes you feel like this, but it's more than that for me. I need you to know I wanted you before."

I desperately need him to know I want to stay with him. Everyone thinks I'm not good enough for Parker, and maybe I'm not, but I want to be.

"Wait. The bond isn't the reason I want you."

"You don't know that."

It makes more sense if it is. All of it is easier to compartmentalize that way.

"Olivia, I love everything about you. Bond or not."

Tears pool in my eyes. It's so quick. I don't understand why his words draw the emotion from a hidden place inside me.

"You don't. You can't. The bond came first and then you just accepted this. It could have been anyone."

"Why do you think that?"

"I ... don't see how."

"How I could love you?"

I nod. "You deserve someone better. Someone who can feel this and will be an amazing mate, who no one would say you could do better with. They wouldn't make this so hard."

He wipes another tear. "Is that what all this is about?" I hide in his forearm, but he turns my chin to look at him. "Tell me why."

"You don't know. You'll hate me when you know. Just tell me it's the bond, and that's the only reason. It's better if that's all this is because then I can't hurt you and you can't hurt me."

"Know what?" He tucks the hair behind my ear, and his voice rumbles in a low hum next to my cheek.

"That I'm the reason for all the terrible things that happened to you. My mom died *first*. It's my fault you never got the pack. It's my fault you have a terrible relationship with your father. It's ... me. I'm your catalyst. Of all the mates you could have had, you're stuck with me. A girl who doesn't care about anything but ballet. Who's a mediocre sister at best."

I'm wriggling away, but Parker won't let me hide. He hauls me beneath him, pinning my hips and kissing the tears on my cheeks away.

"Olivia, who told you that you ruin things?"

"I did. I ruin things for you. For myself. My sisters. My parents ... but I don't want to hurt you. I won't make a good mate because you deserve more. I'm never as good as I should be, and I don't want to let you down. You'll end up hating me, and I couldn't stand it if *you* hated me."

"Baby, relax. Breathe."

I'm crying so hard I can't catch my breath, but Parker's pressure is good. I can't remember the last time I let someone see me cry like this. He's all the things I'm not. We may be alike in almost all aspects, fated parallels, but he's the most solid, confident person I've ever met. Immovable. I grip his arms, grounding myself in their strength.

"It's not your fault. None of it was ever your fault. Things happen. Your mom ... my mom they wouldn't have ever wanted you to think like that. My mom would have loved you. I'm sure she does, somewhere up there in the stars. The bond ... it's a gift. What came first was you and me. I don't need the mate bond to be in love with you. I love you. *You*. Olivia. I loved you before I knew we were mates. You are an amazing sister, and your mom would be so proud that despite everything you've been through, you still held yourself together and your family. But you don't have to do it all by yourself anymore. I found you."

"You found me," I choke.

"I'm not going anywhere. You don't scare me."

There's always been a piece missing. Even when I was certain my ballet form was at its best or my sisters threw me the best birthday party I could imagine, I always wanted more, but I didn't understand what. I thought I could fill that want with more ballet because ballet is the only thing that's ever made me feel whole. But the thrill was fleeting and fragile, like the idea of it had a leak because the thing I wanted was Parker. Somewhere out there I could sense him. My mate. And now I know the success would pale in comparison to being known by Parker Owens.

His kiss tastes like salt, and there's a slight hum in his throat.

"Will you let me make love to you? Show you that it's always been you."

I nod while he wipes the remaining tears on my cheek.

"Okay ..."

He flips us so I'm on top and pulls down his boxers, then with two fingers, he tugs my underwear aside and thrusts inside me. There's a good friction as he stretches me. The whimper that leaves his throat as he drives deeper sends a shiver through my entire body.

"Oh, Parker." My nails dig into his back. "I want this."

"I *know*." He grins, working his hips.

"I love you," I say, clenching around him while the familiar pool of wet heat builds in my abdomen.

The breath sputters from my lungs. I'm so full of him I can't think, but I love watching him watching me. The way he adjusts his weight at every soft sound from my throat. That glossy look in his eye, and those moans of praise from his lips.

Sex for us should be awkward and new—at least for me—but our bodies clear that hurdle for us. There are no awkward bits, just blinding pleasure we both work through.

"Is this how we bond now?" He chuckles as he exhales, kissing my jaw.

"Sometimes. Yes." When it's like this. His love mending me. Filling me completely in a way that reminds me this is the most important thing.

He lifts my shirt over my head so his lips can touch my chest and his tongue can roam and explore anywhere he wants.

I want it to last, but I'm already teetering on the edge. Parker was right, we fit together in a way that's like magic. Like he's made to draw pleasure from me, and me from him. I just want him deeper. I want him forever.

He hooks an arm around my waist, and his eyes flutter when he goes deeper. Parker is endlessly charming. Beautiful.

"My mate," I gasp, and the pressure in my abdomen snaps.

We don't discuss it. It just happens; our orgasms burst at the same time as our bodies blend in a harmonious rhythm. He's deep inside me, chasing our pleasure, with his tongue in my mouth. His arm around me keeps me anchored to him till we're both completely spent. My body shakes around him, and he soothes me.

I stay connected to him, and by his satisfied smirk, I know that's exactly what he prefers.

"Tell me how," I say.

"How what?"

"How to accept the bond."

"You want to be mated?"

I love that flicker of happiness in his eyes.

"Yes. I'm sorry I took so long."

"Let's not do it tonight ... I want this night to be about you and me. And we can make it special. Maybe I can take you on the train to the city, and we spend the weekend. Have you ever been?"

I shake my head, entranced by the thought. A moment alone from the mountain side of Doxlothia. Away from all that's still harboring outside my bedroom walls. The voices. The press. The council.

"Oh, you'll love it. I'll get us a fancy hotel room. We'll finally have a king size bed."

We embrace in exhales of relief. We've been given a gift people dream and write stories about. I don't know exactly what the bond will change.

He kisses me again, and it makes my head spin in a delirious elation. "I'm happy we're doing this the right way. Can I call you my girlfriend for real this time?"

"Yes, I like the sound of that."

All I know is I've been running from Parker since I met him, and I don't want to run anymore.

Chapter Thirty-Eight

Parker

I have to find her.

This can't be it. This can't be the end.

She's gone. Those are the first words to ring in my head when I wake up, and Olivia *is* gone. Her bed is empty while the scent of her lingers on her pillows. The fire in the hearth has turned to ash, and the light from her window is blinding.

I can't believe I didn't hear her get up.

Something is wrong. There is weight in my chest. I grab my phone, and there's nothing but the Rage group chat notifications waiting for me to sift through.

I ignore them and pop in my room to toss on some clothes, eager to find where she went in a hurry. My mind replays the night over and over again, but it's hard to focus on anything other than the ache in my chest. The strange, unsettling electricity under my skin is getting worse. While pulling on my blazer, I realize it's nervousness. I'm hardly ever nervous, not even before games. It has to be her.

My first guess is the ballet studio, but I don't travel far before I see her standing in the Noxx House common room. It's still early, but there's a crowd chatting and moving about for the school day in a blur of purple. The hairs on my arms raise but I don't see any danger.

"Parker." Olivia's eyes are red. She isn't dressed for ballet.

"What's wrong?"

Someone must have died. That's the only thing that makes sense, the only reason I feel like I'm dying when her gaze settles on me.

She takes a deep breath and forces out the words. "I don't want to be with you anymore."

Oh. "What?"

"I want to break up."

For a moment, I think my heart is breaking. But no. This is all her. It's agony. She tries to hide the trembling of her fingers in the hem of her skirt.

The crowd hears, and their mumbling whispers quiet.

"I don't understand. What is this about?" I step forward and she moves back.

I'm replaying our night in an instant. My hands in her hair and all the things she said about love … and wanting this. Did I do something? I felt the connection. The ease in my senses as she fell asleep on my chest. There was no hint of worry or nervousness. We'd laid it all out. She was happy. She was going to accept the bond.

"Our relationship was fake." Her lips barely move when she speaks. Her eyes are fixed past me. "It was all fake. Everything I said was a lie. You should pick a different mate. Because … I don't want to be with you."

My chest tightens and I swallow the lump gathering in my throat. This is my nightmare I tried to prevent. But something is off.

I look around the entirety of Noxx House. There are people everywhere. Some casually listen, and others stare. There's a reason she's doing this in public, and I want to know why. Things were fine a short number of hours ago. She's obviously upset. I can't even focus on the words she's saying because she's in so much pain, and she's hiding it all under a stoic mask. Every beat of her heart sends an ache through my entire body.

"Are you even going to look at me while you break my heart?"

Her eyes flutter to me and water seconds before she says, "Goodbye, Parker."

She barrels out the front door of Noxx House, and I stare at the spot she leaves long enough to hear the voices around me:

"Pathetic."

"I knew they were faking."

"Was the linked mate thing fake too?"

I don't know what's going on, but I will find out.

Chapter Thirty-Nine

Olivia

"What's coming?" he asks as we stare at the darkening sky.
It's bad. The weight of it is smothering.
We can't run from this. It's inevitable.

"I did what you asked."

I swallow the lump in my throat and grip the sink inside the girls' restroom. It's the one in the courtyard that's covered in moss and surrounded by a huge garden that's riddled with bees and snakes.

My fingers clutch the file folder in my hand, holding it up to the mirror to test it. I can see the contents clearly but in the mirror's reflection they're blank.

I awoke this morning, refreshed and eager to talk to Mrs. Vix, when I noticed a folder sitting in a sweeping of dust on the ground by my door. The front was labeled: *For Rabbit. Love, your biggest fan.*

Inside the folder is a detailed account of Parker's life littered in red.

What would you believe? is typed in red at the top of the report. The truth is in black, and the lies are in red. It details doubt surrounding Parker and his rise to team captain: vague accounts from faked sources detailing Parker's family using money to get him the position on the team and how they're using that to get him in the pro Rage league. There's a picture of him patting Ryker on the back, and notes on Ryker's family's involvement in gambling, and a formal news story with eyewitnesses attesting to the story that Parker and his family are involved in some illegal gambling scheme. It's all fabricated to ensure the reasonable doubt of the public.

And it would work.

Parker wouldn't be allowed on a pro team, and whoever this is could ensure that.

At the bottom it reads: *This file is enchanted for your eyes only. Tell him or anyone else and this goes out on immediate release. Don't test me, Rabbit. This is a win-win situation for me. Check your phone for the next instruction.*

The first thing I tried to do was type what was happening into the notes in my phone when an anonymous text popped up:

I see you got my present.

The number was already programmed in as *Your Biggest Fan.*

It was convincing enough for me to follow the instructions to call the anonymous number and receive my next task: break up with Parker in a public space and admit to the fake relationship immediately or the file will go out.

An unidentifiable, robotic voice speaks on the other end of the phone. "Good. Your next step is to take the ferry to The Hunting Grounds tomorrow. They'll be expecting you. The details of The Hunt are in the back of the folder."

"Fine."

I stop and stare at myself in the mirror, wiping the smudged mascara from the corner of my eyes. Parker being targeted is my fault. If he'd never stuck his neck out for me and my sisters, none of this would be happening to him. I don't know who it is. Parker has enemies coming from every angle. Another tear falls when I think of the look on his face in the common room. There has to be a way around this.

"But only if I have assurance that this will be over once I do. I'm not playing this game with you forever," I say, hardening my words.

"I'm just glad you're playing. After The Hunt, you'll be someone else's mate, and it should be the least of your concerns ... but yes, I can provide you assurances. At the west corner of Languid Lake, there's a tower of quartz you won't be able to miss. Come alone. If you don't, I'll know. And bring something sharp."

Someone's else mate. My stomach sours as the plan comes into view. It's about more than humiliating Parker. This person wants to separate us. I'm so numb I don't contemplate the thought of another man's teeth on my skin.

"What is it?"

"You'll see."

The sun is past the high point in the sky by the time I make my way back to the trail that leads to the courtyard. I suck on the blood on my thumb.

"Place your blood on the stone. And secrets done will be yours alone."

The Secrecy Stone is riddled with blood smudges from the top of the magical stone to the bottom. I almost thought it was a joke when I showed up, but marked with a black marker was a place for my fingerprint on top of another. It's smudged on purpose. A quick search of the stone on the forums and school newspaper brings up stories spanning from the start of the university.

The founders first used the stone to keep the location of Doxlothia a secret until it was safe to share. *All secrets have a beginning and an end point with the stone.*

I stared at it for a full five minutes, fighting the urge to turn back. Whoever did this is thinking steps ahead of me. Could I risk Parker's entire reputation? I played through all the scenarios I could think of before placing my bloody fingerprint on the stone. Nothing is worth risking more harm coming to Parker because of my actions.

"How do I know it's your blood?"

"It won't work if not," the voice hummed on the other end.

"I'm not doing this if I don't know if you'll keep your promise."

"Fine. I'll go first. Hold the phone up to the stone." I turned my phone to face it. *"I ,the creator of this secret, will keep this secret and seal it into the stone. I must not tell anyone or release the information contained in the file or any other damaging information on Parker Owens . This information cannot be released by me or anyone else for the term of our arrangement and will be destroyed once the condition is met."*

The stone illuminated briefly as the arrangement set.

"Now, repeat after me: I, Olivia Osborne, will keep this secret and seal it into the stone. I must join The Hunt and stay until completion or suffer my consequence of the release of the file on Parker Owens."

I reluctantly said the words and the stone glowed again.

"What is the point of this? Making me enter The Hunt won't gain you anything."

"Do you really think he'll want you after you agree to be someone else's mate?"

My heart sinks as the castle comes into view, and the memory fades.

When I reach the edge of the treeline and the familiar weight of safety, I try to type out the words to explain what's happening, but my fingers won't move. The stone vow worked.

Another text comes through: *Told you, Rabbit. Now be a good girl and keep our secret.*

"Skipping class now?"

Parker's voice is next to my ear, and I gasp. He's leaning against a tree, his blazer open and his hair messy like he's pushed his hands through it over and over again. He pulls a vial of potion from his pocket and swirls it in the air.

"I thought I'd bring my girlfriend a little gift from our class project."

"I'm not your girlfriend anymore, remember?" Parker's entire livelihood is at stake. This time, I have to protect him.

"Still my lab partner, though." He smirks, eyeing the people passing on the lawn. "Come on, try it."

I stare at the potion bottle in his hand. Maybe he's on to something. Maybe this potion could override the Secrecy Stone and let me say what I need to say.

Hope flutters in my chest when I reach for the bottle, but Parker catches my hand and inspects my palm and moves a finger over my thumb.

"The Secrecy Stone, huh? Tsk." He sighs, then brings my hand to his face and licks my thumb to heal it.

"You should ask before you do that." I still don't know how closely I'm being watched.

"And maybe you should have told me what was going on before you agreed to a secret vow, Olivia." His gaze darkens and sears into mine. "You should have just come to me. We could have figured it out."

His nostrils flare, and he grips the tree beside me. Maybe he's right, but this is his future. Everything he's worked for is on the line. Being on the pro Rage team is his dream, and I have to support that dream like it's mine.

He gives me a bottle of potion. "This is a long shot but might help."

I pop the cork and take a quick sip. Its power falls over me like a fine mist, and I'm lighter. Open. Like my skin is buzzing. My feet stumble back, and the bottle slips from my hand, spilling to the ground.

"It's okay. You're safe." Parker steadies me.

"I know." The words pass from my lips quickly. It's as if the pause before I think the words is gone. "I'm always safe with you."

"Tell me what's going on."

My mouth moves to say the words. *They're framing you. I didn't have a choice.*

"I can't." I wish I could relay the words through our bond.

He sighs. "It was worth a shot. Can you tell me who it is? Is it Barrett? Aster?"

"I don't know who."

"I wish you would have told me. Why didn't you just come to me first? We could have figured it out."

Pressing my fingers to my forehead, I steady my swirling head. The potion is working, though thoughts are popping up one after another too fast for me to catch them.

"No, we couldn't because this is doomed." My eyes widen as I say the words that feel true. The words flow from my mouth with gentle ease. "This was never going to work out."

I can't believe I'm saying it. Maybe I've always known this wouldn't work.

"You really believe that?"

"Parker, if we bond, this is going to be your life. People will always use me to get to you."

"You don't know that."

"Yes, I do. This is proof. If it's bad now, can you even imagine if we complete the bond? Maybe it's better this way ... Maybe we aren't supposed to do it. It's obvious the universe will do just about anything to prevent it from happening, and I think we should just let it keep us apart. We should cut our ties now. Separate. Let all of this craziness die down."

"You're doing it again. Why do you keep pushing me away?"

"Because this isn't going to work."

I'm a coward. I'm mortified by the words coming from my lips because I've hurt him. Parker's shoulders droop.

"So you mean that? You want this thing between us to end?"

"Yes." I struggle to get the word out.

If it saves him from me ruining his life.

He stumbles back, and I grip the tree for support. It's hard to breathe, and suddenly my skin is hot and miserable. It's all ending before my eyes. There won't be any more kisses or any more of his smile. It all hits me at once. Separating is the best option for us, but I can't do this to him. This is a nightmare. My breaths get shorter and faster. I'm hyperventilating, and tears form in my eyes. Before I can bolt, he pins me against the tree with one arm.

"Tell me, what do you need from me?" His voice is a low hum.

"What?"

"Your scent is screaming for *me*, Olivia. So tell me what you want ..." His words are forceful, but his touch softens with his palm on my cheek.

My eyes nearly flutter shut from the relief.

"I can't."

"Why?"

I shake my head, not able to say the things I need to. I don't know what I'm doing. My heart is thumping in my ears, and I don't know if it's from the fear of his words being right or the proximity of his body against mine.

"Fine. You can't say anything about your secret. Then tell me what you need right now."

"I don't get the question. I need to go—"

He presses in, pinning me with his hips, and his eyes lock with mine. "Not before you tell me what you want from me."

He's annoyed and thinks I'm being cruel. My stomach twists at the thought, and the familiar flutter of panic leaps under my skin.

"Our blood is the same now. You smell like me, and mixed into it is so much panic it's making me sick."

"This is just going to make it harder."

I gasp when he palms my face with both hands. He kisses my temple. My cheek. High. Then low. My chin. My ear. I'm dizzy with him. Is it the bond? The potion? Love? Just the love I have for him rolling around in my insides making me think I'm going to be sick without him?

"Don't think … feel … instinct on instinct. Tell me how to make you feel better."

I shake my head, not pulling away. I don't want to. Because I need him. It's agony when he falls away, and he must know because he presses in again.

I'm thinking of the future. How we'll never get another night in bed together. How he's going to marry someone else. How we're going to be separated and there's nothing I can do about it.

He's kissing everywhere but my mouth in a desperate cadence, and it's working. Every brush of his skin heals the ache in my heart. A tear falls and I sniffle, then he's there wiping it. Holding me.

"Kiss me." It comes out in a breath. My heart is bleeding the words. *Don't give up on me. Stay.*

The next second, his lips are on mine in a wash of dizziness and pressure, and we fall into the brush.

I'm on top, fevered and hurried, grasping desperately. His fingers brush through my hair, and my waist. I'm his. He takes my bottom lip between his teeth, and I'm suddenly aware of how good he tastes. It *is* what I need. There's never been anything in my life like this, and I know once my lips leave his, I'll never have it again.

He rolls me onto my back into the tall grass, and I think we'll stay like this forever. Our kisses are doing all the talking—hot breaths and sighs of comfort. We both need it.

Parker fingers the buttons on my collar to snap it open and gain access to my neck, then kisses his mark. The sensation jolts me. It's a reminder of his commitment. His mark on display.

My phone chimes, and I quickly separate myself. A picture of Parker and I kissing in the grass is posted at the top of the feed.

It's captioned. *Broken Up?*

There are already two comments.

Doesn't look like it.

He deserves better.

My phone chimes again. This time an anonymous text: *Bad girl. What will your new suitors think?*

He doesn't know the worst of it yet. The thing I'm about to do.

"You need to stay away from me." I gather myself, dusting off my skirt and the dirt in my socks.

"Do you really think he'll want you after you agree to be someone else's mate?"

Parker will disappear when he knows what I've agreed to.

"We can't do this again. It's over."

I don't look to see his reaction, and I can't stop the tears as I run away.

Chapter Forty

Parker

"How?" I whisper, watching her walk away.

How am I supposed to stay away from her? That's virtually impossible; I warned her.

I shift to clear my head—and because I'm on the verge of doing something that will get me expelled. I know it's one of those fuckers on the council. And gutting any of them won't free Olivia from her vow, but it would send a satisfying shiver down my spine when I tear into them with my teeth. The same satisfaction I get in a Rage match when someone mouths off and underestimates me.

Vows made to the stone can only be fulfilled when the agreement is settled and the agreed upon condition is met. I made one once when my team captain got into a fight with a rival team, and they retaliated by painting the outside of the stadium.

I remember being questioned by the dean, unable to move my mouth to tell her that he started it. I wasn't allowed to tell anyone until the semester ended. Olivia's made a deal she can't get out of, and there's nothing I can do about it.

If I go to the dean, it won't absolve her of her vow. I also have no evidence, and I'm not so sure the dean is interested in helping with an issue that might affect her funding. I'm on my own with this one.

"You're looking murderous this evening," Darien says from close by.

He appears a few feet away in the brush. I've shifted back to my human form and am still shrugging on my pants.

"Five seconds. That's all you get."

"Fine. I heard you're ready to play the game. You know I didn't think it would turn out like this. I was certain Olivia would be the titan here, but I guess the queen needs her knight. And that, you are, her knight in shining armor."

I stop dressing. "You know who's doing this. Is it you?"

"Ah, see I'm sworn to the Secrecy Stone as well. But I do know someone who isn't that would be willing to help you for a price. Well, probably. I'm sure it's high."

"I don't fucking trust you."

"I figured that much. But you really should. After all, who do you think prevented Olivia from being marked against her will at every turn? That night she arrived ... or with Barrett that day in the woods. While I can't tell you much about the night she was drugged, I can tell you that a few more seconds at that party would have been bad for her. Thankfully, I whisked her outside before any damage could be done to your precious mate then followed her all the way across campus to ensure her safety. She found you all on her own, though."

"And I'm supposed to believe that was you?"

"I was watching her all night. There are a handful of people who know what happened that night, and I'm one of them. Only someone who was watching in wait with the ability to sneak around could get her out and pull the fire alarm before that potion started working."

"Why did you do it?"

"As fun as it would be to see that drama unfold, I think this will be the more interesting outcome. The Weres getting what they want all the time is boring."

"You mean it's advantageous for you."

"Now you get it."

It's hard to thank him, knowing he did it for himself.

"Fine. You've been awarded a pass for me not to beat the shit out of you today. Give me the name of the someone who can help me."

Darien's smile widens. "I'll give you one guess."

I ask Zant to have Cane meet in the Rage locker room. He made up some bullshit lie about the future council members needing signatures of all the academic and athletic club captains.

That's got to be why he came into the locker room with a scowl set on his face. He strides in with that stupid slicked-back hair, those expensive shoes that squeak, and the blazer he never fully buttons up.

"I fucking knew it," he hisses.

"Sit," I say, motioning toward the bench.

Zant is close by, saying nothing for once in his life, but he's mostly here to keep me from doing stupid shit. Teammates shuffle around, with a lot of them still in the showers, so steam is floating overhead.

Cane sits with a low growl and a sigh.

"I know you have details on what Aster and Barrett did to drug Olivia that night at the party."

"Who told you that?"

"Not important. But I know you know things ... You might even have proof, and I need it."

Cane laughs a deep belly laugh. "Really? You're asking me for help? That's a first."

"No shit. But I'm willing to bury the hatchet or at the very least allow you to bury the hatchet in my back. We both know that's the only way you'll ever be able to."

"I'm listening."

"Get me proof from that night. Whatever you have, and I'll drop my council nomination."

"Doubt you'd want to be connected to Aster if that gets out," he says.

"You either. Looks like I've done you a favor."

"And why would I do this?"

"Because either way, I'm going to get this information and take them down, so you get the privilege of cutting ties now and staying out of it."

Cane surveys me, and Zant leans against one of the lockers with a deep frown set on his lips. He mouths, *This isn't going to work.*

"Fine. I'll do it, but I want you to step down ... and for you to pledge yourself to my pack."

"What?"

Zant can't keep his scoff to himself in the corner. "Fuck this."

"What's greater than having you out of the way than getting to see the daily humiliation in your eyes for forfeiting your place as alpha and being indebted to my pack?"

I sigh, pushing my hands through my hair. It's not like I thought he was going to easily agree. He wants to humiliate me and impress his father. Being indebted to Cane's pack means whatever I decide to do on my own when I leave Gavin's pack would have to go through him. Probably just means he'll want me to be his errand boy.

"Fine."

"Parker," Zant says, uncrossing his arms and standing up straight.

"I didn't expect you to say yes. You would do that ... all for that girl?"

"Do we have a deal or not?"

Cane stands and holds out his hand to shake on it. "I can get you what you need by morning."

For the first time in my life, I shake Cane's hand. It might be the sleaziest thing I've ever done, but he is the lesser of the two evils I have in my life. I have to pick my battles, and if I need to choose, I'm taking Aster and Barrett off the board.

Zant gives me an earful when Cane leaves, but I'm half tuning him out while rubbing the center of my chest thinking about how miserable Olivia is. I want to go to her, but I have to think ahead about what will fix this in the long term. I'm not giving up and rolling over.

He throws a dirty shirt in my face. "How do you know he won't betray you?"

"Because if he does, I have nothing to lose, so I'll burn this place to the ground."

He sighs. "I don't know if I like this plan."

"I don't either, but it's all I've got," I say, sinking into the bench. "I miss Olivia."

"You were kissing her about an hour ago."

And it felt so fucking good too. She was panicking, but every touch of my lips melted it away.

"Parker!" Evangeline comes barreling into the locker room. "What happened with Olivia? She's inconsolable in her room, and she won't tell me what happened between you two. I can't get her out. I haven't seen her this upset since

...” She eyes the locker room filled with shirtless men in towels. All of them are smiling, and some of them wave till we make eye contact, and I motion for them to steer clear.

“I think she’s being blackmailed by someone on the council and was forced to make a vow with the Secrecy Stone. And she ... she broke up with me for real.”

“Wait.” She hushes her voice. “You made it official.”

“Yeah, for all of a few hours until she told me it was over.”

“Everyone’s saying it was all fake the entire time, and they’re blaming it on her.”

“I know. But I’m going to fix it. I’m going to be there for her, don’t worry.”

Evangeline’s worry makes my skin itch. The need to protect Olivia extends to her sisters too.

“Where’s Emma?” I ask.

“Thankfully, on a trip with the culinary club in the city. Far away from this mess.”

That’s a relief at least. Our phones chime and I sigh. A sinking anxiety follows, and I know it’s bad.

Zant’s voice sounds next to my ear. “You might want to sit down.”

“Why?” I snatch the phone from his hand and read the headline.

Olivia Confirms Breakup with Her Signup to The Hunt This Saturday.

“The Hunt?!”

Zant tugs on my shoulder, but I can barely hear him with the roaring in my ears. The locker room disappears from my sight till all I see is red. The stench of sweat and cologne morphe into nothing. My mouth salivates and my arms itch as the hairs stand on end.

I put out a hand, signaling for them to give me a second. My mate is going to be in The fucking Hunt. This was their plan, the ultimate humiliation. I have to close my eyes and breathe through my nose.

“The Hunt?” Evangeline’s voice is far away.

“It’s how alpha Weres get hooked up with mates,” Zant says.

“She would never.”

“Anyone on the council could have gotten her on the roster.”

My head shoots up. “No fucking way I’m letting this happen.”

“What are you going to do?”

“I’m joining The Hunt.”

Chapter Forty-One

Olivia

"Hi Dad."

I keep my voice low and lay my head on my pillow. The night is heavy as the minutes tick by on the clock above the hearth. My whole body aches even after the bath I took to calm my nerves. I move the hair from the wetness of my face.

"Hey, honey, it's late. Are you all right?"

"Yeah … I … I think I'm going to come home. I hope that's okay. I know I haven't called."

I fight to keep my voice level, tucking my hand between my knees. Going home and keeping a distance from Parker is the best thing I can do for him. Giving the linked mate news time to die down will make him less likely to be targeted so this doesn't happen again. Joining The Hunt means I'll be marked as someone else's mate. Even if I never accept, it will be a public rejection of our bond. I can't imagine putting him through that.

"Certainly. I'd love to have you."

"I have something to do this weekend, and then I'll pack up my stuff. Can you pick me up?"

After stripping my bedding, I put the flat sheet back down to lie on it; it smells like him. That should make it easier to pack, but I abandoned the endeavor to sulk.

"Yeah, anything you need. But did anything happen? Is it about ballet?"

"No. Ballet is … It's not ballet."

I'll give up my spot after The Hunt. I just want this to end. Go back to Groveshire and enter into a smaller local company. I can't watch Parker move on and … whoever I get marked by hopefully won't follow me where I'm going. There is nothing left to think about, only to do what needs to be done.

"I don't think I'm cut out for this here. I thought I was, but … I can't do it anymore. I just want to come home. I'm sorry."

"Sorry? This was *your* dream, honey. I'm always proud of you no matter what you do. *I'm* sorry Doxlothia wasn't what you wanted it to be."

The tears stain my pillow, sinking into the fabric. I wish my mom was here. I was so close to getting everything I always wanted.

"I really thought I could make everyone proud. But none of it matters anymore."

I finally understand why he did it, why my father gave up everything after she died. Because without Parker, I don't care about a spot in the IBCE. I'm doing exactly what my father did except it's worse because he had a better excuse for giving up than I do.

It's better for everyone if I just disappear back to my old life.

"Is this about Parker Owens?"

I sniffle; his name alone is enough to wet my eyes. The council wanted me to play this game, and maybe it's the bond … Or maybe it's the fact I'm hurting Parker. I just don't have it in me to play. I wanted to dance. That's all I wanted to do, and now I can't enjoy what I love here at Doxlothia without him.

"You're in all the papers. I wanted to come see you and meet him, but I knew you probably didn't want to talk to me about it … I mean, wow. You have a linked mate. I can hardly believe it. One of your mother's distant ancestors was a linked mate. That's where you get the eyes from. Lucky. They always said our family was lucky."

"You never told me that."

"There's never been a human pairing for a linked mate before. I never imagined one of you girls would have one. Maybe with your eye color I should have known."

"It's over," I say. "He … he won't want to talk to me anymore."

"Oh, honey. I'm sorry."

"Doesn't matter." I feel more tears coming, so I squeeze the bridge of my nose.

"Your mother ... gosh she loved you so much. She knew you girls were going to shake things up in Vviveren ... that's why she wanted you to attend Doxlothia."

I sit up in bed, wiping my cheek. "She ... wanted us to attend?"

He sighs and I hear a cup being set on our dining table with the faint sound of the records he loves to play in the background.

"You attending the school was your mother's dying wish. I read it in her will, and ... I fought it for a long time, knowing you girls would have to navigate out in the world, especially after how we sheltered you."

"Why didn't you tell me?"

"She wanted you to choose what you wanted, and I wanted that for you too. I enrolled you, not knowing if you'd reject the offer or not. I had to trust Doxlothia was the safest university out there for you anyway. I didn't want to sway you. I wanted you girls to choose your own paths. And she knew the only way I'd ever let you girls out of my sight was that school. I'm sorry I kept you close to my heart for so long."

His voice breaks on the other end, and another tear rolls down my cheek, but this one doesn't sting as much. My dad's fear was always mine. I understand him more than I ever have. He pushed me away because he was afraid and simultaneously refused to let us go.

"It's okay, Dad. I understand."

"It will be good to see you. Get some sleep. And honey?"

"Yeah?"

"Maybe it's not over."

Chapter Forty-Two

Parker

"Don't give up on me." She begs while sobbing into my shirt.

I hold her close, tucking her hair behind her ear. She won't remember us being together here tonight, but I will.

"Never."

The Hunt takes place on the private island that borders the northwest of campus.

We gather by the dock near the guest housing. It's all—supposed to be—voluntary. Those who want to be Were mates for status, love, or any reason, really, sign up each year. *The hunted* are chosen for a reason. They come from money or status, but they do let in a select few from every walk of life. Olivia's eyes were probably her one-way ticket in, adding in that she's a linked mate and has sweet blood would make her desirable to any of the Weres looking for a mate they can use as a bargaining chip.

Not all Weres care about status and pack alliances, but a lot of them do. At least the ones I know.

I check my phone. The news about Aster and Barrett is going to break any minute. Cane provided his evidence by the time the sun came up, as promised—a series of text messages traced back to their numbers discussing tampering with Olivia's drink at the party. I'd given all the evidence to Autumn, the best journalist at the university newspaper, and it took everything in me not to ambush those fuckers in their dorm rooms. But I can't help Olivia if I'm locked up.

I didn't sleep at all. The whole thing made me so enraged I spent the night in my shifted form pacing the grounds behind Noxx House. Olivia calmed down sometime in the middle of the night. I hope she got some sleep.

Chaos will erupt, and I'll be on an island with no service. I can see it all unfolding now. *Aster Carrington and Barrett Hunter Drug Olivia Osborne at a Party.*

They'll want blood. They'll want me.

Well, I'm busy trying to win my girl back from the mess they made.

I text Zant while I wait at the shore for the ferry, begging him to find a way around the Were rule. The only way I think Zant will be able to come is because he's on the council and pays for the food for the guests.

The campus is alive with the news of The Hunt even though it's a private event unrelated to Doxlothia, but since the board of directors is involved the school helps fund and house participants on the private island.

The rocky water bank smells of fish, and every few minutes, another group of people arrive. It reeks of alpha blood, and all my nerve endings are rapid firing.

Gavin is here to see me off. We're gathered by the water while the ferry drifts toward us in the distance. I told him about my plan. He was seconds away from asking his dad for help, but I stopped him. This is my fight. My chance to prove to everyone I'm stepping up and not backing down. Plus, stopping The Hunt is impossible. She's locked in now, and so am I.

"I've set some money back in case I have to make your bail." Gavin's smile is strained. "Keep your head."

"I will. I'm going to get her back."

"I know. I'm proud." He hits me so hard in the shoulder I fall back a few steps. "I'm going to miss you stirring shit up in my pack."

The Hunt is exclusively for alphas. By joining The Hunt, I'm officially accepting my role as an Alpha, and that means letting go of Gavin's pack for good.

"I think you'll like me a lot more now."

He smirks. "Probably."

I smell her approaching. The smell of her perfume and the laundry soap she uses. Her hairspray. Her blood. *Me* all over her.

"Thanks for everything ... Alpha."

Gavin's jaw sets and he smiles, patting me on the shoulder before leaving me to my business—wooing Olivia, which I take very seriously.

"Hi, baby." I stop feet from her, my shades shielding me from the sun beating down. Other than a swarm of other alphas, The Hunt hanging over our heads, and the knowledge the two most popular Weres on campus are about to come for my neck, it's a nice day. Any day I get to see her is a nice day.

Her eyes widen. For once she isn't in her uniform but more of her athletic wear that shows the curves of her stomach and her legs. Those legs, that not long ago, I had wrapped around my waist as I drove into her and forced my name from her lips.

I shouldn't think about it, but I do because she still smells like me.

"Parker. What are you doing here?"

"Looking for my mate. What better way than The Hunt?"

Pretending I'm looking for someone else will prevent her from arguing for the time being. She probably won't believe it, but I want to relieve the guilt wafting off her. Our night together peeled back all her insecurities, and I get why she wants to run and how she thinks it's easier. She's wrong, but she's cute when she's wrong.

Olivia let me into her world but can't keep me out. No matter what they're holding over her head, it won't change my love for her, but I need to show her.

She chews on my words for a few seconds. Her foot taps in the dirt.

"You're here ... for a mate? Someone else."

"Of course. That's why everyone is here."

Something surges in the bond again. Her stomach hurts.

"Well, I-I can't talk to you."

"That's fine. You don't have to. Can't stop me from talking to you though. We're still friends, right? No hard feelings?"

Her mouth falls open, then she closes it, nodding. She actually believes me.

It doesn't look like she's had much instruction other than to meet at the ferry. She follows me up to the line while we wait to board. All the attention on her shifts when the others see me towering over her. I make eye contact with all of them.

After a few minutes of standing, Olivia moves her neck side to side and reaches back to her left shoulder to massage the muscle there. It's strange that I can feel it when I focus on her intensely, right where that knot in her muscle is. I take my hand and softly clamp it over her shoulder. She gasps but submits to my touch as I work my thumb into the muscle.

It's partly to help her relax, and just so happens to simultaneously mark her in more ways than I already have.

She smells like me. Check.

She's got my mark on her neck. Check.

She leans into and thoughtfully sighs at my touch. Fucking check.

I work the knot in her shoulder as the line moves forward. Her heart responds in a rapid cadence, but her anxious scent calms. I don't stop until the knot relaxes under my thumb and she sighs.

"Better?"

Her jaw clenches and she keeps her eyes forward.

"How'd you sleep?" I ask.

She stares at the line of heads in front of us, and there are dark circles under her eyes, which tells me very little.

"No talking. Got it." I smile, the challenge blooming under my skin.

I'm just looking for opportunities to get her to talk to me when I remember morning Parker already prepared for such a thing.

"I brought you this. Not eating while you're anxious is making my stomach hurt."

I hand her a protein bar, and she takes it, nibbling the edge of it as we wait.

The whole lot is buzzing. I look at my phone to see a surge of notifications.

Here we go. Olivia checks her phone, and her eyes widen as she scrolls through the news.

"You did this?"

"Yep."

"They're going to be angry."

"Let them. I'm not scared."

She shakes her head and picks at the skin of her nails.

"I won't let them touch you. Just trust me."

That fidgeting doesn't stop. What did they threaten her with? Surely, it's got to do with ballet. Maybe they're trying to bar her from the IBCE unless she goes through with The Hunt.

Some of the alphas around me move toward Olivia like they want to talk to her, and I stare them down in warning. It's going to be a long fucking weekend.

I keep close. A comfortable distance to not worry her but close enough that I'm behind her as we board the ferry.

I've been on this ferry before, and the familiar scent of the mildew in the icebox and the snack bar floods my senses. There are rows of seats lining the windows inside, and a section to sit in the middle with tables.

She goes to sit next to someone. A Were I'm not the least intimated by, but that doesn't mean I want him sitting with my girl. I press my fingers into the small of her back. It's hidden, not breaking any rules, and I usher her into the empty seat behind and take the spot next to her.

Now her forehead is wrinkled. She's irritated, but she can't tell me. It's kinda cute.

"Don't think any mates will like seeing you sit with me."

Oh, she's jealous with very little pressure.

"I'm not really worried about finding my mate. That will be easy."

Her fingers dig into the wrapper of the protein bar. "Oh, right. Parker can find any mate he wants."

"Sure. Does that bother you? Might I remind you that you broke up with me."

She looks at my lips, then up to my eyes. "Right."

I'm still thinking of that last kiss. It told me all I needed to know. She wants me to save her, and I'm going to.

Outside her window is the calm dark-green sea. I've been to the island once as a kid for summer camp. I remember the rocking of the ferry and my excitement over sitting in a seat by the window.

The boarding hasn't finished yet, but every few seconds, Olivia's chin dips as she nods off while staring out the window.

"Couldn't sleep, huh?"

She shakes her head. Her eyelids are heavy. It's the bond. Her body senses me near. That it's safe and I can protect her.

"You can sleep. I'll make sure no one bothers you."

"Just need to close my eyes for a few minutes," she whispers.

It takes three minutes before she's out, and the sway of the boat brings her head to my shoulder. Her breath warms my arm as she sighs, and all that prickly fear and sadness dissolves from her scent into calm, serene bliss.

Chapter Forty-Three

Olivia

There's no service on the island. I can't tell if I'm extremely thankful or terrified. All I want to do is call my sisters. But it's just one weekend, then I'm free to be back at home alone and sad all by myself.

I stare at the pamphlet in my hands that was handed to me as soon as we disembarked the ferry. We were then separated into groups: hunters and hunted.

As terrifying as it sounds, I was immediately ushered from Parker's side to an area of women and men who might be the most welcoming people I've ever met. All the girls *love* me here. Lots of them come from other schools I've never heard of, and they're free from the Doxlothia bias. Though they know all about it.

I never thought I was the type to care about that sort of thing, but when it's everyone staring and refusing to talk to you while you're already so anxious your stomach is eating itself, it does start to sting. But all the new people tell me how well I hide it, and from the outside looking in, I navigate it all with elegance and grace. If they only knew.

We get a goodie bag full of things for our stay in the hotel, including a T-shirt, socks, and toiletries. I've never been to such a luxurious place before. My room

269

has a queen-size bed and a steam shower. According to the pamphlet and our guide, tonight is the dinner and the welcome ceremony, Saturday afternoon is reserved for mingling, then The Hunt begins after sundown.

"Olivia! Stand next to me." I follow the voice of a girl named Tara who has bright-green hair and silver eyes. "Look, you can see Parker from here."

They don't list the details of the welcome ceremony in the pamphlet, oddly enough, but after we check in to our rooms and drop off our things, we're given the option to linger in the hotel until the ceremony, and it's only the hunted mingling and getting drinks. My plan was to stay secure in my room, but I was quite literally dragged into the lobby with a group of girls who wanted to hear all about me and Parker.

I have zero skills in that area. It almost reminds me of those slumber parties I saw on TV growing up, only we're all over the age of twenty-one and sipping drinks.

Once the sun goes down, we're taken to a garden area. It's open-ended with sliding doors that lead back into the resort. All the hunters are gathered outside in one place in the center. The birds fly overheard, and there's a soft breeze.

I take my place next to her. I do want to see Parker. He's the only thing that's familiar and safe.

"Wow. You're a lucky woman." Tara's eyes sparkle as she eyes him.

They all think Parker is here for me. They tell me about their theories on why we're both here.

Nothing could prepare me for the sheer number of people who know who I am. They say my name like we're friends. Some have even guessed right about the Secrecy Stone rumored to live at the edge of Languid Lake and my involvement in some type of blackmailing scheme. It's like my life is a soap opera to them. Some storybook unfolding before their eyes, and they want to be the one to guess correctly. It should be insulting, but it's comforting to have people believe me for once. And at the same time, unsettling to know how much strangers are thinking of me and piecing my life together. They ask me about ballet too and tell me how amazed they were when they saw my leaked entry tapes.

Here, I'm not Olivia Osborne the Mastermind. I'm Olivia, the ballerina destined to be with Parker Owens, who joined The Hunt to save his damsel.

I wish it were true. That sounds like the best-case scenario, but I'm afraid to let myself dwell on the possibility. What if he really did come for someone else?

I like their stories. There's comfort in how trivial it all sounds.

We stand in a clearing in the trees, and all the hunters are being instructed to kneel in the grass. It's a mix of men and women. Parker is shirtless and crouches to his knees, one leg at a time, while they run shiny silver liquid over his chest. It falls in ribbons over his pecks and down into the curves of his abs.

Our eyes meet. He can smell me.

"We honor a long-held mating tradition of The Hunt. May each of you find prosperity and the one your heart desires. Hold gaze with our moons and receive your place in the universe in acceptance of what will be."

Howls erupt around me as Parker lifts his chin toward the sky. No words come from his lips, but I see the change reflected in his eyes. They glow yellow, and a deep howl rumbles from his chest. His shoulders stiffen, and veins grow and pop from his skin. It's lacing its way into every inch of his body by the second. His canines grow, and his deafening howl radiates throughout my entire body. I may not be able to detect what dominance feels like, but I see it in the faces of the crowd as mouths close and backs straighten. The hairs on my arm prick up, and they move a cup in front of Parker's face that's filled with silver powder. He breathes in, and all the glow runs out of his eyes until they're pure black.

"Breathe in the new breath of your new reality. You are one with the moons."

Parker's body shakes, and his chest shimmers in the moonlight. I let out a breath, and his attention snaps to me. His eyes are midnight black, and he rises to his feet, nostrils flared and shoulders back. I think he's going to run toward me, but with the crack of his neck, his body begins to shift. All I've ever seen are the pictures in my textbook, but this doesn't compare.

He grows taller before my eyes as his chest fills and his shoulders broaden. The hair bursts from his skin, and his forearms swell just before his hands grow larger and claws jut out. His change springs more until the entire group is shifting, and we're all being pushed inside the building. Howling fills the garden. Just before I'm pushed through the door, I see him.

Standing still on two legs, Parker's werewolf form towers above us, and he's a few inches taller than the others. He's at least eight feet tall, with a long stout nose and rows of pointed teeth. With glowing eyes locked on me, he licks his lips. There's a separation in the crowd, then I see all of him. He still looks like a man in many ways, with strong muscle form.

I swear I can hear the word in my head. *Mine.*

The door shuts, closing me off from them, and their howls echo in the night.

"While they're having their first run of the land, you may all prepare for the feast."

Chapter Forty-Four

Parker

This is the most food I've ever seen. I haven't eaten all day—except for a rabbit during the shift? I barely remember picking the fuzz out of my teeth—so I've got hotheaded blood simmering out of control, an empty growling stomach, and the nauseous urge to barf any time I look at the food, because Olivia is still anxious. By mid-dinner, I'm so delirious I've resigned to looking at the wall. Then to Olivia who is across the room with the other hunted. Her under eyes are dark, and she doesn't crack a smile once, only the forced pleasant ones when someone compliments her or asks her about herself. But the girls are being kind to her, and that brings me a little peace.

I'm at a table in the far corner, strategically picked so I could watch over her. There are brass chandeliers in the rafters that cast the room in a warm-yellow glow.

"Are you really not going to eat?" Austin asks me.

The live music starts and the energy in the hall shifts. Some people have already gotten drunk enough to dance. One guy stands up, pitches his napkin on the table, and goes to talk to Olivia. I grit my teeth and grab a few turkey thighs for my plate.

"Owens looks like he might shift," Garrik says.

All the assholes have gravitated to my table, which is the fucking story of my life. I'm a magnet for them. Most of them are acquaintances I've met before in some way or another. A few I used to attend school with in the city. Some are from different universities or different Rage teams.

Gavin would call this "an opportunity for greatness," but I'm not in the mood to be great. The guy across the room is trying really hard to make Olivia laugh by telling her jokes that aren't funny. She's obliging him though with a half-smile and forced chuckle.

"She smells so much like you." Garrik has been staring at her all day. All of them have.

But Garrik doesn't hide the fact he wants her. I smell the shift in his scent when he takes a long look and lingers on her bare legs.

"Probably because a few days ago I was dripping out of her."

His eyebrows raise with that shit-eating smirk, and it does what I want. His attention is back on me as he leans back in his chair and takes a sip of the goblet of wine on the table.

I'm itchy, so I finally take a bite of the cold turkey leg on my plate. "So, yeah, I'd say we're pretty close."

"Yep, he's in love with her," Austin says. He's a trust fund kid and a Rage team captain—the only tolerable one.

"She's in love with him too. That's easy to tell," the tall one, Calix, says. He might be the largest man I've ever seen. I've had to fight him on the ice before. It sucked, but I still won. He's the reason for a lot of the scars on my back.

"Not a dealbreaker for me." Garrik's watching me eat.

"Me either," Calix says. He's got one silver eye and the other red.

"Well, it is for me. Am I the only one trying to find a soul mate here?" Austin asks.

"Yes," the rest of the table says.

They don't ask me why Olivia and I are both here because they don't care. The only thing they care about is how to leverage this for themselves.

"A linked mated with those special eyes at The Hunt makes this the most interesting one yet. Way better than last year." Garrik is back to looking at Olivia. You're not guaranteed a mate, and if someone they want gets taken early on—say some billionaire's daughter—they'll go home empty-handed. "I can imagine it now. An heir with those violet and golden eyes. A boy and a girl with that pretty brown hair of hers."

Oh, this dick is testing me, and so is the other one across the room leaning on the table chatting up my girl. His words have me going places I've never let my mind reach. Olivia's eyes reflected back to me in another man's kids. I'm not even sure I want kids, but I know for sure I don't want Olivia to have some other guy's children. Especially from this asshole who only wants to mate with her for the recognition. Fuck that.

Garrik twirls his fork, setting his elbow on the table and resting his head. "Don't worry. I'll let you come over and fuck her in my house."

My teeth crunch on the bone of my turkey leg, and I spit it on the plate. After grabbing another turkey leg, I drop it with a thud. I focus on the smell rolling off the meat to keep me calm.

"How kind of you," Calix jests.

"Of course, my mark would be on her neck."

"You'd be a kind man and let him take her out too."

"Sure, in the clothes I bought her. With my car. With my money." Garrik licks his teeth.

The whole table snickers, except for Austin. I chew through flesh and lick the bone clean.

"That's not going to work for me because I want to be the only one fucking her," another one says.

I scrape my teeth on the bone, focusing on the taste. The tear. The skin peeling and snapping. *Opportunity for greatness. Opportunity for greatness. Fucking opportunity for fucking greatness.*

"Such a calm alpha," Calix says.

"I'm not worried. You're not gonna catch her," I say.

"You're forgetting we're not all legacy Doxlothia sons. Some of us have been fighting since we were young," Garrik says.

"He's right. I'm itching for a challenge," Calix says.

Fuck these assholes. I drop the clean bone on the table, still crunching on the cartilage.

"Finally some good competition, then," I say, the edges of my vision blurring.

The guy chatting up Olivia's table has her hand.

I grip the table to keep myself from imploding. The others next to me go silent. She accepts. She fucking accepts, and I physically have to look away because I'm going to lose my shit. Or I'm going to throw up. Or maybe fucking both.

He leans to kiss her hand, and she blinks. I'm on my feet before I realize, crossing the room. Who does this guy think he is—

"Move," I say to him. That's as nice as I'm going to get.

"But—"

I move him by simply walking forward. He wouldn't stand a chance against me in a fight. I can feel it all. Like my nose was clogged before, and now all these new senses have kicked in. I take his place by grabbing her hand and moving my other hand to her waist. I'm not as modest as he was. Something in her scent leaps at my presence. Relief. Her breathing is easier. Her eyes heavier.

"Was that necessary?"

I grab her hand and rub the remnants of that scent away with my lips.

Garrik and the others watch us from the table. He's eye-fucking her, and I have a big problem with that, but it can wait.

"You're lucky I don't take you into my room and scent you right now."

Her heart kicks. The scent of her arousal hits me like a freight train, and I don't think anyone could understand the type of restraint it takes not to get pulled down with it.

"I don't like people touching what's mine."

"I thought you said you were here for someone else?"

"And you believed me? When has there ever been anyone else?"

I'm prickly all over and itchy. So fucking itchy. My voice is rougher than I want it to be.

"You shouldn't have come." She sighs.

"Olivia."

I stop swaying, and she waits for me to speak. We're still chest to chest.

"I don't want to be friends anymore."

Her eyes widen, nostrils flaring, and I see something I'd witnessed in her more sacred space. It's the same look when she misses a beat in ballet. She's scared.

"I need more. I need so much more. And I think I've made it as clear as I can make it. Of course, I'm here for you. I'm going to win tomorrow, and I'm going to claim you. Is that what scares you?"

The music lifts, and I thread my arm around her waist. Most people dancing are playfully flirting. There's a photographer in the corner snapping photos of us. I hug her tighter, and one inhale of her scent has my body alive with the itch of shifting. My lips close over my mark on her neck, making the hairs stand up along her skin.

"I can't do this. I shouldn't be dancing with you."

"Then tell me the night we spent together meant nothing. Tell me you didn't feel what I felt and you truly don't love me. You don't have to lie about that. You can tell me now, break my heart."

Olivia stares at my lips. Her scent is the calmest it's ever been. She's leaning into me for support but isn't saying anything.

"You need to think long and hard about what you really want. Because I'm claiming you tomorrow. That's a promise. If you really want to run away, this is your last chance."

She stops dancing and breaks away from me, leaving me in the middle of the dining hall. Garrik's smile mocks me as she disappears into the lobby.

Chapter Forty-Five

Olivia

The steam from the bathhouse is making me dizzy as I stare at the paned glass. The room is lined with opalescent tiles connected with various jewels of jade and sapphire. There are three hot tubs stacked on three levels with white pillars making space in the reverberant room.

Some are sneaking back to their rooms, and others are making out in the other pools. I'd like to go back to my room, but knowing I won't be able to sleep keeps me from retreating there to be alone. Even if the bed has the softest linens I've ever laid my hands on. This is fun for everyone who isn't me—and Parker, if I had to guess. These people probably looked forward to this for months and are treating it like a vacation or some reality TV show.

I need to tire myself out, which shouldn't be hard, considering the only sleep I've gotten was on the ferry. And listening to bachelor alphas talk is bound to put me right to sleep.

Tara was with me for a while before hitting it off with one of the hunters and excusing herself. So it's just me. Alone. Surrounded by what I'm assuming are all very powerful alphas. They pushed the other guys from their spots without having to say a word. Parker waits on the other end of the tub. Too far away to touch. He hasn't moved an inch. He's leaned back with his arms resting on the sides. I hate that he isn't smiling.

His words are still running in my mind. What if Parker wins and we do have the opportunity to complete the mating bond? Should I? Is it selfish to want that still, knowing what I know now? What happens when my secret vow is complete? Will whoever this is let us be together? What if there's just another hurdle to get through?

"So, what do you like to do?" one of them asks. He's got fuchsia irises and long black hair. I wish Emma was here to take the brunt of the conversation. Only, the thought of my sister getting marked by a random alpha werewolf is my definition of a nightmare.

"I dance. I'm a ballerina."

He smiles, and it's not creepy, but I can *feel* Parker's eyes on me.

"Wow. That's so elegant. I'd love to watch."

Trying to be pleasant, I force a smile. The person threatening me told me that I need to play along and mingle with the other alphas. But most men get bored of conversation of dance quickly. They don't take it seriously.

"I bet you dance beautifully."

That's what they see. Some little dainty woman dancing in frilly clothes. If only they saw my bleeding feet or how many hours I pour into it every day. How many dates I'd willingly miss. The tears.

Parker's gaze is even heavier. He's seen all those things.

The guys are a comfortable distance from me. Parker's presence makes me feel safe enough to let my shoulders sink into the water. The water has healing salts and is soothing the lingering aches in my body.

"What do you do?" I ask.

"I'm from Axeleth Academy. Not quite as prestigious as Doxlothia but beautiful and surrounded by water. I'm learning to be a fund manager for the city."

"Sounds interesting."

"It's not. You're far more interesting. You could come hang out, you know? It's practically a beach paradise."

He inches closer. It's so minuscule but enough for our legs to touch. For the first time, Parker's gaze moves to the man beside me, and he tilts his head, unblinking—a silent warning.

He must feel the shift because he leans away from me with a smirk.

"Is he boring you with his riveting conversation on funds and capital?" Another man comes up on my left.

"No."

"Name's Garrik. Parker had lots of lovely things to say about you at the dinner table."

Parker's name sends a shiver down my spine. "I'm sure he did. He's very flattering."

Garrik stares at Parker's mark on my neck. They all see it, but it doesn't seem to bother any of them.

"My little sister wants to be a ballerina. She loves you. If she knew I was talking to you, she'd want an autograph."

Garrik's got charcoal eyes and dark hair with loose curls to match. He runs his wet hands through it to tame it, showing me the scars of claw marks on his forearm.

"She sounds sweet."

"She's six. She's a terror. But I told her I may be able to get her that autograph in person."

My whole body heats. I know what he means. If he marks me and I become his mate, he's likely got a grand house he'd love me to be in. All I can think of is how much my heart would ache being away from Parker. I'll never be able to sleep again and have to get a potion for it. But Parker would be somewhere across the world playing in the pro league, winning. I'm sure of it. Maybe I'm making a terrible choice. I'm ruining everything. I should have just told him when I'd gotten the file and avoided this madness. Why didn't I at least *try* to do this together without running away to fix it on my own? But that's what I do apparently.

That sinking anxiety hits my gut again, and I pinch my arm to snap myself out of it.

I'm not having fun, and I think it's really obvious. If they notice, they don't show it. All I want to do is retreat to my room and collapse into my bed for a good cry so I'm able to compose myself better. I'm having a hard time holding a smile on my face, and that's usually my sign to retreat, but their conversation isn't leaving much room. I'm tired. I'm hot. My head is pounding as the hot water sucks all the hydration from my body.

Garrik keeps saying things in an attempt to make me smile or laugh, and I have to fake it. In any other circumstance, I'd have no problem telling him to go away. I wish everyone would just leave me alone to my misery of the mess I've caused.

"Can we help you, Owens?"

"Nope." Parker swings his head slowly, his arms out and his stance wide. I've never seen him so deadpan and utterly out of emotion.

I meet his gaze, wishing he could read my mind. *Help me. I want to leave.*

"You're boring her," Parker says.

"You know that, huh?" the one with fuchsia eyes says; I never got his name. Or maybe he told me and I wasn't listening.

"You can continue your conversation tomorrow. She's tired. It's been a long day."

"Are you going to make us go?" Garrik says with a smirk.

"Uh-huh," Parker says, like they're boring him.

They hold each other's attention. Each taking up an equal amount of space. I almost think they're going to fight, though Parker never flinches. His breaths are even. He's confident.

"Fine. I'll leave you for tonight."

The others follow his retreat for a towel.

I gasp as Garrik leans in. "But I'd run fast if I were you ... Rabbit."

Rabbit. Does he know about the secret? Did Aster and Barrett send him here for me?

Parker's clenching his fist, with his lips resting on the tops of his knuckles. Once they leave, it's just Parker and me and the mellow sound of water movement around us. The last of the other couples in the other pools retreat too. It must be later than I thought.

In seconds, he's towering over me, with water dripping from his body. My gaze does a slow crawl from his navel to his glistening abs, steam rolling off him in waves.

"You know, we could complete the bond now ... since you're so eager to be a werewolf mate. Then we can be done with this."

He steps between my legs, only slightly brushing my skin, and I avert my eyes but lean into the caress of his lips at my jaw. It's so good. I miss his smell even though now he smells like healing salts.

"Run away together to the city and leave all this behind."

"I have to go through with The Hunt. That's the only way this ends."

"Fine." He nudges my legs farther apart and tugs up my chin up. "But just know, all these guys are dreaming of tasting you in all the ways I already have."

It's more demanding than I'm used to, though I'm not putting up much of a fight.

His lips move to the place that's prickly and heavy from Garrik's proximity. "They want you in their bed."

His kisses breathe life into my skin. Then all I can think about is need. How badly I want him in all ways you could want a person. I will the words to come to my lips. To tell him everything and collapse into him. My body is aching for him, throbbing with need. Is it the bond tying us together?

"They fantasize about taking you to dinner, then taking you home." He sucks at the skin of my neck, just above his mark.

It's always been real to me. But this is—

I gasp from the pressure of him as he places a knee between my thighs. The way he nibbles at me with desire. He's all wet, glistening muscle, and *my mate*.

"Parker," I whisper.

In a blink, his lips are at my ear. "And they're going to keep dreaming."

He kisses down my neck and pins me with his arms on either side of me.

"Do—" I can't say the words. I can't tell him to stop because I can't imagine moving without him touching me.

"Yes?" He runs a finger under the strap of my bathing suit and watches it fall before sucking the skin on my shoulder. A finger runs down the center of my chest. "Say the words. Tell me to stop."

I shake my head. "Don't stop."

"You know it's only been two days since I last touched you like this. Do you miss me already?" He thumbs over my hardened nipples, licking his bottom lips while wearing a hungry smirk. "I can promise no one else will feel the same."

There's frustration in his touch. The way he holds me in place with one arm and teases me with the other. It's firm and punishing.

"This is a compromising position for you, baby. How do you think they'll feel seeing you like this?"

He kisses my collarbone, and my fingers tug in his hair while my head falls back. "Head back, legs open, whispering my name ..."

He's going lower, and my soft sighs turn into panting breaths. His palm cups the small of my back to hold me straighter. It's obvious how much I want him.

How much I love him. And even more obvious how I don't want him to stop touching me. We're made for each other.

My other strap falls, and he whispers, "Why do I feel like you'd let me strip you right now if I asked?"

"We shouldn't."

My phone isn't near. Searching around, I don't see any cameras.

"But you'd like me to make you come, wouldn't you?"

I swallow.

We're completely alone, and he caresses between my legs, and when I squirm, his fingers move under my suit, touching the sensitive skin there but never where I need him.

"Is this casual, baby? The way you want me inside you right now … Would you say this is fake?"

His tongue runs up my neck until it grazes over his mark. My entire body spasms at the pleasure of it.

"I could make you come like this … from my mark. If you hated me, I'd know. It wouldn't feel this good."

I'm shaking my head. Panting. The further I let him go, the more guilty I feel.

But I love him.

I love him.

I love him.

I whimper when he moves his fingers and stops.

"Are you aching that bad for me, baby?"

"Parker. Please touch me."

"Yeah? Why?" His voice is hard against my ear while he runs his fingers back and forth under the edge of my swimsuit bottoms.

"I need you." My voice nearly breaks.

It's an admission to more, and he knows because he melts into me.

"Mate." His breath rushes over my neck before he sucks. My entire body thrums with need, while his tongue teases the delicate skin. There's an ache in my breasts and between my legs when his suction grows harder. "You get whatever you want from me."

The sounds of my panting and the trickling of water echo in the bathhouse, so I whisper his name.

He knows what I want.

Those thick fingers run over my opening, and I'm so close just from his tongue, then he fills me, pressing into me where I ache, and I cry out, the sound ricocheting in the empty bathhouse.

For a moment, it's not enough. I need him buried inside me. I miss him. But he makes it enough. The combination of his tongue on my neck while his fingers are buried inside me draws the orgasm out of me like the snap of a rubber band. That and the memory of him, hands on the headboard, spilling into me.

He kisses my neck while the pleasure spreads through my body, and I ride it out in his arms, gripping the edge of the pool.

His eyes are pure blue. Wide, blown pupils, but soft and contemplative. It's all him.

"You know, I could do so many things right now, including bending you over the side of this and giving you exactly what you want, but I'm playing the long game and finally claiming what is mine. Tomorrow. No more faking."

I lean against him, closing my eyes.

"Parker, I ... I did mean it. I love you. That wasn't a lie."

I don't know what it changes, but I need him to know. No matter what happens from here on out, Parker has to know it was never fake for me, and I do want it to work even if I'm a coward. There's a part of me that still believes. He makes me want to.

My forehead meets his, and he asks, "What do you need?"

"I want to go to my room. I'm so tired."

I'm being lifted out of the water in his arms. He drops me momentarily, shakes out a towel, and wraps it around my waist.

"Hold on to me."

He picks me up like I'm his bride, and I wrap my arms around his neck. His skin is so hot and perfect. I rest my head on his shoulder and close my eyes, pretending for a moment it's just us. No one else matters. I can't believe he's still here fighting for me. It would have been easier to let me go.

Parker keeps choosing me. It's deliberate and calculated and hard. Nothing is easy for him, being here surrounded by these people who do nothing but challenge him. He's doing all of this for me.

"You know ... whatever happens. If this all falls apart, I'd still run away with you. Go to the city just you and me," he says.

"You would ... even if ..."

"Even if. Yeah."

I'm tempted to finish my sentence anyway, but it doesn't matter to him. No matter the circumstance, he'll still want me.

"That's good to know."

Everyone is afraid of who Parker will become, and they should be. He's going to live up to every expectation of greatness, and I want to be by his side when he does.

My eyes open when he places me on the floor. We stay close, with my head pressed against his chest. I want him to come in. I want to give in and take his offer, run away to the city, just the two of us, but that won't solve this. It won't stop people from targeting us. The only way to do that is to fight back.

He pulls a shirt from his bag. "Here. Hopefully this is the last night we're ever apart."

I bring it to my face and inhale. There's something primal about the way it relaxes me.

"So you can sleep."

Just as I contemplate asking him to stay, my door opens. Eva is in my hotel room, in some type of raincoat, and her hair is a mess.

"You came." The emotion of seeing her spills from my eyes, and I wrap my arms around her. "I'm so glad you're here."

"Thank them. It was not easy to get here. We took a fishing boat."

That explains the smell.

When I look back, Parker is whispering with Zant in the hallway.

"Wait, you did this?" I ask.

Zant holds a finger to his lips. "Not easy. All Parker's idea."

Parker is more serious than I'm used to seeing him. He's doing this for me, to prove a point to everyone. He isn't someone to mess with. He's taken his rightful place as a leader, and the world will need to accept it.

I fist his shirt in my hands and take in the scent of it, and with his cologne lingering, I watch him disappear.

Chapter Forty-Six

Olivia

"Mine," he whispers in my ear.

"Oh, this is bad," I say, as Eva and I stare at the envelope that was placed under my door in the night.

It's pictures of Emma on her trip and a typed note. *Enjoy the swim? In case you get cold feet, Rabbit. Step lightly.* The contents are strewn over the hotel bed but Eva can't see them. They're pictures of my sister on the culinary club trip. She's in bright-Luxxia blue, testing out food at different street markets. They're all from different angles where she can't see. The threat is implied.

"What do they say?"

"They're pictures." I whisper.

"Pictures of what?"

My spine straightens.

"Wait, I was able to tell you? These are pictures of Emma on her trip with the culinary club. It's a threat. They're implying they know where she is and that I need to stick to the plan." I try to conjure the words to tell her about the first file and my mouth wont move. Weird. "The contents of this envelope aren't bound to the stone for some reason."

"This place is crazy. We should tell someone. I'll tell someone." Eva's shaking my bed with her fidgeting, so I grab her arm.

"And have them hurt her?"

"We have to do something. Do you really think they would do it?"

"I ..." I didn't know they'd go this far, that anyone would go this far to scare me. Why would Aster and Barrett risk their status to threaten my sisters and me? It must be a retaliation to Parker's article. But still ... "I don't know. But after The Hunt, I'm going to leave Doxlothia and let everything settle."

"What? No way."

"I don't have a choice."

"Well, I'll come with you."

"No."

"But if you go, they win. That's what they want." For once, Eva is making sense.

I scroll through my phone and try calling the anonymous number, but it goes straight to a disconnected tone. Still no service.

I don't understand. I'm missing something.

"Please let me tell someone," Eva begs.

"Tell Parker about the pictures. Tell him ... we have to win this."

Once I leave the room, I'm not allowed back in. Eva's going to have to lie low and out of sight for the day. At least Parker's shirt helped me get some sleep. All of the hunted are isolated from the hunters for the day.

We're put in the dining hall for breakfast, then again for lunch after we're shown the layout of the island, the safety measures, how to call for help, and what to expect while we're there. We all have trackers on our ankles, and there are cameras set up around The Hunting Grounds.

This is a resort, so when the meetings are over, we're allowed more social time.

The sun is setting by the time we can see the hunters again.

I know Parker is on the other side of the wall at times, which should be impossible, but it's a feeling. We're moving around each other all day, and I catch the smallest glimpse of his hair before I'm ushered into a small glass room by one of the pools.

A woman checks me over, makes me sign some liability papers, and asks me one final time if I'd like to back out. My knee is bouncing since all I can think about is Emma. I'm about to ask her for a phone so I can contact my sister when she excuses herself for a knock at the door. I stand by the window overlooking the pool and pillars along the garden, taking in the surrounding trees.

Parker could find me. He's proven himself capable over and over again. Maybe this can still work. I don't want to play the game alone, but we could play it … together. I just need to not get caught by another Were. Easier said than done.

I gasp when the door opens seconds later and Zant appears.

"What are you doing?"

"I came to give you a message. Emma's safe. Gavin's with her. He got in one of his expensive ass private jets to make sure of it. And I have this for you." Zant hands me a small vial with silver liquid. "You'll need this. It should help give you some speed in case Parker needs time to find you."

"She's okay, you're sure?"

"Yeah. You've got people in your corner. We'll figure it out. This is new. I've never seen anyone at the council go this far."

"Thank you for helping. I'm sorry for—"

"You don't need to apologize. You not trusting anyone in this place is more than warranted … but I love Parker. I'd do anything for him, so you better fucking run as fast as you can out there. And expect shit to go wrong. I don't know what they're planning, but since you're always a target, I figured why not give you a little help."

"Got it. I will."

He stuffs his hands in his pockets and turns to leave but stops when he reaches the doorframe.

"I really hope you do care about Parker. I think you do. He thinks you do. He … deserves something good."

Zant's always put together but not today. His hair is messy and he's got stubble on his chin. I wonder if he stayed up talking with Parker.

"Do you really think there's a chance that Parker and I will be able to be together in peace?"

"Complete the mating bond. The higher up Weres will respect it. Even Barrett and Aster. Once it's done, it can't be undone."

"Okay ... tell Parker I'm running to the west."

"You got it. Good luck."

Once Zant's gone, I memorize the map. There are six outposts that the hunted are split up between and shuffled to while all the hunters are let go in the middle of the island. I sip the potion and hide the empty vial before I board the shuttle. There's a waterfall nearby, which means I'm on the opposite side of the island I need to be on. *Perfect.*

I need to stay positive. Parker is fighting. I need to fight too.

"You will have ten minutes to disperse by yourselves."

We're all in athletic wear, shorts, and sneakers. There's an embroidered logo on the polo T-shirt that matches the souvenir I have in my hotel room. My group is vibrant with excitement and laughter. They've waited for this. They want this.

I almost wish Tara and I had the same group, but I use the silence as time to focus on my plan. Just like before a performance, I imagine myself going through the motions, running through the trees and following the river to the north in case I get lost.

It smells of rain, and there's a thick mist settling around us as the sun fades the sky into lilac.

Our adviser has a walkie talkie and is talking back and forth on the position of the others. It's an odd modern element in an otherwise completely archaic tradition.

"Okay, everyone line up." He motions next to a row of bushes.

I note the direction of the lingering sun so I can find the west. I have ten minutes to cover as much ground as possible.

"Remember your safety procedures. This is your last chance to forfeit your run. Any takers?"

The girl next to me giggles. This is my run. My part in the game, and I'm going to play it the best way I know how. There's a relentless hum in my ears as the potion takes its course. There are no cheats in a game against cheaters.

"Alright. Ready ..."

"One."

I inhale. This is a performance. Another dance.

"Two."

Then exhale.

"Three."

At the sound of the whistle, we're all off, and I'm running faster than I've ever moved before. There's no ache in my muscles as I tear through dirt and dead leaves. The voices of the others diminish in seconds.

The sun fades as I weave through the trees, and the moonlight appears through the clouds. There's a lingering soft-purple haze minutes before the night takes over completely, and I stop to catch my breath. The potion makes me move quickly, but my breath still has trouble catching up with the movement.

The reverberating echo of howling evaporates into the air, and my heart pounds. The hunters are coming. I need to move. Now.

I sprint as fast as I can, dodging trees and broken limbs. *Push. Push. Push.* I thank my practice for the stamina to run for twenty minutes straight. Anytime I hear someone near, I run the other way. I'd know if it was him and I'm not far enough west.

It's dark, and I don't know where I am. There's no sun to guide me, only my memory of the map and the trust that I'm still moving west. How fast can Weres move?

I stop at the sound of movement. Wet, sloppy kisses. Hurried breaths. In the clearing are a couple, clearly having found their desired mark, so I move on, running as far as my lungs will allow.

I don't know how long the potion will last.

Something large and dark moves in my peripheral, so I stop. Ten yards away, I spot a silver werewolf with glowing green eyes. They've found me.

I go to bolt in the other direction, and my heart stops. There are two others circling me. None of them Parker. It's so dark I shouldn't be able to tell, but I can. Safety. Sureness. All of it is far. He isn't here.

How? How did three of them catch my scent?

Zant's words echo. *Expect things to go wrong.*

My smell. It has to be my clothes. There must be something they can smell that they like because I should still smell like Parker. Maybe someone tampered with my clothes.

Removing it in one swipe, I throw it toward the werewolves behind me, then bolt in the only opening I see. It works. They're drawn to that scent.

I run till my ankles chafe and my already bruised toenails feel like they're going to fall off. I dart between the trees, stopping only when the noise ceases.

Without Zant's potion, I'd have never made it past them.

Parker. Please, come on. Where are you?

Stripping off my bottoms, I stare at the tree above. I need to move my scent around. Decoys. I need decoys. My fingers snap the bark as I climb branch by branch to place my shorts, then drop back down into the dirt. My whole body aches, and I stumble into the dirt. I have to find the river to the north.

Sprinkling rain cools my hot cheek. I swipe it, along with the sweat, and wipe it on my camisole. *Definitely a good choice for underwear today.* The rain is good and bad. Harder for Parker to find me but easier to hide.

I rush toward the sound of pouring water, but I stop and hold my breath at every snap of a twig. I know it's close, but the only light is from the moon.

At the bank of the river is a werewolf on four legs stalking back and forth. Waiting and sniffing the air, trying to find the scent of someone to hunt. Waiting in the cover of the trees for them to move on, I take off a shoe and place it on a piece of wood, then send it down the river.

My foot snaps a branch, and I hold my breath.

The werewolf's glowing red and silver eyes stare back at me. *Run.*

I run toward the rocks and the embankment, anywhere not out in the open. There's a cave covered by a fallen tree. I don't have time to think if it's a good idea. My feet slip in the mud, so I grip the vines on the inside to keep myself upright.

Howling pierces the air, and mud squelches while the ragged breaths follow me. My body moves on its own until I spot a pool with water rushing in from a hole up above, so I throw my last shoe farther into the cave before diving in.

I submerge myself under the water till the last bit of air runs out and my lungs scream. The werewolf is still there. Brawny shoulders of fur and pure instinct.

I place both hands over my mouth as the werewolf steps in close to the water. I stay completely still, with the waterfall rushing over me. He sniffs the air, his eyes glow in the dark. The waterfall is hiding my scent and frantic heartbeat. I count fifteen seconds before he's out of sight and moving farther into the cave.

I wait another five before climbing out of the water and bolting out of the cave entrance.

I'm soaked and it's slowing me down. My feet are bleeding and so are my knees. Parker has to find me.

A crack of thunder runs down my spine, stopping me in my tracks. Lightning streaks across the sky, and the clouds crowd the full moons overhead.

Where are you?

CHAPTER FORTY-SEVEN

PARKER

"Find me," she says.

They say the first dual full moon after the shift as an accepted Alpha is the hardest. They weren't fucking joking. The rush of it is so intense I nearly throw up. My skin flushes and I brace for what's coming. The throbbing in my skull. The stretching of my skin. Any lingering bonds to Gavin's pack vanish in an instant, and when it's gone, there's just me.

I thought I'd feel empty, but as I stare at my hands in the moonlight and the searing hot pain runs through my blood, I'm whole and free like never before. There's power in my shifted form.

Shit, is this what I've been running from? I guess Olivia hasn't been the only one running.

I've dreaded this moment, but this is what I was meant to accept. I am destined to be a pack leader.

With my nose to the ground, I search for her. The others have already scattered in a flurry of howls and dirt. It should be easy to find her, but my senses are off. I inhale and smell ... nothing. Not even the trees or the soil.

I've never smelled nothing before. I growl, baring my teeth. Someone enchanted me. But how? When?

It could have been my food. Maybe someone had access to the kitchen? *Olivia.*

I'm already heading west like she mentioned, moving fast. Zant warned me someone would try to sabotage The Hunt. That means someone could have enchanted her too.

There's no other option than for me to tune into the bond.

She's scared. Her lungs are burning—she's probably running and hurt. The rain turns from droplets until it's pelting me and wetting my fur. I have to hurry.

Feel for her. I trust the bond. It's all I have to find her. I stop at a riverbank, spotting a shoe floating by. It's hers. I know it even if I can't smell it. Every second, the enchantment wears off. The smell of rain floods my senses. Then the dirt, but it's still faint.

I follow the footprints at the edge. Her heart is racing, and so is mine.

"Where are you?"

I stop. That's Olivia's voice in my head. I don't have time to ponder why. She's close. She needs me. I howl into the night as a warning to other Weres. I'm coming for her, and if they want to avoid a fight, they need to flee.

A broken branch in the distance catches my attention, and thunder cracks and rumbles through the ground.

Her scent hits me.

It's the sweetest, most intoxicating thing I've ever smelled. *Mine. Mine. Mine.* The pull of it is so strong I break into a sprint of pure hysteria.

I need her.

I'll have her.

She can't get away from me. Olivia is mine. My muscles are numb to pain, my senses dull to anything that isn't her scent. I need to claim her.

I stop when a rush of anxiety runs through the bond. She's close. I sniff the air, and the hairs on my back stand on end.

Garrik walks into the clearing slowly. Two glowing orbs locked on me. He's an enormous werewolf with black fur.

Then I see her. Olivia is lying in the dirt and rain, covering her ears from the thunder, then she ducks behind a tree.

"I'm not backing down on this one," Garrik says.

"Good."

I've never been bluffing. This is a fight I won't allow myself to lose.

He keeps his head low to the ground and circles me. I always thought the most important moment of my life would be on the ice, not in the mud and dirt.

The rain falls between us, filling the ground in wet puddles, and the thunder cracks in a dull rumble.

He lunges and I dodge, but he's on my tail and bites into my shoulder. I don't howl at the pain. I don't even feel the teeth dig into my muscle before I shove him to the ground and slash his chest.

I'm vaguely aware of my human senses dulling. That part of my brain is off as the alpha blood inside me relishes the crimson staining my claws. Let's taste. Let's tear. Let's kill.

I go for his throat, biting into fur and skin, and the satisfaction of his blood on my tongue sends me into a frenzy. A deep guttural growl rumbles from my throat, and I lunge at him again, barely missing as he squirms to get away. I give way to the chase, but there's nowhere he can hide. Nothing he can do. He won't get Olivia. He won't win. He'll be lucky to make it out of this alive.

Elation. Pure elation at the hunt is a shot of adrenaline to my heart. I catch him by the hind leg and throw him into the dirt. *Keep fighting. Let's do this forever.*

He flings a boulder at me that narrowly misses and takes out a few trees. There's excitement in that too. I never get to play dirty.

Claws bending into the bark of a tree, I climb. Jumping. Stalking. Watching him look for her like a fool because I'm the one who can sense her. Her scent tunes me back into the bond. I need to see how far Olivia has wandered. I'll have her. Only a few more minutes now.

I jump down onto his back, getting a good cut in before he throws me off. I dig my claws in with full intent to maim him, and he mimics the move with a claw to my chest. With all my might, I clamp my arms around him and take a chunk of his shoulder. Then his arm. He loosens, falling back and yelping, and I advance on him, ready for more.

"Come on," I taunt.

He growls, so I prepare for him to lunge again, but he bows his head, then disappears in the trees, and the echo of thunder follows him.

I'm bleeding. Huffing, I smell for her and follow her scent through the trees. *Mine. Mine. Mine.* I *need* her. I'm close. Her blood, her heat, her sweetness are close. I want to taste her. *Oh, fuck,* I need her. I need her.

I'm going to claim her. She's mine.

She gasps when I tower over her, and she stumbles till her back hits a tree. Those violet and gold eyes flutter while the rain wets her cheeks.

It's see-through. The wet camisole clings to her breasts and the tops of her thighs. Her lips are a cool-pale pink. She looks cold.

I'm going to warm her.

I'm going to ruin her.

"Parker?" She steps forward, her legs bare and knees bleeding. I lean over to sniff her and run my claws through her hair. *My mate. My beautiful mate.*

Nuzzling into her neck, I rub at my mark there, then lick at her wounds. The small cuts on her neck and chest. They heal instantly, and she stares at me in awe. The taste of her blood almost sends me into another frenzy.

"You found me."

With a wild growl, I hoist her over my shoulder, and she gasps, but her scent is calm as I let out a victory howl. The entire forest erupts with the howling cries of the disappointed in the cool night air.

She doesn't seem to mind that she doesn't know where I'm taking her, there's no fighting. I remove her from my shoulder to hold her bridal style as we near the treehouse, and I climb the stairs. She doesn't even shiver when the thunder rolls through the night.

The treehouses are off-limits during The Hunt and only for rent for resort guests, but I can't wait for the resort room. They're going to have to bill me for damages.

I break the door and move her to the upstairs loft, with all clean furnishings, including a ready-made bed. The loft overlooks a small living room area and has a window that takes up the entire wall. It leads outside to a deck being soaked with rain.

I drop her to the wood floor, and lightning illuminates the bedroom.

Finally, I can let go. The adrenaline subsides, and I shift back into my human form, leaving me naked in front of her.

"Mine." The first word that falls from my lips comes from the wolf within. I sniff her neck and groan. "I found you."

She's entranced as I roam her, melting into my touch. Her tattered, thin camisole has holes, and I brush over the skin there. On her breast. Her stomach.

I finally have her all to myself.

"You're bleeding," she says.

"Doesn't matter."

"But—"

"Tell me you want this now. Talk to me."

Her vow to the Secrecy Stone should be settled.

She tests the words. "They ... were framing you. They made it look like you bribed your way to team captain—"

"Wait, this is about ... the Rage team?"

"The folder was slipped under my door, and it had all these falsified testimonies that you were involved in some illegal gambling scheme so you'd never be able to get into a pro team. I wanted to tell you, but they bugged my phone, and the file was enchanted for my eyes only." Her bottom lip quivers.

"You ... did this for me?" I blink. "You seriously thought I cared more about getting into the pro league than being with you? That I'd rather you risk everything you worked for so I could play? You were going to become someone else's *mate* for *me*."

"It would have ruined your entire life and reputation, and I couldn't be the reason something terrible happened to you again. I didn't know if I was making the wrong choice and all I wanted was to go to you, but I couldn't risk it. You were right. I should have just told you. I might be the worst linked mate ever, but I want this more than anything and I love you. I'm so—"

I wipe the tears streaking down her dirt-stained face. "Stop. Don't you dare say you're sorry."

I kiss her salty lips, and it's like that first time in Noxx House. Like electricity free flowing through my veins while I caress her face.

"It's okay now. I'm here. I'm never leaving you. We'll fix it all together," I say.

I can't even begin to think of how with the fresh taste of her on my tongue, but we will.

"I want to be mated to you. Let's seal the bond. Right now." My eyebrows shoot up as she drops her camisole to the floor. "Please."

I kiss her again. "Whatever you want."

Everything else can wait till we're bonded. Complete.

We're wet and covered in dirt and blood, but none of it matters. Our bodies meet in a feral frenzy of lips and tongue.

I need to be inside her.

My shoulders shake as I lift her off the floor by her knees and lay her on the bed. She's completely bare in the moonlight. My skin is on fire, and my teeth hurt. I feel so unhinged. Raw. The wolf in me wants to ruin her. To hear her scream and drain every ounce of pleasure I can from her body. I don't want her to be sore ... but the wolf in me does. I want to fuck her till she can't walk straight.

"It's the first dual full moon tonight after accepting my alpha blood ... tell me if I'm too rough. I'm going to try to be gentle, baby. But I ..." I lean down to kiss the inside of her knee, but that only makes me hungrier.

"You won't hurt me," she breathes.

"I won't hurt you," I repeat, already more sure.

I'm licking her stomach when she says, "What do I need to do to complete the bond?"

"I need to bite you again and then you're going to bite me really hard too."

"Then what?"

"Then I'm going to eat you out, drag you to the edge of the bed, and take you that way."

"You've ... thought about this," she says, gasping when I bite her breast.

Fuck yes, I've thought about sealing our mating bond. I wanted to take her to a fancy hotel room and do it after she had a bath and a glass of wine, but we're both covered in blood and mud, hungry for each other, and I can't wait another second.

"I *need* those two things to happen, but the bond is going to make you uncomfortable, and I don't want to prolong it. Do you understand?"

She nods, so I move to the bed, hovering over her. A faint cry leaves her throat when my teeth sink into my mark on her neck, and it turns into a moan as I drink. The blood bag I was given earlier today doesn't compare.

My ears ring as she cries out. It's just her and me in the middle of the woods. We can be as loud as we want. My inner wolf marks her while the vampire in me is satiated by her blood.

I lick the mark closed and cradle her till she's sitting. The wetness of her lips grazes my shoulder, and I guide her head there.

"I don't want to hurt you ..." Her sigh sets the hairs straight on my arm.

"You won't." I trace her ear. "It's okay."

Her teeth dig into my shoulder. Heat jolts inside me, and I drag my fingers through her hair, groaning from the sudden rush of pleasure.

"How do you feel?" I say, admiring my blood on her mouth.

She licks it from her bottom lip, and the smell of her arousal grows. My girl is turned on by the taste of blood. *My blood.*

"Hot. All over."

"That's how I feel." The heat in my body is growing. The itch spreads from my shoulder down my spine. The bonding process has started.

Chapter Forty-Eight

Olivia

"Parker, touch me." The words come out in a panic as the warmth spreads through my blood with each pump of my heart. He's on top of me before I can blink, running his hands over my body.

I scratch at the mark, and it's burning and itching out of control.

"It's so hot." I dig my fingernails into the skin of my neck, and Parker grabs my wrist.

He peppers kisses over my neck, then licks me, and it's like ice on my inflamed skin. "I'll fix it."

It's the only thing that soothes the burning ache covering me from head to toe.

"Please." I don't know what I'm pleading for, for more of his touch? More of the coolness on my hot skin? Or for him to get inside me, to lose himself completely in this sensation that's growing out of control.

"It's *okay*." His chest heaves with each breath, like he's struggling to hold back, but his touch is barely there, a cooling caress with his cheek against mine. "I'm going to need you to focus on me, baby. Don't focus on anything else."

That's increasingly hard to do when wave after wave of heat rolls through me. I look at my hands, thinking surely there is evidence of burning or welts. But there's nothing. I catch a glimpse of us in the mirror in the corner of the loft, me, starry-eyed with flushed cheeks while Parker kisses me lower and lower. My stomach. My inner thigh. The gash on his chest is nearly healed, but the dried blood is a mess covering his muscles.

"Focus," he demands before kissing below my stomach, and my hips buck into him. Everywhere his lips meet my skin, the coolness of it jolts throughout my entire body. I grasp for him, digging my fingers into his shoulders, and a moan escapes my lips.

This is more intense than the potion.

I'm shaking from the euphoria of his touch. Everything is amplified. He needs to touch me more, to never stop. It's agony not to have him inside me.

He tears into the sheets, holding my hips and pinning me as he takes me with his mouth. The euphoria of it hits me so fast I might pass out. My head throbs with each pulsing beat, but Parker's fingers digging into my hips ground me. Then it's impossible to think of *anything* other than what his tongue is doing. He's devouring me. With a firm grip on my thighs, he holds me despite my squirming. The pleasure is so intense. Every stroke of his tongue has me gasping. I don't think pleasure exists like this outside of magic.

I groan when his teeth enter my thigh. I'm already on the edge, and him drinking is enough for me to spill over. The release floods my senses like ice water. I thrash, but he holds me, placing his mouth at my center, anchoring me.

There's brief relief from the heat, and I look into his darkened eyes, blood dripping from his chin as he licks my thigh to heal it.

As soon as it's over, my body flushes with heat again, and I need it to end.

"It's so much," I say, breathless. "I'm still hot."

He kisses me, and his lips taste of me. "I know. But focus, baby. It's almost done."

His lips meet my chest with cool, thoughtful kisses, then his tongue runs over my nipples. It's like ice. Any added pleasure is an overload. So good it almost hurts.

He spins me, pinning my hips to the bed. When he releases me for a second to adjust, my skin itches.

"Parker, please." I reach for him.

Then his hands are on my hips and running up my back. "Relax, baby. I got it."

He slides into me, and we gasp at the sudden jolt. It's the magic. The bond is solidifying with each thrust of his hips. I bury my face into the blankets, the sounds he's driving from me getting louder. The bond is merging us. Tearing out the old Olivia to make room for the new, and I'm ready for it. To be the other half of a whole.

"You're doing so good." Parker calms me. "Take a little more of me. Just a little more."

My legs shake as he goes deeper, and I'm so full I cry out.

He starts soft, then he pounds into me harder and harder till I can't think. I just need him. I'll die if he stops. The pressure building in my core is unbearable, but my blood races as it climbs. I want him to finish. I think he's almost there, but then he pulls out.

"What are you doing?" I say.

"I want to look at you."

I'm malleable putty in his hands as he flips me, lifts my leg, then slides into me in one fluid motion. This is different. I feel how much he wants me. How good every single thrust inside me feels for him. How he's so close to coming but grasping at the sheets to stop himself.

I feel the bond. What Parker felt but I couldn't.

I gasp.

He stops. "This still okay?"

"I feel ... what you feel."

A wide grin spreads across his face, like that's the best news he's heard all day. "Yeah?"

He goes deeper, and now I know he's right where he wants to be. How the wet heat for him is perfect, and the pressure of me fluttering around him is inching him closer to release. He's so eager to please—

Our pleasure is one harmonious rhythm that bursts simultaneously. Instead of warmth, it's coolness spreading through my abdomen, and as I ride out the end of my release, Parker holds me tight to him till all the heat and itchiness vanish.

I still want to be close to him long after the effects fade. I cling to him, unwilling to lose the connection.

The sound of rain and thunder come back as we lie panting in bed.

Naked and dirty, I turn to crawl on top of Parker's chest, but he stops me.

"Please don't get up yet."

His lips run over my cheek. Rough fingers move through my hair, and he touches me like he's trying to memorize the shape of my lips and nose.

It's done. We're mated. And it is different, but not in any way I thought it would. This was my choice. It doesn't change the way I love Parker; it only deepens our connection.

He is the man from my dreams.

And the boy who pulled me from the water when I was a child. He's always loved me.

"You're my mate," I say, running my hands in his still-damp hair.

He looks as tired as I feel. The rain hitting the top of the treehouse settles around us and it's like we're the only two people left in Vviveren.

"Are you okay?" Parker's voice enters my head.

I suck in a breath. The books only said it was a possibility. Not all linked mates can talk telepathically. I didn't think we—

"Did you just?"

"Yeah. It's okay. I promise." He comforts me with a hand on my cheek. His eyebrows draw together. "Tell me what you're thinking."

"I'm okay." I try back, and his eyebrows lift with the smile on his face. *"I'm thinking you love me. It was never just the bond."*

He smiles. "Never just that. Just you. Always you."

"What are you thinking about?"

"How I need to marry you immediately. Do you think you'll want to take my last name?"

I laugh, placing his hand on my cheek. "We can enjoy this first."

"Oh, I'm enjoying. I plan on enjoying you over and over again." He kisses me on the cheek. "Once you're healed and rested."

"So what happens now?" I say, looking around the room of a luxury tree-house we're definitely not permitted to be in. "Do you think they'll kick us out of here?"

I didn't care at the time, but thinking of someone walking in to find Parker and me naked and covered in dirt would be mortifying, especially if the paparazzi are involved.

I guess I have to look at my life through that lense from here on out. I'm no longer just Olivia Osborne, the ballerina. I'm Olivia Osborne, the ballerina and the first human linked mate in Vviveren.

It's a heavy title, but with Parker, it's not as daunting. Maybe it's something I can be good at. No. I know I can. Just like I know I can play Giselle, my dream role.

"No. I will likely have to pay for the door and the ruined sheets though."

"What about Barrett and Aster? What if they're ... angry?"

He's still inspecting me, rubbing his cheek against mine and his nose down my jaw.

"There's no one in Vviveren that will take you from me. Let them be angry. We're linked for forever now. I'm going to take you to the city. I'll need to build a pack. The moon festival is almost here, and your ballet is coming up soon. It's all up from here, baby."

"You make it sound like it's all going to fall into place now."

"It will. This is like ... like a childhood dream come true. That's how long I've wanted you."

"It's like that for me too."

"Oh, keep doing that." He kisses me with a wide smile.

Parker and I bonded, and my entire life will be different. I'm still going to get into the IBCE, but Parker will be there. He'll get into the pro league, and I'll be there too. I've found my mate and I never have to part from him.

All the dreams of destruction and storms were warning us of The Hunt, but now the threat has passed, and I feel free.

The thunder continues with the barrage of lightning, but I've never felt safer.

Parker pulls me onto a pillow with him. "All of this is pretty rough on your body. I want to heal you."

I smile and wrap my arms around his torso.

"I'm yours. I'm not going anywhere."

CHAPTER FORTY-NINE

OLIVIA

"Hi." The boy on the swing is waiting with a wide smile.

"Parker," I say.

He turns, smiling. "I've been waiting for you. I brought this for us."

Young Parker hands me an umbrella.

"I think it's about to rain."

"Parker." I wake with his name on my lips. The rain has stopped and the light of dawn illuminates the room in a blueish gray, while I stare up at a ceiling made entirely of wooden planks, reeling.

Parker's arms tighten around me tighten. "What's wrong?"

"I remember. We met at the swing every day. There are so many times ... too many to say. And when my mother died, you were there. You let me cry in your arms."

It's all swirling in my head. Every single dream we shared is there. We shared pain, tears, and highs and lows in our dreams, and we never knew.

No wonder he couldn't stop staring the day after he marked me. How do you go back after knowing someone has been with you, caring for you every day since you were children?

"You remember the dreams?" His voice cracks.

I nod, and tears prick at my eyes.

"You let me cry in your arms too," he says.

The early morning gets away from us. I can't stop touching him. He can't stop touching me. When we try, we end up connected again.

Once the light takes over the treehouse completely, Parker ushers us through grounds and back to the resort. Zant and my sister are waiting. I ask Eva if I worried her, and she reminds me there are cameras. There's footage of all of it. Me stripping to my underwear and running through the trees. Parker fighting Garrik. And the moment Parker hoists me over his shoulder and takes me to the treehouse out of sight. Eva assures me I didn't make a fool of myself, though I look like a wreck covered in dirt and blood running around in the rain with nothing but my underwear on. The whole resort is abuzz with the news of the newly mated couples, and many of them are opting to stay for a few more days.

Tara practically tackles me in a hug and introduces me to her new mate, a tall man with golden brown skin named Austin. Parker seems to like him, and it brings me relief she found a good one. She asks us to stay at least one more night so we can have dinner, and I politely decline.

I'm desperate to get back to some sense of normalcy.

We take a private boat back with Zant and my sister, then sneak back into Noxx House. I don't check the forums and only check my phone to call my father to tell him I won't be coming home, and then my sister.

I remember her voice pitching on the phone.

"Why didn't you tell me any of this?!"

"I wanted you to enjoy your trip. You deserved to go."

"Well, don't do it again. If I had known this was happening, I would have helped. At the very least, I wouldn't have functioned as extortion bait. I'm serious. This whole stoic, I handle this on my own crap doesn't work for me."

"Trust me. I've learned."

She must have been eating because there was crunching followed by a muffled change in her voice.

"There are so many things we need to talk about when I get back. I can't believe you and Parker have been sharing dreams since you were children. And you're mated now. I'll need details on that, and not your normal vague, keep it to yourself type ones. You just casually have the best love story ever written in the history of Vviveren? I'm so jealous it hurts. They're going to write books about this."

I rolled my eyes. *"We'll talk about it when you get back."*

Emma's booked on the first train in the morning from the city, along with Gavin who I'll need to personally thank for putting her in a hotel and showing her the city.

We don't leave Parker's bed all day. We deserve just one day—Parker and me, our blissful window, and the snacks stashed in his dresser. Aster and Barrett and their schemes are the furthest things from my mind as he traces circles on my skin and I throw popcorn into his mouth from the end of the bed. Who cares if they're angry? Who cares what they'll try tomorrow or the next day? Parker and I are solid. We can handle it. The bond between us isn't fragile.

It's late when I get a text from Mrs. Vix asking me to meet her to discuss moving forward in the program.

"I have to go to the studio and talk to the director, let her know I can dance," I say, pulling on my school uniform. I've got clean ballet clothes in my backpack in case. "She wants to see me in person."

I stop to look in the tiny mirror Parker has placed beside his door. The mark on my neck has changed. Once dark but now a light-blue crescent of teeth signifying the sealed bond.

"Let me go with you."

I smile, biting my lip. "Don't you have anything to attend to while I'm gone? Moon festival ringing a bell? Maybe you could practice. Gather your team. Talk to your coach."

"Ugh. Quit reminding me to be responsible. You're the only thing I want to think about today."

I lean in to kiss him. "Then you can have a little time to miss me."

"*Tell me everything while you're away,*" Parker says in my head.

I snicker, pulling my hands through my hair to tame it before I disappear into the hall. There's a secret way through the back of Noxx House, and I take a detour through the trees to avoid any eyes. Tomorrow, we deal with the press and the news. Today, I only need to ensure I get to keep my role as Giselle.

"*Let me know if someone bothers you. I'll come save you,*" Parker says.

"I took the back way. So far so good," I say. *"Are you hoping you'll need to come save me so you don't have to do anything responsible today?"*

"Definitely. I'm counting the minutes till you're back in my bed."

I smile. It's going to take some getting used to having Parker's voice in my head like a direct text line.

I double-check the time one more time before heading up the dance studio steps. It's peaceful for a no-school day. I expect to see the door open, but it's sealed with no light coming from inside.

Maybe she wants me to wait for her. I try peeking in the window and stop when I hear footsteps.

"Olivia!" Octavia greets me with a smile and a hug, and I'm instantly relieved. "I saw Parker claimed you at The Hunt. I'm so happy for you."

"How did you see?"

"Oh, the footage from The Hunt gets leaked online every year to the forum. You need to update me. First, they said you broke up, then I saw news you'd been claimed, and you looked more than willing from the videos I saw."

"How much time do you have?" I motion for the door. "I was going to meet with Mrs. Vix. Keep me company while I wait?"

"I have a key! She did mention seeing you tonight. She should be here any minute. She was right behind me when I left the castle."

She reaches for the door handle, and I wait in the quiet of the hall while she unlocks the door.

"I take it you're all healed up and ready for Giselle?"

"Yeah, I think she wants to see me in person to make sure. I brought my clothes to do some variations, but ... I don't want to stay too long."

Normally, I'd pack it in for the night and resign the rest of it to practice. I've had more days off ballet practice than I've had in years. But tonight is for Parker and me.

"I don't blame you. I bet Parker's already missing you."

She opens the door, and we file into the dark room.

"Do you think she'll want to see me dance to prove I can finish my part? I got injured before The Hunt, and she wanted me to come back. But I'm fine now. I'm not warm though."

"Oh, I wouldn't worry. Even if she does, you won't have any issues. You never do. Seriously, you pick up choreography faster than anyone I've ever seen."

The sun is barely enough to bring light into the room, and Octavia steps forward in the dark.

"Do you want me to get the light?" I turn to the wall, searching.

Octavia is facing me, her smile gone.

"What are you—"

She holds out her hand and in one breath, blows a plume of dust and enchantment into the air. It glitters as it falls, leaving me lightheaded.

My vision blurs and I stumble back into weightlessness. Octavia's frown is the last thing I see.

There's nothing to catch me as my vision goes dark.

Chapter Fifty

I sigh. Lying down for a few minutes, I take in the chaos from the last few days, running my hands over the fresh scar on my chest. Everything feels so clear. Completing the bond with Olivia was what I was meant to do. It makes everything else seem insignificant. The deal with Cane. Whatever happens with the council and Aster and Barrett. All of it awaits me tomorrow, and somehow I know it's going to be okay.

Fuck. Now I'm a full-blown alpha. That means I have to start building my own pack. A thought that used to keep me up at night, but with Olivia by my side, it's not so scary anymore. I'm the person I need to be to figure out my own path and make my mother proud. Whatever that ends up looking like.

Ten minutes pass, then I'm on my feet, putting on some pants so I'm no longer naked. I need to go to the rink like Olivia said, but I already miss her.

We're not supposed to be apart after bonding. For the first few weeks, the books say it will be intense. Too much distance will make us both sick. Even across campus will be too much. It's always like that for mates after completing the bond, but it's even worse for linked mates. That's why linked mates have lots of accommodation laws, since being at too long a distance will gradually make us so ill we'll die. It's what inspired *Romeo and Juliet*. A pair of linked mates who were forced to separate both perished centuries ago. Now that we've completed the bond, we'll always need to be in close proximity. No taking separate vacations or work trips.

There's a knock at my door. Probably Zant or Gavin.

My muscles stiffen. Aster is leaning against the doorframe, the flickering hall light illuminating the faint scar above his eye from where I nicked him.

His mouth is poised in a pleased half smile. "Busy man. Heard you solidified things with your mate and wanted to congratulate you."

"Shouldn't you be in jail or something?"

"You'd like that, wouldn't you? Next time you decide to come for my throat, have better proof and make sure your facts are straight. Though, I'll say, I'm quite impressed. I didn't know you had it in you."

"What are you talking about?"

He sighs, stepping into the room and shutting the door. I let him because I'm not scared to fight.

"I take it you haven't had any time to check the updates with your busy schedule, so I'll fill you in. I didn't drug Olivia and neither did Barrett. Your informant was wrong, so I want to find him."

"Wait, back up. What do you mean *you* didn't drug Olivia?"

"Did you really think I'd be so stupid to drug someone on campus? All to get back at you? What would be in that for me?"

I shove him with one hand. "You tell me, you prick. You made her enter The Hunt by framing me."

"The Hunt we had planned after your little stunts. Harmless payback."

"Harmless? You've got to be fucking kidding me."

The heat simmers under my skin, the itch building.

"Okay, let's not be dramatic. My father let me participate in a challenge when I was six, and I turned out fine. Besides, it was obvious you were going to win her *anyway*. Even if you didn't, there was no shot you wouldn't challenge the winner for her. She's your linked mate, and you're a hot head."

I growl, stepping closer, and he straightens his back.

"Then why work so hard to make sure I couldn't find her?"

"Come again?" He sighs, exasperated.

"You had someone enchant me and rig Olivia's clothes."

"Uh. No. I didn't care about the results of The Hunt. Making you both enter was the highlight of my year for entertainment alone. Barrett and I enjoyed the leaked footage."

"What about the pictures of Olivia's sister?"

"Who?" He squints at me.

He doesn't care about Olivia's sisters and hasn't since the beginning. He doesn't know about the pictures either.

It wasn't him.

There's always been more than one person pulling the strings.

"You're telling me ... you are the one who made Olivia join The Hunt, but that was it? What about the council nomination?"

"I can't get it out of him, but Darien is my best guess. Seems to have taken a liking to you. No idea why, you're insufferable."

"I saw the text messages. You were planning on doing something to Olivia's drink."

"It was a joke. We *briefly* mentioned trying to get her drunk at the party. I had the bar double pour drinks, but that was it. Not like she drank them anyway. We thought that's what you were talking about when you ambushed us."

"I thought you drugged her!"

"Well, we didn't."

"You called her Rabbit, the same as the texts she got."

"We all call her that. Darien started it. I'm seeing a pattern. Sneaky fucker. He wanted you to have that council seat, and he has a tendency to get what he wants."

That's rich coming from him. I replay Darien's words in my head. *I think this will be the more interesting outcome.* Interesting for him because he knew who drugged her the whole time. He was leading me toward something.

I harden my voice. "It was Cane who ratted you out."

"You've got to be fucking kidding me. I should have known. He was always slinking around. He's the one who gave me the idea for The Hunt."

"Meaning?" It's coming together. I almost understand.

"We were going to frame you and call it a day, but he thought it would piss you off more."

Cane is the one who drugged Olivia.

He tried to sabotage The Hunt.

He threatened Emma.

Cane is behind it all. We're the target.

My eyes widen. *Olivia.*

Chapter Fifty-One

Parker

She isn't in the studio. What happens after is a vivid harebrained blur. I follow her scent, screaming in my head for her but I get nothing but silence. I can't think as Aster and I wade through the other students in the hallways and the paths outside. I follow the scent to the Central Lawn where Octavia is sobbing in the grass with Darien at her side. He has a handkerchief outstretched to her, while he kneels by her feet.

"I started to think something was wrong, but … it wore off after I put her in the car and watched it drive away."

"What is she talking about?" I hiss.

Olivia's scent is all over her, and all I see is red. Pulsing, bloody red.

Octavia looks up at me. "I'm so sorry Parker."

I growl. "Where is she?"

"There you are asshole." Aster stalks toward Darien.

But not before I wrap my hands around the collar of Darien's blazer. "He's mine."

I can't hurt Octavia so Darien will have to do.

"Is that any way to treat a man who has been keeping your mate safe since the day she arrived?"

"You knew Cane was behind all this and you didn't say anything." I'm about to shift. My body skipped the itch and went straight into the shaking. Aster feels it and he steps back with a smirk.

"I suspected him but couldn't get any definitive evidence because he's good at covering his tracks. It took time to slowly piece that together and his interest in you and your mate starting with the day she arrived. I overheard him making plans to mark her. I could never figure out his fascination with Octavia though. Late night talks and casual drinks together, but Octavia never remembered much about them when I'd ask her."

"It started slow. Too faint to notice till I was missing time." Octavia's voice is a whisper.

"He was drugging her. But like Olivia, I couldn't figure out how or why. They were never alone together. It was always in public with witnesses."

"I don't have fucking time for this." I'm slipping, my claws began to form and snag on the fibers of his jacket. "Get to the point."

"Cane's father has been helping him get forbidden potions. That's what he gave Olivia that night at the party. He befriended Octavia because he needed an opening with your mate."

"We'd drink late at night. I thought he needed a friend. But I'd started to have gaps, like the night of the party. We never talked about you or Olivia." Octavia is talking to me but I'm barely there. "I never thought ... it was me who did that to her. I thought maybe I'd just had too much and started to forget things."

"Olivia, where are you?" There is still no answer.

Memory and motor function charms are forbidden. They don't work well anyway, and they wear off fast. He had to have been drugging Octavia slowly over time for it to work. Getting the potion in her system and then giving her higher doses when he needed to get her to do something. The only way to control someone from a charm like this is if there is already a negative feeling associated with it.

Cane did this. Octavia was just another one of his victims. Who knows how long he's been brewing them.

And now I know he has Olivia right where he wants her. I feel sick to my stomach, and there's heat under my skin. The sickness is starting. She's getting father away. I have to find her. This can't be it. This can't be the end.

"I have to go. I have to find her."

"I can help you with that. You will owe me though." Darien cocks his head with a smirk and I drop him into the grass.

CHAPTER FIFTY-TWO

OLIVIA

"Parker. Parker. Parker." My mind swims as I call out for him.

"I'm coming." His voice is faint as I open my eyes.

My arms are tied behind my back, and there's cloth stuffed in my mouth and covering my eyes. I manage myself to a sitting position, and my feet hit a plush carpet.

I'm so achy. My head is pounding. There's a loud roar I don't recognize. I almost drift out again until a train horn echoes through the room. That's the noise coming from under me. The wheels over the tracks.

"I'm on a train."

Parker doesn't respond.

The ropes around my wrists are so tight it burns when I try to wiggle free.

"Ah, you're up." A male voice I don't recognize is in front of me.

The light is blinding when he removes my blindfold.

Cane.

"Hello, Rabbit." Cane's yellow and green eyes pierce mine.

I haven't thought much of him since that night in Noxx House. I'm next to the warm-yellow light of the bedside table. It's some kind of luxury train car. I'm sitting on a thick ornate comforter, and Cane's in a chair in front of me.

He removes my gag, and I unclench my aching jaw.

"Where's Octavia?"

He has to be blackmailing her or something. There's no way she would do this.

"I don't need her for this. It's better if she doesn't know where you're headed. Sweet girl. Doesn't have the stomach for unpleasant things."

"Why did she ..."

"Because I asked her to." He leans back in his chair, the yellow light saturating his white hair.

"She wouldn't."

"It did take convincing with an added charm. But you know her, she's very ambitious. I think you underestimate how jealousy and envy can change a person. How ... watching someone getting all the things you want can put a sour taste in your mouth after a while. Or when that someone comes in to pilfer everything you have for themselves. For me, it took years, for her ... just a couple weeks of watching you dominate. You got into the company on the first try. Instantly noticed for your natural talents. Then you get the lead for the first- and second-year company. That's when she really started to come around. She worked so hard for all of it, thought she'd have the lead."

I never suspected her. We spent hours together daily. She practiced just as much as me and was always around assisting the director. There was no indication. Not one frown or slipup. I thought she was happy for me.

"Naturally, we are in the same circle, so she opened up to me. Night after night. Drink after drink. It was so easy to do. Little doses of the charm. I could get her to do almost anything."

My head throbs as I lace the pieces together.

He needed me alone.

"It was you. All of it was you."

"Olivia. It's going to be okay. Just stay calm."

"Parker. I'm on a train. It's Cane."

"Don't tell me you figured it out."

I keep careful watch on Cane's hands. He's got on his expensive rings and a gold watch, but no weapons.

"No. I ... didn't have all the parts, but some things didn't make sense."

My throat is dry, and I close my eyes as a wave of dizziness runs over me. I'm warm and growing warmer by the second.

Why would Aster and Barrett, who had everything they needed, put their necks on the line to mess with Parker? It never matched up. There were holes, but I didn't want to see them. Or I never gave myself time to think of them because I didn't understand the danger. I didn't think any of them were capable of this.

"It always had to be someone with a better reason. Someone who hated Parker enough. Someone ... psychotic enough to drug someone and then threaten my sister. That was you. You framed Aster and Barrett."

"They never suspected it. And Aster and Barrett may be filthy rich, but they never had it in them. I dreamed of coming to Doxlothia. Surely, people there would finally match my ambitions. But most of them think too small. They're not willing to get their hands dirty. Not like this. Sure, they'll blackmail or launch smear campaigns. Do anything else, really, but stuff like this is ... beneath them. They wouldn't even commit to slipping a date drug in your drink. No that was 'too far.' Instead, they opted for some brainless idea to get you drunk. Like you were going to just drink with them. Aster took all the drinks himself."

My chest tightens. "You ... had Octavia drug me at the party."

His canine teeth peek out when he smiles. "Didn't even need to be there. I was hoping you'd get marked by someone else. Anyone other than Parker. He'd be devastated, hopefully never talk to you again and then ... you just had to be a linked mate."

"Baby. Talk to me."

"I'm here. Cane has me on a train. It's hot. I feel sick."

"I had to wake up seeing Parker's name as the news spread. Do you have any idea how many times my father called me about it? Every day I had to hear my father's berating."

His whole family is obsessed with Parker. There must be history there. I take in a labored breath. The air from my lungs is hot in my throat.

"He wasn't ... happy. I had to think of something else. Aster and Barrett never would have thought about entering you in The Hunt if I hadn't suggested it. They just wanted to do the framing, but I wanted it to hurt."

The train is moving fast, but that's not what's making me dizzy. My limbs are heavy, and sweat is running down my back.

"What's happening to me?"

"We're quite a distance away from your mate. You're probably feeling a headache. The heat of a fever. Your whole body is aching. I was disappointed to hear Parker was able to complete his bond with you, but that just opened the door to my greatest plan. Mates have to be together once a bond is first completed ... if not, they become very, very sick. I imagine it's worse as a human. No regenerative cells to slow the process. We're on a one-way trip to the city. I'm not sure you'll even make it before your brain is fried from the fever."

I'm too delirious to register the full weight of his words, but I hear him loud and clear. Cane doesn't intend for me to get off this train alive. I try to wiggle my hands free, but my body is growing weaker by the second.

"Why do you hate Parker so much?"

"Haven't you been listening? Because he always gets what he wants!" Cane's yell echoes between us, and I flinch. Nothing but the sound of the train's wheel hitting the tracks follows. We must be in a rear car away from the public.

He leans forward in his chair, skimming my cheek.

"You know, I saw you first. That day in the courtyard while you and your sisters were looking for your house assignments. When I saw you ... saw your eyes, I imagined all the ways I could make you mine. I would have tried to talk to you if he wasn't always around. I tried to play nice with the smear campaign against you and your sisters, but that only made Parker want to protect you more. I would have even given you up to be marked by someone else if it meant *he* wouldn't have you."

Fingers clench in my hair, and he forces my head forward like he's going to kiss me. I jerk away, and pain radiates in my skull. Delirious, hot, and aching everywhere.

"You're a psycho," I say, managing to loosen his grip.

"No. You don't understand. Aside from the dead mother, Parker has gotten everything he's ever wanted in life. And his mother was highly regarded, respected, and loved by everyone on the Werewolf Council. My family has always had to fight hard for our respect. It's toil. It doesn't come easy. When I joined the Rage team, Parker joined too, but he was better. I gave up on that dream, and good thing I did, because he became the youngest Rage captain at Doxlothia. And then he gets not only the mate of his dreams but is a linked mate legacy? With eyes that are meant for me and my bloodline? Parker Owens's name will be known forever, and I can't escape it. He doesn't get to have you too."

"What are you going to do to me?" I whisper. I'm in no place to defend myself. I can't hear Parker anymore, and that's enough to make me panic.

"Me? Nothing. I won't touch you. I'm not a monster. I'll let that bond of yours run its course." His thumb grazes my cheek, and I'm dizzy when I lean away. Those fingers move down my neck till they reach Parker's mark. "Your temperature is already rising by the second."

"Parker, hurry."

"You don't want to hear the statistics of linked mate deaths. Not good odds for him once you go. Then I'll be rid of it all. They'll find your body in the city. No murder weapon. No evidence."

"You don't have to do this. There's still time to go back."

"No one will know. After all, you're known for running. I've got this little piece of paper, and you're going to write on it for me. Let's tell the story of Olivia Osborne, the mate who didn't stop running until it killed her."

I flinch away when he leans forward to undo my hands. There's little relief in it.

"You're too weak to move now anyway." He grabs a pen from his breast pocket. "Now, let's write that letter. Starting with a little note for your linked mate."

My hand shakes as he places the pen between my fingers and I press the pen into the paper. I can't think of Parker's reaction to my death. I have to keep fighting. When I move, a hard object jabs into my hip. My phone is still lodged in my back pocket.

I just need to not pass out before I get it. I try to blink away the emotion of it all. The fear of Parker finding my body. The thought of never seeing him or my family again. My mother wouldn't and didn't give death even the slightest thought. She carried on with a smile and hope in her heart, and so will I.

"Okay, write what I tell you: *Dear Parker, I'm sorry I couldn't stay with you ...*"

This is just another performance, and I've been waiting my whole life for this one. I start writing, hoping I can stay awake.

Chapter Fifty-Three

Parker

Olivia stopped responding to me. Why did she stop?

I slam my fist into the dashboard. My head is pounding.

"We're almost there," Aster says.

"Just stop talking," I growl. His voice and the sound of the engine revving as we drift around corners are setting me on the brink of a full meltdown.

I'm too panicked to give a shit that Aster is my companion for this. There wasn't any time. Darien put an alert out for Cane's car when he realized Olivia had been taken. There's blurry footage of him exiting his car with his pack, and getting on a train with someone tucked under a coat.

I didn't give any thought to grabbing Aster by the shirt and making him drive us in one of his super cars.

He's doing it with ease. The tires screech as we round another turn, and I have to grip the handle above the door.

"Gavin's gathering his pack at the end of the train line in the city. He's tried using his connections to contact the conductor, but it's not getting through. Cane has likely already thought of it. Sounds like he's been planning for a while. There's one little bridge the train goes under. We're going to have to make a jump for it."

"We?"

"I'm coming with you."

"No way."

"I can't have you killing the only witness, can I? Plus, in case you forgot, you're packless. His whole pack is on that train. You need my help."

"Fine. I don't fucking care."

"Olivia. Baby, come on. Talk to me."

It's been more than fifteen minutes since I last heard from her, and I can't think of anything else.

"I can't hear her anymore."

"Well, we're closer to her than you think. We're almost to the bridge."

"Stay awake, baby. I'm almost there. It's going to be okay."

"Why can't I hear her?"

"She's probably just too weak right now. Keep your head. Olivia's one stubborn bitch if I've ever seen one. She'll fight."

Before I can react to that comment, we come to a screeching halt and I'm out of the car before it stops moving. Behind us, members of his pack funnel out of their SUVS and sports cars. We're surrounded by mountains and trees as far as I can see.

I hear the train running on the tracks. Its lights burst through the night, illuminating the mountainside as it grows closer and closer. The ground shakes, but it might be me on the cusp of shifting.

"He'll likely be in one of the back cars."

I shift in an instant. Aster follows suit. Then we charge, running into a full sprint to the edge of the bridge. I'm seconds behind him when he jumps the bridge, and we crash on top of the train car. I run and leap onto the back of the caboose and thrust my fist through the window, the glass bursts and embeds itself in my skin as we scramble inside.

A few members of Cane's pack shift before my eyes. And Aster and I tear into them one by one. They're not a match for us at alpha capacity. I don't think Cane anticipated Aster helping me mow through his pack in the back of the train car.

I leave Aster to clean up the stragglers and keep moving, only injuring them enough so they don't follow.

Her scent is here. I push through the train car faster, knocking over furniture or anyone who gets in my way.

Then I see him. Cane turns around, his eyes glowing.

We're in some type of dining car with tables lining the windows on each side. The hanging lights above the tables shake as the train curves.

Where is she?

"How?" he snarls. I'm expecting him to shift and match me, but he scrambles under the table as I bound forward on all fours.

A gunshot rings through the air.

I stumble back. There's heaviness in my chest. Wetness. I step forward again. Another gunshot.

Then another.

Cane's shaky hand points the barrel at my head, but I knock it from his hand. There's pain when I breathe out.

I slam him into the floor again and again, screaming the words in my head I know he can't hear.

Fucking coward, shift and fight me! I drag him under me by his coat, and a slew of blood drips, staining his pale face.

There's barely anything other than pure instinct to kill.

Cane's frame grows taller and taller as he shifts into a white werewolf, forcing me onto the ground.

He snarls, leaping toward me in the cramped space. My body is slowing, and the power runs from my limbs.

He enchanted the bullets.

It doesn't matter though. Cane is in my way, but he's not about to be. I swipe him across the face as hard as I can and the blood splatters across the window. He lets out an echoing howl. More will come to his aide.

I go for his neck and miss only by a few inches. The enchantment is stealing my strength, but I still get his shoulder, cutting through flesh and muscle, down to the bone. I lock my jaw, shaking him back and forth.

His claws pierce the wound in my shoulder, and I let go. Stumbling back, I growl. I can feel the bullet wounds now. One in the shoulder. Chest. Stomach? Ah, no, missed. It's a little to the left.

"You couldn't beat me, so you cheat. Typical Cane."

He's coddling the shoulder I shredded.

"Who cares about cheating if it gets the job done."

I stumble but catch myself.

His lips curl, showing a long row of teeth. *"Don't look too good."*

"Look better than you."

I need to find her. I'm running out of time.

Pulling a table from the wall, I fling it toward him and bound forward. We struggle against the weakness. The pain. The blood.

His teeth are around my arm, and mine around his other shoulder.

"Stop," he pleads.

I don't. I can't till he's not in my way anymore.

"Fuck, you're bleeding." Aster emerges a little battered.

I let go, my body aching.

"I've got to find her." I motion for the door.

"I got him. Go."

Staring into Cane's green and yellow eyes, I growl. *"If you ever want to finish this, I'll be waiting."*

I let go and run into another horde from Cane's pack, raising my chin and emitting a deafening howl that shakes the walls of the train car.

"Get in my way and you're dead." I stare them down, sprinting forward, and they barely dodge me as they cower and hide.

Her scent is swirling in the air. I'm in the right car. I stop when I reach a locked door. A faint heartbeat lingers inside.

Olivia.

In one blow, I punch through the door, splintering the wood and tearing at it with my teeth.

She's lying on the bed, with her hair wet and stuck to her forehead. Her cheeks are flushed, and her eyes are barely open.

"Parker."

I cradle her in my arms. "I'm here. I'm here."

I'm faster in Were form, and search for the restroom. It's in the next room over, and there's a little tile shower in the corner. It's barely big enough for us to fit in, so I shift into my human form and turn on the cold water.

"I'm so hot," she says, her eyes closing and rolling back into her head.

"I know, baby. It's going to be okay. I'll fix it, just stay awake for me, okay?"

The cold water runs over her, pooling in her lap. It has to be enough, right? She barely stirs, and I move the hair from her eyes.

Under me, a sea of red swirls, but I don't care. She has to be okay.

"Hey, stay awake. Please."

I press my head to hers. Her pulse is weak, but my touch is healing her. It's working. I say it over and over in hopes of believing it.

"I'm so tired. I'm hot. I want to … I … want to stay."

"You will. You're cooling off, it's going to be fine."

"I want to stay …" She slumps into me.

"You will." I close my eyes. My limbs are heavy, and I'm tired. More tired than I've ever been, but I have to stay awake. I have to heal her.

Her grip on my forearm loosens. We're surrounded by red.

"No. No. No. Please don't leave me, baby." I sob.

There's no life without Olivia.

"Please don't leave me. I just found you."

I rock her softly, concentrating on the gentle heartbeat in her chest. The world goes numb around me as I hold her. It's just her and me. Like it's always been. It's how it's supposed to be. The edges of my vision blur.

"Stay with me."

"Stay with me."

"Stay with me, please."

Chapter Fifty-Four

Olivia

The heat is gone, then I'm floating. There's no pain. No fear. Just bliss. I'm the safest I've ever been.

"It will be okay, honey." My mom's voice is there, and it's like she's running her hands through my hair. *"Everything will work out."*

Parker's voice is close by. Barely audible.

"Don't fucking touch her," he snarls.

"They're going to help her. Come on." It's Gavin, I think. "You need help too."

"I have a pulse ... We need to move her."

"He's lost a lot of blood." *Parker is bleeding?*

I don't feel anything in this space, only a growing desire to get back to him. There are so many voices I don't recognize wavering in and out.

"Help him up. We need to keep a connection on their skin. Stay close."

Parker is hurt. He's waiting for me.

Soon there's a faint beeping and the sound of a heartbeat in an echoing room. My heartbeat. I can't tell how long it's been. I want to open my eyes, but my body won't let me.

"Sir, you can't be in here, you need to rest."

"I'm her linked mate. I have to heal her," Parker says, his breathing labored.

"He can stay," another person says.

Then my skin is warm, so much warmer than before.

It only feels like seconds, maybe minutes, before I hear his voice again, but it could've been longer. It's louder this time.

"You're being such stubborn pain in the ass. You gotta wake up. Come back to me, baby." I feel Parker's fingers tracing circles on my arm, up my shoulder, and to the tip of my ear.

I will. I think it, trying to tell him through our bond. The room almost feels solid around me before it disappears again.

"I hope you're dreaming of me." His voice echoes close.

The sun greets me as my eyes fall open. The sheets are pressed, and the smell of linen is overpowered by something much more prominent. I'm being held. There's an arm around my waist, and I lean into the scent of him. He's dirty. Sweaty. But mine.

"Parker," I say, turning to face him.

He jolts up and places a hand on my cheek. "Tell me you're okay. Do you remember what happened?"

"You're here. You're safe," he says, in my head.

"I'm okay. You were hurt?"

"Flesh wound."

"You're going to overwhelm her," Eva says, and I realize we're not alone.

"I remember." I fall into him. "You saved me."

Then he's kissing me everywhere: lips, nose, cheeks, teeth. The kiss of a mate is enough to ease the tension lingering in my chest. I don't hurt anywhere.

"Just to remind you both, we're in the hospital. We. As in your sisters and many nurses are present, so maybe wait to fully make up in the bedroom."

Emma.

I sit up and take everything in. I must be in a hospital in the city because it's all white marble and white linens. The windows are open, showing the city below and the fresh scent of pollen signals me to flowers of all different colors around the room.

"What is all of this?" I stare at the flowers covering my bedside tables and overflowing onto the floor, making out a name on the biggest one. *Darien.* Next to his name is the photo of my mother and Parker's mother.

"I'll show her." Emma places her phone horizontally for me to watch something.

It's a video, and I instantly recognize the wallpaper from the train car.

The camera pans to a shower, and Parker is holding me in his arms and whispering to me. It shows him from the chest up, rocking me while the water covers us. There's blood smeared on his face and in his hair, with what looks like a bullet wound on his shoulder.

"Please don't leave me, baby."

He rests his cheek on my head as he sobs. "Stay with me please. Stay with me. Stay with me."

I reach for him in horror, and he wraps an arm around my waist for comfort.

"The *entire* school has seen this?!"

"Yeah, and they love you for it."

"Who filmed this?"

"It was your phone. Aster found it in the room I grabbed you from, and it was already recording," Parker says.

"The conversations you recorded of Cane and the footage Aster got were more than enough to expose Cane. You and Parker are front-page news. Again."

It's coming back now. It seemed futile at the time to record. I'd managed to wrestle my phone from my pocket when he was interrupted by one of his pack members.

"Wait, Aster helped you?" I turn to him.

"It's a long story. I can tell you about it. Are you hungry?"

I am. My stomach is hollow. "Yeah."

"I'll get you something," he says, getting up to move, but I grab his arm. I'm not ready for him to be out of my sight yet.

"We'll go get it. You both need to eat," Eva says, leaning toward me. "Parker's been refusing food."

"I think the only reason he took water was because the nurse promised you'd wake up," Emma says.

"I had to be sure I'd be right behind you if you didn't wake up," Parker says.

Emma and Eva give an exasperated eye roll.

"Kidding."

"*Not kidding*," he pushes into my mind.

They flutter out of the room, and I reach for Parker's forearm.

"How long was I out?"

"Two days." He palms my cheek. "Felt like forever."

I get lost in his lips. The taste of his tongue on mine and the serene calm from knowing everything is okay now. I lift his shirt to run my fingers over the bandages.

"You were shot?"

"Three times. Cane used enchanted bullets, so healing is a little slower. But I'm okay."

Tears well in my eyes. It's relief. Happiness and sadness. This should have never happened. But it's done. We hold each other until there's a knock at the door, and we reluctantly separate. Two familiar faces emerge.

My father and Parker's. My father is slightly shorter and rounder than Parker's, and when they stand next to each other, I see the stark differences. Even with their similar brown hair. My dad's features are much softer than Mr. Owens's.

I wobble to my elbows to sit up.

"No need to sit up, honey. We've been in and out. Already met. Did the introductions and such."

"Oh. Good." I turn to Parker. "You already met my father?"

"Parker almost took my head off when I tried to come in your room."

Parker rubs the back of his neck, giving me a sheepish grin. "I was a little on edge while you were asleep."

"In his defense, Dad tried to barge in during the middle of the night." Emma skips in, with Eva and Zant in tow. He's holding the plates of food. He winks at me and gives me a little wave while dodging the vases of flowers.

Parker's father stands with his hands in his trouser pockets.

"Thanks for coming," I say, not sure what else to offer.

"You don't need to worry about anything. I've invested in security detail for you and your sisters from now on. Now that you're bonded, I'll ensure nothing like this happens again."

"And Cane is ..."

"Cane will face trial along with his father for the involvement. Octavia too. She was bewitched by Cane, so it's unclear how much she knew. There's still an investigation going on."

I lean into Parker in relief. I think it will be months before I can process everything that has happened.

"I should be apologizing to you. Cane's father ... I've worked under him for many years. I never thought he held malice toward my family. But ..." He looks at Parker, then back to me. "He was originally arranged to marry Parker's mother before she met me."

"Woah, you never told me that," Parker says.

"I never thought the identity of who was important. The separation was messy, but we believed it to be settled. Parker's mother worked closely with him at some points in her career with no issue. But I believe there might have been a history of jealousy I hadn't picked up on. I knew he had ill feelings for myself, but I never imagined he'd passed down all that hatred to my son ... and you, Olivia. I am deeply sorry."

Parker's dad offers me his hand, and I take it in acceptance.

"I have every intention of making this up to you and your family over time for my serious slack of judgement."

In my peripheral, Parker is smiling. Maybe there's room for them to patch up old wounds, and me ...

My father grabs my hand after a few minutes. "You scared me, kid."

"You know I try not to."

"You're one tough cookie. I can't wait to come see your ballet."

What will happen now that the director's daughter was involved in this? Hopefully, they'll still let me dance. I decide not to worry. Things have a way of working out, and as I squeeze Parker's hand and he squeezes back I know I have the most important thing.

"You'll come see?"

"Yes. In fact, I had a talk with the dean this morning. I think it may be time I stepped back into teaching. Doxlothia needs me."

"Really?"

His eyes brim with tears before he hugs me. "It feels right. Your mother would approve. Plus, I'll get to see you all more often."

It's been years since I've hugged my father like this. My family once felt so small and broken, but now I'm surrounded by love, and Parker is too.

"For the record, I like him." He motions to Parker, who's talking to his father and gorging himself on the food.

I smile as my mom's optimistic words echo in my mind.

"Everything will be okay. It will all work out."

CHAPTER FIFTY-FIVE

PARKER

Olivia is beautiful and graceful as she moves across the stage. There's never been a more awe-striking, determined woman. I'm running out of adjectives to describe her. She moves with graceful ease through each variation. Her performance in Act 1 has Zant's mouth falling open.

"I didn't know this is what ballet was like. She's good."

She kept her spot, even after she reauditioned because of what happened with Octavia. And Mrs. Vix had to step down as the ballet director.

This role was meant for her. The stage lights cast her porcelain skin in a dark-blue haze as she dances in her long white romantic tutu. She taught me the differences.

I stay quiet in her head as she performs so she can focus, but as soon as she takes her last step off the stage, I hear her voice in my head and smile.

"How did I look?"

"The embodiment of perfection."

Our whole row is on our feet when she comes to take her final bow on stage. We're right in the front, and I have a bouquet of moon nightingales in one arm and food in the other. I'm dressed in a suit, ready to take her to the city just like I promised.

Her sisters, our dads, even Aster and Barrett came to see her. Though, likely for reputation purposes, is my guess. We aren't friends, but seeing as I now hold a council seat and Aster did help me save Olivia's life, we're working through our differences.

Aster flips me off when I glance over, and Barrett glares at me. He's only here for the photo op of them supporting her. Nothing says *I didn't have anything to do with the drugging scandal* like showing up to every performance and supporting the ballet company with money. They're permanently roped into funding for them.

I wave, knowing I'll be seeing them bright and early at the breakfast table next week.

Gavin and his pack are in the row behind me, and he clamps me on the shoulder for support. And then there's my pack ...

"Your car is here, Alpha." Ryker shows me the notification on his phone. "And your hotel reservation is confirmed."

"We might have arranged a small gift inside." Chase smiles.

"Thank me later." Ryker snickers.

None of us picked it. They came all the way to the city to see Olivia in the hospital when the news hadn't broken yet. They felt connected to me, sensed the danger, and got on the next train in. Packs aren't always chosen. Sometimes, they find you. Maybe it is like Olivia said. There are lone wolves out there that were waiting on me to step up as Alpha.

I'm still adjusting to it. Adding slowly, but it will probably be next semester till I have more recruits. Right now, they both function as my seconds because it just makes sense. They're a good team as my right-hand men. It's weird having them help me with stuff, but they make it funny as shit most of the time, and it alleviates the awkward bits. Zant calls them my minions to annoy them during Rage practice, and they rightfully give him hell for it. I think the whole thing has made the team stronger though. The moon festival is next week, just one more free weekend to catch some alone time with my girl.

I wade through the velvet seats to meet her backstage, and she jumps into my arms.

"I've got flowers, food, and a car waiting to whisk us away."

Her violet and gold eyes glimmer, her hair is in a sparkly bun and looks to be covered in layers of hair spray. "My feet hurt, can you carry me?"

"Can I? I'd love to." I thrust her over my shoulder, still holding the goods. "I'll have the guys come get your bags."

"Congratulations." Darien appears as I spin around and he hands me Olivia's bouquet. "Might want to take a short cut through the woods if you want to avoid a few paparazzi hidden out on the lawn."

More and more are making it past the gate.

"Come to be helpful?" I ask, looking around for his motive, then a man with a camera comes around and snaps a picture of the three of us.

"Won't we look like the best of friends for all of Vviveren."

I push past him toward the back of the theater. You couldn't pay me to care about Darien's social status right now.

"Hope you two come back nice and rested. Lots of council business to attended to Owens."

His voice fades into the murmur of voices backstage.

There are layers of velvet curtains and various people passing us and congratulating her despite her being on my shoulder. I have a ring burning a hole in my pocket, and that keeps me grinning the entire time.

"Parker, your hand is on my ass. People are staring."

"Good. Just how I like it."

EPILOGUE

EMMA

"*Doxlothia's Power Couple Takes the World by Storm.* Wow, what a headline," I say, scrolling through my phone. Cheers erupt in the stadium. The ice is bathed in blue light for the moon festival offseason game. You wouldn't think it's a big deal, but everything is a big deal here. I'm wrapped in a blanket because short skirts and sitting in an ice rink don't mix.

Sports have never been my thing, but supporting Olivia and Parker is pretty much a hobby for me at this point.

"They always exaggerate," Olivia says.

Her hands are covered in mittens. She claims it's because it's cold in the ice rink, but I think she's trying to hide that rock on her hand everyone keeps trying to take pictures of.

"Yeah, okay. I'm just tired of my feed being flooded with my sister making out with her fiancé."

I'm happy for her. Olivia deserves it. Did I kinda want a hot werewolf man to want me? Sure. Did I also want to pursue my dream and enter the culinary club and can't because council member Dacre Everhart decided he wanted to be a dick about it? Double sure.

Now her name is literally everywhere. She's a linked mate. Everyone is obsessed with her performances. All I'm saying is, share the love, sis. Maybe let someone else get a little bit of that magical luck you have.

She hates being famous. I don't understand why. What's so terrible about strangers loving you and bringing you gifts? She still hasn't stopped getting gifts since the whole kidnapping incident. Lucky for them the university is closed to the public and press are only allowed on the campus under strict guidelines.

Parker passes the puck and tackles someone to the ground and the whole stadium stands. Olivia gasps and presses a hand to the glass.

Their notoriety does come with perks. The Doxlothia company and Rage team are required by law to coordinate their dates so the two can always be close in proximity. Which in short means they're never apart. Ever.

Right now, my favorite perk is getting the best seats in the stadium. Parker told me when they have the bigger tournament in the city we get to sit in the special fancy club seats, and I can't wait to test out the food there. I wish Eva were here to keep me company, but she's busy with one of Stelliea's social groups. They handle the merch area.

Parker Owens has infiltrated my life, and he and his pack are literally in my space twenty-four seven. It's nice having a soon to be brother-in-law, especially one who likes trying the recipes I need to test out.

I wasn't paying attention to see the game-winning moment, but Parker is being tackled by his team, and they are cheering his name while the stadium roars.

Olivia beams as she watches them celebrate. They bring out the trophy, and Parker sees her and immediately bolts over to the glass. She moves to the edge of the ice, probably expecting a kiss. Instead, he lifts her, and she wraps her legs around his waist. She kisses his cheek as they skate back to the center, though he's dirty with blood.

They kiss as the cameras flash in rapid succession. The entire stadium is screaming, and they both have blood smudged on their faces. I can already hear the conversations my hallmates will have:

"Did you see when he picked her up and kissed her? Ah!"

"They look so perfect together. Olivia is always so put together."

"The way he looked for her immediately, it was the cutest thing I've ever seen."

I'm so bitter and alone. It's been ages since I've had anyone to share a bed with. And now I'm always with them. The most popular couple in Vviveren, *all the time*. I send Olivia a quick text to let her know I'll see her at the after-game dinner.

I duck between swarms of people sweating and screaming, and run straight into a man's chest. I know it's a man because he smells like the feeling of pulling baked bread from the oven, and he's solid as a rock.

"Watch where you're going," he says.

"Dacre."

Dacre Everhart is only a few inches taller, but he's looking down his nose at me like I'm chewed gum on the bottom of his shoe. Why do beautiful people have to be so evil? I'm not kidding, everyone on the council is easy on the eyes. Dacre's chestnut hair is short and out of his eyes, and I can't help but stare at the tattoos lining his arms.

"You should be careful," he says, and I continue to block his way.

"No, you. You're in *my* space."

"Whatever you say, thief."

Oh, I hate him. I hate him—

"Your recipe sucked anyway," I spit.

Did I steal a recipe notebook from the lounge as a dare? Yes. But it's not as sinister as it sounds. They're hoarding all the good stuff for the culinary club.

"What?"

"I looked at your recipe in the book, and you put too much flour."

"You tried it?"

"Of course I tried it. I'm working my way through them all."

His dark eyebrows twitch, then he points. "You've got icing on your neck."

I'm so confused until I remember I made victory cupcakes for Parker and his team for tonight's dinner. Wishful baking.

He leans in an inch. Two. Three. The slow rub of his thumb sends heat down my spine, and it spreads to my face when he pops the finger in his mouth to taste the icing.

"Too sweet."

"No way. That's my mom's recipe. It's perfect."

He shrugs and waves me off. "Whatever you say, thief."

My mouth falls open to say something witty back, but I shut it.

No further explanation needed. I hate Dacre Everhart.

(Continue Emma and Dacre's story in Bite Me)

Acknowledgements

To my family, especially my husband, for putting up with all the late nights and hours I spent working on this book. Thank you for letting me daydream for a living, for making the best food for dinner every night, and for reminding me to drink water.

Everyone who has read the This Blood that Binds Us series and has continued to support me, I see you. I appreciate you, and I'm happy you're here.

Danielle, my friend who went above and beyond and supported me through every step of this book. I truly don't know how I could have done it without you screaming in my ear how much you loved this book and the characters.

My author friends, for listening to long voice memos and my crises at every hour of the day. You are my little village.

Follow Me

Links to my newsletter/website so you can stay up to date.

Follow me on Amazon so you never miss a release.

Patreon

Instagram

www.ingramcontent.com/pod-product-compliance
Lightning Source LLC
Chambersburg PA
CBHW011317310726
48973CB00011B/2958